# THE Holiday TRAP

# ROAN PARRISH

sourcebooks
casablanca

Copyright © 2022 by Roan Parrish
Cover and internal design © 2022 by Sourcebooks
Cover illustration by Kristen Solecki
Internal design by Laura Boren/Sourcebooks
Internal illustrations by Laura Boren/Sourcebooks and Hannah Strassburger/
Sourcebooks

Published by Sourcebooks Casablanca, an imprint of Sourcebooks
P.O. Box 4410, Naperville, Illinois 60567-4410
(630) 961-3900
sourcebooks.com

Cataloging in Publication Data is on file with the Library of Congress.

Printed and bound in Canada.
MBP 10 9 8 7 6 5 4 3 2 1

*For the change-seekers*

# 1
## GRETA

Snow fell in fat, picturesque flakes, fairy lights twinkled around the stage, and the hum of excitement and cheer that always attended the Owl Island, Maine, Holiday Fair electrified the town square.

Greta Russakoff stood in the center of it all and contemplated precisely how she would murder her entire family one by one.

It had begun as the Holiday Fair always did: Valentine Johnson, the mayor of Owl Island, turned on the lights that illuminated the town square and all the businesses that lined the four streets creating it. She called the Holiday Fair to life amid cheers and whoops from a familiar crowd. And then she called up the volunteers for their annual charity auction.

This year, the charity was the Owl Island Library, and the auction was for a dinner date at Francesca's, Sue Romano's Italian restaurant.

Only this time, after Valentine had called up the usual suspects, another name rang out.

"Our final volunteer is Greta Russakoff. Come on up!"

The smile of holiday cheer died on Greta's lips, and for

one tremulous moment, she thought she'd simply misheard. After all, there were six other Russakoffs in town. They stood all around her: her parents and her four sisters.

But that hope died the same death as her smile when she saw the faces of her mother and her eldest sister, Sadie, who were looking at her with twin expressions of satisfaction.

Her father was pointedly avoiding her eyes, as was her older sister, Tillie, the peacemaker. Her twin, Adelaide, blinked in horror at her but didn't say anything. Her youngest sister Maggie's mouth dropped open, and she mouthed *Oh, shit*, the words swallowed by the murmurs of the crowd.

"What," Greta bit off between gritted teeth, looking between Sadie and her mother, "Did. You. Do?"

"Greta, are you here?" the mayor crooned into the microphone. "Remember, this is for charity."

Valentine was beloved on Owl Island. She had increased tourism and revenue for small businesses, including the Russakoffs'.

Greta added the mayor to her kill list.

Her heart sank as people began to reach out and pat her on the back and smile.

"Go on, Greta!"

"Get it, Greta!"

"Greta, yeah!"

Could you murder an entire town?

"Go get 'em, kiddo," Sadie trilled, and Greta wondered, not for the first time, why Sadie gloried in messing with her more than with anyone else.

*You could just leave*, Greta told herself. *Just turn around and walk away. You're an adult now, and this isn't the damned hunger games. They can't make you.*

Greta squared her shoulders and cleared her throat. "I didn't volunteer," she said confidently and prepared to leave.

Only her words came out as a croak, and she *didn't* leave.

She turned to Adelaide, looking for a rescue or help or… something. But while Addie looked horrified on her behalf, she just shrugged, an I-don't-know-what-to-do gesture familiar from every awkward situation of their childhood.

"Dude," Maggie said to Sadie. "You're such an asshole."

"Greta, go," her mother hissed. "It's for charity!" Nothing scandalized Nell Russakoff like a lack of performative generosity.

Owl Island was a small town. Leaving would mean answering questions for weeks. Which would mean offending people about the auction, a beloved town tradition. Which would mean even more talking to people who'd known her since she was a child and still treated her like she was one.

Greta gritted her teeth so hard she felt a headache threaten and walked stiffly to the stage, taking care not to meet anyone's eyes lest she perish from mortification or reveal previously unknown Medusa-like powers. She stood next to the other volunteers with what she hoped was dignity but would see in pictures later was the pose of someone who desperately needed to pee.

One by one, the volunteers were bid on.

Greta had attended this auction since she was old enough to remember, and since she was old enough to remember, it had been her least favorite part of the holiday festivities.

Still, she went every year because it was a family tradition and because she loved the rest of the Holiday Fair that first December weekend. The auction had even been the occasion of her coming out five years before.

She and Tillie had been in the booth their family ran every fair. The handmade items they were selling changed with the whims of their mother's crafting. One year it had been quilted oven mitts, another it had been felted table decorations, and that year it had been knitted hats and mittens. Tillie and Adelaide were the most enthusiastic crafters and usually made the bulk of the items alongside their mom. Sadie liked to sell things but not make them. Maggie would start one of whatever they were making that year and quickly lose interest. And their father concerned himself with all elements of display, providing snacks, and cheerleading, but didn't have the dexterity for most crafts. His attempts were generally hilarious, though, and every year, they had him try to make one and enshrined it on the shelf above the piano, which now held two decades of misshapen crafts.

In the family booth, Tillie had been showing Greta how to knit a hat for the third time, her attempts at mittens having proven hopeless, and Greta had sworn bitterly as the whole thing slid off her needles.

"Watch your language," her old math teacher Mr. Sorensen had said as he walked past. "Men don't bid on young ladies with potty mouths at the holiday auction."

Greta, home for the holidays from her freshman year of college and high on the freedom of her first months away from her family, had snapped back, "Well, this young lady has no interest in men or being auctioned off to anyone, so that'll work out great for all of us."

Tillie and Greta's father, who'd returned with hot cocoas in time to overhear the exchange, had turned to her with identical hazel eyes—her father's wide and Tillie's smiling. Tillie raised an eyebrow. "Yeah?"

"Yeah," Greta said, starting to shake with nerves. Her whole family—strike that, the whole town—would know in a matter of hours.

She shoved her woeful knitting at Sadie and got to her feet. As she walked past her father, he caught her shoulder and squeezed. When she looked up at him, he smiled and nodded just once. Then he let her walk away to be alone with her thoughts.

Now, she wished desperately for a similar exit strategy, but she was onstage in the middle of the town square with nearly the entire population of Owl Island staring at her.

Just as she was telling herself that it couldn't get any worse, she caught sight of Tabitha Ryder. Greta winced.

Tabitha's smooth blond bangs and elfin face were framed by the faux-fur-lined hood she had pulled up against the Maine winter. She held mittened hands with Jordan Laverty, who was handsome and too infuriatingly kind to loathe the way Greta would have liked.

Hey, at least Greta had a perfectly self-deprecating story to tell when the topic of first loves came up. Not everyone had confessed their love to their best friend and then puked on her shoes. (Although, Greta found out, more had than you might think.)

Tabitha's blue eyes grew wide when she saw Greta onstage, and Greta braced herself for the utter carnage of her heart that would follow if Tabitha smirked at her pathetic misfortune.

But Tabitha didn't smirk.

It was so much worse.

Tabitha, curse the kind soul that had made Greta love her in the first place, gave Greta a look of such pity that Greta felt her insides fold like a paper bag. Gone was the urge to murder.

Now, with Tabitha—beautiful, happy Tabitha—looking at her while holding the hand of her new love, Greta simply wished to disappear.

←→

Greta allowed herself one hour of furious shower wall punching and postshower cringing at the memories of the day before she pulled a wool hat over her damp hair, stepped into her boots, zipped up her heavy coat, and stormed over to her parents' house three streets over, where the whole family always gathered on holidays and Saturday afternoons.

*Close* was the word Greta always used to describe her relationship with her family. Occasionally, as she got older, *tight-knit*. But it wasn't until her friend Ash had returned to Owl Island after leaving for a few years that someone had finally looked her dead in the face and said, "Dude. Your family isn't just close. It's codependent. And weird," he added under his breath as Greta squirmed.

And, okay, she'd always known her family did more things together than lots of people's, but they had a whole *thing* going on, and usually it was great. Her family was lovely and fun. Her sisters—especially Adelaide and Maggie—were her best friends (since Tabitha wasn't in the picture anymore), and she loved having a built-in support network, no matter what happened. But then there were moments like this. Moments when they were intrusive and possessive and infuriating and—

Greta took a deep breath before she opened the door, steeling herself not to give an inch. She couldn't give them a chance to explain, because there was *no* acceptable explanation. She couldn't hear them out, because *no* motivation could justify it. She just had to storm in there, set her jaw, and start yelling. It was the only way to be heard over six other people.

Tillie was just inside the door.

"Are you mad? You're mad. Okay, listen, I can talk to Mom. I think Sadie told her you'd think it was funny, and—"

"*Sadie* told her that?"

"Well, I don't know exactly. I just think—"

"Duuuude," Maggie said, skipping down the stairs. "You looked like you were about to turn into a flock of crows and peck out everyone's eyes up there! Did you see Sadie yet? I bet—"

But she fell silent as their mother walked in from the kitchen, drying her hands on her apron.

"Hi, honey," her mom said with a smile.

"That's what you have to say to me after earlier?" Greta demanded.

"Well, what do you want me to say? That I'm happy my daughter stood up in front of the whole town and glared at everyone?"

"I *glared* because you and Sadie put me in a position where I'd have to do something I hate or publicly offend the whole town. What, did you think I'd be, like, excited about it?"

"Don't be such a baby, Grotto. It was just a joke," Sadie said as she walked in from the kitchen. She took a loud, crunching bite of an apple and cuffed Greta on the shoulder.

"It's not a joke!" Greta seethed with a deep, trembling kind of anger that made her voice come out thin and reedy. "That's what shitty incels and rapey frat boys say when they realize whoever they're talking to isn't going to let them say horrible things. Don't tell me it's a joke to put your sister on a fucking *auction* block for someone to *buy* the right to a dinner date."

"Pshh, it's for fun. It's a holiday tradition," Sadie said.

"Fun for *who*? Not for me, certainly. And I'm *not* going out with Nicholas Martens."

"What do you mean?" their mother broke in, frowning. "You can't not go. It's for charity."

Greta spluttered.

"And you're cool with this," she said to Sadie finally. "I know we fuck around, but you actually think that I should go on a *date* with a *man* who *bought* time with me. Come on."

"Not like you've got any other dates," Sadie muttered. "Whatever, take the free dinner. Nicholas isn't that bad." She waved her hand in dismissal.

Greta took a step toward her. Sadie was only two inches taller than Greta but around ninth grade had decided that she would never lower her chin, so she seemed even taller.

"Fuck you," Greta said. "I *know* you don't think this is cool. You would never do it to anyone but me."

Something flickered in Sadie's eyes, but she just sniffed and the moment was past.

"Now, girls," their mother said. "Stop this. Greta, I'm sorry you're upset. We just thought it might be nice if you gave someone a chance who you ordinarily wouldn't look at twice."

Greta goggled.

"Someone I ordinarily wouldn't…do you mean, like, a *guy*?"

Nell shrugged. "Love is love, isn't it?"

"Yeah," Greta said. "It is. And if I happen to fall in love with a man, then fine. I mean, I probably won't, because I'm a *lesbian*. But you don't get to throw those words around like a flotation device to redeem you from doing something shitty. You *knew* I would hate that. You knew I would've hated it even if it was all women who were bidding on me! I can't believe you!"

Unlike with Sadie, where all strong feeling eventually got expressed as anger, with her mother Greta finally felt tears threaten. It was a betrayal, plain and simple, and while the sisters all messed with one another from time to time, the thought that her mother either honestly didn't know her well enough to understand how much this would upset her or, worse, didn't care was enough to make her cry.

Their argument had brought her father to the living room as well. Always the last to engage, he looked at Greta with sympathy, but she'd long ago stopped thinking of him as an ally. What use was someone who agreed with you if they weren't ever willing to risk discomfort to say so?

Tillie started to chime in with her typical placations, but Greta was done arguing. She wanted her mother to admit what she'd done—even Sadie had done that—and then she wanted to get the hell out of this house.

"Did you seriously not get that I would hate that?" she asked her mother point-blank.

Nell Russakoff's face was the picture of aghast innocence.

"Darling, no. I would never do anything to upset you. I just thought maybe a little push… You can't want to stay single forever. And it's not as if there are many other lesbians on Owl Island…"

But Greta knew. The slight flick of her mother's gaze to the left told Greta that Nell had been perfectly aware how Greta would respond.

"Okay, cool. Great," she said sarcastically. "A push. Well, that sounds great to me. Yup, a push actually sounds like exactly what I need. The hell away from here."

And without another word, she turned on her heel and walked back into the snow.

←→

"I have to get *out* of here. I don't care where," she said to her friend Ramona after relating the incident.

"So get out, babe. I know it's Chanukah and I know your family, but I must introduce you to my friend Boundaries, and her best friend, Also Boundaries."

Greta sighed. She had been introduced to Ramona's friends before. They seemed great. Great and utterly unattainable, like the effortlessly cool people at the parties they'd once attended together.

"I know," she said.

"So go."

Greta looked around the house she'd rented for the last year since returning to Owl Island. It looked nearly the same as it had when she'd moved in—a furnished favor from a friend of Tillie's—except for her plants. Greta's joys, they hung from every window frame and reached for each bit of sunlight they could.

In the second bedroom were her treasures: the carnivorous plants. Her pitcher plants, Venus flytraps, carnivorous bromeliads, and cobra plants. They were helped along by three humidifiers that ran constantly, and she kept the room balmy enough for the tropical species with a heater set to seventy-two degrees.

She walked among them, stroking a pitcher here and inspecting a saw-toothed mouth there. In Maine winters, especially, they required careful attention.

"I can't. My plants."

"Get one of your ten thousand sisters to take care of them."

Greta's nostrils flared. The last thing she wanted was to have anything to do with her family.

"Can you hire someone?"

"It's nearly Christmas, and everyone's busy with their own stuff."

She heard Ramona's sigh that clearly said *You're making excuses, and I don't approve.*

And maybe she was right.

"Look, I'll…um…I'll ask around and see if maybe someone can take care of them."

But she knew the only person she could ask was Ash, and he already had his hands full with more than anyone should have to tend to with the shop and his mother.

"You do that, babe. Call me if you need some sense talked into you. Again."

Then the line went dead, and Greta sat down very carefully on the floor amid the Venus flytraps, wondering if she sat there long enough and still enough maybe they would just consume her slowly and put her out of her misery.

# 2
# TRUMAN

The Garden District was alive with revelers, its grand houses touched with holiday cheer in everything from the subtlest to the most extravagant displays.

Truman Belvedere held the wrapped gift carefully as he strolled past Lafayette No. 1, pausing as he always did to appreciate the roots creeping through the stone walls to meet the ivy that adorned them. The way the tree boughs bent in to shade the sidewalks, beckoning pedestrians inside the cemetery. How the late afternoon sun fell slantways on the graves, offering up the names of the deceased to any who gazed upon them.

Truman loved this cemetery and had visited it often in the eight years he'd lived in New Orleans, beginning with his time at Tulane.

Now, though, rather than stop and walk among the graves as he usually did, he turned the corner and walked past Commander's Palace, toward Guy's house.

He was stopping by unannounced to drop off Guy's Christmas gift, since his boyfriend was taking a trip with his brother for the holiday. Truman was disappointed that he wouldn't get to spend their first Christmas together—and even more disappointed because the announcement had come too late for him to make other plans—but hoped to send Guy off with a smile thanks to the gift he'd spent practically his whole paycheck on. And maybe from the quickie he had planned too.

He'd only been to Guy's house once in the eleven months they'd been dating, but he knew which one it was. A gorgeous gray-and-white Queen Anne with a wraparound porch on the lower level and a step-out balcony through French doors off the master bedroom. The trees were lush and the hedgerow perfectly manicured behind the wrought iron fence.

Guy liked his things just so. And Truman was honored to pass muster.

He crossed the street, nerves singing in his stomach. Nearly a year together and he still got butterflies before he saw Guy. He smiled, picturing the way Guy's severe face softened into a smile when Truman amused him. The way he let his guard down when they curled up together on Truman's couch or in Truman's bed, becoming a younger, gentler version of himself.

Truman knew that was the smile he'd see when Guy opened his front door to see Truman standing there with his perfectly wrapped gift.

Soft music issued from an open window to the left of the door, and white lights twinkled from inside. Guy had always been so vague about certain aspects of his life, and Truman only hesitated for a moment before he let himself peek inside. You could tell so much about someone by their décor, their taste in art, their holiday decorations. He wanted to see the tree that he hadn't been invited to help decorate, the ornaments that, Guy had let slip, he'd collected over the years. Truman made a bet with himself that the tree would be as cleanly and modernly arrayed as Guy himself.

The room was gray and white and navy, appointed with club chairs, a mid-century-modern couch, and an enormous Christmas tree. The white fairy lights that adorned it were evenly spaced around its branches; expensive-looking glass ornaments were hung with an engineer's precision. Truman smiled fondly at the effort that must have gone into the tree and pictured Guy—austere, detail-oriented Guy—listening to Christmas carols by himself while sipping hot cocoa laced with his favorite whiskey and measuring the space between ornaments.

In that moment, Truman forgave Guy for not inviting him to trim the tree. His boyfriend was fastidious and exacting, and he'd wanted to do it precisely as he wished—an ode to the beauty of order rather than a romantic and cozy tradition. It was cute that he had things like this he kept just for himself. Charming.

Smiling, Truman began to turn from the window. He couldn't wait to kiss the hell out of his endearing weirdo. But movement in the room caught his eye, and he ducked out of sight automatically, mortified at the idea of being caught peeping.

But when he peeked again, he saw the movement was Guy, in all his handsome glory, walking into the room. Truman couldn't help gazing at him.

As he watched, someone else entered. Truman had been sure that Guy said he was meeting his brother, not having him over…

The man slid an arm around Guy's waist, and not in a brotherly way.

Truman's stomach lurched.

The man was blond and brown-eyed. He was talking on

the phone, and every few words, he looked up at Guy and rolled his eyes. Guy's face crinkled into the exact expression of warmth and amusement that Truman had thought belonged to him alone.

For a moment, Truman tried to come up with alternatives to heartbreak: it *was* Guy's brother, and they were just very close. It was a friend who had stopped by unexpectedly, just as Truman had, to drop off a gift. It was a coworker who needed Guy's immediate input on an important business matter. It was…it was…

As he watched, Guy pulled the man closer and kissed the top of his head. When a girl of seven or eight walked into the room and held a jar of peanut butter up to Guy, he opened it for her like it was the most natural thing in the world. Then he tugged her ponytail affectionately.

The girl screwed up her face, but Truman had no trouble recognizing the word she said.

*Dad.*

Truman threw up in the hyacinths.

$\longleftrightarrow$

"You did *what*?"

Truman banged his forehead on his friend Ramona's bedroom door.

After leaving Guy's, desperate for space to think, he'd tried to take refuge in the cemetery, but there had been too many people there, wending their way through the crypts, tipsy from twenty-five-cent martinis at Commander's Palace. The idea of being seen in general made Truman's stomach threaten to lurch once more. The idea of being seen by one of Guy's friends, who all lived in the neighborhood, because of course they did…unbearable.

If he'd gone home, he would have sunk into tears and despair. So he'd headed to Ramona's place in St. Roch instead.

"Nothing," he mumbled.

"You did *nothing*."

*Depends. Does vomiting into someone's flowers count as something?*

"I left. Excuse me for panicking when I realized my boyfriend of almost a year has a secret family."

Ramona's eyes got wide, and she shook her head.

"Dog."

Truman should really be getting home to his own dog—his actual dog. They would take their evening walk, maybe chat with Mr. and Mrs. Dinstein if they were on their porch as they usually were. Then they'd go home and watch YouTube videos or listen to a podcast. Then they'd go to bed. Alone. Like they usually did.

Only now Truman groaned, realizing that the reason he usually went to bed alone was probably not, as he'd been told, because Guy had trouble sleeping in bed with someone.

The other lies revealed themselves in a landslide of horror that threatened to crush Truman.

"God," he groaned. "I'm such a fucking chump. He's not going on vacation with his brother for a month, is he?"

Ramona shook her head regretfully.

"How did this happen? How did I do this? How did…I… What…"

He dissolved.

Ramona led him to the couch gently by the arm.

They'd met two years ago when she worked in his favorite

stationery store. Her job had been short-lived, but their friendship endured, and in that time, she'd led him to her couch
gently more times than she should have needed to. Ramona
had an uncanny ability to see things he wished to keep hidden,
and she was disturbingly honest, which meant she didn't allow
those things to stay hidden.

Now, she looked him dead in the eyes, a telltale sign that
she was about to unearth.

"Just say it," he prompted her, ready to get the truth-telling
over with. Suddenly he really, really wanted to bury his face in
a pillow and sob.

"You don't ask for anything," she said simply.

"What?" Truman's spine stiffened.

"Sorry, sorry, edit: Guy is a total piece of shit. Meant to say
that first. It's *not* your fault. But you asked how this happened,
and aside from Guy being an emotional abattoir, it happened
because you do not ask for anything for yourself. You accept
what people give you, and you don't ask for what you need. Or
want. It's a problem."

Truman closed his eyes and let his head fall back against
the cushion.

It was a problem.

He didn't *mean* to not ask for things. When other people
offered ideas for what to do or where to eat, he got excited.
He already knew everything he liked. Their preferences
expanded his own. That was good, right? To be open-minded
and flexible?

But he knew that after a while, people got the idea that
they didn't ever need to ask him what he wanted because they
knew he'd be fine with whatever. And that…that wasn't. That
was the problem part, he was pretty sure.

He cringed anew, remembering the knowing looks Guy's friends had shared the night they ran into them at a restaurant in the Central Business District. Truman had thought they were just a bit snooty, as Guy was, but they had ignored him because they knew he didn't matter. Knew he was just a pathetic side piece. They had been embarrassed for him.

His head spun with shame and mortification, and he winced.

"You're into interior design," Truman said. "Do they make floors that swallow you where you stand?"

Ramona snorted.

"Unfortunately, I think they're still working on that one. But you know, any floor can be used to stand on while asking for what you want and need so that people have a chance of meeting your desires." She squeezed his shoulder to soften her words.

"I've gotta get out of here. Go somewhere no one knows me. Somewhere people won't see me walking down the street and think *There's that pathetic loser whose boyfriend has a secret family*. Well, I guess they're not the secret. I'm the secret. *There's that pathetic loser who's his boyfriend's dirty little secret*. Kill me."

"You know, you're the second person to say that to me today," Ramona mused.

"I'm the second person who asked you to euthanize them because they're dating someone with a whole other life? God, maybe it's you."

Ramona laughed.

"You're the second person who's told me that they want to get out of town immediately."

"God, I wish."

"So go."

Truman sighed. He wished he were the kind of person who left town at a moment's notice. Who gave in to their feelings of heartbreak and drowned them in a fancy bathtub full of wine and cupcakes in a glamorous location far, far away.

But he wasn't.

"I can't leave. I've got Horse, and…"

"People with dogs do manage to occasionally vacation," Ramona chided. "Can you take him with you?"

Truman's first attempt to fly with Horse had also been his last. Usually a chill dog, Horse's horror at flying had been unexpected—and his insistence on sitting in Truman's lap for the three-hour flight to Philadelphia, while sweet, hadn't been received well by his seatmates. Despite Truman's mortified apologies for the whines (Horse), paws in their laps (also Horse), and constant stream of calming baby talk (Truman), his fellow passengers had been neither charmed nor placated.

"Yeah, Horse doesn't fly. It's a whole thing. And it's Christmas, so people have plans. I can't ask them to come over three times a day and walk a dog."

"As I was saying, you're the second person to say this to me today."

Truman opened his mouth, and Ramona clapped her hand over it.

"I *mean* you're the second person who wants to get out of town but has stuff at home they need tended to. So what if you swap?"

He removed her hand from his mouth.

"Swap. Like, swap houses?"

"Yeah! Oh shit, it'd be perfect. You both really need it. How do I end up with all these friends who need my wisdom and guidance so desperately," she mused to herself, flipping through her phone.

"Do people still swap houses? Isn't that, like, the beginning of a true crime podcast or something?"

Ramona ignored him.

"So, it's my friend Greta. We were roommates before I transferred to Tulane. She's great. Terrible boundaries. Wackadoodle family. But a total gem. She just had a fight with her family and wants to leave town. But she has tons of plants. They're, like, her babies. And they need to be tended to. You go to her place in Maine and mist her plants or whatever. And she can come to your place and take care of Horse. It's perfect!"

She sat back, arms spread, clearly quite pleased with herself.

"I can't," Truman said automatically.

She wrinkled her nose. "Why?"

"Because…because I…I just…"

"Exactly. You *can*. You have money, you're not afraid of flying, and you don't like hanging out with your family for the holidays. But you're gonna choose not to because it feels scary and hard. But you know what's also scary and hard, Truman?"

"Lemme guess. Being a miserable, pathetic dope alone at the holidays?"

"Well, I was going to say waking up an old man and realizing that you never took any chances in your life and chose ease over adventure, capitulation over intention, and others over yourself, but yours works too."

Truman laughed despite himself.

"I'll just be miserable and alone in Maine if I go," he warned. "It won't be some cute holiday fantasy."

"Speaking of fantasy," she drawled casually, "isn't the

author of that batshit book you're so obsessed with from there?"

Truman cleared his throat, preparing to say that he wasn't *obsessed*. But it had been his first thought when Ramona mentioned Maine. Agatha Tark *was* from Maine. It was one of the only biographical facts known about her, aside from her insistence on complete removal from public life and her fondness for cats.

The Dead of Zagørjič was a fantasy series Truman had been a fan of since he was a child.

Okay, he'd been obsessed with it.

Fine, he still was.

The Dead of Zagørjič had been the comfort world he'd escaped into any time something bad had happened to him.

Maybe this was meant to be? Maybe he should pack some sweaters and his beloved paperbacks and his journals and his computer, get the hell out of New Orleans, and hole up in Maine like Tark had done.

He was eyeing the wrapped package he'd meant to drop off for Guy. It was a Montblanc Meisterstück Solitaire Blue Hour LeGrand Rollerball pen, and it had set him back nearly $1,700.

"If I sell Guy's present, I could buy a plane ticket."

Ramona looked like the information of how much he'd spent on the gift caused her physical pain, but she just nodded.

"This," she told him with a knowing grin, "is going to be perfect."

↔

Ramona gave Truman Greta's phone number with the strict instruction to text, not call.

"She hates talking on the phone," Ramona said.

"Well, yeah, I'm not a monster," Truman said, shuddering at the thought of a phone call with a stranger.

"You're actually gonna text her, though?"

"Here, look."

Truman tapped in Greta's number and wrote Hi, I'm Truman, Ramona's friend. I hear we have a problem in common?

He held the phone up and pressed Send where Ramona could see.

"Okay, good," she sighed, smiling with relief. "What would you two do without me?"

Truman, assuming that was a rhetorical question, took the opportunity to gather his errant gift and his pride and wave goodbye to Ramona.

Greta texted back as he turned the corner.

*yeah, sounds like we do. are you...into this? i have a LOT of plants you'd have to take care of. A LOT.*

No problem! I'm very responsible. Responsible to a fault, as Ramona would say.

*of course ramona thinks responsibility is a fault lol*, Greta replied, proving that they actually were friends.

I'd need you to take care of my dog. He needs to be walked three times a day. Would that be a problem?

*nope, i love to walk and i love animals.*

Truman felt his mood lift. Could they actually do this? Could he actually get away from the town where everything reminded him of Guy and of his own foolishness? And, in the back of his mind, the whisper: Agatha Tark, Agatha Tark, Agatha Tark.

Sooooo should we do this?

*i think we should*, came Greta's immediate reply. *i've gotta*

*get out of town and away from my family or i'll say shit i regret.*
*well. more shit i regret.*

Yeah, me too. Or, not the say things I regret part bc I actually didn't say anything.

He cringed, remembering his quiet, unobtrusive slink away from Guy's window.

*what happened?*

Turns out my boyfriend of a year has, like, a whole other life? A husband or partner and a kid. And I'm such a fool I didn't even notice.

The words came easily to a stranger, and Truman found himself telling Greta what he couldn't say to Ramona.

I was totally in love with him. But I guess I didn't know him at all, really. What a chump, huh?

Greta's response didn't come for a minute, and Truman's stomach churned as he watched her ellipsis.

*he WHAT!?!? no, yr not a chump, he's a shithead. and his partner doesn't know about you? what is WRONG w people why are they the total worst?!*

A satisfying string of monster and knife emojis followed, and Truman smiled.

The worst part is that I didn't even do anything. I just left.

*want me to go over there and kick his ass?!* came Greta's reply.

Kinda! I just feel like I should've told his partner, right? Like, hey, you're with a cheating jerk, just so you know. Something.

*you're being too hard on yourself. confrontation is HARD!*

Yeah. So what happened to make you need to get out of town?

*oh nbd, just my mother and sister auctioning me off in the public square of our town.*

That brought him up short.

Er. What?

She told him the story of her family and their town holiday festival then, and he commiserated with her plight.

By the time he got home, he felt like Greta needed this just as much as he did.

"Hi, baby," he said as he unlocked the door and Horse trotted up to him. The Great Dane's sleek fur was mussed on one side where he'd been snoozing, but his eyes were bright and he nudged Truman's stomach, eager for their evening walk.

He slid Horse's leash down over his wrist so he could keep texting with Greta, and they set out into the night.

They discussed the particulars and agreed on where they'd leave keys and instructions, and then there was nothing else to say except:

So we're really doing this?

*yeah, we really are!*

Wow. Wow wow wow. I don't do things like this.

*me neither.*

Then there was a pause, and they both sent messages at once.

Truman's said: Maybe that's the best reason to do it. Greta's said: *maybe if we were the kind of people who did shit like this we wouldn't be in our current messes.*

They both liked each other's texts, and the deal was struck.

Fourteen hours later, Truman was on a plane, suitcase packed for a month checked to Maine, his journal open in front of him to a new spread, winging his way toward the unknown.

# A MESSAGE
# FROM RAMONA

**RAMONA to TRUMAN CUTIE and GREAT!A RUSSAKOFF**

I know you've both been feeling stuck, creatively and person-ally. Well, carry an umbrella at all times, cuz it's gonna be raining possibilities and solutions! (Well, snowing them in Maine probably, and shining them down in N.O. ;D)

# 3
## TRUMAN

Truman stretched out on the bed, knocking over the wine bottle he'd just emptied. He reached for it, grabbed it by the neck, and then overbalanced and slowly slid to the floor in a drunken slither that he was extremely glad no one was there to witness.

"Yeah," he said to no one. "Probably no one will ever be here to see me do anything ever again cuz people are bad. Bad, bad. They're bad."

He nodded emphatically and regretted it instantly as his head started to spin. Groaning, he let his head fall gently to the floor. He could just sleep here. Half under the bed was basically like being in bed, right? Yup.

Greta's house was darling. It was small with white clapboard siding and well-worn wood floors. The walls were all white, and there were mirrors and reflective surfaces everywhere that caught the sunlight and threw it around the house.

And every single thing seemed set up for the benefit of plants, not people. There were humidifiers, heaters, grow lights, and a complicated spreadsheet of when each thing should be turned on, turned off, angled, or rotated.

It was a lot, but Truman respected a good spreadsheet.

He'd followed her instructions when he first arrived, then walked into the town square, which was only five blocks away. There he had gathered provisions: three bottles of wine, five kinds of cheese, two kinds of crackers, and four kinds of chocolate, which was all the kinds of wine, cheese, crackers, and chocolate that Muskee's General Store carried.

In just the time it had taken to walk to the store, Truman had already been freezing. Maine, it turned out, was cold. Truman knew this, naturally, but somehow, in the flurry of packing, hiding a key, writing instructions for Greta, and returning Guy's Christmas gift, that knowledge hadn't translated into warm enough clothes.

He'd layered his light autumn jacket atop a button-down shirt and a thin cashmere sweater and looped a woven scarf around his neck, but the wind had blown through it all ten steps down the road, and his shoes were soaked with snow immediately.

By the time he made it home with his groceries, Truman was colder than he could ever remember being. So he'd shucked his clothes, taken the wine, cheese, crackers, and chocolate into bed, pulled the duvet up to his chin, and commenced to spend the evening in a haze of cheese, booze, and the Dead of Zagørjič.

He had read the series so many times over the years that he could open to any page in any of the seven books and know exactly what was going on. Often, he read his favorite bits to cheer himself up.

His current situation, though? Called for a complete reread. He needed to be utterly immersed in the world of Zagørjič. He wanted to sink into the world of Clarion and her hawk companion, Sør, and discover the ability to speak to animals and trees along with her. He wanted to fall in love with the handsome tree spirit, Aerlich, experience the divinity of their romance, and weep bitter tears when he was corrupted by the need to avenge his brother's murder.

Truman had first read the series in eighth grade. He'd encountered it in his friend John's older sister's room one night when he was sleeping over but couldn't sleep. She found him on her floor, halfway through book one in the series, when she got home. At first he'd frozen, because she wasn't known for her sweet temper. But when she saw the way he gripped the book tight, like he was afraid she'd take it from him, she'd sat down next to him and they'd talked about it for hours. She'd let him borrow the whole series—with the threat of certain death should anything happen to them—and he'd been a die-hard fan ever since.

He'd known that Agatha Tark lived and wrote in Maine, but picking up book one, *The Heart Freezes*, after his trek through the winter snow, he felt a new kinship with Clarion when she stands atop Mount Moriah in the gusting snow and wraps an injured Sør in her own cloak. How freezing she must have been! How much she loved the hawk!

Yes, Truman congratulated himself on his newfound empathy and snuggled deeper into the covers to read.

Three hours later, cheese and wine distant memories and chocolate well on its way, when Truman slid to the floor, he just grabbed the duvet and pulled it off the bed onto himself, book sliding with it and landing on his forehead.

He closed his eyes as his head spun.

"What. The hell. Did I do," he mumbled. He was referring, most immediately, to the wine. But the question hung in the air, more all-encompassing than he'd intended.

"How did this happen?" was the obvious follow-up. *How* had he dated a man for almost a *year* and never realized that he had a whole life Truman knew nothing about? Not only that, but *Truman* was the lesser, secret element in an otherwise full life. How had he not noticed he was a mere dalliance? A side character. A subplot in the life of a man who had taken up nearly all his spare thoughts.

Guy had been stern, charismatic, busy. Truman had known from the beginning that he worked a lot. That he had an active social life. That he belonged to multiple organizations. It had all seemed normal.

*Did it really, though? What about all the times you said things to your friends and they looked at you strangely and you realized that things about your relationship were weird? When Guy's parents came to town but you couldn't meet them? When he drove to visit his brother but didn't invite you? When he took you to brunch for your birthday but was busy on his? Come to mention it, the number of brunches you went to instead of dinners...*

"Fuck me."

Truman pulled the duvet over his head. It smelled of lavender, which made him homesick for Horse. He fumbled out his phone to look at a picture of his dog and nearly dropped it on his face, so he dragged himself to a sitting position and scrolled lovingly through the many, many pictures.

Then he let his body do what it wanted, which was to slide back down to the floor, nudging the bed to the right as he slid. He lay on his back and looked at the ceiling. It had an unusual pattern of plaster—almost a sunburst, which reminded him of the healing hut where Clarion finds herself imprisoned in book five of the series.

Turning onto his side, he saw a mark on the wood floor just

under the bed. At first glance, it looked like a wedge patching a hole in the board. But when he nudged the bed aside more, he could see what it really was: a ship inlaid in the wood floor.

"No. No way. You're just drunk. And sad. And jet-lagged. You're drunk-lagged. That's not… No."

But a few minutes later, he still couldn't stop thinking about it. The flashlight on his phone illuminated a wooden sailing ship, set flush with the floor, its prow pointing into the room, its mast jutting proudly.

It was a ship just like the one Clarion touches every night before bed in book six, after Aerlich has turned dark and she has to drag herself to bed without him. She runs her fingers over the ship and imagines that it's taking her heartbreak away—pulling it far out to sea and releasing it for seabirds and fish to pull to pieces.

"Am I in Agatha Tark's fucking house?" Truman breathed. He scrambled for his suitcase and pulled out book six, *The Heart Screams.*

> *Clarion took it for a sigil. An artisan generations before had laid each piece of the Draggør sailing ship into the floor. They were carved from light skrimwood and dark mhyrtlewood—both hard, strong, and nearly impossible to cut with any but the sharpest blade. This craft had been a work of love and obsession. More and more, Clarion believed they were the same.*

"Holy shit!" He squinted at the ship again. "No. No way. It's impossible."

His spinning head insisted that he stop squinting.

He took a picture of the ship, intending to text Germaine and Charlotte and see if it could possibly be true. But somewhere between tapping the button and moving to get back into bed, sleep took him.

↔

Truman groaned as a beam of sunlight stabbed him in the eye.

He was on the floor, in a nest of duvet, pillow, and flannel top sheet that he had no memory of making. His legs were under the bed, and when he opened his eyes, he just had time to see a dust bunny inches from his face before sneezing wildly.

"Oh, Jesus," he groaned as the sneeze threatened to tear his skull apart.

As if in answer, one of the empty wine bottles, apparently dislodged from its rest by his sneeze, rolled across the floor and clunked into his head.

*I'll just lie here for a while.*

↔

The next time he awoke, the sun was less stabby and his hip ached. Truman dragged himself up slowly as different parts of his body complained. He crept to the bathroom and stood under the hot water until vomiting didn't seem imminent.

When he finally opened his eyes, he realized that the bathroom was full of plants. Maybe they were ferns? Two of them hung in front of the small window and another hung on the wall opposite it. There was also something that looked like balls of moss on the windowsill next to a vining plant with beautiful deep purple leaves.

Over coffee, Truman studied the instructions Greta had left and did the morning plant routine of turning on this humidifier and turning off that grow light. One of the humidifiers was for a cluster of carnivorous plants in front of a window in the second bedroom that had been transformed into a kind of greenhouse.

When Truman had heard *carnivorous*, he'd worried that he would have to mess with live grasshoppers or something. But Greta had written that she'd fed all of them before she left and that he wouldn't have to worry about feeding them again for two weeks, at which time there were pellets to give them.

So he simply refilled the humidifier and peeked at the odd plants. Several of them looked like the "Feed me, Seymour" plants, though thankfully much smaller. But a number of them were something he'd never seen before: plants with rounded cup-like appendages in streaks of maroon, green, purple, and red.

"What the hell are you?"

They were absurd and almost beautiful. Truman wanted to touch them but wasn't entirely sure that they couldn't bite off a finger. So he settled for examining them closely.

And when he looked, he saw that one of the medium-sized plants looked withered and brown.

"Oh god, did I kill something already?"

Panicked, he reached in and picked up the pot, peering at the plant. Its soil seemed moist enough, but he had no idea what *enough* meant for ordinary plants, much less something like this.

He ran back into the kitchen and reread the instructions to see if Greta had left contingency plans for such a scenario. There was nothing.

Should he text her? What would he say, though? "Sorry, but I immediately got so drunk in your bed that I didn't notice one of your precious babies that I swore I would care for was in its death throes." Yeah, nope.

Then he remembered the walk to the general store.

"Florist. There was a florist. Florists know about plants, right?"

Right.

He pulled on jeans and a long-sleeved shirt. But remembering yesterday's walk and his own insufficient winter wear, he opened Greta's closet. She wouldn't mind if he borrowed a sweater, would she? No, that was weird.

He tapped a quick message to her: Hey! Hope you're enjoying the warm weather! Unfortunately I'm rather unprepared for the cold. I know it's kinda weird to ask, but...would you mind if I borrowed a sweater?

Her response came immediately. *oh, totally, borrow whatever you want. it's gorgeous here.* And then a palm tree emoji.

He pulled on a gloriously warm woolen sweater and felt much better about leaving the house. Now he just had to find the equivalent for the plant. He pulled a blanket off the couch and wrapped the plant in it as well as he could to protect it from the winter but not squish it in the process, then he set off into town.

It was still bitterly cold, but the sweater made a big difference, and Truman decided to look for gloves and a hat when he got back.

The shop was called Thorn, and it glowed invitingly. Truman rushed inside, cradling the swaddled plant in his arms, and a bell cheerily tinkled his arrival.

A man was arranging roses in a plastic tub with his back to

Truman. He had broad shoulders, thick forearms, and messy brownish-blondish hair that swept his shoulders.

"Just a sec," he called without turning around.

A glassed-in cooler next to the counter held beautiful arrangements. Simple sprays of one kind of flower, riotous mixtures of many colors, and several large arrangements that looked more like art than flowers. Tubs of different varieties of flowers were lined up around the inside of the shop with signs stating type and price and how to make a bouquet of your own.

The walls were painted a soft grayish purple and washed over with irregular swipes of color, giving the subtle effect that you stood inside a flower arrangement. It was lovely and made the scarred wood floors and counter look shabby chic instead of just shabby.

In a red corduroy bed next to the counter, a shaggy black-and-brown dog snoozed, one ear twitching in dreams.

The man turned around, revealing a roughly handsome face and the most gorgeous blue-gray eyes Truman had ever seen. He looked like a sea-torn ship's captain, eyes like a storm. He had a few days' worth of golden-brown stubble on his jaw and lips so lush they almost seemed out of place.

When he took in Truman, his expression turned from impersonal welcome to surprise and then settled in amusement.

"Chilly out there, huh?" he said, raising an eyebrow at the blanket, revealing the patient.

"Oh, no, um. I mean, yeah, it's freezing. But this isn't for me." Truman put the bundle down on the counter and carefully unwound the blanket. "I'm really sorry to bother you, but I'm hoping you can help. I think this plant is dying."

Truman's voice sounded every bit as concerned as he felt, but he would've liked to play it just a bit cooler.

"I know you're a florist, and plants aren't the same, but I don't know anyone here, and I just really can *not* have killed this plant," Truman finished in a rush, looking desperately at the man now joining him at the counter.

He was tall and even broader than Truman had first thought. His eyes were mesmerizing.

He nodded solemnly and examined the plant, peering at it calmly from all sides. Truman relaxed. The plant seemed to be in good hands.

The man stuck a finger in the soil, then peeked at the bottom of the pot, and finally put it back down on the counter and turned his searching gaze to Truman. "Does this perchance have anything to do with Greta?" he asked. His voice was low and smooth.

Truman goggled. So much for secrecy!

"What? No! Um, I mean… Why would you think that?"

"Well. There's only one person I know who collects carnivorous plants."

Truman relaxed again. "Lots of people are into plants. They're very hot right now. Trending." He congratulated himself on keeping his cool.

"Uh-huh," the florist said. "Also you're wearing her sweater. And carrying a plant wrapped in her blanket."

Truman blinked. *Busted.* "Right."

The florist smiled, revealing charmingly crooked teeth and a dimple in one cheek. "You Truman?"

"You knew who I was this whole time?"

The man smiled again.

"So, um. I guess it would be out of the question to ask you not to tell Greta I killed one of her plants…?"

He shrank with shame.

"I don't know," the man said seriously. "Greta is one of my closest friends. And I don't like to lie."

Truman cringed. He was the worst. He'd just suffered the devastation that lying could cause, and now he was asking this man to lie for him? Terrible!

"You're right. I'm so sorry. God, I don't know what I was thinking—lying is the worst. You're right not to lie to people. Maybe I could get Greta a new...whatever that plant is? Oh, god, are they really rare, do you know?"

The florist's expression softened, his stormy eyes fixed on Truman's.

"Hey, don't worry. This is a sarracenia. They require a winter dormancy. You didn't kill it. It's just resting."

Relief shot through Truman like a tidal wave. "Oh, thank god. Fuck, thank you." His head spun with relief.

"Whoa," the man said, and Truman felt a strong hand fasten around his biceps as he slumped against the counter.

"I'm fine, just a little hungover. And jet-lagged. And heartbroken."

A strange, panicked laugh tore out of Truman without his permission, and he closed his eyes as his legs went weak.

The florist took his weight effortlessly, led him behind the counter, and pushed him to the chair there. He disappeared through a doorway and returned a minute later with an apple and a granola bar, holding them out to Truman somberly.

Head rush receding, Truman picked the apple and bit into it. The skin gave way under his teeth to sweet flesh.

"Thanks," he said, leaning against the counter. "I'm okay, really."

"I'm Ash," the man said.

Truman reached out a hand to shake Ash's automatically.

Ash looked amused but shook his hand. Ash's palm was warm and dry and softer than Truman expected.

"So, um, I don't suppose you could leave out the stumbling around hungover part when you tell Greta I thought I'd killed her plant, could you?"

Ash leaned a hip against the counter. "I'm not going to tell Greta."

"Oh. Thanks."

Ash nodded. The dog gave a little yip, waking itself up, and shook itself before coming to stand next to Ash.

"Hey, buddy." Ash scratched the dog's ears. "This is Bruce."

Truman reached out a hand and let the dog sniff his knuckles. "Makes me miss my dog." Bruce gave him a lick and then rested his chin on Truman's knees. "Aww, what a sweetie."

"He's a good dog," Ash agreed.

"Do you like working here?" Truman asked, not wanting the moment to end for reasons he absolutely refused to acknowledge.

Ash nodded. "I love it. People are always happy to come in here. Happy to see me when I ring the bell to deliver flowers."

Truman smiled. "That must be nice. It's cool that people still send each other flowers."

Ash's eyes narrowed.

"No one's ever given me any, so I guess I didn't think about it," Truman stammered on.

Truman had only sent flowers once—peonies for Guy's birthday. He'd received only a terse thank-you text. At the time, he'd assumed Guy wasn't a flower enthusiast. Now, he wondered how Guy had explained them to his husband.

"That surprises me," Ash said.

Truman, flustered, said nothing, just dropped the apple core in the trash can, gave Bruce another scratch between the ears, and wrapped the plant up in Greta's blanket again. "Well, um, thanks!" he said, trying to sound cheery and casual. "Guess I'll let you get back to making people happy. I appreciate your help."

"Truman."

"Hmm?"

Ash held up a finger and walked to the back room again. He reappeared holding a single rose. It wasn't like anything Truman had ever seen. Its petals were almost ruffled at the edges, and its color was caught somewhere between tea and pink. It was the most beautiful rose he'd ever seen.

Ash held it out to him.

"Now you can't say no one has ever given you flowers."

# 4
# GRETA

New Orleans smelled like ozone, frying oil, and a flower Greta didn't recognize. After her flight had gotten delayed twice and then rebooked hours later, leaving her to catch a few hours' sleep using her duffel as a pillow, she had finally arrived. She'd gotten a cab from the airport to Truman's house in a neighborhood called the Marigny that she hadn't been sure how to pronounce until the cabbie had said it.

In the purple twilight, the houses looked like fairy cottages, painted every color of the rainbow. Flowers and fronds spilled from pots on front porches and balconies, giving the whole street a lush verdancy that made her want to run her fingers along it like velvet.

On a number of porches, people sat sipping drinks and chatting, and music drifted through open windows and doors.

Greta was sweating in her winter clothes, the temperature in the seventies, and she grinned, pleased to suddenly find herself in this entirely other world.

Truman's house was what he'd called a shotgun, and when Greta opened the door—the key under the flowerpot just where Truman had said it would be—she understood what that meant. Each room led into the next in a straight line you could (presumably) shoot a shotgun through.

She dropped her bags just inside the door and pulled her suitcase in after her. Before she could even take her shoes off, though, the tallest dog she'd ever seen came trotting toward her from the back of the house.

"You must be Horse."

Greta held out her hand for sniffing, and the Great Dane acquainted himself with all her smells, moving around her in a circle, then coming around to the front and blinking at her expectantly.

"Right, your walk. Give me five minutes."

As if he understood, Horse took a step back and let her into the house.

The living room had a couch, a small television, and a bookshelf crammed with crack-spined paperbacks but was largely taken up by a drafting table packed with markers, pens, pencils, rolls of multicolored tape, paints, and a number of art supplies Greta didn't recognize. A shelf of identical black leather spines sat above the desk. There had to be at least twenty.

Greta couldn't resist taking one down and peeking into it, making a silent promise to Truman that if they were diaries, she would not read them. But no, it was a calendar of sorts, each page a work of meticulous art. It had begun as a blank book and Truman had drawn in different calendars, dates, days, and other lists.

His handwriting was perfect—all capitals like an architect with no variation in size. It was neatly color-coded and decorated, and there was a complicated tracking system for multiple habits that she couldn't quite follow. The entire volume was beautiful and functional, and she decided that this must be how Truman was too. She placed the book back on the shelf reverently.

The bedroom was spotless, with clothes folded and hung neatly, another small bookcase that housed mostly fantasy and mystery novels, and sage-green bedding that made Greta feel calm.

The kitchen was at the back of the house, and it too was organized meticulously, pots and pans hung over a butcher block island and the spice rack alphabetized.

Finally, a small bathroom and shower, with towels the same green as the bedding, and a tiny sunroom that led out onto a long and skinny backyard. There was a lemon tree at the far end of the yard and a brazier in the middle, a chair set on either side of it.

Greta breathed in the subtle scents of lemon oil and barbecue smoke that were coming over the fence from the neighbor's cookout. Her stomach growled.

Back inside, she changed quickly out of her winter clothes and threw on a black ribbed A-shirt with her jeans. She splashed cold water on her face, brushed her teeth, and ran a hand through her flattened hair. She finished with a swipe of black eyeliner that winged out at the edges of her eyes and nodded at herself in the mirror.

Before she had a chance to let the enormity of what she'd done catch up with her, she clipped on Horse's harness, slid her phone, credit card, and keys in her back pocket, and went to explore the neighborhood.

Truman had told her that he and Horse had regular routes they took, but she hadn't been prepared for the dog to practically walk her. She was content to follow him, though, since clearly he knew where he was going.

"Can we stop somewhere so I can get some food, please?" she muttered, amused at the huge dog's single-mindedness. Horse gave a whuffle and threw his head as if asking her to follow him. When they turned the next corner, she found herself outside a barbecue joint with an order window.

Greta stared at the restaurant and then at the dog.

"Can you...understand me?" she said.

Horse blinked his soulful eyes solemnly, and Greta had the distinct sensation that he was saying yes.

"Okaaaaay," she said, more to herself than to Horse.

She ordered a pulled pork sandwich and ate it as they walked. The meat was tender, the sauce tangy and rich, and the slaw a perfect creamy crunch.

Greta congratulated herself on making an excellent decision and rewarded Horse with a bit of meat. He plucked it up from her palm, licked his thanks, and then led them toward home.

Greta had been disappointed to see that Truman didn't have a single plant in his house. Now, though, she could see that the neighborhood had enough plants for her to stare at that she wouldn't have withdrawal. In fact, given the weather, she couldn't wait to explore the tropical varieties that she never got to see in Maine.

"Tomorrow, we're gonna go on a garden walk," she said. "And you're not leading the way."

Horse barked in understanding, and Greta nodded and finished her sandwich. Exhausted, she happily followed Horse back toward what would be home for the next month.

Her phone buzzed with the twenty-billionth text she'd gotten from her sisters since leaving Owl Island that morning. When she'd turned her phone on after the plane landed, they'd cascaded onto her screen in a waterfall of meddling.

You didn't seriously leave town, did you? her twin had written.

oh dang, did u peace out? right before CHANUKAH???, Maggie had texted. respect for this out of character chaos energy actually, then a GIF of a building crumbling to rubble.

Tillie had written simply Are you ok???

The rest of the texts were variations on this theme, except for Sadie's single missive, which simply said: Seriously? You ran away? Are you five?

When she'd gotten to that one, Greta had set her phone on Do Not Disturb, shoved it deep in her bag, and ignored it for the rest of the journey.

This text was from her mother and had somehow circumnavigated her Do Not Disturb orders. Typical.

Did you leave town? Your sisters are telling me you left town. Where are you? Are you all right? Then, as if unable to resist, another text that said, It's Hannukah!

Greta pocketed her phone and let Ramona's words fill her up. Boundaries. She needed to set boundaries with her family, or this would go on the whole time she was here, ruining it.

But her mother's *Are you all right?* wouldn't leave her mind. Her mother worried so much when she didn't know where her daughters were. Of course, she also worried when she did know where they were. But Greta couldn't stand making her worry if she didn't have to. It was selfish and cruel.

So she wrote back to her mother. *I'm fine. I'm in New Orleans. You don't have to worry about me.*

The responses came immediately. So immediately that for a moment, Greta thought she'd sent the text to the family thread rather than just her mother.

Adelaide was first: You're in New Orleans? What are you doing there?

Then Tillie: Who do you know in New Orleans? Do you have someplace to stay?

Then Maggie: oooh, new orleans is supposed to be so rad. where r u staying?

Sadie did not reply.

Rolling her eyes, she switched over to the family thread. Everyone must be over at her parents' house as usual.

*yes, i'm in new orleans. i'm fine. it's great here. i'm staying for a month.*

Replies of a month?, a MONTH?, for a month!!??, and Wait, you're gonna be gone for a whole month??! followed quickly thereafter, and Greta sighed.

They reached Truman's door, and Horse stood respectfully outside it, in case Greta was still having a conversation.

"You're very strange, do you know that?" she asked him.

He blinked slowly and cocked his head, as if to say *You're not the most normal yourself, you know.*

The next morning, Greta and Horse set off for their morning walk early. After her exhausting day of travel, Greta had crawled into bed at 9:00 p.m. and woken up just after 6:00 a.m., feeling deliciously rested and excited to explore.

"Take me to a coffee shop, please," she instructed Horse, just in case he really did understand.

After a few blocks, a coffee shop came into view.

"What the hell, man," Greta muttered at Horse. "This is eerie."

Horse just crossed the street excitedly.

"Hey, it's a Horse," said a man in coveralls on a ladder, fiddling with the rain gutter outside the café. "Where's Truman?"

"You know him?" Greta asked.

"Sure. Comes in all the time."

"Oh, uh, I'm Greta. I'm staying at his place for a bit. I'm from Maine."

She was unnerved by the recognition, something she'd thought she'd left behind in Owl Island.

"Welcome," the man said, sweeping his arms out as if to encompass the whole city.

"Thanks. Er, can Horse go in there?"

"Sure," he said, as if there was no reason a large dog *wouldn't* be welcome in an eating establishment.

Greta got her coffee as well as a treat for Horse, handed to her with a wink by the barista, who also clearly knew the dog.

As they walked, the cool morning heated and more and more people appeared.

Greta kept to one street at first, thinking she'd follow it and see where she ended up. But things she absolutely *had* to see kept revealing themselves around corners and through intersections, and soon she just let her eyes guide her.

Horse, now off his normal route, seemed perfectly happy to walk by her side, a companion rather than a compass.

Greta breathed deeply of the lush plants she walked past, greenery-starved from the Maine winter. Here, ferns and myrtle curled fingers around each other and sunflowers stood tall. Jasmine scented the air, and the porch of a yellow-and-white house was crawling with passionflower. Orange trees grew in a corner lot, the fruit clinging cartoonishly to the trees like something out of a juice commercial. Greta couldn't believe they actually grew like that. She imagined waking on a warm December morning and walking outside to pluck an orange from her own tree for breakfast. The prospect made her giddy.

Greta's love affair with plants had happened slowly.

First she'd been given a spider plant as a gift, and she'd hung it in the window, not sure what else to do with it. When it began sending out arms with miniature versions of itself at the end of them, Greta had been amazed. To see something replicate itself, by itself, without any intervention…it made her think about plants in a completely different way.

Then came another plant and another. She followed Instagram accounts and watched YouTube videos, googled facts, and downloaded apps.

Succulents were her next obsession, and she would drive from garden store to garden store on the mainland, pluck fallen leaves out of the dirt and off the floor around the succulents, then take them home and watch them recreate themselves.

One afternoon trip to even a crappy garden center could yield pocketfuls of leaves. Before she knew it, she had dishes of sprouting succulent leaves on every windowsill of her house. She would check on them each morning, plucking them up to see the whiskery roots that had shot out in the night.

Sometimes they would sit dormant for weeks, and just when they would begin to shrivel and she would contemplate tossing them away, new life would emerge, feeding on the old growth. Self-vampiric, self-creating, they would birth themselves again and again, ad infinitum.

Greta admired them because they could do what she could not: be themselves, over and over, no compromises, no family.

Then winter came, and the weak Maine sun wasn't

enough. So then grow lights and reflectors and heat mats and more. Little by little, her home became a greenhouse. Became a sanctuary for the bits and pieces of plants she rescued and revered.

It was on a trip into Portland that she saw her first Venus flytrap. The world of carnivorous plants swallowed her whole. They were magnificent and fierce, and they fascinated her more with each one she acquired. From the tiniest serrated mouth of a flytrap to the most luridly colored pitcher, they were the most bizarre and beautiful things she'd ever seen.

But like the succulents, they weren't made for Owl Island, Maine. She worked hard to help them thrive, but they were out of their element.

Now, here, in New Orleans—this was where they belonged.

Lost in her thoughts, Greta nearly walked past it without noticing. Only at the last moment did she blink and stare over the fence.

"Are you… That's… Is that…a miniature pony?"

It was standing on the other side of a fenced-in yard, just being a small horse. Greta crept closer, sneaking a look around. No one was in the yard, so she reached out a tentative hand. Did mini horses bite?

But the pony just regarded her calmly and closed its eyes when Greta's hand touched its head.

"Aren't you the sweetest?" Greta murmured.

Beside her, Horse was standing very still, his massive head right at Greta's stomach, but he sniffed at the fence, then yawned and lost interest.

When a couple rounded the corner, Greta stepped away, not wanting to be caught petting a stranger's horse over the fence on her first morning in town.

She crossed the street and kept walking. She didn't know where she was going, but when she crossed Frenchmen Street, the neighborhood changed. She saw bars and clubs, all shuttered in the morning. Then, two blocks farther, it changed again, and print under street names on signs informed her she was now in the French Quarter.

There were more people here, and a number of shops and restaurants, all but the coffee shops not yet open. The streets were cobblestone now, with few cars, and a donkey-drawn carriage, driven by a man in a top hat smoking a joint, clip-clopped past.

Greta veered away from the people, following a small street that was lined with upper-level balconies covered in plants. Unlike Truman's neighborhood, which had freestanding houses, these were a combination of connected houses divided into apartments, lofts above businesses, row homes, and, most intriguing, fences and gates overgrown with greenery, through which the paths to houses set back from the street were visible.

It was at one of these that Greta paused. Bird-of-paradise. They were growing from the ground, huge and stunningly bright, their variously colored beaks spiking in every direction. Greta had never seen anything like it.

There was a low brick wall from which the fence originated, and Greta thought if she could just stand on the brick lip, she could get a better view.

She slipped Horse's leash over her wrist and slid her phone out of her pocket. She couldn't wait to send Ash a picture of the flowers. Bird-of-paradise was one of his favorites.

She wedged the toe of her sneaker between the metal rods of the fence and pulled herself up onto the brick. There were only four or five inches she could stand on, so she kept to her tiptoes and flattened herself against the fence, praying no one chose that moment to look out their window.

From this new vantage point, she could see that the birds-of-paradise grew among luscious passionflowers that vined along the ground and up the trellis on the side of the yard. Closer to the fence, in the dappled shade, grew a bed of ferns, lush and every shade of green.

And on the far side, in the brightest sun...

"Holy shit," Greta murmured. "Is that a fucking banana tree just growing out of the ground?"

"It is," a voice answered from inside the fence.

Greta shrieked and nearly fell off the brick wall. She grabbed at the fence to catch herself and in doing so dropped her phone. It disappeared into the ferns that covered the ground, and Greta cringed.

A woman rose from a patch of sunlight in the corner of the yard closest to the fence, only two feet from where Greta stood. She was tall, white, and looked to be in her seventies, with long silver hair shot through with black, and she wore a gorgeous dressing gown printed with green and gold foliage, which explained why Greta had failed to notice her.

"God, I'm *so* sorry," Greta said, mortified.

The woman chuckled warmly. "Would you like to come in?" she asked.

"In. In? To your garden?"

The woman nodded.

Greta wanted it desperately. She told herself that this was a city and probably you shouldn't just go into strangers' beautiful, luscious gardens in cities because they could kill you and use your body as fertilizer for their plants. But at that moment, she didn't care. If this woman was willing to invite her in after catching her practically draped over her fence, then she couldn't turn it down.

"I would love to."

The woman smiled serenely and opened the gate a few paces down. Greta hadn't even noticed the entrance. On the street side, it had tree boughs growing over it, blocking it from view. It opened in, and Greta unwedged her sneaker from the fence, brushed herself off, and walked through the gate.

"Um, I have a dog here. Is that okay?"

The comment was clearly unnecessary, as Horse could hardly be overlooked since he was big enough to be seen from space.

"It's fine," the woman said. "I love dogs."

The gate swung shut behind Greta, and as if by magic, the street beyond it disappeared. Gone were the sounds of the city waking up. They were dampened by the growth and replaced by the steady sound of a small fountain that burbled cheerily.

Greta blinked. She was in paradise.

The woman plucked her phone from the ferns and held it out to her. "You can take pictures if you like," she said.

Greta felt instantly ashamed.

"I'm so sorry. I didn't see you there. Not that it would be okay to climb on your fence if you hadn't been there. I just— your garden is... And I love... It's... I'm from Maine," she settled on finally.

The woman nodded as if that explained things, and Greta rolled her eyes at herself.

"Your birds-of-paradise are amazing, and I was just gonna get a picture for my friend. He's a florist and they're his favorite flower. I just can't believe they grow here. I mean, of course they grow here. But I've never seen them growing in the wild. Er, not that your garden is wild…"

"Stop talking," the woman said kindly. "Everything's fine. I understand. One plant lover to another, I've climbed many a garden fence myself."

Greta smiled at the image of this incredibly elegant woman climbing anything.

"I'm Greta." Greta sketched an awkward wave. "And this is Horse."

"Pleasure to meet you, Greta. And you, Horse." The woman held out a graceful hand to Horse, who sniffed it inter-rogatively, then gave it a welcoming lick. "Muriel Blondeau," she introduced herself. "You'll stay for coffee?"

"Oh, uh, I don't want to intrude."

Muriel smirked and raised one perfectly arched eyebrow. "Of course you do," she said and swept through the garden into what Greta assumed was the kitchen.

The second she was gone, Greta crouched next to the birds-of-paradise, tracing their magnificent beaks with a gentle finger. The greenery around them set off their spikes of color; the delicate radial blossoms of passionflowers balanced their geometry. Everything in the garden was in harmony.

She found herself next to the banana tree. It was a strange-looking thing, bunches of bananas sprouting from it like the fingers in a child's terrible drawing.

So often with plants, Greta goggled at their beauty, at the elegance of their design. But when a plant seemed to defy grace and order, Greta was reminded anew that beauty was a merely human designation. The thriving banana tree was one of those that reminded her.

Muriel came back into the garden carrying a tray and

gestured Greta to the small table she'd been sitting at before. The chairs were wrought iron and looked to be made of twisted vines. The cushions on them were emerald-green. The table was a similar wrought iron, but its top was mosaic in iridescent shades of green like a dragonfly's wings.

The entire effect was of something that had been upthrust by the very earth and grew into forms nearly indistinguishable from the roots and stems of the garden itself.

"Wow," Greta sighed.

Muriel smiled and placed the glass tray on the table top. It fit perfectly, showing the mosaic beneath.

On it were delicate white china cups with gold-etched rims and peonies. A small glass cafetière was filled with dark coffee, and a pitcher that matched the cups was filled with milk. Pale pink sugar cubes were piled in a clear glass dish, tiny tongs resting beside it.

"Wow," Greta heard herself say again.

It was the most beautiful tableau she'd ever seen.

Then Muriel placed a white china bowl full of water on the ground beside her chair and rubbed her fingers together. Horse walked to her side, licked her fingers, then lay down to drink from the bowl.

"My mother planted this garden," Muriel said as she poured coffee into the peony cups. "Cream and sugar?"

Greta usually drank it black, but she was curious about those pink sugar cubes. "Yes, please."

"She was a painter, and she loved to paint flowers most of all. She planted every flower you can think of, in every possible color. When you looked out the windows into the garden, all you saw was a riot of color and shape, like a pointillist painting. It looked like chaos all together. But when my mother would set up her easel, she would frame the painting exactly right, so that the flowers she painted went together perfectly.

"I asked her once if she had planted them with composition in mind, and she said, 'You don't compose nature. Nature composes, and it's up to you to find the right perspective.'"

"Do you think that's true?" Greta asked.

Muriel nodded. "Perspective is everything."

# 5
# GRETA

They had talked for hours, about plants, mothers, and a host of other topics, and Greta left Muriel's with an invitation to take tea in her garden the following week. She wandered for a while longer before walking back through the French Quarter toward home. As she crossed Burgundy Street, she couldn't believe her eyes. The miniature pony she'd seen earlier was tied to a hitching post outside a bar in the middle of the block. At least she assumed it was the same one. How many miniature ponies could there be around here? She was delighted to realize she had no idea. For all she knew, there could be dozens.

As she approached, a woman came out of the bar, holding a drink in a plastic cup and still talking to someone inside. She laughed at whatever they said, and as she turned, her halo of glossy hair floated back as if in slow motion to reveal one of the most gorgeous women Greta had ever seen. She was white and very curvy, her brown hair a chin-length riot of buoyant curls. She had a large, angular nose, a pointy chin, and huge brown eyes exaggerated with smoky gray eyeshadow. Her mouth was a red moue.

She wore yellow lace tights under gray wool newsboy shorts, black boots, a black T-shirt worn to holes, and a burnt velvet jacket-robe thing in yellow, umber, and black florals.

She slid on large, heart-shaped red sunglasses and spoke softly to the miniature pony.

Before Greta knew what had propelled her, she was standing next to the woman.

"That's a horse." She cringed as the words left her mouth.

"Good eye," the woman said. She was obviously making fun of Greta, but it felt friendly and welcoming rather than repelling.

"God, sorry," Greta said. "It's just, I think I saw it early this morning." She pointed in the direction she thought Truman's house lay in, then corrected herself and pointed the other way. "I just got here. To town. This town."

The woman just let her talk.

"What I mean is I don't really know if this is the kind of place where miniature horses are, like, a common pet, or if this is definitely the same horse I saw earlier."

When the woman just smiled, Greta's traitorous mouth supplied more and more words.

"It's funny cuz this guy is named Horse." She patted Horse's head. "He's not mine. I mean, I didn't *steal* him. I just. I'm house-sitting. House swapping, really. It's his. Dog. The person I swapped with."

*Why don't you give her your ATM PIN and greatest insecurity while you're at it, Greta?*

Greta clamped her mouth shut and shook her head when more nervous chatter attempted to escape.

"This is Teacup. I'm Carys." The woman held out her hand. "And you are?"

Greta shook her hand. "Greta. I'm Greta. Horse," she said again, pointing at the dog.

"Greta and Horse. Got it. And you just got to town because you're doing a house swap with a guy who lives in the Marigny. It's your first time in New Orleans, and you don't quite know your way around yet."

"Yeah, that's… Yup. Accurate."

Realizing that she was still holding onto Carys' hand, she forced herself to release it. Carys looked like a silent film star, with her dramatic nose, huge eyes, and lush pout of a mouth.

"You wanna see some more of it?"

"Huh? Oh. What?"

"Come on." Carys untied Teacup from the hitching post and started to walk down the street, Teacup's hoofs clacking against the cobblestones. After a few steps, she turned, curls flying. "You coming?"

Greta hurried after her.

Carys finished whatever was in the plastic cup and tossed it into the next trash can they passed. "This is the Old Ursuline Convent," she said, pointing. "You know the story of the filles à la cassette?"

Greta shook her head.

"Are you interested in the macabre and supernatural?" Carys asked, her voice that of a natural storyteller.

"Uh. Yes."

Wasn't everyone?

"In the 1720s, the population of New Orleans skewed quite male, making marriage impossible. They required an influx of women, and France was only too happy to scour the streets, prisons, orphanages, and brothels, snatching whoever they deemed undesirable or a strain on the system, loading them onto ships, and sending them to the French colonies in need of marriageable women."

"Jesus. They took them away from their families?"

"A lot of them didn't have families. When they arrived in port, the filles à la cassette trooped off the ship carrying their belongings in casket-shaped chests, their mouths bloody, their skin as pale as death, burning instantly in the Louisiana sun. Or so the stories go."

Carys raised an impish eyebrow and ran a hand through Teacup's mane.

"Until their marriages, they were cloistered here by the Ursuline nuns. One by one, the girls were married off, leaving their belongings behind. Gossip circulated that these were not happy marriages, and some of the girls ended up on the streets, or worse. The mortality rate in New Orleans began to rise noticeably after their arrival. Rumors arose that the girls had transported not clothes in those caskets all the way from France but vampires. The nuns went to the attic where the caskets had been stored and found them all empty."

She paused for effect, and Greta gazed up at the attic windows of the convent.

"Terrified that the vampires would come back to sleep in their caskets, the nuns bolted the door to the attic and nailed the windows shut with nails blessed by the pope. But one of those windows had an uncanny habit of swinging open in the middle of the night."

Greta was hanging on her every word.

"In 1978, some paranormal investigators decided they were going to crack the case of the filles à la cassette. They were denied entry to the convent itself by the archbishop, so they climbed the convent wall and settled in to spend the night there, hoping to see the attic window open…and solve the mystery of who—or *what*—was responsible."

"Did they?"

"The next morning, their decapitated bodies were found splayed across the steps of the convent. They had been completely drained of blood. Their murders have never been solved, but locals speculate the filles à la cassette couldn't have their secrets getting out."

Greta shivered even in the warm sun. She had always loved a spooky tale, but hearing one while looking at the place where it happened was even better.

"So what really happened?"

Carys raised an eyebrow, sphinxlike, and they walked in silence for a moment.

"Chances are that the women were pale and gaunt and ill from being on a ship for five months. Tuberculosis causes the sufferer to cough up blood, which likely explains the blood on some of their mouths. The mortality rate in the city at the time was high to begin with. Lack of hygiene and the weather and swampy environment spawned disease regularly. Perhaps some new disease was brought over on the ships with the girls. But as for the attic window opening and the journalists drained of blood…"

She shrugged elegantly and let the mystery lie.

When Greta and Adelaide were nine and ten, they'd spend stormy nights, of which there were many on Owl Island, trying to scare each other with stories they made up. They'd whisper bits of the tales back and forth between their twin beds until one of them (and it was always Adelaide) got too scared. Then she would pull the blanket up over her head so she couldn't see anything that might threaten her and make a blind leap onto Greta's bed, usually landing half on her and half on the bed, where they would finish the story in squeals, under the blanket, clutching each other for comfort.

A pang of longing for her sister surprised her.

"This is Jackson Square," Carys said a few blocks later.

Greta banished Adelaide from her mind.

"Oh, I walked past here earlier."

"It's the hub of tourism. Everyone visiting New Orleans for the first time ends up here. And so this"—Carys gestured expansively to the square and spun around—"is where we come to take their money."

Greta's stomach gave a lurch. Had she inadvertently gotten taken in by a pickpocket? Was Carys the Oliver Twist of New Orleans? Was Greta about to be used as a diversion because of her obvious infatuation with the gorgeous woman? It would be just her luck.

"Um. Like, *take* their money?" Greta said awkwardly.

Carys raised an eyebrow and said, "Come see." She walked through the square, Teacup at her side, and waved to several people stationed on the steps outside the tall, white church as she passed. She was heading toward the wrought-iron fence that ran around an area of green park in the center of the square. She hugged a tall woman who had a table set up with a sign promising to read your tarot for five dollars and tell your future for twenty, and called hello to a couple whose paintings of the city were lashed to the fence.

From her large bag, Carys pulled a wooden sign and a bowl woven in purple and black and placed both on the ground in front of her. The sign said WILL MATH FOR CA$H.

A family of five walked past and came over to look at Teacup. Carys smiled and said in a voice reminiscent of a carnival barker, "Step right up, folks, and ask me any math problem. Stump me! How about you, buddy?"

This was addressed to the boy, who looked about twelve.

"Umm. 4,567 divided by 8?"

"570 with a remainder of 7," Carys said.

The boy gaped at her.

"You can check me," she said.

He took out his phone and plugged in the numbers. "Whoa. She's right."

"987 times 2,309," his father said.

Carys blinked and nodded, thinking for a moment.

"2,278,983," she said.

"How are you doing that?" the man asked. "Is it a magic trick?"

"Yes," Carys told him, leaning in like she was going to reveal a secret. "It's the magic of math. The greatest show on earth."

The man had no response to this, but at a look from his wife, he put five dollars into Carys' bowl.

She did it over and over. People would be drawn in by the curiosity of a miniature horse, and Carys would offer for them to stump her. Not everyone took the bait, but many of them did—especially men.

When Greta asked if Carys was targeting men on purpose, she said, "Hell yes! Men are four times more likely to ask me questions than women or nonbinary people."

"Of course you've crunched the numbers." Greta laughed.

"Of course." Carys grinned. She was fucking radiant.

"So...*is* there a trick?" Greta asked.

She'd been watching Carys do this for over an hour, checking the answers on her phone right along with the onlookers, and Carys had been right every single time. Once, she'd given an answer and Greta thought she'd made a mistake. But she'd corrected herself instantly.

"Only if you consider my brain a trick," Carys said breezily. She shrugged. "Nah, I love math. I'm good at math. I've always been able to do calculations in my head."

"You're seriously just doing those problems in your head? How?"

Carys smiled. "I don't know. You might as well ask how do you paint a picture or how do you know what words to use in a poem."

"Okay, but those are choices. You could use another word or another color. Math problems have correct answers."

"Right, but it's all just how your brain works. Someone who can render perspective in a painting *knows* which lines and colors will give the desired effect. My brain *knows* how to calculate numbers."

"Damn. Wish my brain knew how to do anything."

Carys cocked her head. "I'm sure it knows *something*."

"Yeah, it knows the birthdays of everyone in my tiny town and when carnivorous plants need to be fed. Impressive stuff."

"Carnivorous plants? Tell me more."

"Do you need to do more math?" *Make more money* was what Greta meant, but it seemed gauche to say it.

"This is more interesting," Carys said and plucked up her sign and her bowl. She deposited both in her bag and said, "Want to walk some more?"

Dazzled by being thought more interesting than making money, Greta nodded. Horse, who had been snoozing at her feet for the past hour, seemed excited about a walk too.

Carys waved goodbye to her Jackson Square compatriots and led Teacup away. "So, carnivorous plants?" she prompted.

"They're amazing," Greta sighed. "All plants are part of the ecosystem, but often it's so much more subtle or removed. Like, a certain animal eats a certain plant and poops it out, and the seeds in the waste grow a new plant and spread its life that way. But with carnivorous plants, it's direct. They attract these insects and just consume them, living because of them." Suddenly self-conscious, she trailed off.

"Yeah, we imagine plants as passive. As something that just sits there. Conceiving of them as predators or hunters goes against what we think of when we think *plant*," Carys said.

"Right, exactly. And what's the line between a plant and an animal when a plant is eating an animal? I mean, insects aren't animals, I know, but it just makes all the distinctions among species and the roles we imagine them to have so fuzzy."

"I love that," Carys said. "Blurring boundaries, breaking down divisions, muddying up categorical expectations. Super queer."

She winked, and Greta felt her cheeks heat.

"You're so cute," Carys said, laughing at her embarrassment.

"You're utterly stunning," Greta said, completely sincerely. "And brilliant. Killer combo." She looked down at her shoes, the toes of her sneakers scuffed and worn.

"This is the Mississippi," Carys said, ruby lips so close Greta could feel her breath.

"Huh?"

Carys' eyes crinkled in a smile, and she nodded in front of them.

"Oh, gosh. A river." Greta hadn't even noticed their approach, so focused on Carys and their conversation. "It's so…" She searched for an appropriately complimentary word. "Brown."

"Muddy waters, darlin'," Carys said.

The river was, at first glance, an unimpressive brown. But once Greta managed to tear her attention away from Carys' eyes—a brown she much preferred—she took in its beauty. The city clung to its curves and an elegant bridge connected it with an island across the water.

Greta pointed at it. "Is that still New Orleans?"

"Yeah, that's Algiers Point. The houses are super cute, and there's a great ice cream place. We can take the ferry across if you like. Although maybe let's wait until we don't have Teacup. She doesn't like the water."

Greta's heart swelled at the idea that she could spend further time with Carys.

A flat-bottomed wooden boat approached with a load of what looked like rebar and other construction materials on it.

"Where's the dock?"

Carys pointed downriver. "A lot of the houses in the Marigny and Treme are built with barge board—wood from boats like that one," she said. "When boats would come down the Mississippi in the nineteenth century, there was no economical way to get them back upriver against the current, so they would be dismantled at the harbor once they'd been unloaded, and the lumber sold cheaply."

Greta turned to look at the city, imagining walking through a house that had come down the river a century and a half before.

"You wanna get some food?" Carys asked. "I'm ravenous."

Greta absolutely did. She wanted this day never to end.

Carys led them through a place she called the French Market and back into the winding streets of the Quarter. "You like oysters?" she asked.

"Yeah. I think Maine oysters might be different, though."

"Shall we find out?" Carys held a hand out to her, and Greta let her palm settle against Carys', savoring the warm press of her skin.

All Greta could do was nod.

They settled on stools at a bar that was open to the street. The man behind the bar nodded at Carys and slid menus in front of them. The words on the menu seemed to blur before Greta's eyes, and she said, "You can just get whatever you want. I'm not picky."

Carys' eyes narrowed as if she wanted to address that comment, but the bartender came back, and she gave him an order Greta hardly understood.

"Do you drink alcohol?" Carys asked.

"Uh, sure."

Carys ordered two Bloody Marias—that at least Greta understood.

"Is that like a Bloody Mary?"

"Yeah, but with tequila instead of vodka."

The drinks were slid in front of them, and Carys took a deep gulp, sighing in bliss. Greta sipped tentatively, and the sharp, rich tomato flavor burst over her tongue. It was sweet and sour and pickles and pepper, and Greta was instantly in love.

"Holy shit, that's so good."

"Right?" Carys clinked their glasses together. "Cheers. Now." She settled her elbows on the bar and looked at Greta like she was getting down to business. "Why the hell did you end up in New Orleans for a month doing a house swap with a guy who names his dog Horse?"

Greta regaled her first with her recent dating app fails, how everyone on Owl Island knew her only as one of the Russakoff sisters and not as herself, and how her parents thought not knowing what she wanted to do with her life meant they could count on her to join the family business.

Before she knew it, she'd moved on to the story of the Holiday Fair. Carys' face told her that she found the notion of auctioning people off just as abhorrent as Greta did, and when Greta got to the part about her mom clearly going along with Sadie even though she knew Greta would hate it, she had to clench her jaw to keep the fury out of her voice.

"So," she finished in a rush just as silver plates of oysters nestled in ice were slid before them, "here I am."

Carys looked at her—really looked—and Greta got the sense that maybe in hiding her fury, something else had leaked out. But Carys didn't push her to say more. "Here you are," she murmured.

They each took an oyster. Carys smothered hers in chili sauce, and Greta drizzled hers with mignonette.

"Cheers," Carys said for the second time, and they touched oyster shells, the pearl-pale flesh quivering as they raised them to their lips.

"Cheers," Greta echoed, her voice just breath as she watched the oyster disappear into Carys' mouth.

The salt sea burst on Greta's tongue, the tang of vinegar and mellow malt of meat. As she swallowed, she felt intoxicated with tequila, salt, and the woman whose thigh pressed hotly against her own.

Lost in mapping the exact topography of where their bodies touched, Greta almost forgot what they'd been discussing. When Carys asked what her family thought of her being in New Orleans, their conversation snapped back into focus.

Greta grimaced. "I've kind of been ignoring their texts," she admitted. "I love them, but I'm just, like, *powerless* against getting involved if I engage. So I've disengaged."

Carys nodded. "What about this?" She arranged the plates of oysters and the cocktails in front of Greta and pulled out her phone. Slowly, she raised her hand and brushed Greta's bleached-platinum bangs to the side slightly. Her fingertips lingered there, and Greta's breath caught. Then she handed Greta an oyster and said, "Smile."

Greta looked not at the camera but at Carys and smiled with everything she had. She was far away from home, far away from everything that had ever made her who she thought she was. She was eating oysters with a gorgeous woman, for god's sake—how could she not smile?

Carys snapped a picture and held her phone up.

Greta looked at a version of herself she wasn't sure she'd seen before. She looked happy—almost carefree. She looked present.

"I'll send it to you, and you can send it to your family so they know you're doing just great."

Greta nodded, still staring at her own smiling face.

"But I'll need your number if I'm gonna text it to you," Carys said, fluttering her eyelashes in an exaggeration of flirting.

"Wow, you play a long game," Greta joked.

"Always."

She gave Carys her number and sent the picture to the family text thread the instant it came through, before she could lose her nerve.

*i'm great and new orleans is wonderful!* she wrote, then put away her phone.

"Thanks," she told Carys.

"You're very welcome," Carys said.

Their gazes caught, entangled. Greta had never wanted to kiss someone so badly in her life. She *ached* to feel Carys' lips against hers.

So of course she changed the subject.

"So, um, what about you? You said you're in grad school for math?"

Carys' slight smile told her that she'd felt it too—Greta's veer away from the moment this was surely building to.

"Yup. Partial differential equations. I love it."

"What will you do with your degree—teach?"

Carys scrunched up her face. "No. I like teaching people how to do math one-on-one, but no way could I deal with a university. All the hoops you have to jump through and the departmental shenanigans. Nope."

"So…you're getting a PhD to…what?"

"To get to do math for seven years!" Carys said, grin so bright there wasn't the slightest doubt in Greta's mind that she truly did love math that much.

"Wow. That's a lot of work."

"It's the most fun. I love grad school. I wish I could stay forever."

She called to the bartender, and he brought out bowls of water for Teacup and Horse.

Greta slipped away to use the bathroom, and when she got back, Carys had paid the bill and gotten them another Bloody Maria each to take with them.

Carys waved off Greta's thanks and asked, "Wanna see something?"

Teacup and Horse seemed just as happy to follow Carys as

Greta was, and they walked back out to the street. Horse had tired of sniffing everything and was now loping easily next to Teacup. At the sound of a noise behind them, Greta turned to see the animals had drifted closer together, Horse's angular shoulder blade nearly touching Teacup's mane.

It was adorable and a sound escaped Greta that she usually only made in response to TikToks of kittens perched on the backs of goats or small cows nuzzling ducklings.

Carys turned to her with a raised eyebrow.

"I think," Greta whispered, "that they might be falling in love."

The second it was out of her mouth, she cringed at her cheesiness, but Carys just glanced behind them and nodded. "Teacup is a total flirt. Love this for him."

They walked downriver, but despite the cool drink she was sipping, Greta felt red-hot.

"So, are you from New Orleans?" she asked.

"Yup. Born and raised. My mom and grandparents too. I wouldn't want to live anywhere else."

"Are you close with your family?"

"Nope. Here." Carys pointed to a set of ordinary concrete steps against a retaining wall. She looped Teacup's lead around the handrail, tying it in a knot. "I'll be right back, sweetie," she said, stroking his nose. "He doesn't do well with stairs," she explained. "But he'll be fine here."

Carys climbed the stairs, and Greta and Horse followed. At the top was a glassed-in overhang and then a walkway perpendicular to the river. When they walked to the end of it, they were a story above the Mississippi and could see for miles.

The sun had begun to set as they walked, and it painted the sky cotton-candy pink, sherbet orange, and a purple the color of a bruise. The clouds reflected them from above, the water from below, the whole vista glowing like a Renaissance painting.

"Wow," Greta breathed.

"Yeah," Carys sighed. "This is one of my favorite spots."

Horse seemed to share her opinion because he plopped down, put his chin on his paws, and stared out at the water.

"Listen," Carys said. "I have to go in a few minutes and get ready for my tour."

"Tour?"

"I give haunted tours of the Quarter in the evenings," she said with a smile.

"I should've guessed from your expert storytelling at the convent."

Carys tipped an imaginary hat in thanks. "Anyway, I wanted to run something by you."

"Um, what's up?"

"It's just, I really. Really. Want to kiss you."

Greta's head went empty.

"Wait. I… Oh. What?"

Carys smiled and stood in front of her. She put a hand very gently on Greta's cheek.

"I would really like to kiss you. And I wonder what you think about that?"

Greta's heart was pounding so hard she was concerned about toppling off the overpass to the ground below—really, this should have some kind of guard rails. It wasn't safe!

"Greta? Are you okay?"

"Huh? Oh, yeah. I'm good. Just trying not to pass out." At the stricken look on Carys' face, she added, "In a good way."

Carys laughed.

"Okay, well, maybe I'll hold on to you just to make sure. And you let me know when you're done trying not to pass out. In a good way."

Carys slid her arm around Greta's waist and rested her cheek against Greta's shoulder. They stood like that for minutes, watching the colors deepen and the city lights begin to shine against the impending darkness.

"Okay," Greta said.

Carys turned to her.

"Okay, you feel good about the prospect of me kissing you?" she said, clearly half joking. "Or your almost passing out in a good way is over?"

"Shut the hell up and kiss me already," Greta said, grinning.

Carys' lips were salt and sugar, her mouth a luscious play of give and take. The kiss was sweet until it went dark and hungry, Carys' tongue sliding against her own and sending shivers through her legs and guts, tingling between her legs.

Now falling off the overpass seemed a possibility for an entirely different reason.

One of Carys' hands was at the small of her back, dragging them together, and the other slid into her hair, tugging just enough to make her gasp.

Greta slid her hand to the nape of Carys' neck, desperate to feel the satin slip of her curls. She felt the curve of Carys' skull under her fingertips and tipped Carys' head back to kiss her more deeply.

The kiss crested and then they broke apart, panting, resting their foreheads together.

"Damn," Carys said as Greta breathed, "Wow."

Carys' grin was everything.

They looked into each other's eyes for a long moment, then Carys pressed a sweet kiss to the corner of Greta's mouth.

"I hate to leave. Seriously. I *hate* it." Her gaze raked Greta's body hotly. "But I have to go change if I'm gonna make my tour."

Greta nodded. "Sure. Of course. Totally cool." She winced, but Carys just smiled. "I might stay here for a minute," Greta said, not trusting her legs to carry her down the stairs.

"Okay. You know how to get home from here?"

"No clue, but I have Google Maps on my phone."

"God bless Google Maps," Carys agreed. She paused. "Can I see you again?"

"Yes. Yes, please," Greta said. She'd never meant anything so much in her life. "You have my number." And, damn, but Carys really, *really* did.

"Yay," Carys said softly. "Bye, Greta."

On her lips, *Greta* sounded like a promise, a flower, a name all her own.

# 6
# TRUMAN

*What would you say if I told you I think I might be staying in a house that Agatha Tark once lived in?* Truman wrote in the group chat.

**I'd say you suffer from an excess of hope**, Charlotte wrote.

*Really??? How can you tell??* wrote Germaine.

Truman smiled. They were precisely the responses he'd expected.

He told them about the ceiling and the way it reminded him of the healing hut in *The Heart Flowers* (book five, in which Clarion has a brief but necessary tryst with a bearling, which strengthens her heart enough that she doesn't give up on her quest). (Charlotte: **circumstantial**; Germaine: *Whoa!!*)

He saved the ship for last.

**Pics**, Charlotte wrote.

He sent pictures.

Germaine replied with a key smash and a selfie with their eyes open comically wide, making a mind-blown gesture.

Charlotte responded, **Hmm.**

Truman rolled his eyes. He adored Charlotte. But sometimes her skepticism bordered on bummer.

**Is there any local history of similar inlays in the architecture? Maybe it's a coastal tradition or signifies something about certain types of houses?**

*Yeah, that Agatha Tark lived in them!!!!* Germaine replied.

I haven't done any research yet, Truman allowed. In truth, he hadn't even thought that there might be other ships, but Charlotte was right.

*Sooooo,* Germaine interrupted. *How are you holding up?*

Germaine and Charlotte weren't only fellow Tark-heads, although their friendship had begun that way. They were his closest friends and confidantes, closer by far than his friends in New Orleans, even Ramona. They'd never met in person, and perhaps they never would. In fact, it was easier to confide in them precisely for that reason.

He didn't need to emote when he felt blank or to rein it in when he felt too much. They hadn't needed to know that he was curled up in bed sobbing when he wrote to tell them about Guy (although Charlotte's murderous reply and Germaine's tender offer for a phone call suggested that they'd had their suspicions).

The truth was he wasn't sure how he was doing. It had been such a whirlwind since he'd gotten to Owl Island that he'd hardly had a moment to think about Guy.

I'm okay. Mostly, I feel like such a fool and I keep looking back at all these obvious signs and being like, Wow, how were you oblivious to the reddest flags in the world? Like, he NEVER stayed over at my place. Well, like three times, and clearly that was when his husband or partner or whoever that was must've been out of town. He never wanted to go out. He talked about himself ALL the time and was it all a lie?! How did this happen?

Truman slumped.

**Look, for someone to do that, they would have to be utterly selfish, entitled, and not care about anyone else's feelings but their own. You dodged a bullet finding out when you did.**

*But it's still super sad!* Germaine acknowledged. *T really loved him!*

**I know, which is why it's so good he found out now!** Charlotte wrote. **Also can we talk for one second about how you found out because you were going over to drop off a surprise gift? Like, paging symbolism 101, your generosity saved you!**

More like my pathetic into-him-ness revealed what a puddle I am. Truman hit Enter so hard he almost dropped his phone.

*Aww, puddle truman*, Germaine wrote, with a string of hug heart emojis.

**I gotta jet, buds,** Charlotte wrote. **Client's here, but I'll chat later.**

Charlotte was a lawyer, and when they'd first become friends, Truman had gotten self-conscious any time he'd say anything slightly illegal, like that he wished he could murder one of his bosses or that he'd picked up a dollar in the French Quarter and not tried to find who it belonged to.

Charlotte had laughed in his face (digitally) and said, **I'm a public defender not a freaking hall monitor. And I want to murder my bosses on the regular, so.**

When Charlotte's name dropped off the text, Germaine wrote, *So how are you really??*

Ughh, shitty.

**I'm so sorry bb.**

I know C's right and like obviously it would've been bad to never know, but...

**But you would've gotten to continue being with someone you loved. I get it. It's not like you just stop loving someone because they hurt you.**

Yup.

For some reason, the image of the florist from earlier popped into his head then. Ash, right. The image of Ash holding out the beautiful rose to him. Ash dropping his large hand on the dog's soft head.

You know, I did meet someone from the island earlier. I wonder if he'd know about whether Agatha lived here...

*Great idea*, Germaine agreed, and Truman sent them a silent bubble of gratitude for always understanding when someone wanted to change the subject.

$$\longleftrightarrow$$

Having mentioned asking Ash about Agatha Tark made Truman realize that there were likely many people on the island who might have known her if she did in fact live here. And since he'd eaten all the cheese and chocolate in the house, he decided to venture back out to the general store and procure supplies for actual meals.

He bundled up in Greta's heavy wool sweater and, since he figured he might as well, grabbed her thick winter coat (too short in the sleeves and too small to zip but still very warm), hat, and gloves.

Owl Island possessed a desolate beauty. The sky was a grayish blue, snow fell softly, and the weathered clapboard buildings stood dignified and remote. Main Street, however, was anything but desolate. Fairy lights glittered the entire length of the business district, looping across the street and up and down both sides. Benches sat outside many of the businesses, and Truman imagined that in the warmer weather, they would be full of locals chatting and sharing coffees.

The streetlamps were charming globes set in metal bases, some with ships on them and some with carved rope, and all the signs appeared to be hand-painted. Particularly charming was one that promised ICE CREAM DREAM and was rendered in drippy pastel writing. It appeared to be closed for the winter. Apparently he'd been so hunched over with cold the previous evening that he hadn't noticed any of this.

Truman passed a coffee shop called Owl Eyes (also sporting a sign that announced it was closed for the season), a hardware store with a sign that simply said HARDWARE STORE, and a drugstore with a faded sign announcing RX & MORE!

The bell above the door in Muskee's General Store tinkled his arrival, and he stamped off the snow.

"Back again!" crowed the woman at the counter.

"Er. Yes. Thought I'd try a food group other than heartbreak," he quipped, laugh-cringing.

"Ah," the woman said and, either from kindness or horror, turned back to what she was doing.

Truman threw pasta, sauce, a few apples, some more cheese, a box of cereal, milk, and some microwave popcorn into a basket. He tried to picture Greta's kitchen to remember if she had a microwave and couldn't. He added a few more things to his basket and lugged it to the counter.

"There you go," the woman said soothingly. Truman felt illogically soothed.

"Um. Are you...Muskee?" he asked.

The woman smiled at him, revealing large teeth and

twinkling brown eyes. "I'm one of 'em. Carla Muskee. This place has been in my husband's family for three generations."

"Wow. Cool."

He fiddled with a pack of gum at the display and then awkwardly added it to his pile so she didn't think he'd messed it up.

"So you know a lot about Owl Island, then? I mean, I assume?"

"I know you're not from around here," Carla said warmly. "And I'm gonna guess that you're a friend of Greta Russakoff's. How'd I do?"

"Does Greta only own one sweater or something?" Truman muttered, looking down at his chest. It wasn't even a particularly recognizable sweater, just a cream-and-brown wool knit.

Carla winked. "My son made that sweater."

"What?"

"Yup. He sells 'em in the back."

Carla gestured past the grocery section to where a few shelves of home goods gave way to a wooden display of knit wool sweaters in the same style as the one he wore.

"Oh, wow, how weird," he said. "I mean, the coincidence, not the sweater. Or not that your son makes sweaters. I mean—"

"I know what you meant," Carla said kindly.

Truman felt his cheeks burn.

"Er, I was just wondering. Do you know of an author called Agatha Tark?"

Carla cocked her head in thought. "Don't think so... Was she the one did those mystery books?"

"That's Agatha Christie," Truman said gently. "These are fantasy books. Thanks anyway."

"If it's books you're after, you should go talk to Maisey and Don over at the Queen Bee." She pointed out the window.

"Okay, thanks."

Once he'd paid, he realized that he'd bought too much to carry home easily. He tucked a few small items in the pockets of Greta's jacket and shoved the handles of two bags up over his wrists, grabbing the others in the most balanced way he could.

"You gonna be all right?" Carla asked. "I could lock the store for a sec and drive you."

Truman was so touched by her kindness that he almost teared up.

"That is so nice of you, thank you, but I'll be fine. See you soon, I'm sure!"

And he skedaddled out the door before she could see the tears that threatened at basic human kindness.

He hadn't always been that way. Somewhere around six months ago was the first time it had happened. He'd been left on the verge of tears when a little girl approached him at the grocery store and told him she liked his shoes. He'd thought little of it, assuming he was just in a strange mood. But it had happened several times since.

Now he wondered if deep down he'd known that Guy was not kind. Was, in fact, so starving him of kindness that the small offerings of others echoed inside him like a pebble dropped into a well.

Did Guy bestow all his kindness on his partner? (For some reason, Truman had been calling him Roger in his head.) Or was he stingy even with him?

Better question: what did you do when all the recent moments of love, desire, and partnership in your life were revealed to be betrayals?

Still better question: how would he ever trust himself again, when he'd proven such a phenomenally bad judge of character?

↤⟶

Truman couldn't see going into a bookstore with five bags of groceries (especially since he was an inveterate browser and it really required both hands and no time pressure of melting ice cream), so he decided to go back to Greta's, put his shopping away, and come back out.

He'd made it within three blocks of home when a vehicle slowed to a stop next to him.

"Truman?"

It was Ash.

"Hi." Truman tried not to sound out of breath and gently suggested to himself that he work on his cardio.

"Hi."

Truman was very taken with Ash's slow, deliberate delivery, as if he thought deeply about each thing before saying it, but at the moment, he felt like his arms were going to detach from his body imminently.

"I was just going to your place. Greta's place, I mean."

"Oh yeah?"

Ash nodded. Truman bit his lip.

Ash blinked like he was waiting for something. "Did you want to get in?" he said finally, as if that had always been implied.

Truman weighed the likelihood of his arms falling off against the likelihood that this florist was going to murder and dismember him and got into the van.

"You're not going to cut me up with shears and then turn my limbs into avant-garde floral arrangements, are you?" he asked.

"No," Ash said evenly. "I'm more into traditional arrangements."

Truman snorted a laugh. "Sorry."

"It's the van, I know."

"Well, it's the stranger thing, really, but the van doesn't help. This is what you use for deliveries?"

"Yep, it's refrigerated in the back. I realize that's another strike against it."

"Yeah, maybe don't put it on your branding. Great for groceries, though."

The corner of Ash's mouth quirked up in the tiniest smile.

"So, serial killing aside, why were you going to my place— Greta's place?"

They pulled up outside the house.

"I was bringing you some things. For the cold weather."

Truman felt the tears from earlier threaten once more. He cleared his throat and slammed the door to give himself a moment to get it together.

What was wrong with him? New Orleans was a congenial, friendly town. Why was he acting like he'd never experienced human kindness before?

The shopping bags cut into his hands even through the gloves, and he rushed to unlock the door.

"Come on in."

Truman bustled the groceries into the kitchen, habit driving him to get the ice cream into the freezer right away. In New Orleans, it would melt on the counter in the time it took to put the rest of the groceries away. Here, he realized, he wouldn't have that problem.

Ash followed him. He placed a thick green sweater and a heavy blue coat on the kitchen stool. "I know you can wear Greta's stuff, but she's smaller than you, so I thought maybe you could use this stuff. The sweater's mine, but the coat's my mom's. She's a little taller than you, but...if you want." He shrugged.

Truman struggled out of Greta's too-small coat. "Does your mom live on Owl Island too?" The coat was a bit too big, but Ash was so large it shouldn't be any surprise his mom would be too. Truman zipped it up and instantly felt over-heated. "Wow, thanks. This is awesome."

"You're welcome. And yes, she lives here."

"Well, thank her for me."

Something flickered over Ash's face, but he nodded. "I will."

# 7
# TRUMAN

"Oh, good, they fit," Ash said as Truman walked through Thorn's door.

Truman had traded Greta's sweater for Ash's in case it was warmer. It certainly had nothing whatsoever to do with wondering what it would smell like. (It smelled like cedar and something bright and botanical that Truman couldn't quite place.) He realized he'd never once worn an article of Guy's clothing. It had been raining one day, and Truman had grabbed Guy's jacket hanging by the door to run down the street to get them coffee, and Guy had stopped him, handing him his own instead.

Truman cringed.

"Yeah. Thanks again."

Ash's hair was in a messy ponytail, and there were thorns all around him. Bundles of different colored roses sat in the bucket at his feet. A soft *ruff* told Truman that Bruce was snoozing behind the counter. He felt like he'd stumbled into another world.

"Do you ever take breaks?" Truman asked.

"Well, not usually when we're so busy," Ash deadpanned.

"Oh, er. Of course," Truman said politely. Then he realized Ash was kidding. "I'm going over to the bookstore. I don't know if you like books, but… Oh! I don't suppose you ever knew anyone who might've lived here named Agatha? Agatha Tark?"

Ash shook his head thoughtfully. "Don't think so. But I was gone for a few years. And I do."

It took Truman a moment to realize Ash was saying he liked books.

"Oh, right, okay. Well, any interest in coming along? Maybe the owners would be more forthcoming with a local around."

Ash raised an eyebrow, but he took off his gloves, pulled on a thick navy-blue pea coat and a wool hat that might have once been maroon but was faded or bleached to a pale pink, and clipped a leash to Bruce's collar. He scribbled something on the back of an envelope and ushered Truman out in front of him. The envelope he taped to the door read *Back soon. If you need flowers, call Ash*, then a phone number.

Bruce howled at the falling snow, shook himself off, then seemed delighted to be outside. He sniffed at the icy sidewalk and licked some snow off the curb.

"So who's Agatha Tark?" Ash asked when Bruce let them start walking.

"She's the author of my all-time favorite series, the Dead of Zagørjič. It's just the most amazingly immersive high fantasy series, with wonderful characters and heartbreaking romance and, god, the settings. Her writing is just so descriptive, it makes you feel like you're inside the story."

"And you think she lived here?"

"It's probably silly, but I know she lived in Maine. It's, like, the only thing I know about her. Her books have a cult follow-ing, but she was super private."

Truman told Ash about finding the ship on the floor in Greta's house.

"Have you seen that before? Is it some kind of…I don't know, Maine thing?"

Ash smiled. "Not that I know of. Wood inlays are usually decorative, aren't they? In the entryway of a house or a fancy parlor or something?"

He made the word *parlor* sound like *Mars*.

Truman's heart sped up. Did that mean it was possible?

Bruce let out a plaintive bark and tried to pull Ash toward the entrance to a restaurant.

"Sorry, buddy. You've got a good few months until barbe-cue season."

Bruce harrumphed resignedly.

A pang of longing for Horse lodged in Truman's throat, and his fingers itched to open his phone to the picture Greta had sent him the day before of Horse standing next to an actual horse. It was a miniature horse that Truman had seen around the neighborhood from time to time, and when he'd asked Greta what was up, she'd written cryptically, *love is in the air*, with a GIF of a cartoon rabbit making heart eyes at a mouse.

The sign for the Queen Bee was a beautifully painted gilt bee against a honeycomb made of book spines. When the door opened, the delicious smell of old books tinged with a hint of mildew filled Truman's nose and put him in mind of quiet afternoons spent reading on the second floor at Crescent City Books as Isabella the shop cat snoozed in a puddle of sun beside him.

"Hey, Maisey," Ash said. Truman hadn't even noticed the

woman sitting behind the counter piled with stacks of books as they came in.

"Good to see you, sweetie. Who's your friend?"

The woman who emerged from behind the counter was a petite white woman with keen brown eyes who looked to be in her fifties. Truman realized that he'd only seen white people thus far on Owl Island.

"This is Truman. Truman, Maisey Osgood."

"Ah, of course. Greta's friend." Before Truman could ask whether perhaps *her* child was somehow involved in creating something visible on his person, Maisey said, "Carla told me you'd be stopping by."

"Wow, that's some phone tree y'all've got," Truman said brightly, relieved that he didn't, say, smell like Greta's shampoo which was handcrafted by Maisey's uncle's step-nephew or something.

"You're looking for Agatha Christie novels?" Maisey asked. "Don!" she called before Truman had a chance to correct her. "Can you take Truman to the Christies?"

"Oh, no, no. Sorry. No, there's an author called Agatha Tark. I think she might have lived on Owl Island back when she was writing—or maybe before. I guess I don't know. And I was really just wondering if you might've known her. Since she was an author, I figure if she lived here she probably came into the bookstore."

"Who's Truman?" came a call from across the shop.

"Never mind, Don!"

"What?"

The man Truman assumed was Don picked his way through the alarmingly full aisles between the shelves.

"Oh, hullo, Ashleigh."

"Don."

They shook hands. Don was nearly as petite as Maisey, with a shock of white hair and tiny round wire-rim glasses.

"Tell Don what you told me," Maisey instructed Truman. Truman did.

"When would she have lived here?"

"Well, I don't know exactly. Let's see, the first Zagørjič book came out...gosh, I can't believe it. It'll be twenty years ago next year. I don't know if she would have been living here while she was writing the series or before. And I don't know how long before it was published she wrote the first book. She's very private."

Don and Maisey wore matching contemplative scowls as they stared at each other, like they were doing a particularly rigorous calculation.

"Doesn't ring a bell," Don said finally. "If she was here in the summers, I wouldn't know. So many tourists come through then, everyone wanting a book for the ferry."

"Smart lady living on the island twenty years ago," Maisey mused. "Well, you know who you should ask, sweetie."

This was to Ash, whose mouth was set in a grim line. He nodded tightly without making eye contact. "I'm gonna." Ash nodded at Bruce, then outside, and swept through the door.

"Sorry we couldn't help, dear," Maisey said. "But do browse and see if anything catches your eye."

Truman dearly wanted to browse, but a glance outside at Ash told him it wasn't the moment.

"I'll be back," Truman assured her. "Oh, and you should definitely stock the Dead of Zagørjič series. It's dynamite. Thanks!"

The icy air stole the warmth of the Queen Bee within

seconds of going back outside, and Truman pulled his borrowed coat tightly around himself.

"So what's New Orleans like?" Ash asked. "I've never been."

"Warm," Truman said bitterly, burrowing even further inside his outerwear as they walked back toward Thorn. "There are touristy areas that are loud and crowded, but mostly it's relaxed. There's great music, great food. It's beautiful. I love the cemeteries…"

Truman had loved spending time in the cemeteries of the city from the moment he arrived for his freshman year at Tulane. He'd grown up in Metairie, near enough to New Orleans that he'd always known he'd go there for school but far enough away that it seemed like a whole other world from the shopping malls and mowed lawns of his childhood.

He'd arrived for new student orientation and been disappointed to recognize a dozen people from high school. In an attempt to leave those days behind, he'd accepted the invitation to party in the French Quarter when one of the girls on his hall had asked him. He'd had fun for the first hour or so, but the longer they stayed out, the sloppier people got.

One girl was standing in the middle of the bar yelling into her cell phone at a long-distance boyfriend who was supposed to have done something he did not do. Two people from his hall danced until they got sick and puked on the curb outside. A boy he'd gone to high school with thought it was hilarious to flip up a girl's skirt, and Truman's stomach lurched with uncertainty. He started to make his way toward the girl to see if she was okay when she turned around and punched the guy in the face, splitting his lip, spilling his beer, and getting them all thrown out of the bar.

That punch turned out to be the high point of the night, and Truman peeled off, making his way back toward campus. He'd had only the vaguest sense of where his dorm was, so he'd let his GPS guide him. When he saw the cemetery to his left on the map, he'd veered toward it and found himself in the dark quiet of the Garden District.

It was such a relief to be away from the din and chaos of the Quarter that Truman hardly cared the gates to Lafayette No. 1 were shut for the night. He skirted its perimeter, appreciating the snatches of music issuing from the open windows of the handsome houses that bordered its walls. He stood on a jutting stone and peeked inside. The darkness was impenetrable a few steps in, but he could make out the ornate tombs just on the other side of the wall.

He contemplated hoisting himself over but decided that getting arrested for trespassing (to say nothing of being haunted) on his first night away from home was not ideal, so he just dropped a pin in his GPS and promised himself he'd come back the next day.

He had, and it was even more beautiful than he'd imagined in the dark. It had become a retreat for him when he needed to get off campus, get away from the stresses of class or the demands of friends. And it had stayed that way until the other afternoon.

The peaceful beauty of Lafayette No. 1 was now enmeshed with the memory of peering through Guy's window and seeing the life his boyfriend actually lived.

"Ugh," Truman groaned.

"What's wrong?"

Ash pulled the envelope off the front door of Thorn and unlocked it, holding it open for Truman. Bruce, apparently thinking the polite gesture was for him, entered at the same time, almost wedging himself and Truman in the doorframe.

"Bruce, you silly thing," Ash muttered, pulling his leash.

Truman smiled. "My dog is even bigger than Bruce," he reassured Ash. "So I'm used to it."

"Yeah? Got a picture?"

"I might have one or two," Truman said breezily, then grinned and thumbed open his phone, which contained 2,786 photos, surely 2,458 of which at least were of Horse.

Truman showed Ash one of Horse with his head thrown back against an autumn sunset. He was standing in front of a brightly painted Marigny house.

"Wow," Ash said. "He's huge. And so sweet-looking."

"Yeah, that's my guy. Horse." When Ash kept peering at the picture, Truman scrolled to the one Greta had sent. "Greta sent this. She thinks Horse is in love."

"With…this small horse?"

"Maybe."

Ash smiled. "Trust Greta to find a miniature horse right away. You want a drink or something? I've got tea and seltzer."

"Sure, I'll take a seltzer. Thanks. Er, is Greta…a horse girl or something?"

Ash looked rather blank at that. "Nah, she just…has a tendency to find the most interesting things wherever she goes."

Then he disappeared into the back of the shop, leaving Truman to wander around. The same bouquets that had been in the refrigerated case before were still there. At least Truman thought they were the same. The buckets of flowers weren't full, but Ash had a number of different kinds. And Truman hadn't seen any customers either time he'd been here. It couldn't be an easy business in the winter on an island.

"Do you do most of your business through online orders or what?" he asked as Ash handed him a seltzer. "Thanks."

"No, not yet. It's, uh, it's on my to-do list," Ash said.

Truman perked up. "Ooh, are you into lists? What do you use? I was just trying a new app the other day, but it wasn't intuitive at all."

Ash cocked his head in that particular way he had that seemed to say *Huh?* and *Why?* simultaneously. "A to-do list is useful," he said slowly. He sounded uncertain.

"Oh, ha, never mind." Truman bit his lip. "I'm a list fiend."

"A fiend, huh?" Ash was watching him intently.

"Yeah, well. So do customers just pop in, then?"

Ash ran a hand through his hair. The hat had made half of it fall out of his ponytail, and it hung in soft curves around his face. "Business is pretty slow in the winter. I've been meaning to set up an online order thingy, but…I haven't."

"I could help, if you want," Truman offered. "That is, I work from home, so I'm flexible, and it's Saturday, so I'm not working at all today. I'm good at…the internet," he finished pathetically.

Ash was rubbing the scarred wooden counter, his capable fingers tracing designs Truman couldn't recognize.

"That's a really nice offer," Ash said slowly.

Truman could see the yearning in his face, but he hesitated.

"Um. I don't have a computer for the shop, and mine is pretty old. But I can get it. I live in the apartment upstairs."

"I can just get mine," Truman said, head already buzzing with how he would set up Ash's website to make ordering easy.

"Really?" Ash asked.

"Yeah, no problem. I'll be back soon."

"Oh, here." Ash fumbled in his coat pocket. "Take the van. It's cold."

He tossed Truman the keys, which fell through Truman's fingers and clanked on the floor. Bruce was happy to participate in this new game, and when Truman got the keys, they were distinctly slimier than they had been.

"You're gonna just *give* me the keys to your van?" he asked. "You barely know me."

Ash raised an eyebrow. "Where are you gonna go, the far side of the island?"

Truman supposed that car theft wasn't a big problem on an island with only three ferries a day.

↔

Truman returned with his laptop, a notebook, markers, and Post-its, delighted to have a project.

"Okay," he said when he was set up at the counter. "What's the website?"

Ash had returned to stripping roses of their thorns, a task Truman had never before contemplated. "For what?"

"For Thorn."

"Oh. Well. I don't…it's not… It's a work in progress," Ash concluded.

"Okay, well, lemme take a look."

Ash grumbled something.

"What's that?"

Ash walked over and typed something into Truman's computer. He'd navigated to the Owl Island Chamber of Commerce website, which had a listing of local businesses. There, in tiny letters, was THORN (FLOWER SHOP). When he clicked on the hyperlink, all that came up was a phone number.

"Ummm…"

"Yeah, well, the progress is…preliminary?"

Truman blinked. "Do you *not* have a website?"

"You don't have to say it like I don't have a soul," Ash grumbled.

"No, no, no, this won't do. I'm going to make you a website. You *have* to have a website." Truman began looking up domains. "Okay, how about *thornflowershop dot com*?"

"Sure, that's—look, you really don't have to…"

"Do you *not* want me to?"

"No, it's just… It's… You don't have to go to all this trouble."

"Okay, then I'm doing it. You'll just need to buy the domain."

If Truman hadn't been looking directly at Ash's face, he would've missed the wince. He clicked on *buy domain* to check the price.

"No worries. It's, like, sixteen bucks a month. That okay?"

Ash nodded and let out a breath. "Yeah. Thanks."

At first, Truman asked Ash question after question about how he wanted the site to look, what fonts he wanted, et cetera. But it soon became clear that Ash hadn't thought about it, nor did he have strong opinions about it, at least not at the moment, so Truman stopped asking him and decided he'd be doing him a favor if he just made all the decisions and offered to change things later.

Soon, he lost himself in the soothing work of fonts, headings, hyperlinks, and SEO. He didn't even realize how much time had passed until Ash put a sandwich in front of him on the counter.

"Where'd you get that?"

"My kitchen," Ash said. He pointed upstairs.

Truman's stomach gave an appreciative growl, and he took a bite. "Thanks, it's really good. What kind of jam is this?"

"Wild blueberry," Ash said. "My mom makes it."

"Wow, first the coat, now the jam. Your mom's totally making my day."

Ash smiled and ducked his head.

"Okay, you wanna see?" Truman asked. "It's pretty basic right now, but I wanted to get your thoughts first. I can change whatever you don't like. Then when we've got it how you like it, I'll get pictures we can add of the bouquets and stuff."

Truman sat Ash in the chair and let him navigate through the site. When Ash looked up, his eyes were wide.

"It's…wow," he said.

He sounded choked, and Truman wondered if perhaps Ash was also starved of kindness.

"I can change *anything*," Truman repeated.

Ash shook his head, and Truman felt a wave of giddiness wash over him.

"No," Ash said. "It's perfect."

It wasn't until Truman was falling asleep that night that he remembered he'd never asked Ash who Maisey had meant when she said Ash knew who they should ask about Agatha Tark.

# A MESSAGE FROM RAMONA

**RAMONA to GREAT!A RUSSAKOFF**

Sorry I wasn't in town to greet you, kiddo, but I know you're settling in. Don't forget to explore the shadowy side of the city, and yourself. It'll make you grateful you're alive!

# 8
# GRETA

Greta joined the group of tourists at the corner where they were to meet for the ghost tour. There were fifteen or so of them in total, mostly couples and families, and Greta amused herself trying to figure out who was into the occult and who had been dragged along for the ride.

In some cases, it was clear—the woman in the pavement-skimming black skirt and tattoos and her polo-shirted boyfriend, the stiff-looking couple in khakis and sneakers and their wide-eyed goth kid—but in others, less so. Like the group of sorority-looking girls clutching enormous grenade drinks and talking animatedly about someone's hot brother. Or the father and son who were both in head-to-toe Dallas Cowboys apparel.

Once, on a family trip to Boston, the Russakoffs had done a historical bus tour. Greta and Maggie had hoped it would be a haunted tour, but it had turned out to be a lot of shit about Pilgrims, the Founding Fathers, and patriotism, which their parents had enjoyed in the vague way of parents relieved to have someone—anyone—else briefly in charge, but had left the sisters cold. Bored and hungry, they'd begun a game of I

Spy that quickly devolved into chaos as all the things they saw were gone by the time the guessing could commence.

Apparently they'd gotten louder than they'd realized, because the next thing Greta knew, her parents were hissing at them in embarrassment to sit down and be quiet. Greta and Adelaide had passed notes in silence after that.

Carys emerged from a doorway, and Greta's breath caught. She wore a spangled black skirt, worn black Frye boots, and an openwork lavender shawl. Her hair was in a messy top-knot, and she wore octagonal wire-rim glasses. Her lipstick was maroon, her luscious mouth curled in a mysterious smile.

"Good evening, y'all. Are you ready to explore the supernatural mysteries of the Crescent City?"

Murmurs of *Yes* and uncertain clapping commenced.

Greta wanted to show enthusiasm to help Carys, but the idea of making a sound in front of other people mortified her.

Carys, however, clearly had no need of her help. She went through a list of rules and then said, "Follow me, if you dare," and turned to stride off into the French Quarter.

At the very last moment, she caught Greta's eye and gave her a wink.

When Carys had texted her, inviting her to come on her tour and hang out afterward, Greta's first response was relief. She'd woken the morning after they'd met wondering if it had all been a dream. Surely, that magical afternoon couldn't have happened? She agonized over how soon was too soon to text Carys and try to see her again.

So when a text came from Carys the next night, she jumped on the invitation.

However, in preparation to come claim the ticket Carys had left for her, Greta had been a tumbleweed of nerves.

Her last date had been six months before—a dating app meetup at a bar on the mainland. It had been excruciating. The woman had been a few years older and asked pointed, derogatory questions about living on Owl Island and the lack of an active queer dating scene.

Greta had left feeling like the awkwardness was all her fault, since she'd admitted to not having had many girlfriends, and her date had said she didn't feel a vibe but that she liked to "pay it forward," so Greta could message her if she had any questions.

"Questions?" Greta had said. "Like…about you?"

"About the lifestyle," the woman had said, and anger curled in Greta's gut, pantherlike and sleek.

What Greta'd wanted to say was, "Lifestyle? Bitch, you live in rural Maine, are, like, two years older than me, and seem to think there's *one* lifestyle that all lesbians share? Miss me with any 'answers,' thanks."

What she'd actually said was, "Oh yeah, sure. Thanks." She'd spent the ferry ride back to Owl Island imagining the mortifying texts her date was sending to friends about the clueless, pathetic woman she'd just had drinks with. Then she'd spent the evening at home wondering why she cared. Why she always cared so damn much what people thought of her.

She'd deleted the app after that.

Now here she was, half a world away, and she still cared, damn it.

Carys came to a halt and waited for the group to catch up. She pointed at a second-story balcony and began to spin her first tale.

Carys was a natural storyteller, and the tour group was rapt. Greta was listening, but she was also luxuriating in the atmosphere. Even though she knew much of the French Quarter was a tourist trap, she *was* a tourist, and while drinking until she puked wasn't a particular hobby of hers, there was something about the place that was captivating. People moved freely from one bar to another, drinking and dancing in the streets, music from street performers bleeding into one another as they walked. There was a freedom here—a different sense of time. And Greta wanted to let it wash her away.

As they approached the next stop, another tour group stood on the corner. "Ghost tour traffic jam," Carys said jauntily. "Let's go up a block, and we'll come back when they're done."

Greta made her way toward the front of the group in an attempt to walk close to Carys, but the father of the Dallas Cowboys–clad father/son duo reached her first and began asking dad questions. What was the population of New Orleans? What was the population density in different neighborhoods?

"I don't know," Carys said easily.

"But, but," the man spluttered, "you're a tour guide."

"Well, if you'd like to know the population density of vampires, that I can tell you," Carys said archly and winked.

"Okay," the man said.

Carys blinked like a silent film star, but the man still stood expectantly.

"That was a joke," she said lightly. "Because vampires aren't real."

The man frowned. "I don't think you're supposed to tell us that on a ghost and vampire tour," he said.

"It sounds like you might enjoy a historical walking tour," Carys said, sounding totally unbothered. "I'll give you a brochure when we get back to Conti."

Then she took a step away from him and held up her hand, stopping the tour.

"Here we are," she said, "at the Ursuline Convent. Would you like to hear about the filles à la cassette?"

Her eyes found Greta's, and she smiled. Greta recognized the place and the story from the other day and smiled back.

"They were rumored to be vampires," Carys said, looking right at the man who'd been giving her shit.

The tour went on like that for another hour and a half, and when they finally rounded the corner to the place they'd met, Greta was tired and very ready to be out of a group of strangers.

She hung back, and several members of the group clustered to ask Carys follow-up questions as well as questions about how to get back to their hotels on Canal Street. A few slipped her bills and thanked her for a great tour.

Finally, even the football fans left, and Carys slumped against the lamppost and pulled off her shawl.

"Thank god," she groaned.

"That must be exhausting," Greta said, approaching.

"Some nights are more than others."

"The population of New Orleans is just under four hundred thousand," Greta offered, feeling a bit silly. "Just, I googled it before I came."

"I know," Carys said and winked. "Thanks."

"Oh, I just thought you told that guy… Oh."

Carys yawned and stretched. "He annoyed me. I'm not Wikipedia. Guys like him want to get the most for their money, so they ask a million questions they don't care about just to feel like it was worth it. I've seen it a hundred times."

Greta nodded and Carys got to her feet again with another stretch. "You wanna hang out back at my place?"

"Yeah, okay. If you're not too tired."

"Just don't ask me any fact-based questions on the walk there and I'll recharge."

"Okay," Greta said before she realized Carys was kidding. "Sorry, I'm really nervous," she confessed.

"How come?"

Carys faced her and seemed to be asking sincerely.

"Well. I guess because you're really beautiful and smart. And you seem…cool? That's not what I mean, but like what cool would mean if it were actually cool. You know?"

Carys didn't nod. She just looked deep into Greta's eyes. Greta's impulse was to look away, but Carys' gaze wasn't challenging. It was open, vulnerable, intimate.

"I hope being nervous doesn't mean you can't still have fun hanging out," she said finally.

Something bright broke open in Greta. Her gratitude that Carys wasn't trying to talk her out of how she felt made her buoyant.

"I'm hopeful," she said and grinned.

Carys' answering smile was warm, and they walked into the night together.

Carys lived in a different part of the Marigny than Truman's house was in, though Greta wasn't clear enough on directions to understand exactly where. Carys explained that the term *riverside* meant closer to the Mississippi, while *lakeside* meant closer to Lake Pontchartrain. And *upriver* and *downriver* referred to the directions of the Marigny versus the Garden District. Greta tried to recreate the route she'd taken from Truman's house the morning she'd seen Teacup in the backyard of Carys' house, but she'd turned hither and yon on a whim that morning and couldn't unravel it.

"So you live…upriver and lakeside of me?"

"Uh. Yes. You wouldn't really use lakeside that way, but it's true. Really, you live in Marigny-Bywater, and I'm in Marigny closer to St. Claude. Here we are."

Carys' house was painted a cheery apricot color, with olive shutters, light pink woodwork, and a bright red door. The porch was white and covered with potted plants, as were the wood steps that led up to it. Lanterns and tiny disco balls hung from the edge of the porch, and bunches of dried herbs and flowers hung between them.

"Come on in," Carys said and opened the unlocked door.

Music greeted Greta as she stepped inside. Then something nearly hit her in the face. She jumped backward and stepped into Carys, who steadied her.

"Shit, sorry!" someone yelled from out of Greta's line of sight.

Carys let out a bark of laughter. "It's king cake season. Don't be alarmed."

Greta didn't know what that meant, but she could now see that what had almost hit her was just a balloon filled with a lot of glitter.

"It's a hazard. If it pops, it'll blast glitter into someone's eyeballs, and we'll get sued!"

"Psh, they'll have to find us first," came the response.

"Hey, y'all!" Carys shouted. "Can I introduce you to Greta?"

Two people emerged from what Greta assumed to be the kitchen, since they were wearing aprons.

"Greta, these are my housemates. This is Veronica."

Veronica was a tall Black woman with her hair braided and pulled into a low ponytail. She wore a black baseball cap with ZERO stitched on it in neon orange, and her owl-printed apron covered mismatched shortie pajamas that showed off her long legs. She was beautiful, but when she smiled, revealing a small gap in her front teeth, she glowed.

"Greta from the far north country of Maine," Veronica said, holding out a hand. "Welcome to paradise."

"Oh, yeah, thanks," Greta said.

"And this is Helen. They don't usually throw things at guests."

Helen was small but muscular, and when they held out a hand, their grin was feral. Greta got the distinct impression that perhaps they wished they could throw things at guests often.

"You won't tell, will you?" they said to Greta.

"Uh, no? Tell what?"

"About the deadly glitter," they whispered.

"Oh. No. Um, what's king cake?"

"So," Helen began, leaning in and fixing her with an intent gaze.

But Carys slung an arm over their shoulder and said, "Can we, like, sit down first?"

They made their way to the living room through the kitchen, and Veronica and Helen stripped off their aprons and sat down.

"You know Mardi Gras?" Helen asked.

Greta nodded.

"King cake is sold for Carnival. You bake a little baby inside, and whoever gets the baby in their slice gets luck and good fortune for the year. Or whatever. But the *point* is that me and Veronica made bank to last, like, six months selling king cakes just for Mardi Gras last year. So we're just making sure our recipe is still bomb and experimenting with…"

They frowned and looked over at Veronica.

"Pizzazz," Veronica finished. "That little something that will set Eleventh House King Cakes apart from the rest."

"Last year, our babies were gators," Helen said.

"The year before that, we painted our boxes with chalkboard paint so we could write people's names and addresses on them. It was cute, but, damn."

"We loaded that first batch in the van, and by the time we got to the first address, the chalk had all rubbed off and we had no fucking idea whose was whose," Helen finished. "Bad call."

"This year," Veronica said, "we're experimenting with tying a glitter-balloon to each box so when someone opens the door, they see it floating there all pretty-like."

"Veronica's afraid they'll pop and blind people, but really I think it'll just add a little sparkle to people's houses."

Carys just shook her head at her roommates. "If you get glitter all over people's houses, they will never order from you again. That shit lasts for decades. Seriously, it's, like, archaeological. PS, please tell me that you didn't have one explode and that's what made you worried, Ronnie."

Veronica and Helen exchanged sidelong looks.

"It's totally fine. We cleaned it up," Veronica said finally.

"Just tell me it wasn't in the kitchen," Carys said hopefully. After a beat of silence, she tried, "Tell me the cabinets were closed?"

"They were!" Helen said triumphantly.

Carys turned to Greta. "Two years ago, we needed purple glitter for our Mardi Gras costumes. We thought we were brilliant because we got these huge bags of glitter wholesale online. When we slit open the box, we must've cut through the bag somehow, so when we opened the box, this mushroom cloud of glitter poofs out onto the floor. It was there for, like, eight months. It got in and on everything, and we were cursing the existence of glitter. Until recently, apparently."

She raised a stern eyebrow at Veronica and Helen, but there didn't seem to be ire behind it.

"I'm Black and trans in the South. I'm resilient," Veronica said with a sniff.

"We were just experimenting," Helen muttered, winking at Veronica.

"I have total faith that y'all won't make me clean up glitter no matter what you do," Carys said, then blew kisses at her housemates and grabbed Greta's hand. "We're gonna go hang out in my room. Happy caking."

"Nice to meet you," Greta said before following Carys.

Helen saluted her, and Veronica waved elegant fingers with a knowing look.

Carys' room was painted midnight blue, and mobiles of geometric shapes hung from the ceiling. She had a large window hanging on the wall that she used as a white board—it was scrawled with equations, dates, and symbols Greta couldn't guess at.

A clothes rack burst with colors, patterns, and textures, and several hats hung on hooks above it. She had a standing desk, and the legs were encrusted with...teeth?

Greta leaned closer to inspect it.

"They're real," Carys said. "Things decompose really quickly here because of the heat, so animals that die get stripped to the bone. I think their teeth are so beautiful."

Never having given the teeth of animals much thought beyond not wanting them to sink into her flesh, Greta was obliged to agree now that she was confronted with them in this context. They were of all different sizes and shapes, some curved, some serrated, and some ground flat.

"It's like what we were talking about the other day—what's the difference between animals and plants when a plant has teeth, basically," Greta said.

Carys nodded and hopped onto her bed, leaning against the headboard. It was a stately affair, with carved posts and diaphanous fabric spilling from the top.

Carys pulled out a glass pipe and some weed. She packed a bowl and held out the pipe and a lighter to Greta. "Want some?"

"Thanks."

Greta sat cross-legged on the bed facing Carys and blew smoke at the ceiling. Carys wiped off her lipstick and they passed the pipe back and forth.

Above the bed hung an enormous painting of a horse rearing against a backdrop of choppy waters. On the horse's back was a figure, her hair flowing around her nude form but failing to cover her ample curves. It was glorious.

It was…

"Is that, um, you?" Greta asked.

Carys grinned and handed her the pipe and lighter.

"Yeah. My friend Edward painted it for me. The horse is supposed to be—"

"Teacup! I can tell."

"Yep. I helped him propose to his boyfriend by doing this personalized ghost tour based on spots they'd been on dates around town, and this was his thank-you."

"His thank-you was to paint you naked?"

"Well," Carys said, blowing smoke elegantly toward the painting, "I requested the subject matter." She grinned.

"Is it, uh… Never mind."

Greta shook her head and closed her mouth. She gazed at the painting, then wondered if it was rude to gaze at a nude painting of Carys. Then she figured if Carys put a picture of herself nude on her wall, she was okay with people looking at it.

"Did I pose for it?"

"Huh?"

"Were you going to ask if it's based on real life?"

Carys had a wicked gleam in her eye, and she pushed her chest forward, posing like the figure in the painting.

"Erp."

Carys laughed. "Maybe you'll find out." She winked and handed Greta the pipe. "Edward added the ocean. I really think it makes the whole thing more dramatic."

Greta giggled.

Carys cocked an eyebrow.

"Sorry, I was just… *Edward*."

"Hmm?" Carys asked, taking the pipe.

"It's like Ed-ward. Like, going in the direction of Ed."

Greta dissolved into laugher and Carys snorted.

"I never thought of that before. Are there other -ward names?"

"Uh… Howard?"

Carys snickered. "You're high. And a nerd."

"A little," Greta admitted. She flopped back on the bed and ran her fingers up one of the posts of the heavy frame. "How'd you get this thing through the door?"

"It was in here when I moved in. Isn't it amazing? There are moon phases carved into the posts on the insides. Not sure if they're original or added later, but." Carys shrugged and blew a series of perfect smoke rings. "Lesbian lunar bed of my dreams." She grinned, and Greta grinned back.

"Are you into astrology and that stuff?" Greta asked.

"I like things that give us shorthands to tell other people about ourselves. Do I believe where the planets were the moment you were born makes a code that determines your personality? No. But I think anything that makes it easier to do self-reflection is useful."

"I should make my sisters get into the zodiac, then." She imagined asking Sadie what her sign was and snorted.

"What's the deal with your family, dude?" Carys asked, lying back on the bed next to her.

"Well, my sister Tillie got married last year to this guy she works with. Adelaide—that's my twin—and Sadie, my oldest sister, work with my parents. They have a real estate business. I've been working there for the last year too. Maggie's still in school."

Carys nodded, listening, but said, "I more meant, what's their *deal*. Like, what's your issue with them?"

Greta sighed. She'd kind of known that was what Carys meant. "You know how when you're little and there's a thing your family does, like drink milk with dinner or buy a certain kind of toothpaste, you just think that's how the world is? And then you meet other families and they drink water with dinner and use a whole other flavor of toothpaste?"

"Yeah."

"Well, my family's just always been really involved in each other's lives. And when we were younger, it was probably pretty normal. Normal enough that I didn't notice much difference when I saw other people's families. And when Sadie, my oldest sister, went to college, she would still call home most days at dinnertime to say hi, and she came home for every break."

Greta hadn't thought it was strange. Sadie had always

loved their dinnertime go-arounds telling about how everyone's day was. She always volunteered to go first.

"Then Tillie didn't go to college. She did an internship
with a veterinarian on the mainland near the ferry, so she kept
living at home. When it was my and Adelaide's turn to think
about school, Addie just assumed we'd go to the UMaine closest to home, like Sadie did. But I...I wanted something else. I
wanted the opposite of Owl Island. I wanted to go to school in
Portland. Maine," she added quickly, since everyone outside
Maine thought Oregon when they heard it.

"When I got in, my mom couldn't even muster fake hap-
piness before she said *You'll be so far away!* Just FYI, Portland
is, like, a three-hour drive plus a ferry ride from Owl Island."

Carys snorted smoke out her nose.

"Yeah. Addie had applied because I had, and she got in
too, but we both knew she wouldn't go. She loves Owl Island,
loves nature. She'd hate being in a city, even a little one like
Portland. Anyway, that was kind of the beginning, I guess.
Sadie said it was selfish of me to go to school far enough away
that I couldn't help Mom and Dad out with the business on the
weekends. Addie was sad I wouldn't be around all the time to
make her be social. My dad said he worried for me in *the big
city*. For context, Portland is *not* a big city by any stretch of the
imagination."

Carys nodded thoughtfully. "And what about you?"

"Me? I...was so excited for a chance to start over that I felt
guilty."

The night before she left home, Greta couldn't sleep.
She'd walked around the only place she'd ever lived, gently
touching the piano, the ragged lines of her father's catastrophic
Holiday Fair crafts, the magnetic calendar dry-erase board on

the refrigerator that told everyone where each member of the family was for the week. Almost as an afterthought, she pulled the cap off the dry-erase marker and left a small note in the bottom right corner of the calendar, beneath Sunday and beneath the list of everyone's telephone numbers. *I love you*, she'd written, then a small black heart. *G.* Five years later it was still there.

"After I left, there was this space between me and the rest of the family that had never been there before. I mean, don't get me wrong, we were always texting and calling, and Addie and Maggie came to stay with me for weekends and stuff. But it was like my world had expanded and theirs…"

She inhaled and shrugged, holding the smoke until her throat stung, then exhaling. She wished the issue would dissipate as easily as the cloud of smoke.

"I mean, I love them. They've been a huge support system for me. Always been there. If I was in trouble, I could call them at any time of day or night and they'd help me. It's just a lot. To feel so…tethered? Surveilled? In college, I started keeping a journal again for the first time in years because before, I'd always known one of my sisters could find it and read it."

She'd stopped when she moved back to Owl Island, though. Even living by herself, she didn't feel comfortable having a journal around. Her family came over so often, and everyone had a key, that she didn't trust it.

"Gah, please make me stop talking." Greta buried her face in the pillow for a moment, then sat up.

"I can't even imagine."

"What? Your family's not codependent and nosy?" Greta tried to laugh it off.

Carys spoke through a mouth of smoke. "Nope. It's me and my mom, mostly. Her parents live about an hour away, but I don't see them that much."

When Greta was little, one of the secret fantasies she indulged in was being an only child. Having time with just her mom or just her dad, with no interruptions.

"Do you and your mom hang out a lot?"

"No. I don't fuck with her if I can help it. Do you mind?" Carys stood and gestured at her clothes. "It's bra off o'clock."

"'S fine."

Greta tried to appear as though her whole attention was on the lighter she held, but she couldn't help glance up as Carys stripped off her bra by pulling it through her sleeve. Her breasts fell heavy and soft, and Greta imagined pillowing her head between them as Carys stroked her hair.

"My mom had me when she was sixteen," Carys went on. "We lived with my grandparents till I was five, then moved out. My mother is…" Greta could practically see her entertaining and then discarding words. "She's very difficult for me to be around, so I try not to be."

Greta passed the pipe back to Carys when she sat on the bed again. Carys lay on her back, took a drag, and held it so long, Greta wondered if she'd swallowed it. When Carys finally exhaled, she closed her eyes.

"Nothing is ever my mom's fault. She doesn't have the life she wanted because people are unfair to her, because they're out to get her, because she had me and missed her opportunities. She's always embroiled in some friend group or romantic drama where she's the victim. She's *always* the victim. It's…" Carys waved the smoke away from her face like she could wave her mother away. "It fucked me up for a long time. Before I realized *she's* the one who's fucked up. Now I try to stay away from her as much as I can."

"Fucked you up how?" Greta asked, putting a careful hand on Carys' ankle.

"It was just us for a long time. So if something was messed up and it was never her fault, then—"

"It had to be yours."

"Yeah. If she didn't show up to a parent-teacher conference, then it was like 'you set me up to fail and look like a bad parent because you didn't tell me about it.' And if I reminded her that I had told her about it, she'd say, 'you know how prejudiced and ignorant people are about single moms and teen-aged moms. You're supposed to be on my side and make me look good. Or do you *want* people to think I'm trash? Yeah, you must want that, because then it looks like you really overcame some hardships.' Et cetera."

Something squirmy settled in the pit of Greta's stomach. "That's awful."

"Yeah. I left for college, even though I love New Orleans, because I needed to get away from her. Now I'll be paying off student loans for an immortal lifetime, yay, but it felt worth it at the time to get away."

"Where'd you go?"

"Atlanta. And amazingly, in Atlanta, when things went wrong, they weren't all magically my fault. I met people who apologized when they messed up. I realized that when everyone you meet has had drama with the same person, maybe it's that person who's the problem, not everyone else."

Carys said this all lightly, but her gaze was fixed intently on the ceiling.

"After college, I wanted to come back to New Orleans,

and I had all this shit planned that I wanted to say to my mom. I confronted her and laid it all out. Her eyes got bigger and bigger, and at a certain point, she just started talking in a low voice. She was saying 'You're a liar' over and over underneath me talking, like she was chanting a spell to ward off my words. And I realized she just wasn't able to see herself the way I saw her. She'd crumble to dust. If she thought of herself as the problem or as doing anything wrong, it would, like, smash the image she had of herself as a good person."

Carys opened her eyes.

"I'm so sorry," Greta said. "She sounds truly awful."

"She's sad," Carys stated. "It's really, really sad when someone's so fragile that the truth feels like an attack. Anyway." She shrugged. "It's better if I don't see her much. And when I do, I just go in like—" She swept a hand down like a forcefield between herself and the world. "Anything she says, I just say, 'okay,' and move on."

Greta lay down on her back beside Carys. "I think it's pretty amazing that you confronted her. Even if it didn't work out the way you wanted. I don't think I could ever do that."

"Confront your family?"

"Confront anyone," Greta mumbled. "Like, I yell at my sisters sometimes, because we fight and we say mean shit all the time, but it's not a real confrontation."

Carys turned on her side and propped herself up on one elbow, looking at Greta. "What's a real confrontation to you?"

Greta turned so they were face-to-face. "A truth, I guess? A hard truth that you tell someone about themselves or about you that you know will lead to strife."

"Hmm." Carys' eyes roamed her face. "What about a soft truth?"

"Huh?" Greta blinked, lost in Carys' curls and skin and eyes and mouth.

"I have this *extremely* soft truth that I would *love* to confront you with…"

Greta smiled and slid her knee between Carys'. "Oh yeah?"

Carys spread her legs in invitation. "Mm-hmm."

Carys' eyelids lowered, and Greta's heart started to beat faster.

Greta trailed her fingertips up Carys' bare arm and watched the hairs stand up. When she reached her shoulder, Greta leaned in and caught Carys' mouth in a kiss. Carys pressed a hot tongue against hers. It was soft—so soft Greta was melting in honeyed sweetness. Then Carys was pressing against her, also so soft, but with an urgency that made her clit throb and her nipples tingle.

"Fuck, you really are soft."

Carys answered with the sexiest, wickedest smile Greta had ever seen. "Sure am. C'mere."

She pulled Greta on top of her and they kissed—wild, deep, lose-your-breath kisses that set Greta reeling.

Every nerve ending responded to Carys; every inch of her skin was sensitized. When Carys tipped her head to the side and licked a line up Greta's neck, Greta shuddered.

Carys *mmm*ed appreciatively and rolled Greta onto the bed.

"May I?"

When Greta nodded, Carys stripped her of her clothes.

"You're so fucking hot," Carys said. "What do you want?"

Greta opened her mouth, but nothing came out. It was clear that Carys sincerely wanted to know. But Greta didn't have any idea what she wanted. Just…

"You," she said, hoping it would be enough.

It wasn't.

Carys stopped. "Do you want me to go down on you or use a vibrator? A strap-on? Dildo? What are you in the mood for?"

Greta blinked. "It all sounds great. Any of it? Sounds great."

"I really want to do what would turn you on," Carys said.

"What if I don't…exactly know what would turn me on?" Greta bit out.

Mortification flooded her. She squeezed her eyes shut, waiting to feel Carys pull away. To see Carys' scornful expression.

"Hey."

Carys lay back down beside her, and Greta opened her eyes a slit. Carys didn't look scornful or horrified.

"It's okay. Do you want to stop?"

"No!" Greta grabbed her arm. "No, definitely not. I just… I'm bad at deciding. Can you just decide?"

Carys said, "Do you mean you get off on being told what to do?"

Greta thought about that. Maybe she should just say yes? But Carys was being so sincere with her, she couldn't bear to ruin it.

"No."

Carys smiled. "Okay, how about I propose something and you tell me what you think?"

"That's perfect," Greta said with relief.

"Okay." Carys reached over the side of the bed and fumbled with the drawer of her nightstand. She came up with a Magic Wand, plugged in and ready to go. "What if I take my clothes off—"

"Yes, please," Greta said enthusiastically.

Carys grinned. "And lie on the bed. And use this on myself. And you lie on top of me so you can reach it too?"

Greta blinked, lust-addled. "Uh-huh."

This time, Carys' smile was sweet and appreciative. She slid her skirt down her thighs, revealing bright red underwear with crisscrossing bands that reached to her waist. They were incredibly hot.

"Damn," Greta said.

Carys raised an eyebrow seductively, then grinned. "I hoped this might happen, so I was prepared."

Greta stripped off her own totally unsexy underwear, and Carys' gaze was magnetized between her legs.

"Can I touch you?"

Greta nodded and Carys swept a finger over her clit. Stars burst all over Greta's body, and she pressed closer to Carys.

"Can I help?" She gestured to Carys' underwear.

"I'm gonna leave them on."

It was only then that Greta even thought about safety, and she felt silly and grateful.

"Good. They're really hot," she said, and Carys smiled.

"Get over here," Carys said. She spread her gorgeous fat thighs, and Greta knelt between them.

Greta had seen Magic Wands online, and her friend Ramona swore by them, but she'd never used one. When Carys clicked the button and it roared to life, Greta's eyes went wide.

Carys spread herself open inside her underwear and guided the vibrator to her clit. Her body jerked when she made contact, and her eyes fluttered closed.

Greta watched, mesmerized, as Carys pleasured herself.

Color rose in her cheeks and her nipples hardened. She was utterly gorgeous.

"C'mere," Carys whispered, and Greta positioned herself over the Magic Wand too. She pressed her hips down to grind on Carys, and a shock tore through her.

"Oh my fucking god," she said.

"Good?"

"It's… I've… We… Yup," Greta concluded.

"This is the lower setting," Carys said impishly and rubbed circles over Greta's clit with her thumb.

"Oh, god. Okay."

The Magic Wand was the most powerful vibration she'd ever felt. She pressed back against it and felt her whole body come alive with the slightest touch.

"Yeah, move however feels good," Carys murmured. She ground the toy against herself, and Greta rode it with her.

The pleasure came first in short, sharp lightning strikes, then as her body grew accustomed to its intensity and she could maintain contact for longer, it was a rolling pleasure that rattled through her and set her on fire.

Carys ran gentle fingertips over her nipples and, when Greta responded, played with them more roughly. With the vibrations between her legs and Carys' hands on her breasts, Greta felt the first twinges of what would build to an orgasm.

"Fuck, yes."

Carys spread her legs wider and pumped her hips up, and Greta leaned down to kiss her. They kissed and moaned into each other's mouths as Greta's weight bore the vibrations deeper into them both. Splayed across Carys' gorgeous body, the angle changed, and Greta began to roll her hips along with Carys.

"You're fucking perfect. Don't stop," Carys chanted.

She threw her head back and grabbed Greta's hips, holding them tightly together.

Greta felt her stomach start to tighten, and her pussy felt swollen and hungry. She and Carys fucked each other, both so close to the edge that every movement caused a moan or a gasp. Greta's thighs threatened to give out and she whimpered.

"You won't squish me, babe. C'mere," Carys said, and Greta let her take her full weight. Carys moaned. "Fuck, fuck, fuck, I'm gonna come," she said breathlessly.

She moved the Magic Wand in circles and her body seized. She threw her head back and let out a silent scream as she came, every muscle rigid.

Greta had never seen anything more beautiful, and she ran a worshipful hand down Carys' face, between her breasts, and down to where the vibrator was touching her. Carys gasped and groaned.

"Are you gonna come?" Carys asked breathlessly.

"Yeah."

Greta was so on edge, she thought anything might tip her over. Carys held the toy firm, and Greta settled over it just right. Every time she moved, she saw the pleasure on Carys' face, her sensitive flesh driven past the point of orgasm.

"I'm gonna come again," Carys murmured.

"Oh, fuck, yes."

Greta watched her writhe on the bed, and the first whimper shot through Greta like a bolt of lightning. She thrust her hips and felt the orgasm gather like a storm, rolling through her slowly at first, then striking with full force. She didn't know how she stayed upright as it rocked her and was only vaguely aware of the sounds that her pleasure tore from her.

When she could move again, she flopped on top of Carys and buried her face in Carys' neck. "Oh my fucking *god*."

"You wanna go for one more?"

"Um? Yeah?"

Carys draped herself over Greta and handed her the Magic Wand.

They held it together and Greta spread her legs and let the toy rumble through her orgasm-primed flesh. For a moment, it was too much, then she pressed it to her opening and felt the vibrations in a whole new way. It happened fast. This orgasm was quiet and gutting, pulling her into the dark as stars exploded behind her eyes, and she buried her face in the pillow.

When Greta returned to earth, she found Carys watching her with soft eyes.

"Wow," was all she could find to say.

Carys smiled and brushed her hair back. For glorious minutes, Greta luxuriated under Carys' touch until she slowly surfaced. Carys smelled sweet and vibrant, and Greta wished she could stay here forever, being stroked like a favored pet. Then her stomach growled.

"Are you hungry? I'm hungry," Carys said.

Greta's stomach growled again and she groaned at it.

"I'll grab us something," Carys said with a smile and a squeeze of Greta's knee.

She wrapped herself in a seafoam-green and cream dressing gown patterned with cranes and swept out of the room.

"Where," Greta said to the spangled ceiling, "the fuck am I."

She let herself drift on the sea of satisfaction and relaxation but was yanked from it by the ring of her phone. It was Adelaide.

"Hey," Greta said, stretching luxuriantly.

"Dude," her twin said. "You've gotta be the tiebreaker. Sadie wants to turn Mom and Dad's photo book into a video, but I think the book is better. Tillie likes both, obviously, and Maggie doesn't like either."

"Well, I'm not there, so I'm not gonna be able to help turn it into a video. If Sadie wants to do it, I don't mind. Not like she has anything better to do."

It was Sadie who answered. "What a refreshingly mean thing to say. Oh, wait, you're always like this."

Greta cringed. "Oops. Hey, Sadie. Addie, let this be your one millionth reminder that you have to tell people if they're on conference."

"You're not! You're just on speaker. Sorry."

"Same point!"

The door opened, and Carys walked in. Greta mouthed *Sorry* and pointed to her phone. *My sisters.*

Carys waved it away and settled back on the bed with a plate of bread, cheese, and grapes. All Greta wanted was to sit with her and eat and talk.

"Guys, I gotta go, okay? Do whatever you want. I'm out this year."

"Wait, *out* out?" Adelaide asked. "But you'll be home for Chanukah?"

"No. I told you, I'm staying for a month."

Carys put a hand on Greta's back and rubbed softly.

"But…Chanukah."

Her twin's voice sounded like she was ten years old again and Greta didn't want to have matching costumes for the first time at Halloween.

Greta pressed into Carys' hand and rolled her eyes.

"Dude, I told you this at the beginning," she reminded Adelaide.

"But I didn't think you meant Chanukah too!"

She sounded genuinely distraught. They'd never spent a holiday apart. Greta felt a twinge of longing underneath the habitual guilt.

"Sorry, Addie. I gotta go, though. I love you."

She ended the call before Adelaide could reply.

"Sorry," she said to Carys. "This looks great."

"Everything okay?"

"Yeah. Every year for Chanukah, we all get my parents a group present. It's been that way since we were little. And every year, it's this whole *thing* because Sadie tries to control it and doesn't want the rest of our ideas but then gets angry if we don't do the work she wants us to do. So inevitably with, like, a week to go until Chanukah, we get it done and it's never exactly the way she wanted, but my parents always act like it's the greatest gift they've ever received."

Carys cocked her head. "Is that bad?"

"No, no. I'm just saying the stakes are low."

Carys nodded and handed her a piece of bread and cheese drizzled with honey.

Greta bit into it, and the tastes exploded in her mouth. Earthy grain of bread, the nuttiness of an unfamiliar cheese, and mellow sweetness of honey.

"Holy shit, this is heavenly."

"I'm glad you like it. Veronica keeps bees over at this community garden a few blocks away, and she makes the honey."

"I've always wanted to see the honey from real bees."

"I'm sure Veronica'd be happy to take you with her."

"I would love that."

"So, your sisters?"

"Oh, yeah, they just wanted me to be the tiebreaker vote. Really, it's silly, because we're in our twenties now, and I'm sure my parents don't need another photo album from us any more than they ever really liked the coupon books we made them with, like, one free kiss from each of us, even though they pretended those were the greatest thing in the world too."

Carys handed her another piece of bread, cheese, and honey.

"Like, we started doing a group present for our parents and a round-robin gift wheel for me and my sisters because we were kids and didn't have any money, but now we all have jobs, and we could just get each other regular presents so it wouldn't have to be a whole thing."

Greta forced herself to stop talking, take a breath, and eat some grapes.

"Sorry, I'll stop talking about this."

"Why do you think your parents are only pretending to like these presents?" Carys asked.

"I dunno, it's silly, right? Your adult children putting on a play or making stuff like kids?"

"I think probably they still love you just as much as when you were little and they still want pictures of you," Carys said mildly.

Greta got distracted watching her suck a bead of honey off her finger.

"Seems like maybe your sister likes an excuse to work on something with y'all."

"Sadie? She just likes to tell us all what to do since she's the oldest."

Greta was half kidding. But only half.

"Sorry to keep talking about my family. Do you have any holiday traditions?"

"Not with my family anymore. For a little while when I was in college, my mom and I would go through the motions. She'd get me random stuff that had nothing to do with my life. I'd put a lot of thought into trying to get a gift that made her feel seen, and she'd be massively disappointed in it, then we'd go to her parents for an awkward dinner."

Carys delivered this statement in an offhand way, but it made Greta's stomach clench with sadness. Then Carys grinned.

"These days, Veronica and Helen and I have a big holiday thing of our own. We invite lovers and close friends who aren't seeing family, and we do it up here." She paused for a moment and looked up at Greta, her whiskey-brown eyes twinkling. "You should come."

Greta smiled and eased down beside her. "Again?" she said.

Carys arched an eyebrow and raked Greta with her eyes. "'Tis the season."

## 9
## GRETA

hows nola??? Maggie's text came when Greta and Horse were on their way to Muriel's for tea.

*it's great! met the most amazing girl and made a friend with an actual banana tree growing in her backyard.*

Maggie sent back banana emojis, then, like a GIRL girl?

*yes, a human girl. woman.*

liiiike ✦???

*total fireworks,* Greta gave in and replied, smiling. An old man walking slowly past her smiled back and tipped his hat.

"Morning," she mumbled.

She was still figuring out the proper mode of interacting with strangers in New Orleans. It was a whole different gestural vocabulary. Coming from a town where everyone knew each other, Greta was used to waving hello. But her experience in Portland, Maine, for college had been one where if you didn't know someone, their overtures generally portended creepiness. Here, though, a thin veneer of formal charm overlaid everything, and it took some getting used to.

She'd asked Carys for a gloss, and Carys had said, "Pretend everyone is your grandma's second-closest friend."

That hadn't been terribly helpful, since Greta's grandparents lived in Ohio and she'd only met them a handful of times. Still, it was better than nothing.

Muriel's garden looked even lovelier than the last time Greta'd been there, and when she pushed open the gate and called, "Good morning," Muriel breezed out of the kitchen door, coffee tray in hand.

"Hello, darling," Muriel said. "I'm so glad you've come."

She put the tray on the beautiful mosaic table and kissed Greta on the cheek. Muriel's silver hair was caught up in a large bun and secured with a silver and turquoise hairpin. She wore a flowing kaftan of yellow, peach, and black in a floral print that reminded Greta of some grand sixteenth-century tapestry.

"Will you help me with the other tray?"

Greta followed her into the kitchen and picked up a tray laden with pastries and fruit. "God, this looks amazing. I hope you didn't go to too much trouble."

"Pleasure is worth a bit of trouble," Muriel said and swept back out into the garden.

"Yeah, okay," Greta said, following.

Muriel poured strong chicory coffee for them both and added cream and sugar. She leaned back, took a deep breath, and sipped the coffee.

"This is one of my favorite things," she said.

Greta was fairly certain she'd never simply sat and enjoyed coffee in her life, always slopping it on her shirt trying to drink it while she watered the plants in the morning or as she got ready for work.

Now, she did as Muriel had done: leaned back, took a deep breath of air that smelled so different from the air at home, and sipped the coffee slowly. She hadn't tasted chicory before coming here, but she enjoyed it—an herby infusion that tasted of river and leaf, particular and assertive.

They chatted easily, about the things Greta had seen in New Orleans so far, about Muriel's garden, and ate croissants so flaky with butter they melted in Greta's mouth and pineapple softer and sweeter than any Greta had tasted. Muriel took the last bite of her croissant and dragged it through the pink-sugared dregs of her coffee cup, popped it in her mouth, and sighed once more.

"I wonder if you'd be willing to help me with something," she said.

"Yeah, of course—anything," Greta said quickly, thrilled to be able to offer something in return for Muriel's kindness and welcome.

"I have several bags I'm donating to a local charity, but they're in the back room, and these hands—"

She held up perfectly manicured hands that Greta had seen shake as Muriel lifted a cream pitcher.

"It's the grip, you see? If you wouldn't mind bringing them to the garden gate, it would be such a help."

"No problem."

They went inside and Muriel led Greta to the back room. Her space was a treasure trove of art, artifacts, draped fabrics, and maps yellowing at the corners. Every bookshelf was full of books stacked sideways and crammed on top of each other, knickknacks strewn in front of them. The floor rugs were layered on top of one another—swathes of elegantly muted patterns in maroon and navy and dusky rose. Every room contained an ornate carved wooden fan and a fireplace inlaid with mosaic tile.

The living room sported the most gorgeous paintings of flowers Greta had ever seen. They were boldly done, each flower recognizable. But the colors were slightly exaggerated and there appeared to be a wash over the composition that blended each edge into the next, like a garden seen while spinning.

"These are amazing," Greta breathed.

"My mother's."

"Oh wow."

She approached the largest of them, hung over the mantel. In maroon, purple, and cobalt blue, Muriel's mother had rendered frothy peonies, delicate wax flower, and serrated thistle, each flower with its own texture but layered like a living bouquet. From the upper left corner, a hand reached down as if about to pluck one. It leant the whole composition a sense of menace: life that could be ended at any moment, nature at the mercy of human caprice.

"It's a little upsetting," Greta said.

"I agree."

As they passed into the back room, Greta caught a glimpse of still lifes in a very different style. She pointed. "Are those your mother's too?"

"No, those are mine."

"Muriel, I didn't know you painted too!"

"For the joy of it, not to share."

Muriel's paintings lacked the drama of her mother's. In its place was a serenity, a sense of collaboration with nature rather than its agony or ecstasy. One large painting was only foliage, so many greens it felt like being inside the color itself. Another was of the birds-of-paradise currently growing outside. Though the flowers brought drama of composition and form, the painting was still earthy and calm.

"Why don't you put any of yours out in the living room for people to see?" Greta asked. "They're beautiful. Really different from your mom's but beautiful."

Muriel smiled. "Iris's paintings are my public face, these my private. I like to remember their differences. It reminds me of how different I am from her."

"And that's…a good thing?" Greta ventured.

Muriel nodded. "We honored one another's differences. It's the only way we were able to have a relationship."

"Sounds nice." Greta hadn't meant it to come out sounding bitter.

"Oh dear. Are you and your mother too similar?"

"Nah. I mean it sounds nice to honor the differences instead of have them be a point of contention. My mom wants me to be like her, but I'm not, and she takes it as an offense. Like I'm choosing to be different from her because I don't respect her. Which isn't true."

"What do you respect most about her?"

Greta blanked.

Her mother was always anxious, always seemed to be okay only if her children were fine. She never admitted to doing anything because *she* wanted it, only because it was "the right way." She didn't ask Greta's dad to do anything around the house, even though he never did anything on his own.

*Fuck, do I not respect my mother?*

"I don't know," she said, horrified. "God, I'm awful. All I can think about are the bad things."

"We all judge our parents, Greta. They're the people who teach us what the world is, and when we're old enough, we learn that they're wrong in ways they didn't even know. That's because the world is different for us."

"Seriously, though, all I can think of is that she raised five kids, and I refuse to respect my mom only for child-rearing. I'm disgusting."

Muriel smiled and squeezed her shoulder. "It's a mindset, dear. If you think about it when you're talking to her, I'm sure you'll find things to respect. Respect isn't the same thing as like."

She walked into the back room, leaving her paintings behind.

As Greta carried Muriel's bags to the garden gate, she tried to replay the last conversation she had with her mom to find things to respect. Nell had been worried that she was in a city alone, sad that she was gone during the holidays, and resentful that Greta had left "because of something so silly."

So her mom judged her too.

"Muriel? Do you *feel* wise? And if so, when does it start?"

Muriel chuckled. "I don't feel wise. I feel certain. It's wonderful. It started gradually, I suppose. The more experiences I had, the more things fell into slightly more predictable patterns. It meant I had to do less work to understand people's motivations and behaviors and my own responses to them. It meant I knew I had a limited amount of time on earth and could more easily choose how to allocate my resources. Maybe in my early forties? Don't rush it, darling. You'll get there, but you can't shortcut it—it's these experiences you're having now that allow you to feel certain later."

"I don't feel certain about anything," Greta admitted.

"I think that's fairly normal." Muriel sounded utterly unconcerned.

"But, like, not even about what I want to do for a job. I don't want to end up mindlessly becoming...I don't know, an *accountant* or something."

"I doubt there's much chance of that," Muriel said with a wink.

Greta started to take it as a compliment, then remembered that earlier in their conversation, she'd mentioned how bad she was at math.

"Still," she grumbled.

"What would you do all day if you could choose?" Muriel asked.

"Something with plants."

"There you go," said Muriel.

"I don't know what I could do with plants that would actually make a living, though," Greta said and sighed.

"Don't mistake not knowing with there not being an answer. There's some wisdom for you. Now, it's noon. Shall we segue from coffee to champagne?"

Greta grinned. "You're so fucking cool."

"I'll take that as a yes. Do an old lady a favor and fetch it from the refrigerator?"

Installed back in the garden with flutes of champagne, Muriel regarded Greta fondly. "Don't worry," she said. "Plan."

Hours later, leaving Muriel's tipsy and delighted, Greta repeated it to herself as she made her way home.

*Don't worry; plan. Don't worry; plan. Don't worry; plan.*

# 10
# TRUMAN

"We should definitely get ones with you in them," Truman insisted.

"What? No. Why?"

Ash stood in the cool morning light, hair in a messy bun, waxed-canvas apron over a baby-blue wool sweater fraying at the cuffs and collar. He held a bouquet of pink and yellow ranunculus in one hand and shears in the other.

Truman snapped his picture. "Because."

He held up his camera to show Ash. Everything was soft and pastel except for the pop of sunshine yellow and the hard line of Ash's stubbled jaw.

"That's...that's a hell of a picture, Truman."

"Thanks. I just got this camera last year. I'd only ever taken pictures with my phone before that, but I love it. Okay, now show me some of the bouquets you'd have the stuff to make anytime, and we can photograph them."

Ash snipped, twisted, and pulled so quickly Truman hardly noticed he was seeing bouquets come together. So far, he'd only seen Ash slow and deliberate, but this was him adroit and in total control. Truman wondered which version of Ash he would see if they—

*Nope. No. Nuh-uh.*

"What do you do for work?" Ash asked as Truman stuffed down all thoughts of Ash in bed and began to photograph.

"I'm an accountant."

"Come on."

Truman looked up. "What?"

"You're… Sorry. I thought you were…" Ash shook his head. "That's not what I was expecting you to say."

"What were you expecting?"

"I suppose some kind of photographer or social media management…thing. An accountant is like…my great-uncle Morty."

"Well, sure, me and your great-uncle Morty are like that." He held up crossed fingers. "Nah, I'm not creative really."

*Truman is our practical child.*

"How's that? You're being creative right now."

Truman waved that away. "This is just practical. Like, you need pictures for the website so we're taking pictures. My sisters are the creative ones. Miriam is a painter and Eleanor is a singer."

Ash put together another bouquet, this one darker and more somber. "Do you like it? Accounting."

Truman looked through the camera's viewer at the beautiful colors and forms. When he'd started college, he hadn't known what he wanted to study. He was curious about all the subjects and excited to learn. He'd hoped interest and skill might make the choice for him, but he liked most of them, was good at most of them. He found himself, at the middle of his junior year, meeting with his advisor and having no clue what he wanted to major in, much less do after college.

Sent away with the mission to pay attention to what he particularly enjoyed the next semester, he found an intro to accounting course unexpectedly soothing. In a moment when everything seemed to be moving quickly and unexpectedly, Truman enjoyed the neat boxes of data and predictable equations.

There were solutions in accounting, and if you simply followed the process the correct answer emerged like magic. There was no uncertainty, no second-guessing. Just clean, definitive numbers.

"You're a natural," his professor had said, and he'd been equal parts flattered and embarrassed. When he'd gone home for his mother's birthday in April and told his family he was going to major in accounting, his eldest sister, Miriam, had laughed.

"That's so totally adorable," she'd said. "It's like when you were a little boy and you dressed in that tiny suit!"

The tiny suit in question had been for Christmas and insisted upon by his parents, but he'd enjoyed putting it on and playing dress-up even afterward.

Eleanor had agreed. "Super cute. You, like, balance us out!" The two had slung their arms around each other's shoulders, their usual competitiveness evaporating in the face of a common noncreative. "I can't wait to tell my friends my little brother is a gay accountant," Miriam had said and ruffled Truman's hair.

Did he like it?

"I enjoy the order of it. I like organizing things. But it doesn't, like, make my heart sing, I guess," Truman said, an extreme understatement.

"What does?"

"Hmm."

Truman turned around to find Ash's broad chest closer than he'd expected. He straightened up and swallowed the lump in his throat.

Ash's eyes were as deep and vast as the ocean. He handed Truman the bouquet he'd just finished, and Truman held it for a moment before his brain caught up with him and he realized it was for photographing.

"Um. Do you really want to know?"

Ash nodded, as if it would never occur to him to ask a question to which he wasn't interested in hearing the answer.

"Bullet journaling."

Ash paused. "Sorry, I don't know what that is."

Truman was used to this. He pulled out his phone and opened Instagram.

"So, it's a whole system of organization, but it's thoroughly customizable to each user. You begin with a blank notebook—I like a dot-grid paper—and an index where you write down where each thing is. Then you lay it out however you like." He scrolled through examples of people he followed.

"So it's a calendar, planner, to-do list mash-up?"

"Yeah, exactly. Some people really turn them into amazing works of art."

Truman opened one of his favorite accounts. She used watercolor in a different palette each month, and for December, she had used black paper that she speckled with silver ink stars, then painted the aurora borealis as the backdrop for her weekly spreads.

"This is gorgeous," Ash said. "God, it must take forever to do this for every week."

It did take a great deal of time, but Truman was rarely

happier than when he was sitting at his drafting table, listening to *ShadowCast*, his favorite podcast, a New Orleans–based true crime show, and dreaming up his monthly themes and weekly spreads as Horse snuffled sleepily beside him.

"I love it. Mine aren't nearly as elaborate as this, though."

"Do you have an account on here where I can see yours?" Ash asked, peering more closely at his phone.

"Not yet."

It was a dream of Truman's that he was trying to work himself up to. But he knew his stark black-and-white spreads could never compete with the gorgeous, colorful, creative art that people posted.

"But, um, I do have my journal here, if you want…?"

Ash nodded emphatically.

Truman lifted the sleeve he kept his journal in and slid it out. As usual, just feeling the heft of paper and ink made him happy.

He placed it on the counter and tried not to look as Ash flipped it open, but he couldn't help himself. He could see the spot of Wite-Out on the *y* in February, the place where the ink of a new, untested pen ghosted through the paper in week two of March, and the smear where he'd erased the pencil lines in April's border before the ink had been completely dry.

"It's not very—" he began to say, just as Ash looked up at him.

"Holy shit. This is…*amazing*. This is art. You just make this up?"

Warmth fizzed in Truman's gut. "Well, I look at a lot of other people's work online," he said. "And I'm in a group where we share ideas, and—"

Ash had gone back to flipping through. "But you use this. For your actual planner?"

"Yeah, that's what it is."

Ash seemed mesmerized. "This is amazing," he muttered again.

"Thanks. If you're into it, I can totally show you how to do it," Truman offered, realizing perhaps Ash's awe was more for bullet journaling itself rather than the particulars of Truman's interpretation.

"Oh, no, thanks. I'm not…organized." And Ash went back to poring over Truman's bullet journal.

Truman took a mental photograph of Ash's face that he could call up later, whenever he had the guts to actually start an Instagram.

"Wow, so you keep track of a lot of stuff in here, huh?" Ash had flipped to his habit trackers.

"Yes. I like habits."

Ash looked up, listening intently.

"It's…I dunno, I like seeing all the stuff I do. It makes me feel more like I…do things?" Truman ended awkwardly.

"It's an accounting," Ash said, and Truman nodded. Then he saw the tiny smile playing at the corner of Ash's mouth and realized he was teasing him.

"Haha."

Ash smiled. "It's cool," he said. "It's like you're having a whole conversation about your life, just with yourself."

"God, when you say it like that, it's the saddest thing I've ever heard," Truman said.

"Why?"

"I guess because it's by myself?"

"I said *with* yourself," Ash said, and it was clear that to him, that was different.

The bell above the door tinkled for the first time since

Truman had been in Thorn, and a woman in a red wool coat walked in, unwinding a thick scarf. "Hey, Ash," she said.

"Hey, Sadie. How's it going?"

"Pretty good. Glad it's the weekend."

The woman had wavy blond hair, brown eyes, painfully upright posture, and gave the distinct impression that she made herself at home anywhere she went. Her expression softened then, and she asked, "How's your mom doing?"

Ash nodded and mumbled something and then turned to Truman. "This is Truman. He's the one who—"

"You're the one who house-swapped with my little sister," she said, eyebrow raised. "Sadie Russakoff." She stuck out a hand with a bloodred manicure.

"Oh, wow. Yeah, hi. I'm Truman, from New Orleans."

Sadie Russakoff gazed at him steadily, like she was reading some kind of usage instructions only she could see. Her grip was overly firm, like she was used to having to prove herself, and her hands were soft.

"So what's New Orleans like?" she said finally.

Truman, tongue-tied and convinced that Greta's sister already hated him, replied, "Um, warm."

"That sounds nice right now," Sadie said, cocking her head to the snowy outdoors. "Ash, I want to grab a bouquet of those purplish-gray roses you sold me last month?"

"Sure."

Ash ducked into the back room, leaving Truman with Sadie.

"So…" he began.

But before he had a chance to think of any small talk, Sadie said, "Is Greta okay?"

"Uh. As far as I know, yeah."

"She just *left*. She didn't tell *anyone* where she was going. We could have heard about a *plane* crashing and not even known she was *on* it."

Sadie's expression was tight, her voice intense.

"Um, she definitely didn't die in a plane crash. If that helps," he finished weakly.

Relief, irritation, and temper warred on her face.

Even without remembering which sister Greta had said was responsible for volunteering her at the Holiday Carnival, Truman felt pretty sure it was Sadie. He could practically feel the desire to rant about Greta emanating from her.

Truman wished he were confrontational. He wished he were the type of person to say, "Oh, and you're her big sister who purposely did a shitty and homophobic thing that you knew she'd hate just because you could. I *wonder* why she left town at Chanukah."

But if Truman had been that person, he would also have marched up to Guy's front door in the Garden District, rung the bell, and announced loudly to Guy's partner/husband that he was being betrayed.

And he hadn't.

He wasn't.

Truman searched his brain for words and what came out was "So, um, who are the flowers for?"

Sadie's smile was ice cold.

"Me."

"Oh, cool. Awesome. That's...yeah, I like flowers too. Wonder why I don't get them to have around. Maybe I should get some for my place—er, your sister, uh, Greta's place. Um."

Sadie raised her eyebrows and gave him a tight-lipped smile that was just the barest flex of her lips and said clearly *I don't care what you do because you made me experience a moment of self-consciousness and I didn't like it.* She took her phone and occupied herself with ignoring Truman until Ash returned with her roses.

"Okay, bye," Sadie said. Then, at the door, she turned and said, "We should grab coffee some time."

For one horrifying moment, Truman thought she was speaking to him. But then Ash, to whom she was, of course, speaking, made a noncommittal *sure mm-hmm* sound, and the bells tinkled Sadie's departure. Air suddenly filled the room again.

"She's…" Truman didn't finish the sentence and didn't need to.

"Yeah. We were in the same year at school. She asked me to the homecoming dance," Ash said.

Truman snorted, trying to imagine earthy, calm Ash with Sadie. "And how did *that* go?"

Ash looked confused for a moment. "It didn't. I'm gay."

Truman was fairly certain that if a picture had been snapped of him at that exact moment, his mouth would have made a perfect O of surprise.

"Sadie tried to play it off as a joke, like *Oh, yeah, I meant as friends, obviously!* Except we weren't friends. I think she wanted me to be her gay best friend or something."

"Gross."

"And she hated when Greta and I became real friends."

"So I guess you won't be grabbing that coffee anytime soon?"

"As the kids say, el oh el," Ash said with totally flat affect.

"Yeah, she clearly hated me for facilitating Greta's departure."

"I'm sure." Ash smiled and went back to flipping through Truman's bullet journal.

"I am too," Truman blurted out.

"Are too what?" Ash murmured absently.

"Gay?"

Truman hadn't meant it to come out as a question.

Ash looked up from the notebook, eyes mesmeric. "I know," he said softly.

Truman tried to think of some joke to break the tension, but he couldn't come up with anything that didn't sound like a bad stereotype.

"Greta told me about why you wanted to get out of New Orleans. I hope you don't mind. She didn't know we'd ever meet."

"Oh. No, it's fine."

"I'm really sorry."

"Seriously, I don't care. Not like I'm in the closet."

"I meant about your boyfriend. What was his name? It was something really douchey."

Truman snorted. "Guy."

"Guy, right. Anyway, it really sucks that he did that to you. And to his partner."

"Yeah."

"Can I ask you something?" Ash said after an awkward pause.

Truman nodded.

"Do you wish you'd never been with him? Do you wish you'd made a different choice from the beginning?"

Truman considered the good times they'd had together. The things he'd learned from conversations with Guy. The places they'd been. There had been beautiful, fascinating, joyful moments.

Hell, he'd thought he *loved* Guy. But now, looking back, the beautiful, fascinating, and joyful times were only a handful of marbles dropped into an empty jar. If the relationship was a spreadsheet, there were only a few scattered entries in the positive columns and box after box of red. *Where*, precisely, had he come up with the sum of love?

But then he thought of the men he'd dated before Guy. They were looking better just at the moment, by virtue of not possessing entire secret families (at least as far as Truman was aware), but not by much. And all of them had ended leaving Truman wondering what he'd seen in them to begin with.

"I feel like I'm supposed to be like, no, I don't regret it because I learned x, y, and z important lessons that will change the way I relate to people in the future or whatever. But honestly? Yeah. I regret it. I wish I hadn't wasted the last year of my life on someone who turned out to be a shitty person."

Ash nodded.

"But, that said, there's no point in regretting it really, right? Because it's over and I made the choices I made and I can't change it."

"Right. Yeah. You can't change it."

The bitterness in Ash's voice gave Truman pause.

"Is there a choice you wish you'd made differently?"

Ash ran a rough fingertip over the velvet edge of a white rose. "No, I guess not. Sometimes stuff just doesn't…turn out how you imagine."

Before Truman could respond with a hearty "Ain't it the truth," Ash said, "Well, it's getting near closing time, so…"

It was a polite dismissal, and Truman was shocked to realize that, one, he'd spent the whole day at Thorn with Ash, and, two, he was disappointed to leave.

"Oh, right, sure. I'll just get these pictures uploaded and then we can talk pricing and delivery and everything."

He gathered his laptop and journal and bundled it and his camera into his bag. He was all ready to head home. Alone. He dawdled with the zipper of his coat for a moment, trying to figure out if it was pushy to ask if Ash wanted to hang out again.

"Maybe...maybe tomorrow. If you're free, I mean. You could come back."

Relief slid through Truman's veins like a drug. He let the smile that threatened peek through, and Ash blinked like he was surprised at himself.

"Yeah. Yeah, I could probably do that."

The warmth of Ash's parting smile stayed banked in Truman's chest even as he walked home in the cold.

# A MESSAGE FROM RAMONA

**RAMONA to TRUMAN CUTIE**

You make the life you want one choice at a time!

**TRUMAN to RAMONA WILDE (who works at Pen Man Ship)**

You're v cryptic lately.

**RAMONA to TRUMAN CUTIE**

Things are only cryptic until you know what they mean :D

**TRUMAN to RAMONA WILDE (who works at Pen Man Ship)**

I know what cryptic means lol what are you talking about?

Ramona?

Ramona.

-__-

**RAMONA to TRUMAN CUTIE**

*GIF of an octopus*

# 11
## TRUMAN

The truth of Truman's work was that, thanks to some spread-sheet hacks he'd created, he could do his nine-to-five work-load in about four hours a day, except during tax season, so he rose early, made coffee, and banged out the day's work well before noon.

Not wanting to seem overeager, he headed to the Queen Bee before going to Thorn. He spent a pleasant half hour or so browsing the shelves, reading bits of this and that, before Maisey bustled in, arms full of packages. Truman rushed to grab a box that was teetering dangerously and slid it onto the counter.

"Oof, thank you, dear," Maisey said, plopping the rest of her armload onto the floor beside the counter.

"Can I give you a hand with anything?"

Maisey waved away his offer with a flick of her hand but gestured him close. "Just picked these up from Maureen." She didn't elaborate on who Maureen was. "She saves them for me."

Maisey opened the box Truman had saved from falling. He didn't know what he'd been expecting, but it certainly was not a box full of hundreds of eggshells.

"Oh, um. How nice."

Maisey snorted, eyes sharp. "Eggshells are a tool of protection and nourishment. Ground into a fine powder, they can be used to cast a circle or draw growth energy to you. They're also excellent for sigil work."

*Oh, dang, Maisey's a witch!*

"You just have to make sure you boil them first," she instructed. "You don't want any salmonella in your circle."

"No, of course not," Truman murmured. He imagined a magical circle vomiting from food poisoning. "My friend Ramona is really into magic and stuff."

"Magic," Maisey said, "is all around us."

"I wish," Truman muttered.

"You might be surprised, Truman. Perhaps you need to pay a little more attention to the signs you're being given."

"Signs?"

But then Truman remembered Ramona mentioning Agatha Tark when she told him Greta lived in Maine. And he remembered Ramona's text telling him it would be raining possibilities. He *had* been inundated with a slew of ideas for Thorn and for his own potential business ventures since then…

"Signs, synchronicities, call them what you will. They're an indication from the universe that you're on the right track."

Truman nodded, unsure how to ask what it indicates if you puke in your boyfriend's flower bed after learning he led a double life. "Synchronicities like…?"

"Oh, like, if you're talking with a friend about wanting to redo your kitchen, and later that day you run into another friend who is redoing their kitchen. That kind of thing."

Truman wasn't sure about all that, but he nodded politely.

Maisey started moving the bags to the counter and Truman bent to help her. They were mostly books, with a few random gardening tools mixed in. As Truman lifted the final bag onto the counter, the bottom ripped and a large, hardcover book slid out. On the cover was a botanical sketch of a rose stem. It was titled *Thorns*.

Truman's eyes widened and visions of Ash danced in his head.

"Yeah," Maisey said with a knowing smile. "Kinda like that."

*It's just a sign that it's nice you're helping Ash get Thorn in working order, that's all. Nothing to do with Ash himself.*

Maisey was watching him intently. Flustered, he shrugged into his coat and shoved Greta's knit hat over his head. "Is there a place I can get take-out coffee on Main Street?"

"Yes, the Hardware Store." She pointed across the street to the store called the Hardware Store.

Truman cocked his head. "But, like, good coffee?"

"Oh yes, best in town. Tell Bob I sent you."

Truman thanked her.

"Oh, Truman. Did you boys talk to Julia about the woman you were trying to find?"

"Who's Julia? Sorry, I'm at capacity with all the new names."

"Ashleigh's mother. She knows everyone. Well. Sometimes."

"Oh. No, not yet. Thanks."

The bell tinkled cheerily behind him, and Truman crossed the street.

Ash's mother? Why hadn't Ash suggested her as a source of information? Clearly they got along fine if he'd borrowed her coat for Truman.

*Maybe he doesn't want her to meet you.*

The door to the Hardware Store didn't have a tinkling bell but an ancient buzzer that sounded somewhere in the depths of the shop.

Truman had planned to walk across the street and poke his head in for a moment in case Maisey was watching him, then go find a real coffee shop. But there, just inside the door, was a coffee setup that looked inviting.

"Truman!" boomed a voice from his left, startling him into a display of snow shovels.

"Uh, yes?"

A large, bearded man emerged from between the shelves. He wore padded Carhartt overalls, an orange-and-brown flannel shirt, and worn work boots. "Maisey told me you'd be stopping by."

"How?" Truman muttered, alarmed. Did the Owl Island phone chain have the power to disturb the space-time continuum?

"You'll be wanting two coffees, yes? Cappuccinos? Lattes? I've recently gotten very into cortados."

"Wow, um. Yeah, two lattes, I guess. Thank you."

Instead of moving behind the coffee counter, the man held out a meaty hand to Truman. "I'm Bob. Welcome to Owl Island."

"Wow, thanks."

Truman begged himself to stop saying *wow*.

Bob chattered about Owl Island while he made the lattes.

"Would you like some muffins to go with your lattes?" he asked, and Truman noticed for the first time that the back counter held a bakery tray. "Kenny's boy makes them. But of course you won't be knowing Kenny. Landon's a good kid. Well, not a kid anymore, I guess. Nearly thirty. Excellent baker."

"I'd love some muffins," Truman said enthusiastically, concerned that he might soon know more about Kenny and Landon than he did about his own friends if he didn't interrupt.

Bob handed him a bag and a cardboard coffee carrier. "On the house. Welcome."

"Oh, no, I couldn't—"

"You can and you will."

"Wow, thank you very much."

"Come back anytime. And send Ashleigh my best!" he called as Truman opened the door.

↔

Truman walked into Thorn ready to make a joke about the whole town saying hi to Ash but was saved from it by nearly running into a broad-shouldered man made even broader by a cartoonishly square gray wool overcoat.

"Excuse me, sorry," Truman said, sidestepping the man.

He ignored Truman. "Think about it," the man told Ash flatly. Then his voice softened and he added, before leaving, "My best to your mom."

"What was that all about?" Truman asked, unloading the coffees and muffins on the counter. "Also, hi."

"Hey," Ash said. Today, he was wearing a brown-and-gray sweater in the same style as Greta's.

"Lemme guess." Truman pointed at the sweater. "Muskee's?"

"We'll make an Owl Islander of you yet," Ash said, as if this were a fate worse than death. "Thanks for the coffee. What do I owe you?"

"Nothing. Bob sends his best."

Ash smiled.

"I used to work at the Hardware Store." Like everyone else so far, Ash managed to imply the capital letters in the name. "For three summers in high school."

"At the risk of stereotyping, does *everyone* on the island know every single other person?"

"Nah. It just seems like it. But most of us with businesses on Main know one another. We try to help one another out, recommend that people check out all the other shops during tourist season. If I needed supplies for the shop, I'd get them from Bob. If he needed flowers, he'd get them from me. Being on an island makes it hard to order online. You can. It just takes longer. But we try to support one another."

"That's really lovely."

Truman indulged in a dreamy fantasy of running his own business for a moment, then remembered the man he'd passed on the way in.

"So was that guy, like, the Owl Island Mafia or something?"

"As close as we come to it," Ash muttered. "That's Carlton Crimm. He's the largest landowner on the island, even though he lives on the mainland. He, uh, he wants to buy the shop."

"Oh, wow. Would you still work here?"

Ash shook his head. "Nah, he won't keep it Thorn. He's already bought three of the adjacent properties, and he wants the land. He has plans to build a hotel spa thing. For the tourists."

"Oh no! You won't sell, will you?"

It hadn't occurred to Truman that Ash might own the building, but he supposed real estate in rural Maine wasn't as expensive as in New Orleans.

Ash was chewing on his lip. "I might not have a choice." He looked around Thorn, and Truman couldn't help but notice he seemed resigned. Then Ash made a sound of disgust and said, "You wanna get out of here for a while?"

"But what if customers come?"

Ash shrugged, and Truman thought he might be seeing part of the problem with Thorn's cash flow.

Still he said, "Okay."

"Come on, Bruce," Ash said as he pulled on his coat. "Walk."

At the word, Bruce sprang from a dead sleep like he'd been reanimated with a zap.

"Dingbat," Ash said affectionately. Bruce barked in acknowledgment.

"D'you want me to—okay!"

Truman grabbed the bag of muffins and the coffees and followed Ash, who was already out the door. This time, he didn't bother to leave a *Back soon, call Ash* sign on the door.

Ash turned away from the other shops on Main Street, rounded the corner away from Greta's house, and strode off, Bruce keeping pace. Truman power-walked to catch up, sloshing some latte on his—well, Greta's—glove.

When Truman caught up, Ash scrubbed a hand over his face.

"Sorry, I just had to get out of there. Felt like the walls were closing in or something."

Truman held out a latte, because sometimes when the walls were closing in, there was nothing you could do but attempt to caffeinate them back into position.

"Thanks."

"So, forgive my inferences, but context clues suggest that Thorn isn't making enough money, and you might need to sell to Mafia guy because he's offering more money than you could make?"

"You got it."

"Well, while I'm Sherlocking, can I assume that your mother is not in good health and that that's part of the problem?"

"Yeah."

They walked in silence for a few blocks, but now it didn't feel awkward. It felt contemplative. Companionable.

"The building used to be a kind of Army surplus meets random fishing and boating stuff shop when I was little, but it had been abandoned for years when I bought the building. It wasn't up to code, the plaster was crumbling, and the apartment upstairs was…well, let's just say I stayed at my mom's for a month while I made it livable. It was *very* cheap. I did all the work on it, with some help from Bob."

Ash lifted his to-go cup in salute, like it stood in for the man himself.

"He kept coming over to give me things and saying that people returned them and he couldn't resell them. It was total crap, of course, but I was desperate so I shut up and accepted it. Now I just deliver a bouquet of flowers to his house every week to say thanks. Not that it'll ever even out."

Truman's heart swelled at the image of Ash honoring Bob's generosity every week forever.

"Anyway. Now that it's fixed up, Carlton's offering about ten times what I paid for it. I don't know, I've got a little time to figure it out, but…"

He trailed off as they turned another corner, and the rocky coastline came into view. Once exposed to the water, the wind whipped them, but the sun shone brightly, sparkling off the wavelets and shadowing the giant-tumbled rocks.

"Wow," Truman breathed, awed, and for the first time that day, it was exactly the right word. "The ocean is absolutely gorgeous."

"That's Penobscot Bay."

"Oh. Great word. Is the bay different than the ocean?"

"Nah, not really. Same water." Truman smiled as Ash continued, "The Penobscot are the Indigenous people whose land we're on. It's a mispronunciation of the Algonquin for *the people of where the white rocks extend out*."

And extend out they did. There was a line of rocks that looked like they made a path of steps into the water. Truman felt like at the right moment, he would be able to follow them down below the waves into a salt-crusted crystal palace.

"Wanna sit?" Ash tugged lightly on Truman's jacket and pointed at a flat-topped boulder.

They picked their way across the rocky shore, Bruce trotting easily alongside them, and sat down. It was immediately more comfortable. The sun warmed their faces, and two large boulders buffered them from the punishing wind. The smell of salt and the sound of the waves were lulling, and Truman sipped his latte in a state of unfamiliar bliss.

"My mom has early-onset Alzheimer's," Ash said, sipping his own coffee and gazing out over the bay. "She was diagnosed three years ago. That's why I moved back to Owl Island."

Truman felt like he'd swallowed a stone. "I'm so sorry, Ash. That's…damn."

"Lots of the time, she's okay. Like her old self. Around dinner, though, she gets really confused. And at night, she sometimes freaks out, doesn't know where she is. She…" He didn't finish the thought.

"And you take care of her."

"I try."

Ash paused for long enough to eat half of a blueberry muffin. Long enough that Truman wondered if the kind thing to do would be to change the subject. But then Ash continued.

"The thing that's most important is that she has consistency in her life. Routine. It helps. And she's lived on Owl Island for forty years, so I'm not going to stick her someplace where she won't know anyone. Where no one will know who she used to be."

"But that means you have to be here. And you don't like it?"

Ash shook his head. "I like it. A lot, actually. I'm not real social, as you might have gathered." He gave Truman a self-deprecating smile. "I enjoy the peace here. And it's a beautiful place to live. It's just… Being here means being alone, mostly."

He said it so softly the wind almost snatched the words before Truman could hear them.

"You've got Greta, right? Well, usually."

Ash murmured his assent, and Truman realized that he meant alone in terms of romance, intimacy, a partner.

"Oh, I see. That's so hard." Truman imagined Ash late at night, hair rumpled and beautiful eyes tired, grief-stricken at the loss of who his mother once was, yearning for comfort, for conversation, for love, and finding himself perpetually alone. "That's so, *so* hard."

Ash shoved the rest of his blueberry muffin in his mouth and patted Bruce's head. Truman's heart ached for him.

Truman wasn't good at aching.

He hated problems that didn't have solutions, and he hated doing nothing, even in the face of a problem *without* a solution. He wished he had the power to comfort Ash in some deep, fundamental way, but he didn't. There was only one thing he had the ability to do.

"If Thorn was doing better, that would take some of the stress off, right? Give you some more options at least?"

"Yeah. Definitely."

"Then that's what we'll do!" Truman pledged.

Ash reached out and put a hand on his knee.

"Thank you," he said, voice choked up. And a wave broke over the rocks, salty droplets spattering their faces.

A sign.

←→

They were sprawled on Greta's couch in the living room, Ash having decided that since he'd already closed the shop for an hour, he may as well leave it shuttered to dream up ways to save it. Truman chose not to make the first thing on the list *maintain regular hours* because it seemed passive-aggressive, but he added it as a large bullet point in his mind.

"This," Truman said, "is a brainstorming session. That means there is no idea too silly, big, small, or seemingly bananas to go on the board. Just shout them out, and I'll write them down. Okay?"

The board in question was a large freestanding mirror from Greta's bedroom onto which Truman had taped scrap paper.

"Okay."

Ash, it turned out, was terrible at brainstorming. He seemed to need to work out every detail of something in his mind before he'd speak it aloud.

After fifteen minutes of encouraging *okay, and*-ing, Truman said, "That is not a *storm*! That's like a-a-a leaky faucet!"

Ash let out a choked sound that was half giggle and half harrumph and wholly undignified. Truman grinned.

"Just...don't second-guess your ideas," he said. "No bad ideas in a brainstorm! Like, okay, how about, um, a flower of the week sale where one kind of flower is half off. It'd get people in the door, but then they'll see the other stuff and want those too. You can make a sign to put in the window."

Ash's brow was furrowed, but he was nodding. "That's a really good idea."

"Yay!"

"Maybe I could do a punch card thing where if people buy ten bouquets, they get the eleventh free?"

"Yes, love it, creating customer loyalty and incentivizing purchase through gamification. Uh, I was a business minor," he added when Ash raised an eyebrow.

"Lucky me."

"Are there any flowers that are super cheap for you to stock?"

"There are a few that are always cheap, but they aren't very popular. Then, in the summer, there are always people who grow wildflowers that you can get pretty cheaply. But they're not what people think of as florist flowers, you know?"

"Okay. But what if you did some kind of specific and different kind of bouquet? Like, if you did wildflower bouquets in recycled jars or something and sold them as picnic bouquets for tourists. Or—wait, better—sold them as a souvenir of Owl Island. You could have little clear stickers with Thorn and an owl on them to put on the outside of the jars. Then you could tie the bouquet with colored twine or something with a loop and say that as soon as the flowers start to wilt, they should hang them upside down and dry them as a souvenir. They could keep the dried flowers in the Owl Island jar. And you could sell it for more because they get a fresh bouquet, a souvenir glass, and a dried bouquet that'll last."

"That's…also a really good idea." Ash looked thoughtful.

"What are you thinking right now?" Truman asked, energized with ideas and wanting more.

"I'm thinking that I don't have the cash flow to print stickers, much less signage and labels and all this stuff. I want to do it, I just…"

"Okay, money is always a sticking point, but there are ways around it."

"Ways around money? I'd love to hear them."

"Well, I'm still holding out hope for the toppling of the white supremacist capitalist hetero patriarchy, but in the meantime, I meant something slightly lower key. Do you know someone with a printer?"

"I know Greta," Ash said, and he pointed at the small desk setup she had in the bedroom.

"Oh, right, of course. All you'd need to make the stickers is a design, some clear sticker paper, and a printer. You can ask Greta to use her printer, and I can totally make a design for you. Then, you have six months till tourist season, which is plenty of time to save all your jars. You can ask people in town to save theirs for you too. It'll look cool if they're all different. More bespoke. I mean, if you want?"

Ash blinked owlishly at him. "You'd really want to do that?"

"Make you a design for stickers? Yeah, of course. And as for the signage, that's easy."

Truman explained how he could use recycled materials, repurpose stock, use a profit-sharing model with artists to sell merchandise in the store. The ideas fell into his head, one after the other, like raindrops.

Ash was nodding, eyes wide.

Finally, Truman forced down his excitement at giving Ash multiple new income streams and focused on Ash's unblinking eyes.

"You look overwhelmed. Are you overwhelmed?"

"I'm... Yes. I'm overwhelmed."

Truman dropped onto the couch beside him and forced himself not to spout off any more ideas, even though his mind was spinning with them. Flower crowns for summer tourists' children, and winter greenery wreaths for the holidays, and a partnership with a local restaurant to provide centerpieces for tables, and...

"Well, the trick is to just break each thing down to its component parts, make a to-do list, and do one thing at a time." Truman jumped up again and grabbed one of the blank notebooks he kept for just such occasions. "Here, this can be yours."

Truman sketched the Thorn logo on the front of the notebook, outlined it with his favorite Micron 0.2, shaded it in with his 0.5, and started to add Ash's name with a 0.8.

"What's your last name?"

"Sundahl," Ash said. "But you really don't have to—"

Truman added it to the cover, then drew a flower next to *Ash* and a sun next to *Sundahl*.

"Okay, so we can write down all the component steps to each project and then go from there. Ready?"

Ash gulped.

"So, how about—"

"No. I'm..." Ash got jerkily to his feet. "I'm not ready. I'm really sorry, Truman. I've gotta go."

Truman knew not everyone had the yen for brainstorming that he did, but really, they were just getting started.

"Oh. Okay. We can pick this up later if you want?"

"It's not… This is… You've been so kind, but I just…I can't do this right now. I'm sorry."

He had his coat and boots back on before Truman rose.

"Ash, I—"

"Sorry, Truman. Sorry," Ash said with an agonized look. Then he opened the door and strode quickly out into the darkening evening.

Truman shivered even after the door was closed.

Had he gone too far? Was the notebook too much? Or had Ash simply withered in the face of Truman's organizational zeal?

He dropped onto the couch and threw an arm over his face. All his excitement about the ideas for Thorn had deflated.

Hey, he messaged Germaine and Charlotte. What percentage of budding friendships are ruined by one side's over-enthusiastic brainstorming about business ideas, would you say? Because I might have just demonstrated that it's a drastically underrepresented category of social destruction!

He added laughing and crying emojis, then the clown face.

*Oh no, Truman!* came Germaine's quick reply. *The florist?*

Yup. A rose emoji, then a frowning emoji. I brainstormed him right into a panic about his business.

**Psh, wimp**, Charlotte wrote. **Him, that is.**

Maybe I was a little, um. Overenthusiastic.

*One of your most endearing qualities!* wrote Germaine.

**If flower boy can't see that you have great ideas, then he doesn't deserve you. Or them.**

*Yeah*, Germaine wrote. *Real talk, are you INTO flower boy?*

Stop calling him flower boy, it makes him sound like he's a child in someone's wedding. And NO. I am done with men.

Truman searched for a GIF of someone from a black-and-white movie dramatically collapsing onto a fainting couch, but before he found it, Charlotte replied.

**You'll never be done with men, Truman. You're a hopeless romantic. Emphasis on hopeless.**

Haha, Truman wrote.

But. Was that true? He'd never thought of himself that way before.

*It's true, T*, Germaine wrote.

What? No I'm not! Circumstantial evidence!

**Not what that means**, Charlotte replied immediately.

Joke alert, C.

**Getting facts wrong is not now and will never be funny.**

Truman snorted.

**Okay, you want proof? Your favorite part of TDoZ is when Aerlich begins to stray toward the darkness and Clarion pines over him for LITERALLY the rest of her life.**

THAT is your proof??

Germaine sent a screen of broken hearts.

*I kinda agree, boo*, Germaine wrote. *Like, I love Aerlich, as you well know, but by book six I really wanted Clarion to be with Illonial.*

Truman's blood boiled as it always did when this came up.

She can NOT be with Illonial. He doesn't love animals!!! It's like the basis of her whole interaction with the WORLD!!!

Charlotte sent a thumbs-down emoji.

**People can be in love and not share all the same interests**, she wrote.

That's NOT a partnership! Clarion and Aerlich were so connected and they had the same worldview and values. They were a team and they faced the world together until—

Truman broke off because it was too painful to rehash Aerlich's fate.

Charlotte sent a laughing emoji and wrote, **SEE?**

*You're a super romantic, babe*, Germaine agreed.

Truman wasn't sure how to render the sound of a grumble in a chat, so he wrote, GRUMBLE GRUMBLE GRUMBLE.

*It's not a bad thing*, wrote Germaine. Of course they would think that.

**It's not bad, just unfortunate for you since you couple hopeless romanticism with a total inability to request what you need**, Charlotte wrote. Then, **Oops, did I say that out loud?**

Go on, then.

Truman figured if he was gonna get roasted, then he may as well get specifics.

*I think what C means is that you're very giving to the people you date, but you're not always...you don't always...*

**You don't tell anyone you date what you want from them. You just take what they give you and make up a story about how that was what you wanted in the first place. It's bad.**

Truman blinked. Then he read it again.

Germaine sent an open mouth emoji, making it abundantly clear that they and Charlotte had discussed this behind his back and Germaine hadn't thought Charlotte would say it to his face. Well. Chat face.

It was painfully close to what Ramona had told him after the Guy fiasco, but he figured he'd just double check. Triple check.

Do I really do that?

*Yes.*

*Well, you're just so generous that you can find ways to make almost anything be nice or sweet, even if it's...*

**Not**, Charlotte concluded.

Quadruple checked.

Truman cringed. He thought about the time that Guy had said "I have something for you," and Truman had gotten so excited, thinking that Guy had gotten him a present, which would mean Guy had been thinking about him. Then Guy had pulled Truman's pen out of his own pocket and said, "You left this in my car."

Truman's stomach had dropped, and he'd swallowed hard to dispel the disappointment. But by the time he'd gone to the grocery store that evening, he'd rewritten the story: it was *sweet* Guy had taken the time to return his pen because he didn't want Truman to be without it.

Of course, now he realized that Guy had returned the Micron because he didn't want his husband to see it in the car and know it wasn't Guy's since it wasn't a two-thousand-dollar fountain pen.

Truman drooped.

He remembered Abel, the guy he'd dated before Guy. Abel had asked what he wanted to do one weekend, and Truman had told him he'd love to go out to dinner together. He hadn't *said* he wanted a romantic meal. But it had been what he was picturing: candlelight, soft music, decadent food, and deep conversation. Abel had shown up with a sack of take-out tacos, then dragged him to a club where his friend's band was playing. The next morning, hungover and exhausted, Truman had told himself that it was romantic that Abel had wanted Truman to meet all his friends.

Oh my god, I'm a disaster. I'm a disaster romantic.

**Yup**, wrote Charlotte.

*Weeeeeeeeelllllllllllllll.* It was the closest Germaine would ever come to pronouncing it the truth.

So what do I do?! How do I fix it!?

*I don't think it's something to fix, bb, it's kinda just your personality.*

**Oh, it's 100% fixable**, Charlotte disagreed. **You just have to realize that "romance" is a cultural concept, constructed from outdated and fictionalized notions of subjugating one's autonomy to the notion of partnership. Then, every time you find yourself having these yearnings for shit and you don't know why, ask yourself, "do I want this because movies and pop culture have trained me to believe I'm only loved if someone else gives this thing to me?" and soon you'll see that you can tease apart your actual, individual desires from the mess of capital-R romance that society spoon-feeds us.**

There was silence then.

Finally, Germaine wrote, *OR you can just be honest about what you want, to yourself and to the next person you date. It's ok to want things!!!*

They added, *(also, C, are you using talk-to-text cuz hot damn).*

**Circling back to the issue at hand**, Charlotte wrote, **what does flower boy look like???**

Truman laughed. He felt his cheeks heat for no reason. He sent them the picture he'd taken of Ash the day before, drinking in the soft blue and pink of his sweater and lips, the bright yellow of the ranunculus. The stormy blue-gray of his eyes.

*I'M SORRY WHAT* came Germaine's instant reply.

Charlotte wrote, **Oh, Truman.**

So he's handsome! It's not like I'm in love with every handsome person in the world! He's not just his looks. He's also really sweet and kind and generous and he takes care of his mom and he makes beautiful bouquets!

*Take that*, Truman thought.

*Oh, Truman.* This time it was Germaine who wrote that.

GRUMBLE GRUMBLE GRUMBLE, Truman wrote once more.

He thought about how he'd gone to the Queen Bee that morning to avoid seeming overeager to get to Thorn. How the press of Ash's thigh against his as they sat on the flat-topped rock at the beach had made him want to lean into Ash. How he'd looked at the pictures he'd taken of him a dozen times last night. He'd told himself he was picking the best one for the website, but...

Oh no. Oh no no no. Oh fuck, Truman wrote.

*Oh, shit, it's bad. T swore.*

**Truman, I would like to remind you that you're there for A MONTH**, Charlotte wrote.

How can I have a crush on someone—I got my heart stomped on literally fourteen seconds ago???

*I don't think there's a timeline on it, boo.*

**Probably getting your heart crushed just makes you \*more\* likely to crush on someone**, Charlotte mused. **Because you're looking for an object onto which you can project your truncated feelings.**

HOW DO I MAKE IT GO AWAY??!!

**Just stop seeing him,** wrote Charlotte.

*Aw, why do you want it to go away?*

Because we have JUST established that I am a disaster romantic!!! Nothing good will come of this! My heart is already smashed. What if Ash, like, vaporizes it??

**Well, it wouldn't be Ash that did anything, it would be your own thoughts and feelings about the situation,** Charlotte corrected.

Truman pictured Ash holding the šilpka that Clarion used in the Dead of Zagørjič. It emanated pulses of magic that turned an enemy's mind inside out.

He shuddered and hugged himself. But then he imagined spending the next three and a half weeks on Owl Island, knowing Ash was near and not seeing him. Walking past Thorn to get groceries and avoiding him. He hated that thought even more than he hated the thought of getting his heart vaporized.

Shit, I do like him, Truman wrote.

**You poor soul.**

*Eeeee!!!* Germaine sent a screen of heart eye emojis.

I'm gonna go take a bath and drown my sorrows. In wine, I mean. Not in the bath. I mean, not literally in the bath. I mean…

**We know what you mean. You're not killing yourself. That is a good choice.** Charlotte sent a thumbs-up emoji, then a bathtub emoji.

Germaine wrote, *Good, take care of yourself. Things will look brighter in the morning!* <3

**Literally,** Charlotte added. **Sorry, sorry, ok bye.**

Truman turned on the taps in Greta's clawfoot tub. She had a jar of bath salts with thyme and rosemary in it that he sprinkled into the tub. The aroma rose around him as the herbs hit the hot water, and Truman took a deep breath, trying to relax.

"Ooh, Ash could sell flower-scented bath salts at the shop!"

The thought hit him, accompanied by a surge of excitement. He caught himself just before he pulled out his phone to text Ash. Then he realized it didn't matter, because Ash had never given him his phone number.

"Ugh, pathetic," he diagnosed. Suddenly the thyme and rosemary didn't seem so relaxing. Instead, he pictured himself as a turkey about to be brined in savory herbs. He certainly felt like a fucking turkey. He found some lavender and added it to the bath, hoping to conjure a vibe of calm rather than poultry. He'd just take a bath, read, and go to bed. Alone.

Truman grabbed book two of the Dead of Zagørjič, *The Heart Soars*, and a bottle of wine and slid into the hot, herb-scented water.

# 12
# GRETA

The boardwalk twisted around moss-draped live oaks and through the bayou. The sign in the parking lot of Barataria Preserve had warned visitors not to allow small children or dogs too close to the water's edge and to listen for the telltale rattle of snakes.

Greta was in love. In love with the gothic drips of moss and the warmth in December and the murky-sweet smell of the bayou and the risk.

"So what was Greta like as a roommate?" Carys asked Ramona. It had been Ramona who suggested Jean Lafitte Park as a destination hangout when Greta texted her about meeting up. As a New Orleans transplant, she knew all the best local spots but had also once been a new arrival who'd learned the city.

It was a Tuesday morning out of tourist season, and in the twenty minutes they'd been walking so far, they'd yet to see another soul. They'd yet to see an alligator either, and Greta kept her eyes peeled.

"She was a dream roommate," Ramona said breezily. "Clean but not super neat, slept like the dead so I didn't have to tiptoe around all night, up for hijinks and late-night snack runs, great conversationalist, and very open to letting me boss her around. Perfection."

Greta snorted.

"Boss her around?" Carys asked curiously with a raised eyebrow.

"Oh, you know. Very open to hearing about all her faults and the behaviors that were holding her back in life." Ramona gave her a wicked grin.

"The real question is were you actually good at knowing them?" Greta said.

But the truth was that Ramona had changed Greta's life more than she knew. Well. Maybe she did know. When Greta had been left alone in her dorm room with the hugs and tears of her family still imprinted on her skin, all the elation she'd felt at being free of them evaporated. She'd sat in the quiet-loud of move-in day and found her head strangely empty. She knew she should start unpacking but couldn't quite get up off the bed.

When the tall girl with white-blond curls, blond eyelashes, and the coolest gray eyes Greta had ever seen breezed into the room, stuck her hand out, and said, "I could murder a slushie. Wanna bounce?" Greta had followed her. Once her legs were moving, it was easier to talk. Once she talked, it was easier to think. And once she could think, she thought *Holy shit. I'm in Portland, drinking a slushie that I don't have to share, in the flavor of my choice, and I can do…whatever I want.* It had blasted through her like a gust of wind off the ocean, sending shivers down her spine. Or maybe that was the slushie. Ramona would go on to teach her a lot over the next year, but Greta had never forgotten that first, unintentional lesson: sometimes, when all else fails, get off your ass and get a slushie. Or, you know, a whatever.

"Of *course*," Ramona said. "I give stellar advice. Giving advice and being able to take it are two entirely unrelated gifts, I'll have you know."

Carys smiled at Greta. "So what was a really good piece of advice you gave Greta?"

"Oh god, allow me to flip through the veritable card catalogue of options." Ramona struck the pose of *The Thinker*. "So it was fall semester and Greta had made the horrible mistake of signing up for a psychology lab from seven to nine on Friday evenings."

"It was the only one with slots left," Greta editorialized.

"And there was this Halloween party going on at our friend Mika's place. Tons of great costumes, weird spooky games, the works. I tell Greta she's gotta skip lab that week because we need plenty of time to get our costumes ready."

"What were you?"

"Dude," Ramona said, "she was Harriet the Spy, and she was so freaking cute. She had her hair in a braid—it was long then—and the red sweatshirt jacket and her little black-and-white notebook. Adorable. I was Joan Jett."

Ramona struck a pose that was presumably supposed to conjure Joan Jettiness. Carys raised an eyebrow and winked.

"Anyway, it's six p.m., and no Greta. It's seven p.m., and no Greta. And I realize: this bitch has actually gone to her psychology lab in the monkey building on the Friday night of Halloween."

Greta scanned the water for alligators, a smile on her lips. It was nice to spend time with Ramona again. Just being around her made Greta happy.

"I got ready all by my lonesome," Ramona said with a tragic frown.

"You got ready with Jill and Santos, thank you," Greta corrected.

"Fine. *Any*way. When it's nine thirty and Greta's still not back, I go to call her, and do you know what happened?"

"No, no," Greta interrupted. "You went to call me and realized I'd been calling you for an hour and a half but you'd left your phone on silent."

"Yeah, fine. So I pick up my phone, and can you guess what happened?"

Ramona actually paused to allow Carys time to guess.

"I don't dare," Carys said gamely.

"This absolute ninny had gotten herself locked in a monkey cage!"

Greta felt her face heat.

Carys looked to her, clearly waiting for her revision of that sentence.

"I did," Greta confirmed. "Not *with* a monkey. But there was this extra cage, and I was moving some of the supplies into it, and the door shut behind me."

"Oh my lord," said Carys.

"Yeah, the rest of her lab group didn't show up—obviously, since it was the Friday of Hallo-freaking-ween—so she was just stuck in there, like." Ramona made like she was clawing at a cage and Greta snorted. "I went down and let her out. God knows what might've happened if I hadn't!"

"You also magnanimously brought my costume so I could change *in* the monkey cage because you said there wasn't time to go home." Greta turned to Carys. "We lived four blocks from the psych lab."

Carys grinned.

"We were already *very* late to the party," Ramona explained. "Missed the costume contest!"

"Which you wouldn't have won anyway."

"I might have." Ramona sniffed.

"Rebekah was dressed as a full-on owl with wings that flapped and her face covered in real feathers. You would not have won."

"Well, I guess we'll never know now, will we?"

"Lucky you have Mardi Gras now for any costume cravings," Carys said.

"Hallelujah. Thank god I ended up someplace primed to appreciate me."

Something moved in the water to Greta's left.

Slow and ineluctable, an alligator rose.

"Holy fucking hell," Greta breathed.

In the flesh, it was terrifying. A dinosaur. A predator. It looked fake, like the plastic and resin models she'd seen all her life. And that just made it scarier. But the way it moved was hypnotic, arms dragging its muscular bulk from the water.

"Gah." Ramona shivered. "They're so toothy."

"A friend once took me canoeing underneath I-10," Carys said softly. "There hadn't been that much rainfall lately, and the water was low enough you could see the roots of all the cypress trees. So we're just getting high in the middle of the water, letting the boat drift because there was a lot of surface crud and rowing was hard. And something moved out of the corner of my eye. A gator was *in* the tree. Like, sunning itself on a branch eight, ten feet above the water. The thing could've just dropped into our canoe like a spider."

"They *do* that?" Greta shuddered. "What did you do?"

"Nothing," Carys said with a shrug. "It seemed pretty happy where it was. But it was freaky."

Greta made a mental note to never go canoeing in the bayou. The alligator had closed its eyes, and Greta crept closer. There was a small lookout area that bumped out into the water, and she turned into it and crouched low, peering at the alligator through the wooden slats. The animal opened an eye lazily, and its jaw followed. The teeth didn't look as sharp as Greta would've thought. Then its jaw clamped shut with the force of a bear trap and she shuddered.

A hand touched her shoulder and she jumped.

"Sorry," Carys said. "Just me." She held out a hand to help Greta up.

"Thanks."

Carys didn't let go of her hand when they started down the boardwalk again, and Greta squeezed it. Carys squeezed back.

"So what are you gonna do, Gretzky?" Ramona asked, using the silly nickname Greta hadn't heard in years. For the first six months of their acquaintance, Ramona had used a different nickname for her practically every day.

"Do about which particular fuckwad of my life?"

"Uh. All of them? Any of them?"

Greta didn't have an answer.

"Are you at least gonna get off that damn island where your family runs your whole life? You've heard about her family, right?" Ramona said this last to Carys, who nodded.

"I want to."

"Well then," Ramona said, as if simple desire was all it took to remake a life.

As if to underscore the point, Greta's phone rang.

"Hey, Maggie," Greta said. "What's up?"

Ramona made a face to Carys that said *Did I tell you or what?* and she and Carys walked a few steps ahead of Greta.

"What's up is I need you to weigh in on this whole Greg situation, because if I have to talk about it for one more single minute with Sadie, I'm going to perish."

"What's the Greg situation?"

"Omigod, Addie didn't tell you? So Tillie's bringing Benjamin to Chanukah, obviously."

"Obviously." Benjamin was Tillie's husband.

"And Naveen is coming to hang out with me."

Naveen was Maggie's best friend/maybe-boyfriend. She'd never admit he was, but they seemed more intimate than friends sometimes.

"So Sadie has decided that she and Addie should bring dates."

She said *dates* like it wasn't a real thing. Which, on Owl Island, it kind of wasn't.

"O-kaaay?"

"Obviously Addie isn't gonna."

"Obviously."

"So now Sadie is saying she's bringing this *Greg* person, and I guess he works in the post office, but…"

She didn't have to finish. It was clear what had happened. Sadie, jealous that anyone might have anything she didn't, had roped some random gentile she probably met while picking up a package into being her plus-one to Chanukah dinner. She would fawn over him performatively, Mom and Dad would ask him personal questions because they'd think he really was her date, and he'd become deeply uncomfortable, which would make Sadie double down. Hell, she might even date him for a few weeks after the dinner just to make a point. She'd done it before. Not that she'd think of it that way.

"Yikes," Greta said. "That's shitty and I feel for this Greg, whoever he is, but you know Sadie. If she's made up her mind… And let me repeat for the one hundred thousandth time: I will not be there, so I don't know what you want me to do."

"Damn," Maggie said. "Not fair. I wanna be not here."

"So leave," Greta said. It felt easy and reckless to say the words. It felt amazing.

"I can't."

And for the first time with one of her sisters, Greta didn't say *I know* when she knew what they meant. Instead, she said what Ramona—and now Carys—would say to her.

"Why can't you leave?"

"Because it's Chanukah. Mom and Sadie would roast me alive."

"I left. I'm not roasted alive."

"That you know of," Maggie muttered.

Greta's stomach clenched. "What are they saying?" she heard herself ask. All the ease and recklessness of the moment before rushed out of her like a punctured balloon.

"You know," Maggie hedged.

"Tell me."

"How sad it is that we won't be a family. How Mom hates to think of you all by yourself for Chanukah. What did they do to make you not want to celebrate with us. *You know*."

None of this was surprising to Greta. But it hurt anyway. How did it hurt anyway?

She walked in Carys and Ramona's wake, watching the sun filtering through the trees to spangle on the light wood boards. She smelled the lichen and the dusty moss. She listened to the knock of woodpeckers and the splash of some submarine battle playing out in the bayou to her left.

It hurt because she felt guilty. And she felt guilty because she didn't want to hurt anyone.

*Cool, so not wanting to hurt other people means choosing to feel hurt yourself. Great calculus, Greta. Guess Muriel was right about you not accidentally ending up an accountant.*

"I didn't do anything wrong," Greta said, her voice rising.

"I know, bro," Maggie said.

Carys looked back at her with a raised eyebrow and a concerned expression. Greta sighed and smiled.

"So if you want to leave, you should leave," Greta said.

"Yeah," Maggie said. "I know." For a second, Greta thought she was going to say something serious, but she just concluded, "I've got a million Amtrak points."

"Good," Greta said. "Listen, I gotta go. I'm seeing alligators."

"Like…up close?"

"Very fucking close. Love you, bye."

"Send pictures!" Maggie was saying as Greta hung up.

She rejoined Ramona and Carys.

"Which of the brood was that?" Ramona asked.

"Maggie."

"Aw, Maggie's my favorite one. She's had, like, less time to be in your family so she's slightly more functional."

"Okay, enough about my family. Can we just take some pictures of terrifying dino monsters now?"

"Yes. Yes, we can," Ramona said.

Carys took Greta's hand again and brought it to her lips, a silent question: *Are you okay?* Greta squeezed her hand in reassurance. When Carys slid a hand to her nape and rubbed gently, Greta *hmm*ed and pressed closer.

"You're such a cat," Carys said fondly.

Greta blinked at her, then licked her lips and pressed her forehead to Carys'.

"Meow," she said and caught Carys' mouth in a kiss.

←→

Greta was walking Horse at dusk, the skies over the Marigny dimming to a sherbet swirl of peach and purple, when she called Maggie back.

Maggie was the sister she felt she knew both most and least. Most because she'd observed Maggie's entire life from a vantage point of three years' wisdom. Least because she'd left for college when Maggie was fifteen and Maggie had been gone at college by the time she moved back to Owl Island.

But she couldn't stop thinking about Ramona's offhand comment. Ramona'd only met Maggie a handful of times. Once when she'd accompanied Greta home for Passover on Owl Island, twice when Maggie had come to visit for the weekend, and once when the whole family had come to Greta's graduation.

Still, blunt though she could be, Ramona did have an uncanny sense of people even after meeting them for the first time. She'd been the friend in college who had disliked Chad "Morty" Mortimer, whom everyone had loved for his easy-going, somewhat awkward charm and his ability to spend his family's money in ways that benefited whatever friend group he was with at the time. Morty, who ended up getting kicked out of school their junior year when a woman took to social media to expose him as a rapist after seven allegations of sexual assault were deemed not worth "ruining his life over" by the administration.

"Oh good, the crocodiles didn't get you," Maggie answered the phone.

"Alligators," Greta corrected absently. "Okay, is our family totally fucked?"

"Yes," Maggie said without missing a beat. "But I love us so much."

"Dude, I'm just here in this totally new place, meeting people, and it's like with this distance and without context, it feels so clear to me that we don't communicate well and we're too judgmental and bossy with one another. *So* clear. But then I imagine us being any different and I just draw a blank."

Horse nosed at the iron gate in front of a beautifully painted teal-and-cream house, and a chipmunk darted away.

"I was listening to this podcast the other day," Maggie said. "I forget the name, but the lady was talking about how with individuals, it's fairly simple to change our behavior because we're only answering to ourselves. We can integrate new habits and thoughts and change our perspectives, boom, boom, boom. But then it gets super more complicated when you add in other people, because you don't have control over them, and the dynamics that you've established and ingrained over years of being together kick back in. It's like grooves in mud or something. You can try and drive a different way—crisscross them or whatever—but with the grooves there, the easiest thing is always gonna be to slide back into them."

"It never really seems to bother you, though."

Maggie snorted. "It bothers me," she said definitively. "But I just think of it as the *my family* part of my life, and it's only one part."

"I don't think I have that sense of discrete parts. To me, it's like this constant background noise. Or, no, not background—more like fog, and if I wander close to it, I get lost in the fog even if I'm doing my own thing."

Greta turned the corner at the antique store/bookstore that was never open and headed toward the river.

"Wanna know a secret?" Maggie asked.

"Obviously."

"I'm not coming back to Owl Island this summer. Naveen and I are gonna drive cross-country, then stay with his brother in LA, then make our way back east via Canada before fall semester. I'm not moving back after I graduate either. That's why I can't leave now. I'm saving up."

Greta felt her eyebrows pull high and her mouth open. She was making a face of horror, even though what she felt was excitement for her sister. She forced her eyebrows back to neutral and let herself smile.

"That sounds really fun," she said.

"Right?! Anyway, don't tell anyone. I'm gonna wait till the last minute to tell them because I don't wanna deal with it. Naveen's brother's awesome. He cuts hair for work, and then he does these paintings where he takes a picture of how the cut hair falls on the floor and sees it as shapes to guide the paint. It sounds disgusting but they're *amazing*. I'll send you his website."

"Sounds great, Mags."

Greta realized she'd gotten turned around listening to her sister talk and was now looping back around toward Frenchmen Street. She could hear the first stirrings of music and a crowd.

"So what's the deal? Are you never coming back either?"

"Huh? I didn't say that."

"Dude, come on. You're loving it there, no?"

She was, but that wasn't the same as never going back. She had a job in Owl Island, a house. You didn't just up and move away from everything you knew after being somewhere for less than a week…right?

"I am loving it," she conceded. "But it's been, like, five seconds."

"You're super into this girl, you're hanging with Ramona, and you've sent approximately seven hundred pictures of flowers to Ash."

"How do you know that?"

"I saw him at Muskee's the other day. Omigod, speaking of: he's so into Truman. Have you talked to him about it?"

A pang of guilt twisted Greta's stomach. She hadn't talked to Ash at all. They'd never really had a phone relationship—she usually just stopped into Thorn—but she should definitely text him.

"No, I owe him a text that isn't all flowers."

"Well it's de-*light*-ful. He's all moony. Anyway, are you? You totally should. We could announce it to the family together. They couldn't kill us both. It would be too suspicious."

Greta imagined staying. She imagined walking outside without a winter coat. Having a garden where the plants of her heart thrived year-round. Learning a new culture, a new region. She imagined waking up wrapped around Carys, making her coffee with lots of cream and sugar, bringing it to her in bed. She imagined kissing Carys' lips and brushing back her curls to nuzzle her neck.

She sighed with pleasure, but it was too soon. She could just imagine Carys' expression if she said, *Hey, I like you. How about I move here?*

"I just mean…what if you did?"

Reasons why it would never work automatically scrolled through Greta's mind like a ticker tape.

"Well, I don't have a job—"

"You can get one."

"Don't have a place to live—"

"You can find one."

"I don't know how I'd be able to get all my plants here—"

"It's called a moving company, and I refuse to believe you don't understand that."

"Haha. I don't know."

"Dude, these are not problems. They're, like, normal parts of moving that anyone over the age of twelve knows. What's the actual issue?"

"What if I move here and I'm just as miserable as I always was at home?"

The words came out of her mouth before she even registered their truth in her mind.

"Whoa."

"Sorry, I just mean—"

"No way. Do *not* apologize. I just never knew you were straight up miserable."

"I mean, I'm not really. I…"

But as she looked at the night blooming around her, she could acknowledge that she really, really was.

There weren't opportunities for her on Owl Island. Summers were nice in Maine, but she hated the cold weather, hated the feeling that as of November, the whole world shut down until May. She felt trapped, an ineffectual Persephone, doomed to the underworld to wait out half her life until spring came.

She hated how homogenous the island was, how she'd only

learned about lives that were different from hers secondhand, through books or movies or social media.

"I guess, yeah, I don't love it. I adore Ash, of course, and Addie, and all of you. But there's just…"

"Nothing there for you."

"Does that sound so awful?"

"Dude, no! Why should you have to stay someplace just cuz it's where you happened to be born? It's silly. You should be somewhere that nourishes your damn soul."

"When'd you get so wise?" Greta teased.

"Oh, I've always been like this," Maggie said breezily. "You all just never noticed 'cause I'm the baby."

"Clearly, you've benefited from the experiences of your sisters before you."

"Yeah, probably, but mostly I think it's just because you all already had each other so I kinda hung out on my own."

"What? No way. We always let you hang out with us."

"Yeah, *let* being the operative word. You let me tag along. But tagging along was boring, so I did my own thing. No one noticed since I wasn't like Adelaide tattling to Mom and Dad when she got left out."

Greta laughed. Addie had been an inveterate tattletale from about seven to twelve.

"I'll have to share that perspective with Ramona. Her theory was that since you're the youngest, you've just had the least amount of time to be poisoned by our family culture."

"Ha, Ramona. She's such a weird bitch, I love her."

"I will let her know."

"Wanna know another secret?" Maggie asked.

"Of course."

There was an uncharacteristic pause, and when Maggie spoke she sounded almost shy. "You're my favorite sister."

The favorite game was one that all five Russakoff sisters had played often over the years. Someone did you a favor, you told her she was your favorite. Someone borrowed your shirt and ripped it, you told her she was your least favorite. It meant everything and nothing.

But this wasn't part of the game. Maggie sounded sincere.

"I'm serious. I know you and Addie are twins so you, like, have to be each other's favorites or whatever, but I just wanted you to know."

Tears pricked Greta's eyes. Her brave, sweet, wild little sister thought of *Greta* as her favorite.

"Thank you," she said. "For real. And honestly, yeah, Addie is my twin and I know her better than anyone, but that doesn't mean she has to be my favorite."

"And, ugh, whatever, favorites are kinda toxic, I know. It's fucked up to need to rank things because it implies there's a single best thing, and that's such a shitty capitalist mindset. But you know what I mean. I love you—yeah, that's the one."

Greta grinned. "I love you too."

"Okay, good. Well." Maggie's voice was a little rough. "I gotta go eat. I'm glad you called."

"I'm glad I did too."

Greta slid her phone back into her pocket, vibrating with a kind of giddy excitement in the aftermath of the conversation. It wasn't about whether she was going to move to New Orleans. Not really. It was about what she had the capacity for. And suddenly her capacity seemed limitless.

"I could move here. Or anywhere. I can do whatever I want," Greta whispered to Horse.

Horse nuzzled her stomach, as if to say, *You absolutely can! Let's keep walking, huh?*

Without realizing it, Greta ended up on Carys' street. It was rude to just stop by, surely. Maybe she could stroll past and shoot Carys a quick text, like, *Hey, I'm nearby. Wanna pet Horse?*

"We'll just walk by, okay?" she said to Horse.

Horse loped easily down the street in front of Greta, almost like he was leading her to Carys' house.

But before she had the chance to recompose the text in her head, they were nearly at Carys', and there she was on the porch with Helen and Veronica.

"Greta?"

"Uh, hey," Greta said, flustered. "We were taking a walk and...um."

"Come have a drink!" Carys waved her onto the porch.

Greta wasn't sure if she should hug Carys or kiss her, so it was a relief when Horse interposed himself between her and everyone on the porch.

"Well, who's this angel?" Helen said. They crouched down in front of Horse and let him enthusiastically lick their face.

"This is Horse. He...uh...he's this person Truman's dog and..."

"Oh, Carys told us about your house swap," Veronica said. "I love it. It's so early two thousands."

"Uh, thanks?"

Carys was smiling and looked pleased to see her. She waited until Helen was fully licked and then squeezed past Horse to slide an arm around Greta's waist.

"Hey," she said. And if Greta hadn't known there were people around them, she would've sworn there was no one else in the universe. She lost herself in Carys' whiskey-gold eyes and heard herself say hi back. But all she could pay attention to was the soft kiss Carys pressed to her lips. She tasted of berries and smoke and the honey that was just her mouth, and Greta wished they could live in that kiss forever.

"Drink?" Helen asked, holding a teacup out to Greta.

"Thanks. What is it?"

"Blackberry lemonade with a little moonshine thrown in for sparkle."

They went inside the house, and when they were gone, Carys whispered, "A *lot* of sparkle."

"My aunt taught me how to make it," Veronica said.

"You know how to make moonshine?"

"I know how to make anything you want." Veronica waved an elegant hand, and Greta believed her.

"Carys was telling me about your beekeeping. I'd love to see that sometime, if you ever want any help."

"Sure. Come along tomorrow, if you want."

"Really? Yeah, I'd love to."

Helen came back onto the porch and set a bowl of water in front of Horse.

Greta thanked her and settled onto the bench with Carys, looping Horse's leash loosely around her foot.

The drink tasted like berries and fire and summer, and Greta was instantly obsessed. "This is amazing. You should bottle it!"

"Right? This is what I've been telling them," Carys agreed. "Y'all need to just open a restaurant, seriously."

Veronica and Helen exchanged a look that said they'd discussed this.

"Opening a restaurant is a hard-core nightmare," Helen said.

"We love life too much to ruin ours," Veronica agreed. "However, we *should* find a way to sell this stuff to someone who wants to stock it in bars and serve it at local restaurants. Maybe after king cake season."

"Well, if you want any help, I'd love to," Greta said. "My family has a business, and I've worked there, like, since I was born, so if I can do anything—I mean, if I...I dunno, if I end up back here ever."

She let the sentence linger in the air, trying it out for the first time.

"You think you might end up coming back?" Carys asked.

The newfound sense of possibility from before still lingered, but Greta didn't want to freak Carys out.

"Yeah, I...I hate Owl Island. I mean, it's lovely in its way, but. I was just talking to my sister, and she said there's no reason to live somewhere forever just because you were born there. And I kinda never thought of it like that. But she's right. Right?"

"Oh yes, absolutely right," Helen said immediately. "I, par exemple, was born in a shit-stain of a town in rural Texas because my parents make bad choices. Was it nightmare fuel? Yes! Did I leave the second I turned sixteen? Also yes. Because of course in Texas, we're allowed to get married at sixteen—nope, that's definitely not still a child—and leave our families, thank fuck."

They passed a hand over their face in a *phew* gesture.

"So my queer ass married this random, left town, made him divorce me, and now I wouldn't cross the state line if all Louisiana were on fire, thank you very much."

"Well, there's the water right there, so," Veronica said.

"Exactly. I'd wade into gator-infested waters before stepping a toe into Tex-ass."

"Are you from here?" Greta asked Veronica.

"I'm from St. Bernard Parish, yeah. But I'm a different person than I ever was when I lived there. Might as well be a thousand miles away."

Helen high-fived her.

"Classic tale of quote unquote 'boy' realizes she's a girl, girl tells parents, parents care more about preconceived notions and egos than about girl, girl leaves, and shit gets a million times better for her."

Sitting there, surrounded by three people who all had families far worse than her own, Greta wondered if she was just ungrateful.

"How do you know if you'd be better off without your family?" she asked.

Helen refilled her cup, and Carys slid a warm hand on her thigh.

"I don't think it's so cut and dried," Helen said. "Like, I still talk to my parents. They love me. They just have lives that aren't the one I want. If they wanted to come visit me here, I'd be down. I just won't go back there."

"Yeah, it's about choosing how you want the people in your life to make you feel," Carys said. "You can decide you only want people in your life who make you feel respected, cared for, listened to. Then you communicate that to them, and if they repeatedly make you feel disrespected, neglected, or ignored instead, you stop giving them your time or energy."

"Family's hard because it's rarely all bad," Veronica said. "There's all those pretty memories of good times too. Times y'all baked cookies or picked flowers or whatever shit white people do in Maine."

Greta snorted, remembering times she really had baked cookies and picked flowers with her family.

"And it feels like if you cut those people off from your future, then you lose the folks who knew that part of your past," Carys said. "But it's not true. You keep those memories no matter what, because they're yours. They don't belong to the people you shared them with."

Helen and Veronica looked at each other knowingly, and Greta got the distinct sense this was a conversation they'd had before.

"This is a thing, huh?" she said.

"Oh, honey. This is a *thing*," Helen said, and Carys and Veronica nodded meaningfully.

"Do you not have queer friends or something?" Veronica asked.

"No, I do."

Greta thought of Ash first. Then realized that most of the queer friends she'd made in college she only texted with on rare occasions. They'd lost touch because most of them hadn't stuck around Maine after graduation. Or if they had, they'd stayed in Portland and rarely left.

"Well, maybe not that many," she revised.

They sipped their drinks, and Veronica and Helen started talking about a mutual friend whom Helen had seen the other day and had an update on.

Carys turned to Greta. "Would you really move here?"

In the (admittedly short) time Greta had spent with Carys, she'd always seemed confident and breezy. But a note of vulnerability crept into her voice now. Her eyes looked uncertain but hopeful. Heat flushed through Greta. Had Carys been playing it cool only because Greta was leaving soon? Had

Greta's concerns that she was rushing into things by imagining moving here been unfounded?

Greta twined her fingers through Carys'. "I really like it here. And…um…" Her heart started racing and she could feel heat move from her chest to her neck. "Like, no pressure, obviously, but I really like you, and…"

Carys smiled, showing her overlapping front teeth that Greta loved. "I really like you too, Greta."

The flush spread up to Greta's cheeks, and she ducked her head. "I'd have to find a job and a place to live and…move… I don't know. It's a lot. But maybe?"

Carys nodded, smile dimming a touch. "Well, if you start really thinking about it, let me know. I'll get on the queer phone tree and find you something."

"There's a queer phone tree here? That's amazing!"

Helen, Veronica, and Carys laughed.

"It's not really a thing. It just feels like it is," Carys clarified. "This is a small-ass town."

Veronica and Helen nodded.

Greta looked around at the sprawling city, the new friends she'd made, the woman she was quickly falling for.

"It feels pretty damn big to me."

# 13
## TRUMAN

Truman stood under the hot water and cursed his existence. Well, wine's existence.

"Stop buying wine and there won't be wine to drink," he told himself logically. But the words hurt his head, so he decided not talking was best for the moment.

In fact, after several days of nonmiserable having a purpose that had interrupted his original plan of sulking all alone, he was right back where he started. He was toweling off and contemplating simply crawling back into bed and continuing his interrupted self-pity when his phone chimed.

The text was from Greta: *can't say i've gone there (lezbian) but lemme know?*

Confused, Truman looked at the message above it. He'd apparently sent it at 11:12 p.m. and had no memory of doing so.

To his utter, stomach-churning horror, it read, Is ash a good kiss? Lookslike he would be bc of his mouth right>?@!

"Oh god. Oh god, oh god, oh god."

He squeezed his eyes shut tight and sent up a prayer to that same, unbelieved-in god: *please let that have been the only text.*

He opened his eyes just enough to see the screen and saw that it was definitely not the only text.

"Oh, kill me."

11:02: hi greta! We're gona save thorn! For ash

Greta had replied, *that's great!*

He'd responded with a GIF of a little girl crushing a soda can in her hand. Then he'd written, Ash is so nice but mean.

Greta had sent a question mark and said, *elaborate pls.*

He had written Exactly.

Clearly realizing he was intoxicated, she'd just sent a laughing emoji and apparently put her phone aside before she had seen his final message. About kissing. Ash.

"Kill. My. Soul."

Truman collapsed onto the couch and quickly replied, LOL a drunken imp stole my phone and texted totally unrelated-to-life things apparently pls ignore everything.

Then he pulled the blanket over his head. Only it wasn't a blanket; it was Ash's sweater.

Feeling extremely fail, he added, The plants are doing great btw!

*generally i find when drunken imps steal yr phone they tell the truth*, Greta replied, devastating any remaining shred of Truman's dignity. *yay plants! the flora here is outrageous and dreamy, ps. horse is also great—i'll send pics later :)*

Truman walked into the carnivorous plants room and saw another one had turned brownish gray. He prayed that it was one of the ones that went dormant in winter.

"Either that or I ruin everything I touch, sooo."

He went through the routine for the rest of the plants and, satisfied he didn't seem to have killed any of the others, checked them off on the spreadsheet.

He dragged himself through a few hours of work, but his mind was ticking away in the background. He'd come to Owl Island to get away from New Orleans and the shame and heartbreak he'd experienced there. His feelings about Ash weren't really about Ash, right? They were about Guy. Guy, who had been dazzling and intimidating and hot and unattainable and, finally, a bad guy.

But it hadn't *just* been to get away from Guy and memories of him. Or to avoid the people who might have witnessed his mortification. Was it? Truman liked New Orleans. But he'd just kind of…stayed there after college.

*No*, the little voice in his head that sounded half like Ramona and half like Charlotte said. *You stayed there because Anthony was staying and he told you it'd be fun if you were there. Then you had two job offers, one that was on-site and would've netted you colleagues and contacts, and one that was work from home, and you chose the one that was work from home. You chose the one that might as well have been anywhere and left you the freedom to pursue your own interests or chat with your friends about TDoZ during work hours.*

*Then you and Anthony broke up and you met Javon, and so on and so forth.*

"Ugh. Me."

Truman updated the spreadsheet he'd been working in, uploaded it to the client portal, and decided he needed to do something just for himself.

What did people do just for themselves?

Uh. Run? Yeah. People ran to, like, feel alive and feel their blood pumping, and…probably feel secure that they could outrun a murderer. Truman should run! He should use his time on this beautiful island to become a runner—it was perfect.

He changed his clothes and popped in his headphones and chose a playlist that someone on Spotify had named "MURDER YR HEART RATE," so that sounded promising. Then he set off down the front path at a dead run.

The plan was to run to the beach. It would be such a great endpoint for his very first run. He'd take a picture of the waves lapping the rocky shore and caption it *First run of what I'm sure will be many more. #Runninglife.*

Since the way he'd reached the beach before was from Main Street, that was the direction he headed.

Running felt amazing. Running felt like flying!

By the third block, running no longer felt amazing. Running felt like dying.

He rounded the corner to Main Street gasping for air, then crossed the street.

One moment, he was upright, wondering *Can lungs become shredded bags of air from gasping for breath?* The next moment, his sole hit a patch of slush and he was pitching forward, airborne, into the street.

He landed with a splat that knocked the tiny amount of air still in his shredded lungs out of him and tried to scramble out of the street to avoid being run over by a car or trampled by a mule-drawn carriage, then remembered he wasn't in New Orleans. He was on Owl Island, and there was no traffic and (probably) no mules.

Truman groaned and began the slow process of dragging himself upright and seeing if any part of him was broken, crushed, or missing.

After only a second, though, warm hands were on his face and a familiar voice was asking if he was okay.

Ash.

"I saw you go down through the front window," he was saying, voice concerned.

Truman was still gasping for air and couldn't respond.

"Truman? Can you not breathe? Shit, let me call someone." Now he sounded panicked.

Truman shook his head and grabbed for Ash's arm.

"No, no, I'm okay," he gasped.

"You sound really bad. Maybe you broke a rib or punctured a lung. Your breathing—"

Truman snort-gasped in mortified laughter. "I'm fine. Just. Out of. Shape."

Finally able to stand, Truman let Ash help him up. Concern etched lines on Ash's handsome face, deep enough that Truman could tell they were habitual. Ash couldn't be more than a year or two older than him, but already he'd had so much occasion to worry.

Ash slung an arm around his waist and helped him across the street and into Thorn, even though Truman could've made it fine on his own. Ash smelled like woods and flowers, and Truman wanted to press his face to Ash's broad chest and breathe him in. But he didn't, because he was sweaty and breathless and covered in slush and probably stank.

The moment the door opened, Bruce padded over and nosed in Truman's crotch. Truman chose to take it as friendly concern.

"Here, come with me," Ash said, and it took Truman a moment to realize Ash was speaking to him and not the dog.

"Oh, me. Okay."

He trailed after Ash through the area behind the desk to a staircase. At the top, Ash opened the door to an apartment.

It was spare but neat and had a calm, if faded, aesthetic that reminded Truman of beach glass blasted smooth by moody waves and capricious sun.

He was led to the middle of the living room, gentle light spilling through the thin blue curtains, and Ash encouraged his jacket off. Ash's hands moved over him with gentle precision—checking for damage and resigned to finding it.

"I'm really fine," Truman assured him. "Embarrassed mostly."

"I didn't know you were a runner."

"Uh, I hope after what you saw you now know that I am not."

"I just saw you slip."

Ash still had one hand on his elbow, like he didn't want to break contact.

"I'm not a runner. I never run. I…" He was already filthy and pathetic, so he figured the truth could only benefit him at this point. "I wanted to do something for myself because I came here all heartbroken like a stupid, heartbroken fool, and then I met you and I got all *bleargh* when you left yesterday, but it's really not about you. It's about Guy. Guy's his actual name. I know, it's confusing. It's about Guy and my stupid heartbrokenness, but then there's you and there was the wine, and I was just gonna go run to the shore because it was so beautiful and, like, heart-expanding yesterday, so I *ran* and then. Well. Then I fell. Anyway. I'm fine. I mean, physically. Obviously I'm a ridiculous mess in every other way," Truman finished with laughter bordering on the frantic.

Ash was watching him with a line between his brows. "Do you want to take a shower?" he asked.

"With you?"

The words were out of Truman's mouth before they passed through his conscious mind. Ash's eyes widened.

"Ohmygod, no. I'm sorry. Obviously not with you."

Was there a mortification greater than cringe? Because if there hadn't previously been, Truman was sure this was it.

Ash gave a tiny smile, and Truman swallowed hard, trying not to cry.

To avoid this still-greater horror, he turned and headed quickly for the bathroom. He threw open the door, ready to escape Ash's beautiful, serene blue-gray gaze, and came face-to-face—well, nearly hanger to eyeball—with the closet.

"It's...um..."

Ash pointed through the kitchen, and Truman squeezed his eyes shut tight. He gave a weak thumbs-up sign that he hoped would forestall all other communication and headed in the direction Ash had pointed.

Safely inside the tiny bathroom, he turned on the shower and sagged onto the toilet lid.

"Omigod, kill me."

Once, his freshman year of college, he'd done something mortifying at a floor party—he didn't remember what it was now, which should have been a comfort—and had fled to the communal bathroom to hide. He'd said something similar, and a voice, strange and inhuman in the echoey bathroom, had responded, "Don't tempt me."

Truman had been so startled he'd almost fallen in the toilet trying to get out of the stall. By the time he did manage to extract himself, there was no one there to be found.

He choked on a giggle thinking about it and stepped under the hot water.

To calm himself, he imagined what Germaine would say. Probably something like *You just tripped! It's not a big deal. And Ash is just a person. So talk to him like a person.*

"Just a person," Truman repeated.

When he got out of the shower, there was a soft knock on the door.

"I have some clothes for you."

"Okay."

The door opened just far enough for Ash's arm to come through. Truman took the clothes, heart beating quickly.

"Thanks. You can...um...go down to the shop if you need to. I can meet you down there."

Ash made a sound that could have been assent or thanks and closed the door.

The sweatpants were gray and the long-sleeved T-shirt was a faded blue. No, not faded. Ash's things weren't faded, they were softened. Every color, every fabric, soft and worn in. It reminded Truman of Ash himself.

He tried to towel his hair into some semblance of order. The shirt was far more casual than what he generally wore, but he liked it. It said that Ash cared about comfort more than what people thought of him. It wasn't a true thought for Truman, but he wished it were.

Outside the bathroom, it was cold. Not wanting to rifle through Ash's possessions looking for a sweater, he plucked a cream-colored blanket off the couch and wrapped it around himself. Then he padded down the stairs in Ash's too-big but very warm wool socks.

Ash was standing at the counter, fiddling with a white rose, a frown etching the line between his brows deeper. He looked up and his eyes widened slightly.

"We've got to stop meeting like this," Ash said.

"Huh?" Ash plucked at the blanket wrapped around him and Truman said, "Oh, ha."

Ash stripped off his own sweater and handed it to Truman. It was still warm from his body, and Truman let himself relax into the warmth of the garment's hug.

"Listen," Ash said just as Truman said, "Sorry I…"

Truman closed his mouth and gestured for Ash to go ahead.

"I freaked out yesterday." Ash flushed. "You started talking about to-do lists, and I just…"

"I got totally overenthusiastic. I knew it. I told them."

"No, you didn't. Wait, told who?"

"No one," Truman said quickly and clamped his mouth shut.

"It wasn't you, that's what I'm trying to say. I'm…"

Ash put his forearms down on the counter and dropped his head between them. His voice, when the words came, sounded echoey, like it was coming from underwater.

"I'm kind of barely keeping it together right now. The shop is fucked. My mom is… Anyway." He lifted his head. "When you started getting to the part where I'd have to do *more* work to make these ideas happen, I just panicked. Because I feel like I'm already drowning."

Bruce came and nuzzled Ash's leg in comfort, and Ash scratched between his ears.

"I'm sorry I ran out last night. I had to get to my mom's and I just… Yeah. Anyway, all during dinner with her last night, I was thinking about what we discussed. The ideas are great. I just need to work myself up to taking on new things."

Relief flooded Truman. Not only had he not scared Ash away, but here was a problem he could actually solve!

"Okay, I know I'm just jumping right back in, but I have lots of ideas of how you can make these changes without doing much more work."

Ash's eyes lit up for a moment. "Yeah?"

"Well, can I be totally honest?"

Ash nodded.

"Okay, you don't really have many customers. So during work hours, it would be a better use of your time to implement these new projects rather than stocking the store with stuff no one buys. And you could save some money by not buying as many flowers for a little while, since people aren't coming in, and put that money toward these new projects."

Ash looked around at the empty shop. "Yeah, it's pretty grim, huh? I swear half the people who come in do it out of pity."

Truman held his tongue.

Ash nodded slowly—a working-through-things kind of nod. Finally, he said, "Okay. Let's do it."

"Yeah? Great! Oh hell, I don't have your notebook. I can go home and get it, though!"

"We can just use regular paper," Ash said and pointed to a pile of scrap paper.

It made Truman's brain itch, but this wasn't about him making things pretty, it was about Ash. Besides, he could always copy it all into Ash's bullet journal later.

Satisfied with the promise of future notebookification, Truman assented.

He cursed himself for not having his usual Pigma Micron in his pocket. One more strike against running. But he grabbed a stack of scrap paper and got ready to make an action plan.

$$\longleftrightarrow$$

Three hours later, sprawled on the shop floor, Bruce lolling happily between them, they had a plan. It was a good plan,

Truman knew. But he also knew that even the most perfect plan wasn't worth anything if it failed to be executed. And Ash was struggling. Even when he could see the appeal of things, he didn't trust that people would buy them. Even when he recognized their utility, he doubted his ability to carry them out.

But Truman knew Ash could do it, and he was here to help. The fact filled him with a deep and thrilling sense of satisfaction. He was excited to start. And beneath his anxieties, Ash seemed excited too. His eyes were lit with purpose, and he'd seemed to genuinely enjoy teasing Truman about his handwriting. (He'd called it a font.)

"I've gotta start cleaning up," Ash said. "I need to stop at the store for some groceries before I go to my mom's."

"Do you cook for her every night?"

"Most nights. Well, lots of times she cooks, but I go over there and I bring the groceries."

And just like that, the life drained out of Ash's eyes, excitement and teasing replaced with his habitual weariness.

"Do you want some help?" Truman offered. "Or company?"

Ash looked pained.

"Never mind," Truman said quickly. "Sorry. I didn't mean to intrude."

"It's not that. It's…she's worse in the evenings, and sometimes she gets confused about who people are. It just might be disorienting."

"I totally understand," Truman said. Then he had an awful thought. "Does she know who you are in the evenings?"

"Sometimes."

"Who does she think you are when she doesn't know?"

"Um. Sometimes my dad. Sometimes her friend Mark.

Sometimes she doesn't know who I am and she tells me to get out of the house."

Ash's low voice got tight at the end of his sentence. Truman couldn't imagine how painful it would be for your own mother to think you were a stranger.

Ash obviously took amazing care of his mother. Truman wondered if anyone ever took care of him.

# 14
# TRUMAN

"I asked my mom if she remembered an unfriendly recluse who lived on the island."

Ash and Truman were in Thorn, hanging flowers up to dry that were on the edge of being unsalable.

"Oh yeah?"

Ash gave a snort of laughter. "Yeah, and she looked me in the face and said, 'You?'"

Truman laughed.

"I'll try her during the day when she's more herself and see."

"Thanks. I've been rereading the series, right, and now that I'm here, I'm noticing all these things that feel so familiar to the books. Like, there's this cave in book 3 that Clarion has to sleep in to stay protected from a magic storm, and the description is of this place that's a hole in the rock of the world, a maw with jutting teeth and the drool of the ocean draining from it as the tide goes out. It reminds me so much of what a cave on these shores would be like."

Ash was making a strange expression. "There is a cave like that. On the other side of the island from where we sat."

Truman's heart soared. "For real?!"

Ash nodded. "I can show you if you want?"

"Um, *yes*, I want!" He pulled out his phone but decided to wait and send Germaine and Charlotte pictures instead. "When?"

"Uh, now?"

Truman tried to make himself say no, but between running the shop and caring for his mom, Ash didn't seem to have any downtime.

"We can talk about shop plans on the way," Truman promised.

They got in the van, Bruce choosing Truman's lap as the place he'd like to ride and licking the window until Truman rolled it down. It was cold, but Bruce helped keep him warm as they drove. Ash stopped at a kind of turnaround dead end.

"This is the north point of the island. It's rocky enough that no one lives over here. The road doesn't go any farther, but we can walk."

Bruce, thrilled to be outside and seemingly impervious to the wind whipping off the ocean and finding its way into collars and sleeves, barreled out of the car and began sniffing wildly.

Ash clipped on his leash and gave him a hearty pat, then began picking his way over boulders.

"Try and step where I step," he called over his shoulder.

Truman did as instructed gladly, since some of the boulders seemed more like seesaws if you stepped in the wrong place.

"This is safe?" Truman called, imagining his foot sliding off a slick rock and his leg lodging in a crevice between them.

"Ya know. Don't try this when they're covered with snow. But yeah, it should be okay."

"Not comforting," Truman muttered.

*It should be okay* was what Ramona had told him when she took him to the gator preserve, and three minutes after that, a gator had almost snapped his face off. Truman redoubled his efforts to step where Ash stepped, even though he was fairly sure there weren't alligators this far north. Once you've seen them in the water, you never forgot it.

They rounded a curve in the coastline, and then it came into view.

"Oh my god," Truman breathed. "This is it."

It was just as Agatha Tark described it in *The Heart Stops*. From the outside, it looked like a head rising from the ocean— oops, the bay—gaping maw dripping with saline froth. Inside, the light narrowed to a triangle that drew you in. At the bottom, jagged rocks jutted up like teeth, rimed white with salt.

He fumbled for his camera and managed a few pictures with shaking hands.

If there was a ledge on the left side of the cave with fossil traces, Truman was gonna lose it.

"Can we go in?"

"Yeah, just watch the foam. It's slippery."

Bruce bounded over rocks to the mouth of the cave easily, and Ash followed. For a large person, he sure was light on his feet. Truman followed, forcing himself to look at where he was stepping rather than stare in wonder at the cave. But as he got close, he couldn't help peering deep into its darkness.

It was vertiginous and the cave echoed the sound of the waves back at him like a giant ear.

"Whoa!"

Ash's arms shot out, and Truman stumbled into them on his last step into the cave.

He found himself held tight against a broad, warm chest. Ash wrapped his arms around him and said very softly, "You okay?"

"Ugh, yeah, sorry, jeez. I promise I don't usually wander around just falling over. Today isn't indicative of my typical ability to, like, be upright."

He felt Ash smile against his hair and then let him go slowly.

Reluctantly?

Truman didn't let himself believe it. That was what got you into trouble: believing that people who caught you so you didn't faceplant into rocks had feelings for you because they didn't let you face-plant into rocks.

The cave was bigger than it had looked from outside, the ceiling vaulting to an apex. Something roosted there. In the book it had been *atbaj*, batlike creatures with heads on both sides of their bodies so they could sight for predators in 360 degrees. But as he watched, one of the creatures descended, and Truman saw that they were seagulls perched high above.

He walked to the left-hand side of the entrance, but there was no ledge, just sea-wet stone and sand clinging in the crevices. Same on the right-hand side. Truman didn't want to be disappointed—after all, it could still very well be the place; surely, authors added fictional details all the time—but he was.

As he approached the triangle of light making it through, he realized that the cave went farther back than he'd first realized.

"Is it safe to go through here?" he asked Ash.

"Yeah, just don't be surprised if you find sixteen-year-old me and my buddy Lorin trying to do witchy sea rituals in there."

"I'm very intrigued, and I do want to hear all about that in a minute."

Truman crouched low to get through the opening and looked around the dimly lit area. Once through the entrance, it was tall enough to stand at full height and roomy enough for three or four people.

And there, on the left-hand side of the rock...

"Holy shit," Truman said worshipfully.

It was a stone ledge. When Truman shone his phone's flashlight on it, he could see whorls of fossilized shell studding its worn-smooth surface. He ran a finger over them and got goose bumps.

He was standing in a place where Agatha Tark had surely stood, was touching the rock she had likely run her own fingers over. The same fingers that had penned the Dead of Zagørjič.

Truman took pictures of that too, and with a flash, they came out well. The flash also made visible something scratched into the wall at the corner of the ledge. Truman got on his knees to peer at it closely.

There, incised in stone, was the symbol of owl wings surrounding a diamond. The sigil of Illmarčzia.

Truman couldn't breathe. Was this how paleantologists felt, unearthing proof that dinosaurs walked the earth? He let his knees give way and sat on the floor, blinking up at the sigil.

"You summon anything in there?" Ash said breezily, sticking his head in. "Hey, what's wrong?" he said immediately at whatever he saw on Truman's face.

Truman pointed and blinked.

"Oh, yeah, isn't that cool? It's been here as long as I remember."

"It's her. It's really her."

Truman explained about the sigil, and Ash sat cross-legged beside him.

"Wow, I can't believe that all the times I came here as a teenager, I was seeing something from the same author you were reading thousands of miles away."

Truman felt a tear tickle his cheek before he was aware he was crying.

"Oh, hey," Ash said. He looked stricken.

"I'm just overwhelmed," Truman assured him. "You don't know what this means to me."

"I'd like to," Ash said gently.

At first, Truman wasn't sure how to put it in words. Then he just started talking.

"When I first read the series, it was like a whole world opened up to me that I'd never known could exist. I don't mean because it was fantasy. I mean because it was these people living in ways and having thoughts and feelings that I'd never experienced. And even though it was fantasy, the things they went through and did felt more real to me than my own life. I was twelve when I read them, and it opened up all these new thoughts, I guess. Like it was a lens I saw the whole world through."

Ash nodded.

"So I started to apply everything in my real life to the books. Or, no. I brought the lens of the books to bear on everything in my real life? Anyway, it was a kind of…I mean, I'm not religious at all, but it was kind of like a bible for me. I admired the characters so much, so I used their strengths and ethics as a guide for who I wanted to be. I asked myself if Clarion would be proud of me for a certain behavior. If yes, I felt good. If no, I knew I should've done something different."

Truman trailed off, contemplating what Clarion would

think about his recent relationship with Guy and realizing she would be horrified. She had stepped away from her lover when he made choices she couldn't endorse because she had only been interested in a love that was a true partnership. She would *never* have allowed herself to be treated the way Truman had. She would never have settled for a love that was strangled and conditional and all on someone else's terms.

She would be ashamed of him.

It walloped him. Here he sat, in a place that felt sacred with Agatha Tark's presence, and his role model would be ashamed of how he had behaved. How little he had valued his needs. His ethics.

He felt slightly sick.

"Truman?"

Truman tried to swallow with a totally dry mouth and choked a little.

"Are you all right?" Ash put a hand on his arm.

No. He was decidedly not all right. But he wanted to be—*could* be, he thought. He needed to do better. Be braver. He needed to take a deep breath, figure out what he wanted, and try to be honest about it. When he put it like that, it sounded so easy. But Truman's guts knotted and his fingertips tingled.

*Just be brave. Be brave like Clarion and tell the truth.*

"I like you!" Truman blurted out. "We just met, and I'm, like, actively still heartbroken over this shitty person, but every time I see you, my stomach is like Jell-O, and I want you to like me!"

Ash's eyes were wide and he was blinking owlishly.

"You don't have to say anything, but I've been a coward about my feelings for basically my whole life, and Clarion would be ashamed, so. Are you happy now?"

This last he yelled up at the cave, and it sent echoes tumbling around them.

Ash smiled. He let out a small, undignified sound that might've been a choked-off giggle. Then he stopped trying to hide it and started laughing. It was booming in the small space, and Truman covered his ears.

"I'm sorry," Ash said between laughs. "It's not funny at all."

But he kept laughing.

"Is this a panic response?" Truman asked.

Ash shook his head and clamped a hand over his mouth. "I just haven't laughed in a really long time," he managed. "I forgot about it."

"You forgot about *laughter*? What are you, a Dickensian street waif?"

Ash snorted with more laughter.

"Well," Truman sniffed, "I'm so glad my confession can provide a reminder of what true hilarity feels like."

Ash grabbed his knee and shook his head. "No, no. I'm sorry. It's not like that at all. I swear."

His grip on Truman was firm and warm. Truman instructed the nausea roiling in his gut to recede.

"Okay," Ash said, getting himself under control. "Fuck, I'm so sorry. I was *not* laughing at you. Well. I was laughing at *you*, but I wasn't laughing at your feelings at all. It was just that you yelled it like you were mad about it, and it came kind of out of nowhere for me. And I'm really sorry I laughed. I like you too. Obviously."

*Obviously?*

"Uh, it isn't obvious to me," Truman said.

"No? I gave you a rose the first time we even met."

"Well. People give their friends roses."

"We weren't friends."

"Okay, but I *do* this! I take ordinary, nonromantic things and make them into this whole narrative where someone is romantic and kind and lovely, and then it turns out they have husbands and children and are actually just using me as a fuck piece on the side," Truman blurted.

"Don't call yourself that," Ash said softly. "Your boyfriend was an asshole."

"Yeah. But then what does it say about me that I fell for him?"

Ash looked at him very seriously. So seriously that Truman got scared and dropped his eyes to the floor. Ash put a hand under his chin and gently raised it. His eyes burned.

"It says that you're kind and generous and probably give people the benefit of the doubt even when they don't deserve it."

Truman swallowed hard and blinked fast to keep from tearing up.

"I—"

But before he could say anything, Ash's phone chimed. Which was a relief because Truman had had absolutely no idea what he was gonna say.

Ash was looking at his phone intently, then cocked his head and glanced at Truman. "You think I'm probably a good kisser, huh?"

"What!?"

Then Truman remembered his amnesiac text to Greta the night before. "Oh god," he groaned.

Ash smiled. Not a smile of amusement but one of pleasure. "Truman."

"Nope."

"Truman, hey."

"I can't believe she told you!"

"She's my best friend," Ash said gently.

"She's my…my… Yeah, fine, she's my nothing. Fair point."

"So."

"So."

Ash looked at him and quirked an eyebrow.

"We can't kiss now!" Truman exclaimed. "You just got a message from your friend about a drunken text I don't even remember sending. That is *not* romantic."

Ash's smile was warm and fond and grew into a grin. "Okay," he said. "I disagree. But I get it."

"You disagree? I drank a bottle of wine in the bathtub and got sad cuz you left our brainstorm and I was thinking about your lips?"

Ash shrugged. "I'm not, like, up on my grand gestures or anything. But I think kissing after you yelled your feelings at me in the middle of the ocean after we discovered that our teenage years are kind of mystically linked by the cave that we're currently in all alone is, yeah, kinda romantic."

"Grumble, grumble, grumble," Truman said. Because when Ash put it that way, damn it, he was right.

"Did you just *say* grumble?"

"Okay, c'mere."

"What?"

"Come here. You're right, it is romantic."

"Well, now you're glaring at me, and it's not seeming that romantic anymore," Ash said.

They both fell silent.

"This is super awkward now, huh?" Truman said miserably.

"Yup."

"Should we go?"

Ash nodded and stood. He held out a hand to Truman, and his grip was warm and sure.

Truman let himself be pulled up, and then they were standing face-to-face in the dimness of the cave.

The blue-gray of Ash's eyes was swallowed by his pupils, and Truman wished they were lit by candles the way Clarion and Aerlich were the first time they sought refuge in the cave. The flickering light would carve Ash's jawline and cheekbones, glow in his eyes, and paint the fine honey hairs of his eyelashes gold.

They stepped closer.

"Is it romantic now?" Ash murmured.

Truman nodded and slid his hand to the back of Ash's neck, cradling his skull, his thumb rubbing the sensitive skin behind his ear.

Truman tipped his head up and Ash bent to meet him. Their lips hovered a centimeter apart, and Truman could feel the pull between them. He closed the distance and caught Ash's lush mouth in a kiss. His lips were just as soft as Truman had imagined.

It began as a slow, tender exploration. Then Truman hooked his arm around Ash's waist and pressed them closer together. Ash deepened the kiss and Truman's stomach flipped. He was breathless, weightless.

He twisted his fingers in Ash's long hair and touched his tongue gently with his own. He felt Ash shudder, then found himself pressed to the rock wall of the cave. Ash's hand cradled his head, and he relaxed into the firm hold of rock and Ash.

The kiss went on and on until Truman was light-headed and breathing hard. Then Ash broke it, groaning, and rested his forehead against Truman's.

"Damn," he murmured.

Truman couldn't agree more. He sagged in Ash's arms, and they slid to the floor again, grinning at each other. Ash reached out and traced his cheekbone, then dragged a fingertip over his lips. They felt kiss-stung and hot.

Truman, too comfortable to move, said, "Can you reach my phone in my pocket?"

Ash cocked his head in question but slid his phone out and handed it to him.

Truman opened the text thread with Greta and, in full view of Ash, wrote Can confirm. Those lips were made for kissing. Twelve out of ten would recommend.

He held up the phone and Ash grinned. In the cave he'd read about at twelve years old and never thought was real, Truman sent the text. Then he leaned back in for another kiss.

# 15
# TRUMAN

Truman and Ash left the cave and bundled into the van like giddy teenagers, giggling when Bruce howled at the ocean, chortling when a gull almost flew into Ash's windshield, and snorting with disgusted laughter when Bruce sat between them with a dignified expression, like a third person, then farted so loudly he scared himself and rocketed back into the rear of the van to recover.

Back at Truman's house, they made cocoa to get warm and then flopped onto the couch.

"And we'd bring candles in our pockets and stick them to the floor, but it wasn't that big in there, so once Lorin almost lit their knee on fire."

Ash was regaling Truman with his teenage attempts at witchcraft in the cave.

"What were you trying to conjure?"

"I'm not sure we even knew, really. But going through the rituals felt important somehow. It's like we wanted *something* to happen. Something that would tell us we weren't alone in the world or that there was power we could tap into."

Truman understood.

"I still feel that way, I think. Like there's forces out there that I can feel working, but I want to know how to tap in. Not god or anything. More like…something outside that's made of the same stuff as something really deep inside me that I don't even know how to access."

Ash's hair was a windblown cloud around his shoulders and his cheeks were pinked from cold. He tipped his head back and looked up to the ceiling. "Do you ever think maybe it isn't something that's out there but just something we choose to do? Like…that there's this…I dunno, this well of power and control that we can tap into inside ourselves. But then the world gets in the way. The world, circumstances, other people, like, squeeze it out of us. Make it smaller and smaller until it's gone."

Truman reached a hand out and found Ash's rough fingers. He twined their hands together.

"Yeah, maybe. Then you have to get away from that stuff to refill it. Or…biggen it. That's not a word. Biggen? What the heck?"

"Enlarge?" Ash offered.

"Yeah. Like, for me, that's how the cemeteries at home are. It's not *because* they're cemeteries Or, not mainly. It's because they're these repositories of so much history and feeling. Over the decades and centuries, so many important emotions have happened there. It becomes like a bottomless source of feeling and beauty and personal history. So spending time in them always fills me back up. I leave feeling like that well or whatever is bigger, deeper, fuller."

"I feel that way about the ocean," Ash said. "Especially in the spring, when the air is warming up but the sea is still holding on to winter. It's a never-ending engine of change. It never looks exactly the same for two seconds in a row. It's so deep and vast that things inside it are unlocatable. You could just disappear into it and have a whole world of possibilities. Just looking at it, especially when no one else is around. Especially in the moonlight. Fuck, it's so magical."

"I love hearing you talk like that," Truman said.

"Like what?"

Truman shrugged and flipped over on the couch to face Ash. "Like, often you're so practical and, like, controlled. It's cool to hear you be more expansive."

"I *am* pretty expansive," Ash said.

He said it with the inflection of a joke, but Truman didn't laugh. "I can tell," he said.

Ash's teasing expression turned serious, and he put a hand on Truman's arm. "You are too."

The words sounded pat, but Truman could tell he meant it.

"I don't always know how to talk about the things I think about," Truman said. "I wish I were creative like my sisters and I could paint about them or something."

Ash screwed up his face. "Uh, are you kidding? You're creative. You came up with thirty creative ideas to grow my business. You made a whole website. You take beautiful photographs. And you're basically obsessed with an epic fantasy series that you've said determines the goals of your life. What on earth makes you think you're not creative?"

Truman smiled at this characterization but brushed it away. "Nah, that's just, like, business strategy and unhealthy escapism. My sister Miriam is a painter and my other sister Eleanor is a musician. Like, they're proper artists. I'm an accountant, for god's sake."

Ash frowned.

Growing up, Truman had watched his sisters cultivate their arts. It had always been the two of them, occasionally in collaboration, more often in competition, but always the two of them making something while Truman only consumed. His nascent passion for order and neatness was deemed oddly charming, his inability to settle on a major an indication of his lack of vocation.

He knew his parents were glad—well, relieved—that he had a safe, practical job that paid the bills. But there was never much to say about it, so they never said much. Whenever they talked, they would regale him with the ins and outs of his sisters' lives and careers. Their album releases, art openings, reviews in journals. His own work, by comparison, had no peaks, no climaxes, just steady work day by day until tax season, when he was busy doing many tiny things over and over at volume.

So he didn't blame them for not having anything to say about it. He himself had little to say. So he'd talked instead about his actual passions. He'd told them about the fonts he created for titles in his bullet journal, about the new pen he'd found that flew over paper with the smooth glide of bike wheels on fresh macadam. He'd told them how creating a system for planning out and recording the events of his life made him grateful for each day because his system honored every hour of it.

But they'd just nodded politely and said it was lucky he was so good at keeping himself organized. They'd said it was nice he had something to keep him busy. They'd said *You could just buy one with the dates and lines already in it, right?*

"There are lots of ways of being creative," Ash said.

Truman nodded. He was sure Ash was being genuine, but

his words sounded a little too much like what Truman had told himself as a balm to his sisters' dismissal of him, and it made him squirm.

"Do you want to watch a movie?" Truman asked, wanting to turn off his brain.

Bruce lifted his head as if to say that he certainly wanted to lie on the floor at their feet for two more hours.

"Sounds good," Ash said.

"What are you in the mood for?"

"Something magical," Ash said with a wink. "Do you want some more cocoa?"

Truman held his cup up with a nod. He guessed Ash knew where everything was since he likely spent time here with Greta.

Truman found an old movie that promised witchiness and starred people whose names he vaguely recognized.

When Ash returned with the cocoa, they settled in to watch, Truman pressing his knee against Ash's thigh and moving close enough that their shoulders touched. Like this, if he turned his head, his face was close enough to Ash's that he could see every freckle and hair and line.

The movie was fun and silly and seemed to involve a subplot about poison that had nothing to do with the magic of an actual magical potion, which Truman found unsatisfying. But there was a black cat and an underground music club and a number of gorgeous antiques.

Truman turned to make a snarky comment about the protagonist's hat to find Ash's eyes closed, lashes fluttering appealingly. His lips were slack, and in the light of the television, the dark circles under his eyes were more visible. Truman turned the volume down three clicks and enjoyed feeling Ash's warm weight next to him.

The shriek of a phone sometime later made Truman jump and Ash lurch upright with a gasp. It was Ash's phone, and he snatched it up with a look of disoriented panic.

"Hello? Oh damn. I'm so sorry, Marjorie. Thanks for calling. No, no, I know. I will. Is...is she okay? Yeah. I'll be right there. No, I'm not at home. Yeah. Okay, thanks again. Thank you. Bye."

Ash was trying to shove the phone in his pocket and gather his things at the same time. Truman's stomach fell.

"Hey, hey, what's up? Is it your mom?"

"I can't believe I fell asleep. I never do this. I should've been there hours ago."

Ash's face was tight, his eyes wild. Truman tried to catch his arm to tell him it was okay, but he never stopped moving.

"I'm really sorry to run out like this again," Ash said miserably.

"Let me come with you. I can watch out for Bruce."

"Oh, shit, Bruce!"

Ash doubled back, eyes wild.

"Ash, stop for just a second." Truman caught his shoulders. "Let me come with you. I can drive. I can hang on to Bruce. That way, you can take care of your mom."

"I don't wanna make you do that."

"You're not making me. I'm offering. Please."

Ash blinked owlishly, then bit his lip and nodded. "Okay, thanks."

They piled back into the van and drove downtown, where they pulled up at a house around the corner from Thorn. The front door opened before they reached the door, and a curly-haired white woman in her fifties waved.

"Hey, Ash."

"I'm really sorry," Ash said by way of a greeting.

"That's all right. Julia and I were just having a little chat, right, Julia?" she said heartily.

The woman who followed her out the door looked a lot like Ash. She was tall, with ash-blond hair and blue-gray eyes, but she looked disoriented, and she was wringing dry, reddened hands.

"Ashleigh, I couldn't find you," she said. "You're out too late."

"I'm sorry," he said gently. "I was watching a movie with my friend. This is Truman."

Julia perked up. She held out a hand to him, and Truman shook it.

"Hi, Truman. Call me Julia. It's always nice to meet Ash's friends."

"Nice to meet you, Julia." Truman searched for something to say. "You've got a great son."

She smiled. "I agree."

"Do you want to go have dinner, Mama?"

"I am a bit hungry," she said. "Should we stay at your house?"

"Nah, let's go home to your house," Ash said.

"I like your new couch," Julia said. "Much more comfortable than the old one."

"Thanks," Ash said and held out a hand to her.

"Hi, Brucie bean," she said, crouching to scratch behind Bruce's ears. He greeted her enthusiastically, licking her face and putting his paws on her shoulders.

"I'm so sorry, Marjorie," Ash was saying softly.

"Never mind that," Marjorie said, waving him away. "No harm done, and it was nice to chat with Julia for a bit."

Ash closed his eyes and shoved his hands in his pockets

like he was preventing himself from doing something. When he spoke again, his voice was choked, though with emotion or regret Truman couldn't tell. "I really appreciate you being so understanding."

"Sweetie. There are a lot of people on this island who've known Julia a long time. We want to help you. I don't know why you won't let us."

"I'm…I…thanks. I've gotta go."

Marjorie watched them from her front stoop as they walked to the van, and she raised a hand in farewell. Ash was helping Julia into the van, and she was telling him that she knew how to get in a car, so Truman waved back.

Ash got his mom settled in the passenger seat, then crouched in the back of the van with Bruce and directed Truman. They pulled up in front of a picturesque cottage with a wraparound porch, a chimney, and white-painted clapboard siding. But as they approached the front door, the details came into focus. The paint was peeling, the porch sagged, and several boards' ends had popped up. There were parts of the siding that looked rotted, and the front door opened with a wailsome squeak.

Inside, the house was open and airy, but even at first glance, something was off about it. There was a hand mixer in the magazine rack, a pile of folded clothes on top of the mantel, and a decorative birdcage with a single dusty light bulb inside.

Ash bustled around the house, putting things quickly to rights and talking to Julia all the while. Was she warm enough? Did she know what she wanted for dinner? What had she and Marjorie been talking about?

It was a perfectly choreographed ballet, and Truman stood there, holding Bruce's leash and feeling useless.

"What's your name, dear?" Julia asked him as he followed them into the kitchen.

"Truman."

"Like Truman Capote," she said with an engaging smile.

She twisted her hair up and secured it with a pencil. She was really quite beautiful.

"Yup."

It was always preferable to get Capote over Harry S.

"I read *Breakfast at Tiffany's* when I was thirteen, and I wanted to run away to New York City."

Truman grinned. "I know what you mean. I saw the movie in college, and it made me wish my life was glamorous like Holly Golightly's."

"Oh, no," Julia said, brow furrowing in a way that made Truman worry he'd upset her. "Holly Golightly's life isn't glamorous. It's an eggshell of glamour with nothing inside: easily shattered and impossible to fill. She's miserable. Don't you remember the end?"

Truman did not, in fact, remember the end.

"She's the cat, dear. We're all the cat. Poor slobs with no names."

"I didn't like that movie," Ash chimed in.

Julia turned to him and cupped his cheek. Then she winked at Truman. "Ashleigh hates charming people."

Truman was about to laugh, but Ash said, "They're slick and glib and I don't trust them."

"Should I be...insulted by that?" Truman had always rather thought that being charming was positive.

"No, because you're not."

Well, that answered that question.

Julia seemed to have recovered from her concern about

Ash, but as he boiled pasta and defrosted sauce from the freezer, she peppered him with questions about when he got his new couch and whether Marjorie was a good roommate.

Truman couldn't be sure, but he thought Ash was just making things up. From what he could piece together, Ash had once lived in the house Marjorie now owned. In her confusion over him not showing up when he usually did, Julia thought she was supposed to go to his house and ended up there.

Confusion aside, Julia was lovely to talk to and told stories that Truman thought might be at least fifty percent fiction—she seemed to have a love of literature and movies and to shift seamlessly from her own experiences to those she'd read about or watched. Still, dinner was entertaining, and Ash seemed to relax once they'd sat down.

In the middle of a monologue about *In Cold Blood*, Julia trailed off, her eyelids heavy. "Ashleigh?" she said. "Did Claire get home yet?"

Truman watched as Ash's face aged ten years without moving.

"No, Mama. She's not coming home tonight."

"She's not?"

"No, she's out of town."

Confusion flickered on Julia's face for a moment, but it was her attempt to hide it that was heartbreaking.

"Of course, I know she's out of town. You don't think I know where my own sister is? She's visiting that boy. I don't like him. He's too old for her."

Ash nodded. "Yeah, I don't like him either."

Julia's face smoothed back out into a serene mask, but her eyes were far away and they stayed that way.

After dinner, Ash settled Julia in front of the TV, putting

on an old movie that she liked. "I'm gonna go get some sleep, Mama," Ash said.

Julia cupped his cheek.

"You do that, sweetheart. You look very tired."

"I am," Ash said. His voice cracked.

They got their coats and boots on as she stared at the television, but as they opened the door, she called, "Capote!"

"Uh," Truman said. "Yeah?"

"The Clutters thought they were safe because nothing like that had ever happened before. But there's a first time for everything."

Truman blinked. It was a common cliché, but in the context, he found her words chilling. "Yeah, I guess that's true," he said.

"Okay, goodnight, Mama," Ash said and quickly shut the door. "I'm so sorry," he said. "I'm so fucking sorry."

"Hey, hey. You don't have anything to be sorry for. What do you mean?"

Ash shook his head. "Nothing. Never mind. Sorry."

They drove back to Thorn in tense silence. It turned out there was a side entrance that led directly upstairs, and Truman went inside with him without asking.

Ash stripped off his coat and boots and poured food into Bruce's bowl. Once Bruce was happily snarfing it up, Ash sat down on the couch and closed his eyes.

Truman wasn't sure what to do. He wanted to comfort Ash, to reassure him. But maybe Ash was one of those people who got mad if you saw them when they were vulnerable and would make him feel bad.

"I don't think I'm gonna be very good company right now," Ash said finally.

"Is that a polite way of asking me to leave, or you wanna hang out but you actually think I won't like how you are?"

"Um. The first because of the second?"

Truman sat next to him. Very gently, he began to untangle Ash's hair. Ash closed his eyes again and leaned closer to Truman. Ash's hair was fine and thick and clearly tangled easily. Slowly, Truman worked out the tangles until he could run his fingers through it.

When he got to the back of Ash's hair, a tear slid down Ash's cheek.

Truman wiped it away with his thumb and pressed a gentle kiss to the damp skin. Ash drew a shuddering breath. When he spoke, his voice was choked and low.

"It's like watching her get erased. And when she's not there... She's the only person who knows so many things. My childhood. My... And when she's gone, those pieces of me are gone. And the way I remember her...it's all getting replaced by this...this not-her." He squeezed his eyes shut, and tears spiked his lashes.

Truman dragged gentle fingers along Ash's scalp.

"I love her so much, but I...I don't know how much longer I can do this. I feel all scraped out."

"Come here," Truman said softly and wrapped Ash in his arms. He had to go up on his knees to do it, but he wanted Ash to feel held, supported, taken care of.

For a moment, Ash was rigid in his arms, but then he let out a breath and sagged against Truman. "That sounds so damn hard."

Ash put his arms around Truman then, hugging him back. They clung together, and Truman had the strangest feeling of familiarity. He felt calm and capable and like he'd been here before. It felt wonderful to hold Ash. It felt right.

# A MESSAGE FROM RAMONA

**RAMONA to GREAT!A RUSSAKOFF**

I'm so glad you've found your hive, G! Now go woo your queen

**GRETA to RAMONA KNOW-IT-ALL**

*wait how'd you know about the bees?* 🐝

**RAMONA to GREAT!A RUSSAKOFF**

I know shit. When will you learn?!

# 16

# GRETA

The community garden where Veronica kept her bees seemed to be three or four lots that once had houses on them.

"They started it after Katrina," Veronica explained. "A lot of properties never got rebuilt, and there was a period when we had the chance to claim some of the properties that were quote unquote 'undesirable.'"

"What made them quote unquote 'undesirable'?"

Greta felt foolish the moment the question was out of her mouth.

"They were in poor Black neighborhoods."

The garden was divided casually, some plots larger, some smaller, some with plants sown in immaculate rows and others in a state of overgrown abundance. People had built all sorts of potting benches, shelves, raised beds, and other unidentifiable structures.

Veronica's plot was at the far corner of the garden.

"People think the bees are gonna get out and sting them, so they want me as far away as possible," Veronica said with a sneer. "They don't get that the bees can leave whenever they want, that they've got no interest in stinging people unless people try to kill them, and that it's these bees that are pollinating their damn vegetables."

The hives looked like Styrofoam coolers on legs, and there was a large plastic barrel resting beside them. Tools Greta didn't recognize lay tidily on a warped wood shelf.

"Did you build all this?"

"Yeah, all the wood is salvage. After Katrina, there was all this wood from the houses left. Some of it rotted, but a lot of the structures here are from busted-up houses. So when I got this plot a few years ago, it was here. I just repurposed it. Okay, you wanna see the bees?"

Greta nodded. "Do you wear one of those suits?"

"Nah, not with my bees. I know them. They're gentle as hell. Just wanna eat pollen and chill. They won't hurt you."

"Eek, okay."

*Don't flinch, don't flinch, don't flinch*, Greta commanded herself.

Veronica took the cover off one of the boxes to reveal the wood frames inside. Bees buzzed lazily on top, and Veronica hummed to them. The buzzing was a quiet thrum that Greta could feel in her chest and temples and fingertips.

Veronica slid a wooden frame out of the hive. It had bees clustered on one corner, and they quickly flew back into the hive. The frame, free of bees, looked like a solid pillar of wax.

"This is the cap." Veronica pointed at the wax. "Once the honey is made, the bees put this beeswax cap over it to keep the honey in. It's got a lower moisture content. To get at the honey, we gotta scrape it off. Hand me that?"

Greta handed her the tool she was pointing at. It looked like a cross between a bread knife and a machete.

Veronica positioned the frame over a metal bucket and slid

the instrument along the wood, slicing off the wax cap. Golden honey glistened underneath, shining in the morning sun.

"Wow," Greta breathed.

"Taste it," Veronica said. She ran a finger over the fresh honey and brought it to her mouth. With closed eyes, she savored the honey. "It's my favorite taste in the world."

Greta scooped a fingerful of honey off the comb and tasted it. A flavor more complex than the honey she was used to burst on her tongue. It was sweet and floral and herbaceous and *fresh*. It tasted like nature. Alive.

"Damn."

"Right?"

"I knew how honey is made, but there's something wild about seeing *how* it's made."

Veronica nodded. "When I started, I did all this research. My grandpa had kept bees when I was little, but I never knew how to do it. I looked up everything, thinking I wouldn't do it right. But then when I started, it was like I didn't really need to do anything. The bees do it all. They know what to do and when and how, and I just needed to not fuck up collecting what they made."

"Nature! It's so magical," Greta crowed, overwhelmed with elation. "That's how it should be. So I'm really into plants—all plants, but I love carnivorous plants. And in nature, they know just what to do. Then my dumb ass has to live in Maine, where no carnivorous plant would ever want to grow because it's winter for, like, half the year."

Veronica shuddered at the idea and made a face Greta wholeheartedly agreed with.

"I know. I hate it. So I have to do all these things to try and mimic nature, basically, to just keep them alive. But like, if a Venus flytrap were growing right here, it would thrive. I wouldn't have to do anything, because it would be in the place it was meant to be, and…yeah."

"Girl, just move here," Veronica said.

"I wish it were that easy."

"It is that easy, if you let it be. You know moving somewhere doesn't mean you have to cut all ties, right? You can still talk to your family, still visit."

"Yeah, I know."

"So what's the deal? And if it's that you don't wanna freak Carys out, do *not* worry. She's learned better than anyone that shit ain't about her."

"Oh?"

"Yeah, you try growing up with a narcissist mother who blames you for everything. She's done some deep work."

Greta was torn between wanting to ask a hundred follow-up questions and not wanting to seem like she was pumping Veronica for information. She decided that no matter how much she wanted to know more about Carys, it was Carys she wanted to hear it from.

"It's not that. Not really. My parents moved to Maine when they got married. Neither of them got along very well with their parents. We're the only Jewish family on Owl Island. Key word, *island*. And it's not like people were openly anti-Semitic, mostly. We're not really religious or anything— well, I'm not at all—but when I was little, it was all Christmas this and Santa that as the default. Growing up, anytime there was a holiday, everyone else celebrated it and we never did, and vice versa. One of the first times I remember realizing my family was different was when my older sister Sadie started school and came home really sad because everyone exchanged

Christmas cards and she realized no one was going to mention Chanukah."

She remembered Sadie's face. She'd been so little, but she had set her shoulders and said maybe she should make Chanukah cards for everyone instead so she could teach them about it. Their parents had told her she certainly could do that if she wanted, and Sadie, ever stubborn, had. She'd come home crying two days later because her classmates hadn't wanted the cards or the explanation that went along with them.

By the time Greta'd gotten to school, she'd expected it and hadn't bothered correcting anyone. Who cared what her classmates thought anyway? But Sadie had been angry with her, accused her of erasing her identity. Of course, what Sadie hadn't known—what even Greta hadn't understood at that time—was that there were pieces of her identity more fundamental that weren't out in the open yet either.

"I don't mean to make it a bigger deal than it was, but there were all these times when it was just us—every Easter, every Christmas, blah, blah, blah. We just were always the only ones who knew what that was like. We were our own little group. And it happened naturally, so I never thought about it until I was older. I don't know if that's how it started or what. But we're all really used to being together, to having each other's backs. Only now, it's like… I didn't really choose it, and it's grown into something that feels stifling instead of supportive."

Veronica nodded. "When you're part of a minority, you wanna find the people who are like you and can understand your experience. Thing is, if that's only a couple of people and they're not the ones you want to spend your time with, you get group identity, but you lose your own. So you gotta be some-where that has enough people like you to find the ones that get you but also that you wanna be with."

Veronica uncapped frame after frame as she talked and slid them into the plastic barrel.

"When I was first coming out as trans, I hung out with the few trans people I met. But I realized pretty quickly that it was *only* being trans that we had in common. So then I started finding people who were also politically radical, and Black, and queer, et cetera. And the more kinds of people I met as my authentic self, the more I felt like I could be that and still have my people around me. My hive."

She winked and Greta grinned.

"Are you the queen?"

"Obviously. Okay, you ready for some honey?"

"What is this?"

"A centrifuge. You spin it and the honey flies out of the comb. Then we collect it."

"You *made* a centrifuge?"

"Well, it's really an old rain barrel I found, but yeah, I put a crank on top so it can spin and made little things to fasten the combs in there. You wanna spin it?"

"Okay."

Veronica fastened the top on the barrel and showed Greta how to spin it. They checked every minute or so until Veronica deemed the honey extracted.

"See, there's just pollen left." She pointed to some yellow residue on the wax. "It's got carbohydrates in it, so they'll eat that if we put it back in the hive."

She slid the frames back into the hive one by one. They had only extracted honey from about a third of them. Veronica explained that they couldn't do them all at once because the bees needed something to be working on.

At the bottom of the barrel, honey gleamed.

"That is amazing," Greta said for the one thousandth time since they'd arrived.

Veronica grinned. "Well, aren't you delightfully easy to impress."

"What? No! This is legitimately amazing!"

"I agree." Veronica pulled a large glass jar from her bag. "Hold that steady for me, will you?" She upended the plastic barrel, and honey poured into the jar. "Now we can take this home and strain it. I used to do all of it out here, but someone kept stealing my strainer. Grab that bucket?"

Greta picked up the bucket with the wax from uncapping and followed Veronica out of the garden.

"Some people think that bees have healing properties," Veronica told her as they walked back. "That spending a lot of time around them improves your health. Their buzzing creates a frequency that heals."

"I've heard that about cats' purring."

"Yeah, me too. Apparently some people with asthma can be treated by breathing beehive air too. I dunno, but I believe it. I always feel better after I've been with the bees."

"That's how I feel about my plants," Greta agreed. "I miss them. Is that weird?"

"Not to me."

As they approached Veronica's street, Greta wondered if she should warn Carys that she was going to be there. Was it intrusive to just be in her house, even though she was there with Veronica? Then again, Carys knew she was going to the garden with Veronica this morning, so…

"Carys isn't home," Veronica said.

"Stop reading my mind," Greta grumbled.

"Then stop being an open book," Veronica teased, nudging Greta's shoulder with her own.

"Am I really that obvious?" Greta asked miserably.

"Yeah. Really, really obvious."

Greta groaned.

"It's a good thing, Greta. You're just genuine. It's nice."

"Genuinely a huge dork," Greta muttered.

"Yeah, well. There are way worse things to be. Anyway, she's on campus, so you don't have to stress-slash-hope she'll walk in every second."

"Thanks."

Greta's embarrassment was forgotten when they got into the kitchen.

"So you can use heat to filter honey. That makes it more liquid, which makes it easier to get the little bits out. But I don't like to because the heat kills all the good, nutritious antibacterial stuff. I use two different sized filters and just let gravity do the work. First I run it through the larger one, then the finer one."

Veronica showed her, and they poured the honey first through the larger filter and left it to drain.

"Honestly, if there's a small amount of pollen that doesn't get filtered out, that's fine by me," Veronica said. "It's good for you."

She turned to the bucket of wax capping.

"Now this shit? Is delicious. Here, you can chew it like gum. But don't swallow the wax."

She gave Greta a small piece of wax. When Greta bit down, honey oozed from the wax and coated her tongue.

"Holy crap. It really does feel like chewing gum!"

"Yep. Nature's candy. Fuck, good job, bees."

"Good job, bees!" Greta crowed, filled suddenly with an elation that came from experiencing this amazing process, hanging out with a new friend, and the mysterious sense of possibility rushing through her.

Veronica grinned.

"Okay, so now we put some water in here and then heat the bucket to separate and melt the wax."

The water slowly came to a boil, and the wax began to melt.

The sound of the front door opening shot Greta to attention. Was it Carys, home from campus?

"Dude, it smells like heaven in here," Helen called from the front room. "Will I ruin the bee vibe if I smoke some weed? Oh, hey, Greta! Awesome."

Helen was pulling off a purple polo shirt and khaki pants as they walked into the kitchen. In black boxer briefs and a white A-shirt, they stuck a finger into the filtering honey and ate it with relish.

"Get your dirty-ass, fried green tomato fingers out of my honey, you absolute ferret!"

"I washed my hands before I left the restaurant!" Helen insisted, sounding offended, then wrinkled their nose. "But actually, my tip money is filthier than the deep fryer."

They washed their hands, then slumped into a kitchen chair and pulled a pipe and a bag of weed from the space between two cookbooks in the corner of the retro kitchen table.

"How was work, dear?" Veronica trilled.

"Terrible as always, darling. How are the bees?"

"Wonderful. And Greta didn't even scream or run away when she met them."

Greta's stomach fell. "Did you think I would?"

Veronica snorted.

"No. That's what I did," Helen confessed. "I didn't *scream*, thank you. I might have *cried out*, but I am not in the habit of being swarmed."

"First of all, that's not what Jenna's sex party friends tell me, and second of all, you were decidedly *not* swarmed. Three bees flew toward you and you ran like…like some member of the Saints whose job it is to run really fast."

Greta had the vague idea that the Saints were a football team but wasn't entirely sure.

"An-y-ways," Helen said, "I'm glad we have honey, and do you want?" They held up the freshly packed pipe.

"Sure." Greta took it from her.

"Blow the smoke away from the honey, please," said Veronica.

Helen rolled their eyes at Greta but nodded.

By the time they finished the bowl, the beeswax was ready, and Veronica took a silicone mini muffin tin from the shelf.

"Hold this cheesecloth on here?" she asked, and Greta did.

The water had mostly boiled out, leaving Veronica pouring the melted beeswax through the cheesecloth, which caught a skin of impurities.

"I love this part," Helen said.

With a practiced hand, Veronica poured the clean beeswax into the muffin cups. "Now, we just let it cool, and we have fresh beeswax," she said triumphantly.

She had already moved the honey on to strain through the finer strainer, and now she poured it into two jars. One of the jars she slid into the cupboard next to the window. The other jar she wrote something on and handed to Greta.

"Huh?"

The lid said *V's Kick-Ass Honey* and the date.

"You helped. You get honey."

"Seriously?" Warmth suffused Greta like a hug. "That's... wow. Thank you. I love it."

She felt surprisingly overwhelmed, holding in her hand the precious distillation of the work of flowers and earth, sun and bees, Veronica and heat and knowledge.

"So what are we making with this batch of wax?" Helen asked, rescuing Greta.

"Dunno yet."

"Dang, I wish I wrote letters. Then I could make cool seals out of beeswax and stamp them with my initials. It'd be awesome," Helen mused.

"Well, write someone a letter then," Veronica suggested.

"Ugh, no." Helen looked horrified and Greta laughed.

"Do you put the king cakes in boxes?" Greta asked.

"Yeah, why?"

Greta shook her head. "It's probably silly, I don't know. I was just thinking about what you said about seals and how you were looking for something unique for the packaging that maybe wasn't glitter. What if you closed the boxes with bees-wax seals and imprinted them with the name of the business? You could make business cards for the lemonade too and put them in the boxes with the cakes. Or stick them into the seal? Then people would smell the beeswax every time they opened the box to eat the cake and be reminded."

She trailed off because both Helen and Veronica were staring at her with wide eyes.

"Yes," Helen said.

"Fuck yeah," Veronica agreed. "This is correct. Because

we've talked about wanting to sell that damn lemonade for two years but we haven't done it yet. It's sweetened with my honey, so that's the connection. And I've been selling my beeswax to local chandlers, but I'd make way more money making the candles myself and selling them. They're pretty easy to make, and wax is the biggest expense. Damn. Yup."

"Too bad you don't put candles in a king cake," Helen said.

"What if you made king cake candles?" Greta offered. "I think it's kinda gross, but people love those candles that smell sweet."

"Oh, damn," Helen said, nodding. "We could be like, 'Do you wish you could get king cake all year round? Now you can!'"

"Write this shit down," Veronica said to Helen, who was already scrambling for a pen.

"I wonder if there's a way you could reuse honey jars to make candles in, or candle jars to put lemonade in," Greta mused.

"Maybe we can," said Helen. "I'm writing it down."

"I could grow lavender and other herbs and flowers you could flavor the lemonade with or put in the candles," Greta said dreamily.

She realized she must be pretty high, because the notion of moving to New Orleans and growing lavender for a business with two people she'd just met filled her with pure elation.

# 17
## GRETA

Shortly before 7:00 a.m., Greta approached the gate of a lavish home in the Garden District, checking the address on her phone for the third time.

She was here as Muriel's guest, but she didn't see Muriel anywhere. In fact, the only people about were a few kids scampering for a school bus.

Just as she had decided to slink away unnoticed, Muriel strode elegantly down the street in a red wool cape and flowing teal pantsuit, a group of equally well-dressed seniors following in her wake.

"Greta, dear." Muriel kissed her cheeks. "I'm so glad you could make it. I'll introduce you to everyone inside. Come along."

Then she swept through the gate and up to the front door, the rest of the flock following in a colorful vee.

Greta suddenly felt very underdressed in her black jeans, boots, and buffalo plaid flannel.

Muriel didn't knock, simply stood quietly at the door, so Greta joined the back of the group. Precisely at seven, the door opened, revealing a grand entryway with gleaming pale pink marble floors, soft green walls edged in elaborate gold moldings, and a white marble table directly in the center that held the largest arrangement of flowers Greta had ever seen.

"Welcome, welcome," boomed their host, a petite Black woman who appeared to be in her sixties or seventies and was wearing an equestrian-style outfit.

Muriel and the woman exchanged cheek kisses, and the greetings commenced. When their host had kissed the last cheek and murmured the final welcome, Muriel slid her elbow through Greta's and walked her over.

"Camilla St. James, may I introduce my dear new friend, Greta Russakoff."

"Welcome, dear. How do you do?"

"Hi, hello, thanks so much for having me, Ms. St. James. Um, sorry, I didn't know this was a fancy occasion, so I didn't dress up. Sorry. Your house is amazing."

"Oh, it's not fancy," her host said with a rich laugh. "Just a few old friends getting together for some flower talk. And please, call me Camilla."

"Okay, well, thank you for having me, Camilla."

Camilla kissed her cheek and herded everyone through into a magnificent sitting room, wallpapered in a bold rose print against a black background. The furniture was a damask of the same print but with a pale yellow background, and a huge piano sat in the corner with a freestanding ashtray next to it, topped with fluted amber glass. A chandelier dripped crystals in the center of the molded plaster ceiling.

"Wow," Greta couldn't help muttering under her breath as they trooped through.

A thin, stooped man with a ring of white hair, wearing a blue linen suit that bagged at the shoulders and knees, turned to her. He had sharp blue eyes and wild eyebrows, and when he spoke, it was with an accent Greta couldn't quite place.

"You should see her Christmas parties," he said with a wink. "Trees up to here."

He raised an arm to indicate height, but since he was a small man, the effect was comical. Greta smiled.

"When do the Christmas decorations go up?"

"December the fifteenth and not a minute sooner."

It was December thirteenth. Greta raised her eyebrows, hoping she was conveying polite interest. She knew that people often had specific times that they put up or took down Christmas decorations, though she didn't know why.

"I'm Marvin Kann."

"Greta. Nice to meet you."

They shook hands, then followed everyone else through the house.

They ended up in a solarium at the back of the house. It had light green tile floors, and the entire room was clad in metal wrapped windows. Greta's breath caught at the soft morning light that made the plants glow like jewels.

And what plants they were! Towering monsteras ten feet tall with aerial roots dripping to the ground like the tangle of wires to a soundboard. A jade plant—no, tree—with a trunk as thick as her arm. Flurries of hanging philodendrons snaked their tendrils across the ceiling. Geraniums and orchids, begonias and ferns. Each area of the solarium was like a microclimate of sun and heat and humidity perfect for each plant.

The glass almost melted away as the plants inside blended with the plants outside in Greta's vision.

On a low shelf in the very far, sunniest corner of the

solarium was a magnificent euphorbia cactus that had to be at least twenty years old.

All Greta wanted to do was examine each plant, run her fingers along their leaves and nodes and spines and spikes, and fill her lungs with their fresh, sweet air.

But the company was gathering in the ring of chairs at the center of the solarium, and Camilla was wheeling a tea cart over to them. It was laden with a silver samovar of tea and one of coffee, a three-tiered serving plate of delicate pastries and tiny sandwiches, and three carafes of juice—orange, apple, and a reddish purple one that might've been cranberry or could've been anything.

They ate and drank and Greta attempted to stay close to Muriel and not spill anything or get crumbs on the immaculate floor as she listened to the conversations around her.

They were inaccessible to her at first—grandchildren and mayoral scandals, mutual friends and a newspaper story she hadn't read—but as the plates were cleared and the coffee cups drained, the conversation turned to plants, and Greta felt every muscle relax.

They didn't have an official name for their klatch, but Greta came to think of them as the Garden Gang. They were all over sixty, mostly single, and passionately loved plants. They'd begun meeting once a month to help one another with garden projects, swap bulbs and cuttings, and visit botanical gardens together. However, they had, in their third year, begun to have aspirations larger than simply meeting up socially and sharing their love of gardening.

One of their number, Tangerine Huang, was on the city council and suggested they volunteer to plant flowers and other sustainable plants in a neighborhood park that was being rebuilt. After that, they volunteered with community centers, schools, and neighborhood project crews and had been doing so for the last six years.

Greta said she could imagine them turning up en masse, dressed in their linen suits, jodhpurs, and flowing colors, while the other volunteers looked on in awe.

"We dress as we please," said Olive Martelli, a large white woman with bright orange hair and cat's-eye glasses studded with rhinestones. "One of the privileges of maturity." She pronounced it *ma-toor-ity*.

"Who gives a toss what people think," chimed in a man whose name Greta never knew. He looked like an Edward Gorey drawing come to life, so she named him Edward in her mind. He was wearing black-and-white-checked pants that ballooned at the thigh and narrowed at the ankle, a cropped black matador-style jacket, and bright yellow ankle-high Wellingtons.

Camilla stood and the conversation quieted.

"Shall we?" She gestured dramatically to the garden that stretched beyond the greenhouse.

The Gang rose too, several of them swapped their shoes for sneakers or boots, and they proceeded outside through a panel in the solarium that Greta hadn't realized was a door.

Camilla's garden was as dramatic and beautiful as she was, even in December. Pink snapdragons and purple alyssum bloomed along the iron lace fence that demarcated her property from First Street, rose bushes stood against the fence on the other side, and swathes of growth meandered between them, creating pockets of privacy, one of which housed a white iron table and chairs and another of which contained a wooden chaise longue with a peach-and-white-striped cushion and a table beside it shaped like a pineapple.

"If you would be so kind," Camilla said, "I'd like to plant calendula and dianthus today. And in the vegetable patch, mustard, radish, and turnips. Then if we could mulch the tropicals, I'd be simply delighted."

"You have a vegetable patch?" Greta asked. She had assumed the garden was purely decorative for some reason.

"Oh yes. Would you like to head up that planting today?"

"Oh, I…to be honest, I don't know much about growing vegetables. I'd love to learn, though."

"Excellent!" Camilla clapped her hands together. "Toni should teach you all about it. She's a veggie whiz."

A broad, stooped woman in a large black hat gave a wave. She gestured Greta over and led her to a raised bed behind the chaise longue. Greta hadn't noticed it before because nothing appeared to be growing.

Toni pointed at several mounds of dirt. "Those are the potato mounds, so we don't want to plant radishes close to there. Mustard is good as a border because it has those beautiful yellow flowers."

Greta nodded along, trying to commit everything Toni said to memory. Three others had followed them to the vegetable patch, and under Toni's guidance, they began to sow mustard seeds around two edges of the bed and turnips inside them.

"You do the radishes, dear. Young knees," one of the women said, directing Greta to the middle of the bed and handing her three paper envelopes, each with a different variety written on it. Cherry Belle, White Icicle, and French Breakfast, they said.

"Should I mix them up or keep each type together?"

"Camilla likes them mixed together," Toni replied. "Three inches apart."

Greta knelt in the dirt, happily interplanting the

exotic-sounding radishes. She was used to the calm that came from repotting her plants, fertilizing them, and trimming away dead leaves. But kneeling in the dirt in December, with plants thriving all around her, filled Greta with hope.

She *wanted* this. She wanted to be in a place like this, teeming with life year-round, full of people and possibilities. She'd never done much gardening outside. The growing season in Maine was fairly short, and her indoor plants took most of her energy. But the idea of growing her own vegetables, having a plot in a community garden—hell, having even a little bit of space in this climate where things could thrive. She *wanted* it.

When the radishes were sown and the group headed back to the others to mulch, Greta snapped a picture of her hand in the dirt with greenery all around her and sent it to Ash.

*playing with plants in december wth!?* she wrote and added a heart eyes emoji. *how are you?*

Then she slid her phone into her back pocket and went to learn how to mulch tropicals, whatever that meant.

↔

After a much-needed nap (six a.m. was not her preferred time to rise), a long walk with Horse, and a lot of googling how to grow tropical plants and vegetables in the New Orleans weather, Greta got ready to meet up with Carys, who'd texted earlier to invite her to a pool party.

Greta threw on a sports bra and some tank underwear beneath her jeans and A-shirt, hoping Carys' friends were okay with impromptu swimwear. Carys hadn't said anything else about the vibe of the party except to say there would be food, drinks, and a special guest.

She walked to Carys' and found Carys, Helen, and Veronica sitting on the porch, sipping their famous lemonade. Greta's heart filled with joy, not only to see Carys but Helen and Veronica as well. She liked them both so much. After only knowing them for a short time, she felt like they were her friends as well.

"Hi there," Carys said warmly and wrapped her arms around Greta's neck, pressing a kiss to her lips.

Greta's whole body lit up. She wanted the hug to last forever.

"How was school and the square?" Greta asked.

"School was medium. One of the students in my 12:30 is this boat-shoe wearing, floppy-haired creep, and he doesn't take notes or anything, just leers at me the whole time."

"God, I'm so sorry. I didn't even think that your own students might be like that."

Helen snorted. "You should hear one of the evaluations she got at the end of term last year."

Carys grimaced. "I knew exactly who it was too. Little shit. Anyway, the square was good. Teacup and I hit the jackpot with some kind of water polo team. What the hell even is water polo? But they were buzzing with performative testosterone and loudly wanted pictures with Teacup and to ask me math problems, so I raked it in."

"Suffer from their creepiness in class, take their money after," Greta said.

"Exactly," Carys replied.

"So where are we going?" Greta asked as they began to walk.

Veronica balanced a large jug of what Greta presumed was her lemonade on her shoulder, so Greta hoped they weren't walking too far.

"Our friend Rae house-sits for this family. The husband is

some kind of tech dude, and the wife owns an art gallery here and one in LA. They go to California all the time, and they have a pool, so Rae will have us over. It's pretty sweet."

The house was tucked behind a gate that surrounded overgrown shrubs whose tendrils crowded the path to the front door. It looked unassuming and modest through the foliage—nothing you'd notice from the street. In fact, Greta realized she'd walked past this corner several times since she'd arrived and never noticed it.

Helen opened the unlocked door, and they entered another world.

Inside was cool and serene, and Greta found herself in a foyer that more closely resembled a gallery than a hallway. There were canvases hung salon style on both walls, from paintings so tiny they appeared to be done with a single strand of hair to photographs blown up to the size of a door.

And there, in the middle of the wall... Greta gasped.

"Is that...that's not an original Mimi Nakaya?"

"Yup," Carys said.

"Holy shit."

Greta walked gingerly into the living room, as if there might be famous, priceless objects lying on the floor and she didn't want to step on them.

The house opened up into room after room, nothing like the shotgun style that Greta had become accustomed to. It had clearly been gutted and renovated, its modern open plan a showcase for the many objets d'art that stood on pillars and shelves as well as lining the walls.

"Eleventh House!" someone called. "Yay!"

"Hey, Rae," Helen began, but before Greta could turn to see their host, someone else yelled too.

"Incoming!"

Greta heard a sound that she couldn't place. A strange low snuffling that moved close to the ground.

Suddenly, from around the corner, running straight toward them, came the source of the noise.

A pig.

"What the—" Greta got out before Carys and Helen both knelt and stopped the pig in its tracks.

"Hi, Madame Snortface," Carys said affectionately.

"Well, hello, Snoots McPigfeet," Helen chimed in.

They both patted the pig on its sides and scritched between its ears.

Greta turned to Veronica questioningly.

"No, ma'am," Veronica said. "I do not approve of this situation."

"Is this a pet?"

"Well, you can't expect people who think they're special to have a dog or a cat, now can you? This pig is half their personality."

Greta looked around at, presumably, the other half. The art all over the house seemed under distinct threat from the pig before her.

"Weird," Greta pronounced. Veronica nodded definitively.

"She's sweet," said Helen, giving the pig another pat.

"As someone with a non-cat, non-dog pet," said Carys, "I beg you not to judge."

"Oh, shit, sorry," Greta said, having forgotten Teacup for a moment. "Teacup doesn't seem like half your personality at all," she quickly added.

Carys winked at her. "I'm not offended. They got the pig for their daughter, actually. She loves him. His name's Scribble."

"Uh, hi, Scribble," Greta said and reached out a hand.

The pig was solid and bristly, and Greta took her hand back.

Carys and Helen both seemed to glow with affection for it. Greta caught Veronica's eye over the pig's back and was gratified to find her wearing an expression of eye-rolling displeasure that matched her own feelings.

Having received his pats, Scribble waddled past them and collapsed inelegantly onto a pile of cushions in a corner of the room.

"Aw," said Carys.

Greta was filled with a warm glow. "You love all animals, don't you?"

Carys grinned.

"They're all so cute, and they're just totally themselves. Scribble just spends all his time being a pig. He's not trying to do anything else. It's aspirational."

"You don't even know," Veronica chimed in. "This girl thinks squirrels are cute." She shook her head like she'd delivered a terminal diagnosis.

"They're *adorable*," Carys said. "They're just like…kittens, but with jobs."

Veronica snorted, Helen smiled knowingly, and Greta couldn't see anything but the sincere warmth in Carys' face.

"You're a smush," Greta said.

"Total smush," Helen agreed.

Carys rolled her eyes. "Whatever," she said, mock annoyed, but she leaned into Greta's shoulder, and Greta slid an arm around her waist.

Veronica headed into the kitchen, and they followed. Unlike the rest of the house, the kitchen didn't seem to have been renovated. It was a galley, small and cramped. There were decorative jars of olives and peppers on the stovetop.

"You don't need a functional stove when you only eat take-out sushi," Veronica explained under her breath.

On the countertop beside the stove, snacks were laid out. Hummus and pita, grapes, cheese and crackers, cookies, alcohol, and cans of LaCroix in several flavors. Veronica slid her pitcher of lemonade in the refrigerator.

"Oh, good, there you are. Thanks for coming."

The speaker was a tall butch in a pink short-sleeved button-down with green flamingoes on it, cutoff jean shorts, and a green baseball cap worn jauntily to the side that said *Vroom* in gold embroidery.

After their greetings, Carys put a hand on Greta's shoulder. "Rae, this is Greta. Greta, this is Rae. They're our host for the evening."

"Hey, thanks for inviting me," Greta said.

Rae had a mischievous smile and twinkly blue eyes.

"My pleasure. So happy to share the bounty with a new arrival."

"And what a bounty it is," boomed the same voice that had yelled *Incoming*. "Hey, I'm Matthew. He/him."

Matthew was large, tall and broad and fat, with beautiful gray eyes and hair the color of fire caught up in a high ponytail.

Greta introduced herself in kind, held out her hand and found it squeezed warmly.

"Carys, you scamp," Matthew said. "What a hottie."

"I agree," Carys said, squeezing Greta's shoulder.

Greta flushed, flattered and unsure what to say. She didn't think of herself as hot. Some days, she liked how she looked just fine. She knew people responded to her big blue eyes and bone structure, and she enjoyed bleaching her hair to a striking platinum, but when she looked in the mirror, usually the first thing she saw was how uncertain her eyes looked and how stubborn the cut of her jaw was.

She ran a hand self-consciously through her hair and ducked her chin so Matthew wouldn't see her blushing.

"You're adorable," Carys said, putting a hand on the back of her neck.

"Okay, okay, enough of this," Helen said. "I'm going to the pool."

The house was arranged in a semicircle around the patio and pool area, with a sliding glass door out of the kitchen on one side and the master bedroom on the other. There was a wooden deck around the house, with pockets of planting that shaded benches and a wrought-iron table and chairs. It stepped down to the cement and tile patio that stretched around a kidney-shaped pool.

One end of the pool was shaded by trees Greta didn't recognize that dropped pods into the pool when the wind blew, and the other side was in full sun. Chaise longues and side tables were clustered around the pool and held three more people who stood to greet them.

Carys made introductions, for which Greta was grateful.

Tana was a middle school teacher with a huge grin who swore more than anyone Greta had ever heard. After greeting everyone, she and Veronica holed up on a chaise and began intently discussing a book they were both reading.

The man named Jacob seemed to be Matthew's boyfriend. He looked like he could be an underwear model but was actually a painter. He was as shy as Matthew was gregarious, and though he smiled warmly at everyone, he seemed happy to listen rather than participate in the conversation.

Lur was originally from Cuba and had come to Tulane for

grad school the year before. She studied sociology, as did Rae, and they'd met at a lecture and become fast friends. Lur was interested to hear about Maine—since arriving in the U.S., she'd only traveled around Louisiana and Texas.

As the sun set, solar-powered lights began to glow around the yard. It was a warm evening for December, and people began to get in the pool.

Veronica had on a stunning white bikini, Jacob and Matthew both sported cute swim trunks, and Carys undressed to reveal her gorgeous curves in a high-waisted suit that looked like something out of a glam forties movie.

Suddenly, Greta felt self-conscious.

"Aren't you coming in?" Carys asked.

"Oh, well, I didn't bring a suit," Greta hemmed. "So I'm just wearing a sports bra and underwear."

"No one cares. Don't worry about it," Carys said.

"Are you sure?"

Lur had unwrapped her dress and was sliding into the pool in a belted red one-piece that showed off multiple pin-up tattoos.

"Absolutely positive," Carys said. She pressed a kiss to Greta's lips.

Then Helen stripped their T-shirt and jeans off to reveal they were wearing nearly the same thing as Greta.

"See?"

She nodded, relieved.

The water was warmer than she'd expected. In Maine, even in the summer, the bay and ocean were chilly, and Greta had tightened her muscles in anticipation. But this felt like stepping into a cool bath, and Greta relaxed and let the water hold her.

They bopped a ball around for a little while, but mostly people just kept chatting, only in the water.

"How was your gardening thing this morning?" Carys asked.

"It was so cool," Greta said and told her all about Muriel's friends and the work they did helping get plants and flowers into more neighborhoods in the city.

"Hey, Tana," Carys called, and Tana swam over to them. "Were you telling me about doing new after-school activities with your kids?"

"Yeah, we're doing this whole fuckin' programming initiative right now. If the damn school will cough up the money."

"Are you doing anything with gardens?"

"Shit, yeah. We're trying to get some of those fuckin'... whaddaya call 'em? Wooden beds?"

"Raised beds?" Greta offered.

"Yeah, those. I read that growing your own shit makes kids more excited to eat their vegetables or some crap."

Greta smiled and imagined Tana swearing this much around middle school kids.

"Well, Greta is a huge plant nerd. Would you ever want someone to tell the kids about carnivorous plants?"

"Carnivorous plants? Oh *hell* yes, they would love the shit out of that. Middle schoolers are psychopathic monsters, just as a rule, so they love anything that's fucked up!"

"Great," Carys said and squeezed Greta's side.

"If you're looking for people to help with building a garden, I know this group. They're pretty rad older people who've done a lot of volunteering with different communities," Greta offered. "I could ask if they want to help?"

"Dude, if they wanna volunteer, I will abso-fucking-lutely take them up on that because we have no damn money."

"Cool, Greta can ask them about helping with the garden, and she can do a thing about carnivorous plants," Carys said.

"Hell yes! I'll get your number when we're not, ya know, in a pool."

"Okay, great, thank you."

Greta's head was abuzz with all the things she wanted to show the kids about the amazing world of carnivorous plants. First she'd have to get some here—it was much more interesting if she could demonstrate the way they consume and how they move. Surely there was a local plant store that had them in the city, given the climate.

Carys nuzzled her neck, and Greta turned into her embrace.

"Wow, thank you," she said. "I never would've asked anything like that."

"I know," Carys said. "But sometimes you can't wait around for someone to notice you've got something to offer. You've gotta offer it."

Greta thought of all the times she'd hoped for opportunities to be presented to her. She'd worked hard to always seem responsible and dedicated. But she'd never been a squeaky wheel. She'd watched as other people were chosen for opportunities she would love to have and always figured it was because they were more qualified or more appealing than her.

Girls she'd wished would ask her out but that she'd never tried to ask out. Jobs she'd never been offered because she didn't make her interest known.

Damn.

"Yeah, you're right."

Carys backed her against the side of the pool and kissed her.

"Do you think I could...do that?"

"Of course you could, babe. Tana just invited you."

"I guess I mean really *do* it. Like…when I was hanging out with Veronica the other day, with the bees, I was imagining what if I did live here and I grew lavender to scent her and Helen's candles, and it seems like such a dream. But…"

She could picture how it would go. Her parents, devastated that she wanted to be so far away from them, feeling awful because she didn't want to join the business. Adelaide, feeling abandoned. Ash, her best friend who needed someone to have fun with, to vent to, as his mom slipped further and further away.

"I don't want to let everybody down," she finished.

Carys' eyes were sympathetic, but her voice was sure. "What about letting yourself down?" she said gently. "What about staying someplace that doesn't nourish you, just because you think you owe it to other people?"

Greta's throat tightened. That *just* was harsh.

"They're my family, and they depend on me," she said.

"Do they? Do they really depend on you, or do *you* have this idea that you have to stay and it's not really about them?"

Carys ran a hand over Greta's wet hair, but Greta pulled away.

"It's not like that," she muttered.

Carys just looked at her steadily, ready to listen, but her question hung between them. Greta didn't have any proof. Didn't have anything to hold up to Carys and say *See, they need me* that she hadn't already shown her.

Greta lifted herself out of the pool, and Carys let her go without comment. She grabbed a towel from the stack. Her legs prickled with goose bumps, and her stomach was in a knot as she walked inside. She poured herself a glass of Veronica's lemonade and gulped it down. It was delicious. She poured another and went to find a bathroom, needing a moment to collect her thoughts.

The bathroom was tiled in iridescent cobalt blue from floor to ceiling. It felt like being inside a wave. When Greta sat down, the toilet let out a beep, and she nearly jumped out of her wet underwear.

The toilet was some fancy toilet-bidet combination with multiple settings. Who the hell were these people, and why did they need toilet settings? Greta punched a button on the control panel and was rewarded with a jet of warm water to the crotch.

She snorted and hit another button. A soothing hum emanated from the toilet, and the seat got warm.

"Oh my god. This is absurd."

She stood and sent a picture to Ash, who thought even asking for food without one of the listed ingredients made you high maintenance. Then she sat down on the toilet and downed the second glass of lemonade.

She'd thought Carys understood. Understood how hard it was, how much pressure her family put on her, how much they expected. But apparently she thought Greta was just lying to herself.

When she got up, the toilet let out a noise that sounded like it was sad to see her go.

"Get in line, buddy," she slurred and giggled to herself.

Reluctantly, she left the world of blue tile and almost immediately ran into the pig.

She swore and contorted herself to avoid falling on top of it. Instead, she pitched to the side and landed in a heap on the floor. Scribble stuck his snout into her armpit, gave a snuffle, then collapsed on top of her instead.

"God damn it," Greta muttered resignedly.

Which, of course, was when Carys, Matthew, and Veronica walked into the room.

Matthew's laugh boomed in the quiet of the house and startled Scribble, who attempted to get to his hooves, but he couldn't get purchase on the floor.

"I did not come to this party to watch some white girl from Maine get Mason Vergered," said Veronica and turned on her heel.

Greta didn't know what that meant. She scrambled to her feet, but the room spun and she found herself on the bed.

"I got it," Carys' voice said from what seemed like far away.

Then warm hands were pushing her hair back.

"You okay?"

"Mmf," Greta said.

"You have some lemonade?"

"Mm-hmm."

"Helen put twice the usual amount of moonshine in," Carys said.

Greta's head spun. It took her a moment to remember who Helen was and what moonshine was. Moonshine. So pretty. The way it looked gilding Carys' brown curls.

When she looked up, she saw that her hand had found its way into Carys' hair, the damp curls dotted with pearls of water that *plock*ed onto the bed.

"Greta, I like you a lot. I think you're so lovely and sweet and intensely hot. But I'm never gonna lie to you about this stuff. So I'm sorry if this wasn't the right time to talk about it, and I'm ready to whenever you are. Okay?"

"Never?"

"Nope. Not even when it would be nicer to."

Greta felt a mix of relief and fear. Then her head started spinning, and she let it fall to the pillow.

"Will you stay for a minute?"

"Yeah, I'll stay as long as you want."

# 18
## GRETA

Greta woke in Carys' arms. It took her a minute to realize they were in Carys' bed rather than her own, or Truman's, or the rich pig people's. Warm light streamed in through the window and twinkled in the cut crystals that hung on the sill, throwing sparkling rainbows of light over them.

"So gay," Greta murmured with an affectionate smile.

Carys kissed her. "I'll show you so gay."

They kissed sleepily, lazily, and Carys nuzzled Greta's neck.

"How're you feeling?" she asked.

Greta took stock. Her head was throbbing and her throat was dry, but physically, she felt better than she'd expected. Emotionally, on the other hand, she felt anxious. Had she ruined everything last night? Would it be horrible and awkward and stressful?

"Okay," she said.

Carys passed her some painkillers and a glass of water. "Good. What are you doing today?"

"Nothing." Greta never did anything. "Um. Gotta walk Horse, but other than that, nothing."

"Want to explore with me?"

Greta sat up. "Wait, really?"

"Yes, really," Carys said, smiling. "Why?"

Greta shook her head. "Nothing."

Carys waited.

"I thought maybe you wouldn't wanna see me again after last night."

Carys sat up too and put her hands on Greta's knees. "Why wouldn't I want to see you again after last night?"

She didn't sound like she was playing oblivious but like she wanted to know Greta's interpretation of what had happened.

"We had…a fight? A difference of opinion. And I got accidentally drunk and fell asleep."

"Having a difference of opinion's really common," she said gently. "Just because I like someone doesn't mean I have to agree with everything they say or do."

"Right."

But Greta couldn't quite swallow. *Wasn't* it a problem if you wanted different things? Believed different things? If you were in a relationship, that is… But they weren't, really, were they? Because Greta would be leaving at the end of the month.

The thought came so quickly and so automatically that she squeezed her eyes shut.

*I don't want to leave. I want to stay here.*

The other voice in her head simply said *But you can't.*

"What's going on for you right now?" Carys asked.

"Ugh. Voices in my head fighting." Greta rolled her eyes at herself, hoping for levity. But Carys nodded so sincerely that Greta took a deep breath and went on. "I want to stay here. And there's this voice in my head just saying over and over, *You can't.* And it's…I don't know how to make it shut

up. It makes me feel guilty and freaked the fuck out and—"
She broke off because she was scared she was about to start
crying.

"Why guilty?"

"Because," Greta croaked, "I don't want to disappoint
my family. They've always been there for me. I know I bitch
about them a lot, but I don't know what I'd do without them.
They're all I've ever known, and if they leave me—" Tears
welled in her eyes.

"Hey, okay, come here."

Carys' strong arms wrapped around her, and Greta let the
tears come. She tried to stay quiet, but it was no use. Carys
stroked her back as she cried.

"You were talking about feeling guilty to move here and
leave your family. But then you said you're worried they'll
leave *you*. Why would they leave you?"

Greta hadn't meant to say that, but once it was out of her
mouth, she realized it was true. She wasn't just afraid of letting
them down, although that had been what she concentrated on
because it was what she could control. Tears leaked from the
corners of her eyes, and she ducked her chin.

"Because if I leave, what if they don't…"

"Love you anymore?"

Greta nodded miserably.

"Oh, sweetheart," Carys said. Her voice was exquisitely
gentle. "If your family stops loving you because you make a
choice that's best for yourself, that's not love. That's control."

Greta sobbed.

She knew her parents loved her. She knew her sisters loved
her—even Sadie. So why was she so damn scared?

"They do love me," she choked out.

"I believe you," Carys said. She stroked Greta's back and her hair and her cheeks.

"But they'd be so hurt if I leave." And if Greta hurt them, they could hurt her back.

"Why would they be hurt?"

"Because it means I don't love them."

"Does it?"

"No!" But that was what they'd think, wouldn't they? That she was abandoning them, breaking the unspoken Russakoff covenant of sticking together, their family unit against the world.

"You think they'll interpret you leaving as not loving them?"

She nodded.

Well, okay, not all of them would.

Maggie wouldn't. Maggie would think it was kick-ass if she moved to New Orleans. She wasn't even going to be on the island after this semester. Tillie would miss her, but she'd never be mad about it. Sadie would make her feel bad. But Sadie made her feel bad even when she was there.

Her dad would miss her too. But he would get over it. He got over everything.

Adelaide. What would her twin think if she left? They'd spent their whole childhoods doing everything together. But in the last few years, Greta realized they had less and less in common. She loved her sister fiercely and knew the love was returned. But they couldn't spend all their time together effortlessly anymore. Their interests had grown in different directions.

Her mom. Greta loved her mother, but they just didn't mesh. She didn't like how her mom treated her. Like an extension of herself. Something she had rights over, like an arm or a leg. Like she understood everything about Greta, only she didn't—she just interpreted it all as if Greta felt the way she'd feel in the same situation.

When Greta would tell her, no, that wasn't how she felt, her mother would look at her with surprise. *Oh*, she'd sniff. And that would be all. But Greta *knew* that it meant *How did you go from being a person I knew and understood to one who insists on thinking the opposite of everything I do just to prove you're not like me?*

How would she take Greta's leaving? Like a power outage or a fraudulent credit card charge: something that wasn't behaving as she wanted it to.

And damn, that didn't paint her mom in a very flattering light at all.

She said as much.

Carys replied, "When I told my mom that I didn't want to see her anymore, she told me I was ungrateful. That she'd put her whole life on hold to raise me. That everything she should have been got messed up because of me. And now I had the audacity to not even want her in my life." Carys shook her head. "I knew how she was by then. She would blame the sky for raining if it meant avoiding responsibility. I told her it was her choice to have me. She could have had an abortion. She could have given me up for adoption. Hell, she could've left me at a fire station. But she chose to have me and raise me. And now I was a person, which meant I got to make my own choices. She started sobbing and screaming about how I wanted to punish her and hurt her."

"Damn," Greta said. "That's...that's so horrible. I can't even imagine."

"It was all about her. It wasn't about me or about my choice to cut her out of my life at that time. Now, my mom's a covert narcissist, and I'm not saying that your family is. My point is that sometimes you have to hear an exaggeration of something to realize when it's happening a little bit."

Greta let that sink in.

Wasn't she describing something very similar? If she moved here, it would be about her. Her choice. Her desire. Her life. And if her family made it all about them...maybe that wasn't her problem?

Her heart leapt, but her traitorous mind rebelled. *Making decisions all for yourself that hurt other people is the definition of selfishness. Don't you think Mom and Dad have done things for you that they didn't want to do? Of course they have! That's just part of being an adult.*

"Do you think," Greta began slowly, "do you think it's selfish to make a choice you *know* will hurt someone?"

Carys cupped her cheeks. "No."

"Even if you *know* it will?"

"No. You don't hurt people by choosing yourself over them. They hurt themselves with what they think about it. It's not your job to fold yourself up so small that your edges never bump into anyone else, babe. What kind of life is that?"

Greta thought about those words the rest of the day. As they made eggs and toast and ate in the back garden with Teacup. As they caught the streetcar to the Garden District. As they wandered along Canal Street, trying on ridiculous outfits in the secondhand stores and choosing their dream furniture from outrageously priced antiques.

She couldn't remember a time when she hadn't folded herself as small as she could. Couldn't remember a time she didn't consider choosing what she wanted over what someone else wanted selfish.

Growing up with four siblings, it had been drilled into her at an early age: you did what served the greatest number. There was never going to be enough money for each of them to get the DVD they wanted, so they got the one they could all compromise on. They couldn't buy each of them a new sweater of their choosing because they all had different favorite colors, so they got one that wasn't overtly hated by any of them.

What that had resulted in her whole childhood was everyone watching movies they didn't hate but didn't love. Everyone wearing a sweater that was the slightly wrong size and a color they didn't like. Not a big deal when you were talking about a movie or a sweater.

But when you were talking about choices that affected your whole life, didn't compromise result in everyone getting something that no one really wanted?

*What kind of life is that?*

A wasted one.

"Okay," Carys said. "This is one of my favorite spots."

They stood in front of a cemetery with high stone walls and an iron gate thrown open to the sidewalk lined with live oaks.

There was a small cemetery on Owl Island, but it didn't look anything like this. It was crooked and sea-blasted, stones worn almost blank by salt and time. This was laid out like a small city, with sidewalks in rows and crypts that stood above the ground. Each was grand and some even had wrought-iron fencing around them like a house. The wall they entered through looked like safety-deposit boxes. Carys explained that they held remains.

"The aboveground tombs are expensive, so this is a cheaper option. Also, the tombs can't be opened for a year after a body is interred. So if it's a family tomb and someone else in the family dies, say, eight months later, they can't reopen their family crypt, so lots of families have a secondary spot in the wall to put a body in until the crypt can be opened again and the body permanently interred."

"Why can't they be opened?" Greta asked, visions of ghosts and vampires swimming deliciously in her head.

"I think it was probably a health thing to prevent diseases back in the day? A lot of people here died from yellow fever."

"Oh," Greta said, slightly disappointed it wasn't more supernatural. "That makes sense."

"I see. You wanted some spooky shit, huh?"

Greta grinned. "Kinda."

Carys took her hand and they walked through the narrow pathways, weaving between tombs and around gravestones until they came to a tomb near another gated entrance to the cemetery.

This was an aboveground tomb, but where most had a flat slab of marble or stone affixed to the front with decorative fastenings, this tomb's was missing. She could see directly into the open crypt. It looked like an oven, with a slab in the middle and space above and below it.

Carys crouched down, and Greta followed suit.

"If you look closely, you can see some bones still in there," Carys said, pointing to the back corner of the tomb.

Something white gleamed in the dimness of the dirt, and Greta squinted to make it out. It could've been bone. It could also have been plastic or stone, but for the sake of the spooky vibes she wanted, she chose to believe Carys' story.

"I'm kinda surprised no one's taken the bones," she said.

"Oh, babe, if you steal bones from a grave in New Orleans, on your own head be it." Carys shivered.

"I didn't know you believed in the ghost tour stories you tell."

"What I like about ghost stories is that even if things didn't happen precisely the way the story has come to be told, they still point to the fears and taboos that are real." She shrugged. "Do I believe stealing a bone from the cemetery would immediately bring the ghost of that person down on me and spell my imminent death? Not really. But I think that the kind of person who would disturb the remains of someone who's died—of someone's beloved family member—is also the kind of person who would make other choices in their life that would lead to chaos, discourtesy, and negative consequences. So I guess it's a shorthand?"

"Like a math formula," Greta said.

"Yeah, kind of. Not that it's guaranteed every time, but it's suggestive anyway."

"That was a very practical answer. But *do* you believe in ghosts? Or vampires or any of that stuff?"

After a minute, Carys said, "I believe there are things I don't know or understand. I believe there's stuff that happens that can't be explained by the materialism that quote unquote 'realists' insist on. I guess I believe there's stuff now that was unthinkable five hundred years ago, because we didn't know about it, so why wouldn't the same be true of five hundred years from now?"

Greta nodded.

"What about you?"

As a child, Greta had wandered along the rocky shoreline

of Owl Island with Adelaide. They had stared out at the bay until their eyes crossed, trying to see mermaids emerge from the prickling foam. For a year or so, Greta refused to turn her back on the water, convinced that one of the creatures that lurked within it would scramble onto land and fell her with a single strike of its fangs to her vulnerable throat.

It had been a story as real to her as Tillie's fear of the dark or Maggie's brief but intense conviction that their house would catch on fire.

With time, she grew out of it—or perhaps grew *into* the… what had Carys called it? The materialism that realists insisted on?

But she'd never stopped hoping they were real.

Because if the scary supernatural things were real, then it stood to reason the wonderful, magical ones were too. And Greta had always, always hoped to be in the presence of magic.

"I don't know about vampires and ghosts specifically. But I know that I want the chance to experience magic."

The second it was out of her mouth, she braced for a feeling of foolishness, but it never came. Instead, Carys' eyes burned and she found herself pressed up against the side of a tomb and kissed breathless.

A lizard scampered away between the sun-warmed stones.

A spark kindled between them, and Greta mapped Carys' lush curves, sliding a hand from the small of her back down to squeeze her gorgeous ass. Carys shuddered and pulled away. She grabbed Greta's hand and, with a fiery look, pulled her to the corner of the cemetery, into a circle of tombs overhung by the branches of a willow tree.

Carys backed her up against the brick wall, under the cover of the tree. She kissed Greta's lips slowly, then with more tongue, until Greta was moaning. Carys' touch sent fire through her veins and made her cunt pulse.

Carys slid a hand into her jeans and traced her damp slit. When she circled her clit with a clever finger, Greta gasped and buried her face in Carys' shoulder.

"God, you feel like magic," Carys murmured.

"You feel like magic," Greta tried to reply, but it came out a lust-slurred garble.

She squeezed her eyes shut and concentrated on Carys' fingers, teasing her flesh until she was wet and swollen and squirming, trying to get contact everywhere.

"You're so fucking hot," Carys said, voice gone low and rough. She pressed her hips against Greta's thigh and ground against her, shuddering.

Carys' fingers slid inside her, and Greta's legs went limp. She squeezed around those fingers, and Carys worked her expertly as she murmured all the things she wanted to do in Greta's ear.

"Oh, fuck," Greta groaned. She was a tinderbox, a fire-cracker, a moaning, panting mess of pleasure waiting for the lick of flame that would explode her.

Carys leaned in close and scraped her teeth against Greta's neck.

"Fuck, yes, please," Greta begged against Carys' skin.

Carys hummed her pleasure and sucked at Greta's neck. Paroxysms of pleasure shot from her neck to her crotch, and when Carys closed her teeth around the spot and pressed her gorgeous tits against Greta's, the spark flared.

"Oh god, I'm gonna come," Greta said through clenched teeth.

"Yes, fuck." Carys' voice was midnight and then she went

back to biting Greta's neck and fucking her to within an inch of her life.

Tremors of pleasure began to shake Greta from her core, and when Carys swirled a thumb over her clit, her body clamped down in an orgasm so explosive that she nearly slammed her head into the wall. She screamed silently, biting on her own fist to dampen the sound.

Carys curled her fingertips over Greta's G-spot, and another wave of orgasm gripped her.

She rode it out, blasted apart by pleasure, her heart thumping and the blood pulsing through her, leaving shivers of orgasm in its wake. When Carys slid her fingers out and brushed Greta's clit again, she was so oversensitized that she jerked away and wrapped Carys in her arms to keep her still.

"Ohmygooodd," she moaned. "You're outrageous."

Carys hummed her satisfaction and laid a kiss on Greta's hair.

Suddenly, Carys tensed, and Greta tuned back in to the world around her. Voices were approaching, and she could hear someone say, "Is this the corner where…"

Carys turned them so her own back was to the approaching tourists and slid her hand out of Greta's pants. With a dark look, she licked her fingertips, and shuddered with lust.

Two women rounded the corner and pointed to the tomb next to Greta and Carys, talking about it. They wore khakis and cotton sweaters and looked like they might be mother and daughter or perhaps sisters. They were reading from a printout, and both had cameras around their necks.

Carys gave a casual wave as she stood in front of Greta. "Enjoy the boneyard," she called jovially as they walked off.

Greta snorted. "Oh god," she groaned and collapsed onto

Carys' shoulder. She concentrated on making her legs support her weight and then pulled Carys back toward her. "What can I do for you?" she asked, running an appreciative hand over Carys' breasts.

"Mmm, nothing. I feel great."

"Are you sure?"

"I'm very, very sure," Carys said.

She raised the hand that had been inside Greta to her nose and breathed in deeply. Greta trembled and flushed. She buttoned her jeans, then kissed Carys deeply.

"That was magical, thank you."

"We make our own magic, darlin'," Carys said.

# 19
# TRUMAN

It was an uncommonly sunny day for December—or so Ash said; Truman was used to it being a pleasant seventy-five degrees all month—and they were in Thorn. Ash was on the phone with a local farm on the mainland, discussing wild-flower sourcing (and rolling his eyes rather dramatically at Truman in response to whatever was being said), and Truman was finishing up his own work for the day before he could get to the project he was excited about: designing a new logo for Thorn.

Ash said a relieved goodbye and buried his face in his hands on the counter in front of Truman. Over the last several days, Truman had learned that Ash *loved* having his hair touched, and he couldn't help but see this most recent flop as a bid for him to run his fingers through it.

He scratched Ash's scalp, and Ash let out a rumbling moan that tumbled through Truman from his scalp to his crotch.

The door swung open in a clanging of bells, and Ash jerked upright. It was Carla Muskee, lugging a large cardboard box.

"Hi, Ms. Muskee," Ash said as Truman said, "Hello, Carla."

"Heard you were lookin' for jars," she said and slid the box onto the counter. "This the kinda thing you're after?"

Truman peered in at a jumble of different sized glass jars. A few had brands stamped into the glass, but most were exactly what they needed.

"Yes, thank you!" Truman said.

Ash narrowed his eyes. "Who'd you hear that from?"

"Oh, here and there," Carla said with an expansive wave and a wink at Truman. "Also heard you might be looking for artists' work to sell in the shop. Ted's been doing these watercolors lately. Good stuff. Should I tell him you want them?"

"Oh, um…" Ash looked desperately at Truman.

"Okay, so what we're looking for are greeting cards with original art on the front," Truman explained. "So that when people come in to buy flowers, they can get a card to go with them."

Carla nodded. "All right, I'll let him know."

"Best if they're flower related probably," Truman added. "Wait, is that your son who makes the sweaters?"

"Mm-hmm."

Truman wondered if there was anything to be made of that. He could see the bullet journal page of artisan craft ideas now…

"So I'll tell everyone you want more jars, then?"

"Yeah, thank you."

She gave a crisp nod and moved to the door. At the last moment, she turned back to Ash. "It's good what you're doing here, son. I'm proud of you."

And before Ash could say anything, she closed the door firmly behind her.

Truman caught the soft look in Ash's eyes before they became shrewd.

"Here and there, huh?" Ash said.

"Well, when I stopped to get coffee at Bob's this morning, I mentioned it to him because it looked like he had a million jars lying around. I guess I should've remembered that if you say something to one person on Main Street, you've put out a neon sign."

"Thanks," Ash said. "Once Ms. Muskee knows, everyone knows. So I guess I'll clear out some shelves in the back to store them."

"Yay!" Truman couldn't help feeling giddy with excitement. There was nothing like seeing an idea become a reality.

↔

By four that afternoon, Truman had to admit they had a huge problem. It seemed like everyone in town had dropped off jars. One after another, they came into Thorn with boxes of jars. And not just business owners but random people on the island.

Truman had turned someone away who'd just brought in a bag of dirty peanut butter jars.

"We need to be clearer about what kind of jars we're looking for," Truman said, trying not to breathe in the stench of old peanut butter.

"Yeah, good luck with that," Ash said, and Truman realized that maybe there had been something to his intention to write an email to the local shopkeepers detailing what he wanted.

But the straw that broke the camel's back was someone

named Darnell Waters. There was the beeping that signaled a truck backing up and then a shout from outside that sounded like "Yo, Ashleigh!"

Ash let out a long-suffering sigh, and Truman followed him outside. There, half in the street, was a garbage truck.

A skinny white guy with shockingly blond hair jumped down from the cab and pointed to the back. "You wanna go through and get the jars?" he said.

Truman couldn't tell if he was serious, joking, or being an asshole.

"You know what, Darnell, I'm actually good on jars for the moment. I've gotten a lot of them today."

"Oh," he said. "There are some really good ones in there, though, probably."

"Yeah, I appreciate it, but I'm not going to sort through the recycling for them. That's why I asked people to save them for me."

"Oh." Darnell seemed disappointed. "Maybe next week?"

"Nah, I'm honestly never going to want to sort through the recycling for them. But thanks for thinking of me, Darnell."

Darnell climbed back into the cab and rolled the window down.

"Okay, well, I'll save you some good ones, though. See you next week."

He waved and drove away.

Ash let out a bone-deep sigh and lifted his face to the sky.

"I'm sorry," Truman said. "I did this, and I'm sorry."

"It's fine," Ash said. "It was nice of you to tell people for me, really. You couldn't know that people really, *really* like to help."

He said *help* like you might say *desecrate the dead*.

"Yeah, I think I'm getting that. Do you know that guy?"

"Yup, we went to high school together. He…uh…means well?"

"Clearly," Truman murmured.

↔

That night, Truman was working on a spread in his bullet journal and listening to *ShadowCast*, which made him miss Horse. He'd given up on having a notebook for Ash. Ash didn't write anything down, just seemed to remember everything. But Truman liked a clear accounting of everything, so he'd been keeping it in his own journal.

Now, when he finished the day's entry for Thorn, though, he found himself jotting down ideas for a new section of his bullet journal on some scrap paper.

It started with doodles of flowers. Since he'd been spending so much time at Thorn, he'd begun appreciating them more. Especially since Ash kept sending him home with little bouquets. He sniffed the one Ash had made him today. It was a purple flower he always forgot the name of and some delicate Queen Anne's lace.

He was sketching a border around the page, made of stems with the flowers exploding in the corners. Truman wasn't the best artist, but his lines were minimal and clean, and he felt he captured the essence of whatever he was drawing. Once he'd created the floral border, he wrote: *Stickers, dividers, bookmarks, printables, lists.*

He stared at the list he'd just made and at the bouquet in front of him, then around Greta's house, filled with carnivorous plants in all their strange glory.

He pulled out his phone and messaged Charlotte and Germaine.

What if I started my bullet journal Instagram with the goal of designing my own line of planner stuff?

Charlotte wrote back immediately: **Yes, do it.**

"Well, that was startlingly positive," Truman muttered.

Germaine's response didn't disappoint: *Hellllll yes you should you'd be brilliant!!!*

Truman flipped back through the last eleven months of his bullet journal. There was a lot of material there. A lot of things that he could turn into pages people might like to buy and use.

He didn't hate his job. It had a lot of advantages for him, which was great, and the work itself was okay. But the idea of doing it forever was depressing. What if this could be a way out? A way of creating a different cash flow that might eventually allow him to leave it?

He drew a bath and slid into the hot, herb-scented water. This time, it wasn't a bath of sadness and wine but one of possibility, and he texted Ash: You should carry floral bath salts ;)

$$\longleftrightarrow$$

The invitation to dinner had been hand-delivered, slid under the front door when Truman woke up.

MAISEY AND DON OSGOOD INVITE YOU! A HOLIDAY DINNER, TONIGHT, 7:00 P.M. FESTIVE DRESS ENCOURAGED; GIFTS DISCOURAGED. WE'D LOVE TO SEE YOU THERE!

*Tonight* had been written in over the scratched-out date, so clearly most of the invitations had gone out earlier.

Ash was attending the dinner as well, he found out when he texted What does "festive dress" mean?, so they walked over together.

When they got to Maisey and Don's house, it became clear that "festive dress" meant everything from Christmas sweaters to puffy-painted and bejeweled red turtlenecks, from spangled green dresses to somber tweed jackets paired with maroon ties.

Ash was wearing jeans and the pastel blue sweater that made him look utterly huggable. ("It said festive dress was 'encouraged,' not mandatory," he'd explained when Truman asked what was festive about it.)

Truman himself had borrowed a red sweater that he'd found in Greta's closet. He didn't think she'd mind, but it was rather snug under the arms and a bit short in the sleeves, so he tugged them up to the elbow as if he was warm, though he wasn't.

"Truman, I'm so glad you made it," Maisey greeted them. "Sorry for the last-minute invite, but you weren't even here when they went out."

"Thanks so much for having me. Is this an annual tradition?"

"It is. We've been having these dinners since we got married. Is that Greta's sweater?"

"How can you tell?" he said, startled.

"Greta wears it to this dinner every year. Even though the Russakoffs are Jewish, Greta always said she didn't have any blue sweaters for Chanukah so she went with this one."

Truman smiled at the idea that he and Greta had the same impulse, and as soon as they'd made their way inside, he took a selfie and texted it to her.

*are you taking over my life!?* she wrote back with a GIF from a movie he didn't recognize that said *SWF*.

"So you see," Ash said, "I'm wearing festive clothes because I'm wearing a Chanukah sweater."

Truman smiled. "Did you know Greta wore this sweater here every year?"

"No. I haven't been in years, actually."

"Oh. Did you not get invited? How *do* people get invited?"

"Nah. I was gone for a long time, and then since I've gotten back...I guess I haven't felt much like doing this kind of thing."

"So what made you come this year?"

Ash squirmed and blinked owlishly. "Oh, well. I don't know. Just felt like it, I guess."

Before Truman could tease him about that being a total nonanswer, Don came downstairs and began making the rounds. When he reached them, he slapped Ash on the back and squeezed Truman's shoulder.

"Good to see you boys here. Ash, glad you changed your mind. Make sure you get some of the sweet potato casserole. I made it using my secret ingredient." He winked. "And don't bother asking, because I'm taking it to my grave." He turned to leave. "Oh, and the eggnog's got quite a kick."

"You changed your mind?" Truman asked, eyeing the buffet table for the eggnog. "How come?"

Ash mumbled something that sounded like "*Fridunnow.*"

Truman cocked his head in question, and Ash let out a sigh.

"Because I wanted to hang out with you," Ash said.

Truman felt like a balloon had inflated in his heart and he was being pulled upward by the string. Since their kiss in the cave, they had sat close and hugged, and Truman had touched Ash's hair a lot. But they hadn't kissed again. In fact, Truman had started angsting about whether maybe Ash had only been moved in that moment to kiss him but wasn't actually into it.

But Ash's face was not the face of a man who wasn't into it.

Aware his mouth was hanging open, Truman closed it with an audible snap. He slid an arm through Ash's and squeezed.

"Whaddaya say we get some of this eggnog?"

"I hate eggnog, but yeah." Ash smiled and squeezed Truman's arm back.

The dinner was served buffet style, with guests filling their plates and mingling in Don and Maisey's living and dining rooms. As the night went on and the eggnog and wine flowed, Truman found himself hearing snatches of gossip about everyone in town. He also heard no fewer than five people exclaim about how surprised they were to see Ash.

Truman found himself drawn into a discussion about business tax itemization and left with several requests to do people's taxes. Then Ash subtly gestured him over to the corner. Assuming Ash was looking for a rescue, he squared his shoulders and approached.

"Ginny, this is my friend Truman. Truman, Ginny does that journaling thing you do."

"You do bullet journaling?" he exclaimed and was delighted when she nodded. His delight grew when she pulled her journal out of her bag.

"I need a cover for it," she said idly, smoothing a bent corner as she opened it to show him.

Truman mentally added *protective covers* to the list of things he could potentially sell.

Ginny's style was completely different than Truman's. She

used a lot of stickers and washi tape, which made for a riot-ously colorful journal. She also tried different media through-out the year—watercolors one month, colored pencils the next. Truman admired her flexibility.

They got to discussing the spreads they were most recently using, and Truman found himself confiding in her.

"I've been thinking of starting up a little side business, actually. Designing stickers and page borders but also print-able spreads kind of based on my style of hand lettering."

He showed her a few pictures he'd taken of his bullet jour-nal spreads.

"God, these are gorgeous," she said. "Totally not my style, but I have a friend who does BuJo, and she's always looking for bold, minimalist stuff like this. So much of the stuff that's out there is a little more flourishy, you know?"

Truman nodded. "Yeah, I feel like it could be something people might be into," he ventured.

"If you're interested, my friend—different friend—has an online shop where she sells her stuff. I can send you the link if you wanna check it out. And I'm sure she'd be happy to talk with you about how she started it. All that stuff."

"Yes, please! I'd love that."

$$\longleftrightarrow$$

And so Truman left the party with a promise from Ginny that she'd connect him with her friend and a date to go over to Ginny's for coffee and to discuss bullet journaling the follow-ing week. He was giddy with it (and the eggnog didn't hurt) as he and Ash waved their goodbyes and ventured out into the cold night.

He slid his arm through Ash's and tried to skip. Of course, since he hadn't informed Ash of this plan, it was not successful.

Ash chuckled. "Are you tipsy?"

"Nah, just happy. Well, a tiny bit tipsy, but mostly happy. I like Ginny. Thanks for introducing us. Did you go to high school with her too?"

"Ginny? No, Ginny moved here a few years ago when she married Mort Hazeldon. She's, like, ten years older than me. Do we look the same age?"

Truman came to a halt and made a show of peering at Ash's face. Of course, this was really just an excuse, because Ash's face was quite wonderful and he enjoyed looking at it. When Ash became uncomfortable being stared at, Truman shrugged.

"I'm terrible at guessing people's ages, actually. Everyone twenty to forty looks the same age, basically. Unless they dress like parents. Then they look older."

"That why you dress like a parent? To look older?" Ash teased.

Truman feigned outrage for a moment, but he knew it was true. He'd once heard someone say that you either dressed to express who you were or to hide it. His khaki pants, plain button-down shirts, and subdued ties were perfect for work, but they certainly didn't express his personality.

"Okay, well, why do you dress like…however you dress?"

"I just wear what I like," Ash said simply. "You want to come in for a bit?"

They were standing outside Thorn.

"Definitely."

Bruce was ecstatic to see them, and Ash took him outside for a turn around the block while Truman made them some hot tea.

When Ash returned, they settled on the couch, intertwining their legs since there wasn't quite enough room.

"That was fun," Truman said. "People here are really nice."

"Yeah, they're all right."

"They seem to like you an awful lot."

"They love my mom. They feel sorry for me," Ash said matter-of-factly.

"Do you want to know something embarrassing?"

"Always." Ash gave a ghost of a smile.

"Well, I know you're not sure about being back here, and you came because of your mom. But that's a great reason. You know why I'm in New Orleans?"

He made sure Ash was looking right at him.

"Because this guy I was dating three years ago told me to stay. No, really," he said at Ash's expression of doubt. "It's way worse than you're even imagining. Tyler and I hooked up at this party senior year of college, and the next weekend, when everyone was discussing what they were doing after college, I said I didn't know what to do, and he was like, 'You should stay here. We'd have fun.' So I did. I signed a lease. I got a job. I was grateful that someone had told me what to do so I didn't have to decide on my own. And I like New Orleans. I've had a good time the last three years. But come on…"

"But you seem so…decisive," Ash said.

Truman snorted. "I mean, I am when it's about other people's stuff. I don't know. My friends say I'm bad at advocating for my own needs but I'm good at meeting other people's."

"Are they right?"

Truman sighed. He was fairly sure you weren't supposed to air all your worst qualities to people you had crushes on.

But…maybe that was exactly why his other relationships didn't work out. He'd been trying so hard to be the version of himself that was *best* or *most palatable*. Wouldn't it be a refreshing change to go into things knowing someone's actual weaknesses?

"Yeah, it is true, I guess. I go along with what other people want too much. I make up stories about why it's all fine, and meanwhile, I just decide to change what I wanted to fit with their needs. It's…pretty pathetic, huh?"

Ash's brow furrowed. "Not pathetic. But probably not great for you." He picked at a split in the couch cushion. "Have you been doing that with me?"

Truman started to say no right away, then forced himself to really think about it. Had he? "Well. No, actually."

"Okay, good. Don't, if you can help it," Ash said.

Truman let out a bark of laughter at the idea that he could just *stop* doing the thing that had been his biggest problem in relationships. Then he started to giggle because what if—*what if?!*—that was actually all it took to stop doing something that didn't serve you. To…stop doing it.

"Are you okay?"

Truman was lost in helpless giggles, and those turned into hiccoughs. He nodded, then shook his head.

"What if…what if that's…all…it took?" he choked out, hysterical with a laughter that had nothing to do with humor and everything to do with absurdism.

Ash looked at him strangely, clearly not seeing the humor. "I think that is all it takes," he ventured. "It's just difficult to do it."

That made Truman laugh harder. "I'm sorry, I'm sorry," he said. "It's not funny. I just can't stop laughing. Phew." He breathed deeply through his nose in an attempt to get himself under control. There was something about Ash that made him feel like he was pulling an all-nighter with friends all the time. Something giddy and special and difficult, but you knew it was going to be so worth it. "Why do I have so much fun hanging out with you?" he burst out.

Ash's eyes went wide. "I have *no* idea. People don't think I'm fun."

"What? Why?"

Ash shrugged.

"To be fair, I didn't say *you* were fun. I said *I* have fun with you," Truman clarified in the spirit of not subjugating his own needs, desires, or feelings.

"That's very true," Ash acknowledged with a small smile. He tucked his hair behind his ear. "I have a lot of fun with you too."

"Yeah?"

"Yup."

"Sleepover!" Truman crowed. It tracked in his head, because of thinking about an all-nighter, but Ash's eyes got wide once more.

"Yeah?" he said.

There was something reluctantly hopeful about his expression, like he didn't quite believe Truman meant it. All of which made Truman even more determined to show Ash that he loved spending time with him and did find it fun.

Truman nodded. "Movie?" he suggested. "What's a good sleepover movie? My sisters used to have specific fun sleepover movies, but whenever I went to sleepovers, everyone wanted to watch horror movies." Truman shuddered.

"I'm not a fan," Ash said.

"No, me neither."

They scrolled through their options, discussing things they'd seen and wanted to see and weren't in the mood for, and eventually Ash tossed the remote between them and said, "I really don't care what we watch."

Truman picked it up. He'd wanted to find the perfect movie, but maybe there was no such thing. "Okay, let's see what the universe wants us to watch," he said, then closed his eyes and began to scroll up and down, back and forth. He counted to fifteen, then pressed Play.

He opened his eyes to see what they were watching.

"Oh my god, seriously?"

Ash snickered.

It was a documentary about metal refineries in Canada.

"Lemme try that again," Truman offered.

This time, he landed on some animated children's program featuring a magical bear and her friends.

"Er?"

"I really don't care," Ash said.

And Truman realized Ash meant it. He didn't mean he didn't mind which of five things he liked they watched—he honest to god did not care. Which either meant he was totally disengaged. Or…

Ash's arm slid around Truman's shoulders. "This okay?" he murmured.

"It's perfect," Truman responded truthfully.

He let his body melt into Ash's. Ash smelled so good. Truman wondered what he smelled like everywhere. He put a hand on Ash's thigh and traced designs there with his fingertips, appreciating the give of skin and the resistance of muscle beneath.

On the screen, the animals frolicked in some kind of submarine, but Truman didn't pay it any mind. He was utterly concentrated on the tiny movements of Ash's fingers against his arm. Every nerve ending sparked with fireworks at the contact.

They turned toward each other, foreheads pressed together and limb heavy against limb.

Truman's breath was slow and shallow, and he closed his eyes to breathe Ash in.

"Truman," Ash murmured.

"Can I kiss you?" Truman asked.

He opened his eyes to find Ash's blue-gray gaze intent, his pupils blown. "Fuck, please. I thought maybe you didn't want to."

"I thought *you* didn't want to."

Ash smiled and slid a hand to Truman's jaw. "I assure you, I want to."

Truman brushed his lips over Ash's. He couldn't believe he got to do this. Then he leaned in for a real kiss. Ash's lips were full and firm, and he kissed with a desperate sweetness that stirred Truman's desire to a pulsing need deep in his gut.

He couldn't get close enough.

Truman threw a leg over Ash's thighs, and Ash hauled him onto his lap.

"Fuck, yes, c'mere."

Ash held him close, and Truman deepened his kiss, sweeping his tongue against Ash's and sucking on his mouth to taste every inch of it. Ash shuddered when Truman ran fingertips down the side of his neck, so he pressed kisses there instead. When he licked at the crook of Ash's neck, he jerked and groaned.

Truman latched on and sucked at the skin there, which resulted in a gratifying shudder and Ash's hand clutching at his back.

"Oh my god," Ash groaned as Truman redoubled his efforts.

Before he knew it, Truman found himself lying on top of Ash on the sofa, their bodies perfectly aligned.

Truman was hot, his skin so sensitive every touch set it on fire.

He pulled his shirt off, needing to be rid of it.

"Can I?" he asked, tugging on the hem of Ash's sweater.

Ash stripped it off quickly, and when their mouths met again, the heat of Ash's chest and stomach, lightly furred and firm, made Truman moan in appreciation.

"You're so fucking hot," Ash said, brow furrowed almost like it vexed him.

"Look who's talking," Truman said and kissed a path down his belly. He made an interrogative noise, and Ash kicked his pants off. Truman did the same. Ash's cock lay straining toward his belly, and his eyes burned hot as he watched Truman.

Slowly, Truman lowered himself down on Ash once more. Their erections met and Truman had to bite his lip to keep from crying out with the exquisite sensation.

"Lemme hear you," Ash murmured.

The shaky, lustful noises that spilled out of Truman's mouth as they ground together embarrassed him at first. But they clearly turned Ash on, so he decided to stop worrying about it. Soon, they were thrusting against each other and groaning.

Using muscles that Truman had appreciated but never seen in action before, Ash crunched up and pulled Truman higher on his body.

"Can I touch you?" he asked, cupping Truman's ass.

"You can touch me anywhere," Truman breathed out.

"You have the most gorgeous ass," Ash murmured. "Every time your back's to me, I want to walk right up to you and press myself against you, feel your perfect ass."

Truman groaned.

"Don't stop talking. Damn."

"Yeah? Okay."

Ash ran a fingertip between Truman's cheeks and lingered on his hole.

"I want to press against you, then pull your pants down, bend you over, and bury my face right here."

He whirled his finger, making Truman's breath catch. Exquisite frissons were shooting through him, scrambling his ability to think.

"I want to spread you open behind the counter, right there in the open so that if a customer came in, you'd just have to wait. Then I would take the softest rose I could find, and I would tease your hole with it until you were begging me to open you up and fuck you until you screamed."

"Oh my *god*," Truman groaned.

"Too much?" Ash asked.

"No no no, nope, no. Definitely not."

Ash kissed his cheek. "C'mere."

Truman was led to Ash's bed, mind utterly scrambled with lust.

"Can I play with you?" Ash asked, breath hot against Truman's thighs.

"You can do whatever the hell you want with me. No, seriously, please."

Ash chuckled softly. Truman heard the sound of a pop, and

then Ash's fingers were back, rubbing around his hole, slick with lube.

Truman pressed his cheek to the bed and tried to shove his ass back onto Ash's fingers, but Ash seemed to enjoy tormenting him.

"So damn sweet," Ash said. "You're so hungry for me." He rubbed Truman's hole so slowly that Truman felt light-headed.

"Oh my god, don't stop," he begged.

"I won't."

Ash kissed the base of his spine, then slid a thick finger inside him. For a moment, Truman's body resisted, then his muscles gave way, and all he felt was the exquisite intrusion.

Ash explored his body with a singular focus, noting every moan, gasp, and twitch to map Truman's pleasure, until it felt like he'd turned to jelly around Ash's fingers. An insistent buzz grew and grew, and when Ash curled his finger against Truman's prostate, a wash of exquisite pleasure overwhelmed him.

"God, you're so perfect," Ash muttered.

"You're so perfect," Truman tried to reply, but it came out garbled.

"Do you want to come like this?" Ash asked.

Truman nodded and then shook his head and nodded again.

Ash smiled indulgently, then eased his fingers out. Truman keened with the loss but Ash just kissed him, then flipped him onto his back. He slid his fingers back in, and from this angle, the pressure was unbearably perfect. Truman felt like he was unspooling into a supernova of pleasure, bits of him lost among the stars.

Ash's erection was a heavy brand against his thigh, and he

cupped his hand over it, feeling Ash's breath catch. Ash thrust against him as he worked him with his fingers until they were both moaning and sweating.

Ash closed his other hand around Truman's cock, and Truman nearly screamed, so utterly sensitized that he almost couldn't stand it.

"Omigod, don't stop," he begged. "Please, please don't stop."

Ash, eyelids heavy with lust, did not stop. He swirled his fingertips over Truman's prostate with such perfect pressure that Truman felt his muscles beginning to tense. A light stroke over the head of his cock, and he was gone.

"Omigod, omigod, Ash, I'm gonna, ohhhh god."

Truman's back bowed off the bed and his orgasm ripped through him, locking every muscle in ecstasy. He clawed at the bedsheets and grabbed Ash's shoulder to anchor him to reality as his body shuddered out of his control.

He was vaguely aware of Ash murmuring warm, appreciative things as he came back to himself. He groaned and then gasped as his body twitched with an aftershock of pleasure.

"Truman, god," Ash groaned. He was looking at Truman with such affection and admiration.

"You," Truman accused. But there was no end to the sentiment. "Can I touch you?"

"Yeah, if you want. Um, I'm…it's not gonna take much."

Ash's teeth were gritted and his chest flushed. Truman eased him down beside him and slid his fist over Ash's hard flesh. He stroked slowly and firmly, watching Ash's cheeks flush red and his eyes roll back in his head. He considered teasing him but decided to save it for next time. Right now, he just wanted to see Ash come his brains out.

Truman added a little lube and then stroked him hard and

fast, pressing a finger under his balls. Ash's body locked up, mouth opening on a yell.

His orgasm was explosive, nearly doubling him over, and Truman didn't think he'd ever seen anything hotter than Ash's fist driving into the bed with pleasure, then pulling the pillow over his own face as he cried out his release.

Truman lay down next to him and gently removed the pillow from his face.

"Fuuuuck," Ash groaned. "You destroyed me."

"You destroyed me first," Truman accused matter-of-factly, burying his face into Ash's shoulder. Ash's arm came around him and pulled him close. Truman kissed the skin in front of his mouth until Ash stroked his head.

"Damn. Okay."

Ash sounded conclusive.

"What?"

"Well, just, I'd been wondering what it would be like. And it was so much better," he said reluctantly.

"You're a big nerd," Truman murmured.

"Yeah."

They lay entwined, and Ash's warm palm stroking up and down his spine lulled Truman closer and closer to sleep.

"Maybe this is the solution to your fashion problem," Ash muttered just as Truman was drifting off.

"Hmm?"

"Maybe you're not supposed to wear any clothes. Maybe you're just meant to be naked all the time."

Truman grinned with delight. "Yeah, I think you solved it."

"Mm-hmm," Ash congratulated himself sleepily. "Solved it."

Then he gave Truman a pat on the ass and dragged him even closer.

# 20
# TRUMAN

"I have an idea," Truman said into Ash's shoulder.

Still half-asleep, Ash made a sound of lustful assent and slid his hand down Truman's spine.

"No, no, a business idea."

Ash squeezed his ass.

"A *flower shop* business idea."

Sleepy blue-gray eyes blinked open and focused on Truman.

"Hey," Ash said.

Truman watched as delight, then surprise, then hope crossed Ash's face. How had he never noticed how expressive Ash's face was before?

"Hi." Truman brushed Ash's hair out of his eyes and pressed a kiss to his stubbled cheek. "So I have an idea," he went on.

Ash schooled his features into a listening expression, but his fingers still explored Truman's skin like he was convincing himself Truman was real.

"Okay, so, you know how everyone gets those ugly red plants for Christmas?"

"Poinsettias," Ash said absently.

"Right. What if you gave them another option? What if you ran a special on red roses for Christmas—er, I'm assuming most people on the island celebrate Christmas? Just because… it's very…homogenous."

"Right," Ash confirmed. "Greta's family is Jewish, and the Pivens practice Buddhism, but they still come to all the Christmas things in town."

"Okay, so, red roses with greenery—still red and green— and we could find some kind of Christmassy name to call the bouquets, and then you put a big picture of one in the window with a sign that says, like, 'Tired of having the same poinsettias every year? This Christmas, try roses!' Or something like that."

Ash's brow was furrowed but he was nodding. "I'd need to start small, because I don't have the cash for a big outlay right away."

"Yeah, start with a few people, then you imagine they'll tell their friends."

"The thing about poinsettias is they last all month. Roses only last four days. Five at most."

"Oh. Right."

"I like the idea, Truman. Really."

Ash stroked his cheek.

"Aw, Ash, it's okay. I like telling you ideas. You don't have to do them. You know about the actual *flower* side of a flower shop and I don't. You won't hurt my feelings by telling me the problems with my ideas."

Ash ran a hand through his hair. "Are you sure?"

"Yeah. That is, as long as you're not mean about it, I'm sure."

"Well, I like the roses idea. I wish I had the money to do rose bushes. Like, little miniature red rose bushes instead of poinsettias. People could plant them outside in the spring. But they take a lot more care. Most people just throw the poinsettias away."

He was staring at the ceiling as he spoke, and Truman got the feeling he was seeing a new side of Ash. An unselfconscious, less-filtered side than the Ash who couldn't even brainstorm without feeling like his ideas were too unpolished.

Ash cupped Truman's face. "It's a good thought. Thanks."

"You're welcome."

Ash kissed him slow and sweet, and Truman found his thoughts moving far from business.

"I have an idea," Truman said.

Ash started to move away from him. He slid a hand down Ash's spine and grabbed his ass.

"Mmm, yes, please."

↔

Truman finished his work for the day, then decided to check out what kinds of holiday fare the shops on Main Street had on offer. He told himself it was research for Thorn, but he was just in the mood to poke around.

Muskee's was his first stop. He hadn't explored the non-food offerings yet.

Carla was washing the counter when he came in, and she waved a hand in her customary greeting.

"Hey, Carla. How's it going?"

"Can't complain, can't complain. The Larson girl just spilled a blue Gatorade on my counter, but what can you do?"

The back of Muskee's General Store was divided into roughly five sections: home goods, clothing, bath products, décor, and a collection of things that Truman could only reconcile into a category called Maine things. There were spoons with Maine written on the handle, candles with cabins on them, plaid towels, cast-iron doorstops in the shape of bears, et cetera.

Truman picked out some extremely Maine soap for his mom and headed to the counter.

"Do you mind if I ask you some questions about business on the island?" Truman asked.

"Shoot, kiddo."

Truman did. He asked the same questions to Bob at the Hardware Store, the Osgoods at the Queen Bee (where he found a lovely coffee table book about the history of horse racing for his father), and several other shop owners up and down Main Street.

He came away with a lot of information that didn't surprise him in the least—online shopping and big box stores had completely eviscerated the economy on the island, except in the summer, when the island became a tourist destination. But he also gleaned some that he couldn't have known without their insight, *and* an idea. An actual idea that he thought might work.

Ash was behind the counter at Thorn, glaring at a calculator when Truman arrived.

"Did that thing wrong you?"

Ash looked up and his face softened. "Hey." He came around and wrapped Truman in a warm hug. "God, you're freezing. Get in here."

Truman did not point out that he was already in here. He

just burrowed his admittedly freezing nose into Ash's warm shoulder and breathed in the scent of the man mixed with the light floral scent of Thorn.

"Okay," he said after he'd smelled his fill. He was buzzing with excitement. "I have an idea."

Ash's eyes went lust-dreamy, and a slow, promising smile bloomed.

"Er, no, a business idea. But a good one! I think. Well, you decide. Okay, so I just talked to a bunch of the business owners on Main—I was doing some Christmas shopping anyway." Truman held up his bags, lest Ash think he was *only* poking his nose in. "I asked them stuff about their bestselling products and what the challenges were to their businesses. Super interesting, by the way. Should I be a business coach? Anyway. They all agreed on one thing."

"The business owners of Owl Island agreed on something? Was it that Jim Musgrave shouldn't be allowed to cook out on the beach?"

"What? No. Wait, what does he…cook? You know what, never mind, if y'all have some kind of *Fried Green Tomatoes* barbequeing people situation going on here, I don't wanna know. I'm sure you have your reasons. But listen, okay? They all agreed that one of the reasons there isn't more business is because there isn't that much to do here, so people leave the island to do activities and end up shopping on the mainland while they're there."

Ash nodded.

"Okay, you already knew that. But my point is that what we need here are things to *do*. Things to keep people here so they have an opportunity to shop."

Ash nodded again.

"We've been thinking about things you could sell. But what about experiences? Here's my thing: you do a weekly, or monthly, or whatever, event at Thorn. People pay a fee to come, like a date night or a friends' night out, or just something fun to do on your own. Whatever. Then you have a bunch of flowers here, and some vases and jars. And people drink wine and arrange flowers, and they pay by the stem on top of the fee to come. Then you can use the fees they pay to come to buy the flowers, because they'll prepay when they sign up. And you'll make your money on the flowers they use and the arrangements they take home."

Ash was blinking slowly, thinking expression firmly in place.

"Maybe you charge for the wine, maybe the wine's free because the more they have, the more they want to stay and chat and make bouquets. We can price it all out. Oh! And maybe you partner with one of the restaurants and you do it there, where there's more space. They can sell food and wine, so you don't have to deal with it. You can have the tubs of flowers and all the tools set up on the tables. And you can go around helping people arrange. Maybe you even have a few arrangements around the restaurant so people get inspired."

Truman was buzzing with excitement.

"It helps the restaurant, it helps you, and maybe people would even come from the mainland if they hear of a quaint date night or friend hang option on an island. So then they end up coming on the ferry early to be here on time, and then they're here so they go to the local shops, spend money, all that."

Ash was silent for a long time, eyes narrowed, looking around the shop. Truman forced himself to be patient.

"That," Ash said finally, "is a damn good idea."

Truman's heart soared. "I could help you plan it. We could see about partnering with—"

Ash interrupted him with a kiss and looked deep into his eyes. "Where the hell," Ash asked, "did you come from?"

"New Orleans," Truman said with a wink.

Truman's phone rang.

"Oh damn, it's my mom. I'm gonna." He gestured to the phone and Ash nodded. "Hey, Mom."

"Truman Alexander, where on earth are you?"

"Uh. Maine."

"I know you're in Maine. That lesbian girl at your house told Miri."

Truman rolled his eyes at "lesbian girl."

"Well, if you know, Mom…"

"What on god's green earth are you doing in Maine? D'you fancy freezing to death?"

"I do, yeah."

"Truman."

"Don't worry, Mom. I've got warm clothes, and I'm staying at Greta's house—that's the *lesbian girl*—so I'm not gonna freeze to death." Then her words registered. "Wait, Miriam went to my house? Why?"

"She's your sister, darling."

"Yeah, I know. But she never told me she was coming or anything."

"Family doesn't need to ask, Truman. Family is always welcome. She was very irritated that she made the trip all the way there only to find that *person* in your home."

"Yeah, see, if she had texted, then she wouldn't have suffered the irritation of finding I wasn't at home."

Truman would have been willing to bet everything he owned that Miriam had been in town for reasons entirely unrelated to familial closeness and had wanted to crash with him for the night before heading out to wherever her next stop was.

"Listen, Mom, everything's fine. I just wanted to get away for a while. Take a vacation. That's all."

Vacation was a word he knew his mother could understand. She was forever planning her next weekend getaway, even though she rarely got farther away than Texas for a spa weekend with her girlfriends.

"Hmph," his mother said, powerless in the face of the word *vacation*. "Well, I hope you get your fill of the freezing north. You can show me pictures at Christmas. Speaking of which, I need to discuss your father's gift with you. I've had my eye on…"

Truman let his mother's voice wash over him. It was nice to hear a familiar accent after being on Owl Island, but he found himself irritated with her faster than he usually was. Every year, she discussed elaborate plans to shower Truman's father with a Christmas gift of his dreams, and every year, Truman's father said in no uncertain terms that what he wanted for Christmas was a new golf club and a weekend at the races.

Truman simply *mm-hmm*ed in the right places and watched Ash looking something up on his phone. Truman hoped it was flower-arranging event related.

"Truman!"

"Uh-huh, yeah?"

"Don't you think that's simply perfect?"

"Yes, Mom, perfect. Listen, I've gotta run because I have a work call in a few minutes, okay?"

As his mother sighed, the door to Thorn opened.

"Goodbye, dear. Do try not to freeze to death."

"Yeah, I'll try. Love you, bye."

Speaking of mothers, the woman who'd just entered Thorn was Ash's.

"Hi, Julia," Truman said.

"Mom, hey. You okay? What's up?" Ash asked, checking the time and crossing to her.

Julia squeezed Ash's shoulders and smiled easily. "Nothing's up. I'm just popping in to say hello and buy some flowers."

Ash gave her a look. "Mom, you can have whatever you want, but I'm not taking your money."

"That," she said with a pat to his cheek, "is a singularly terrible way to do business." She turned from Ash to Truman. "Talk some sense into my son, would you? His generosity is borderline self-destructive."

Truman snorted at this perfect distillation. "Damn, she's got you pegged," Truman said.

"Yeah, yeah."

Julia winked and began perusing the flowers. "Do you have any peonies, darling?"

"Yeah, in the corner there." Ash pointed at a bucket of furled yellow and pink peonies, their petals a tight promise.

"I love peonies," Julia said to Truman.

Ash was biting his thumbnail, and Truman had the sudden conviction that Ash ordered peonies for this very reason.

"What's the occasion, Mom?"

"I'm having some lovely young people over for coffee tomorrow."

"That's nice," Truman said as Ash said, "What? Who?"

"You remember Mallory and Jack's son, Bradley?"

Ash nodded.

"And the McFaddens' cousin?"

"Uh, Tania? Tori?"

"Tori, yes. They're coming for coffee. Bradley wants to be a journalist, and he's started writing freelance. And Tori's a filmmaker. Well, she wants to be. They're so interesting, and we got to talking, and I invited them over tomorrow."

"That's really nice, Mom. I hope you have a great time."

"I'm sure we will," she said breezily.

Truman watched Ash. His expression was perfectly fixed between joy and pain.

"Can I wrap those up for you?" He slid the flowers Julia had chosen from her hands. "Truman wanted to ask you something."

"I did? Oh! Yeah. I'm trying to figure out if someone used to live on Owl Island. She would've been here more than twenty years ago, and she would've lived in Greta Russakoff's house. She was a writer and wasn't very friendly…maybe didn't socialize with anyone."

"Are you talking about Marlene Travis?" Julia's whole face lit up. "She rented that house every summer for seven years. Had to be, oh, well, actually, she started coming two summers before Ash was born, so, twenty-eight years ago?"

Disappointment ripped through Truman to hear that it wasn't Agatha Tark. Then a small voice that sounded very much like Charlotte said, *Hey, dipshit, ever heard of a pen name?*

"Marlene was my dear friend," Julia said. "I was devastated when she stopped coming." She chuckled. "Didn't socialize. That's an understatement. She couldn't stand most people. Don't know why she let me befriend her. Maybe I was just persistent enough."

"Was she…um." Truman swallowed hard. "Was she working on a book when you knew her?"

"Oh yes, she was always working on something. She would not pick up the phone or answer the door until three p.m. because she was writing. But whenever I'd ask her to read what she wrote, she said no. I asked her what her book was about, and she said it was none of my business." Julia chuckled fondly.

"Holy crap," Truman breathed. "Agatha Tark. Um, do you know where she went when she stopped coming to Owl Island?"

"No, I never knew much about her life outside the summers. She didn't keep in touch during the rest of the year, but then there she'd be, come June first, like clockwork. Until one year, she just didn't come. I never heard from her again."

Ash shrugged on his coat and, holding the wrapped bouquet of flowers, put his hand on Julia's shoulder. "Can I walk you home, Mom?"

Julia turned to Truman and raised a honey-brown eyebrow, as if to say, *Isn't my son sweet and overprotective?* She took forty dollars out of her wallet and placed it on the counter. Then she held her arm out to Ash.

When he opened his mouth to complain, Julia covered it long enough to say, "Goodbye, Capote." Then she swept out of Thorn, Ash trailing in her wake.

# 21
# GRETA

Carys collapsed onto Greta's bed, arms out, with a groan. Horse licked at her hand sympathetically. She'd been holed up at Greta's for the last forty-eight hours, grading all the math finals for her students.

"Five left. Only five left, then I'm on break. I can feel my soul attempting to leave my body."

Carys never sat on chairs properly. She always sat cross-legged or with one knee up, or she contorted into uncomfortable-looking positions on the floor.

Greta, who was reading a mystery she'd bought at the cute used bookstore she found the other day, lying next to her, stroked her hair. Carys had been balancing a clipboard on her lap, and when she'd collapsed, the clipboard had landed on the pillow.

"Want to take a break? I've gotta take Horse for a walk."

Carys groaned again.

"Nah. I wanna push through. I'm gonna finish these and then I'm gonna get ice cream and not think about my students for three glorious weeks."

Greta kissed her goodbye and slipped out the door with

Horse. She'd loved having Carys staying with her the last two days. They'd made dinner together and watched movies when Carys took breaks. Greta had gotten to see what Carys looked like in the shower and see her hair long down her back spring up into curls as it dried.

It felt…intimate. Private.

Greta let Horse lead her through the streets of the Marigny. It was late afternoon and the light was beginning to turn peach at the edges. Greta was filled with a deep sense of satisfaction. Fulfillment she'd never had before.

She popped into a corner store to buy ice cream for Carys' end of exams celebration. She didn't know what kind Carys liked best, so she bought four and headed for home.

Carys was back at work, this time on the floor.

Greta held up the bag of ice cream.

"I wasn't sure what kind you like, so I got a few." She crouched on the floor and kissed Carys. "Do you want some now?"

Carys blinked, her expression unreadable. "No, I was going to go out and get some when I finished."

"Yeah, that's why I got it."

Greta put the four pints in the freezer and settled back on the bed.

"That was a sweet thought, Greta, but like I told you, I wanted to do that when I was done. It was going to be like a marker of finishing, and I always go to this place and get a cone."

Something tightened in Greta's stomach.

"Oh. Sorry. I didn't mean to mess up your tradition."

"It's okay—you didn't know. We can still go get cones and eat that later."

"Okay," Greta said. She'd never done something nice for

someone and had them reject it before. Carys said it was fine, but Greta felt uneasy.

An hour later, Carys threw down her clipboard and crawled into bed with Greta.

"I'd like to thank the academy for giving me this honor," she murmured to no one. Then she threw an arm over Greta's stomach and kissed her neck.

"Hi. You done?"

"Mm-hmm."

"Congratulations, yay."

"Thanks," Carys garbled. She nuzzled in closer.

"Did you wanna go get your ice cream cone to celebrate?"

"Mm, I'm so comfortable," Carys said. "Maybe later."

Then she promptly fell asleep.

←→

The next week was the best of Greta's life. Carys was on winter break, so her days were free, and she only had a couple of ghost tours scheduled so her nights were mostly free too.

Greta went to Muriel's for morning coffee and asked her if the Garden Gang might be up for helping Carys' friend Tana's students build raised beds at their school, and Muriel called around and began planning all the materials they could donate.

Ramona and Greta got stoned and wandered through the aquarium, renaming all the marine life and sending Carys nature documentary-esque videos of their explanations, which Carys found extremely amusing. When they collapsed in a pile of giggles in front of the sea lion display, Ramona told Greta that she seemed happy, and Greta told her, without any irony, that she'd never been so happy in her life.

And that weekend would be Eleventh House's annual holiday party, so every evening, they planned the food, worked on decorations, and explained their traditions to Greta, who was thrilled to participate, especially since one of the traditions was that you elaborately wrapped up something you had on hand to give as a gift, then everyone swapped back at the end of the night, unless you both liked the trade. That way, everyone got the fun of opening presents without the pressure of having to buy anything.

Two nights before the party, they'd been sitting around brainstorming menu ideas when Carys had come up with the idea of making Veronica and Helen's signature lemonade into Jell-O shots that they cut out with holiday cookie cutters into festive shapes. That idea was deemed perfect, so they spent the next twenty-four hours making batches of lemonade, mixing it with gelatin, and refrigerating it in rimmed sheet pans.

They began with the cookie cutters Helen had—Christmas trees, angels, et cetera. Then Greta decided to freehand a Star of David, and when that worked, they abandoned the cookie cutters altogether and started cutting out whatever shapes they wanted.

Carys' pièce de résistance was an octopus, Veronica's was an owl, and Helen's was a ghost, because they claimed that every holiday sucked in comparison to Halloween. Greta tried her hand at a menorah, which came out looking suspiciously enough like Carys' octopus that Greta cracked up and declared octopuses officially Jewish and the new mascot of Chanukah. She texted this to Maggie and Adelaide, along with a side-by-side picture, and Maggie responded *Christian hegemony has long kept this secret but the octopus has been reclaimed!!!*

Intermittently, as the trays of Jell-O shots firmed in the

refrigerator, they made paper chains out of Carys' old math handouts and strung them along the high ceilings of the living room. They grabbed LaCroix cans out of the recycling and cut them into stars that they strung together on dental floss. Veronica said she'd seen it in the window display of a tattoo shop in Philadelphia once, years before.

The next day, Veronica and Helen kicked Carys out of the house, insisting that they be able to create the party food with no distraction or oversight, so Greta and Carys spent a sweet day wandering through antiques shops in the French Quarter and discussing their dream homes.

Greta's dream house was a rambling Victorian mansion that she'd once seen on Instagram. It would be painted flat black with shiny black trim and a bright teal door. (The color of the door changed every time she'd recently seen something in a color she liked.) Its entire back half would be all glassed in so that every room was full of plants, and it had an elaborate bathroom with a huge jacuzzi that was tiled in all cobalt-blue glass. She remembered the feeling of being inside a wave in the pig bathroom, even if she remembered little that came after.

Carys' dream house was a Frankenstein of a Greek Revival mansion, like her favorite house in the Garden District, and a rambling farmhouse, complete with a weathered red barn. She wanted to fill it with chandeliers that dripped crystals, phonographs, fin-de-siècle candelabras, and lavish velvet furniture.

Both Greta and Carys wanted animals that could wander in and out of the house and its grounds, and both agreed that their dream houses needed secret rooms hidden behind book-cases that would swing open silently, revealing nooks covered in pillows with miniature refrigerators for snacks. They would be big enough to read or nap in and would never be revealed to any but the most trusted guests.

They had just left the third antiques store and were about to stop for beignets when Carys froze, and Greta, who'd been walking just behind her, slammed into her back.

"What's wrong?"

Carys began to turn around slowly.

"Carysanne," called a loud voice.

Carys swore under her breath.

"That's my mom."

"What do you want me to do?" Greta asked.

But Carys didn't have a chance to answer.

Carys' mother was taller than she was, and her hair was blond with brown roots. Greta knew she was only forty or so, but she looked older.

"Hello, darlin'," she trilled. She pulled Carys in by the shoulders and kissed her cheek. Carys stood frozen.

"Hi, Mom."

"It's so good I ran into you, because I wanted to invite you to spend Christmas with your grandparents and me. And before you tell me about how busy you are, I won't take no for an answer this year."

She started talking fast, about plans and timing, but Carys cut her off.

"No thank you."

Carys' mom paused for a moment, eyes narrowing slightly and nostrils flaring.

She then pivoted to Greta, and her face changed completely. Eyes wide and twinkling, she grinned at Greta and held out her hand.

"Well, hello there, Carysanne's friend who she was too

rude to introduce. I'm Shelly." Shelly gave Greta a scandalized smile that was clearly meant to be a shared meditation on Carys' failings.

Greta didn't know if she should shake Shelly's hand and say hello or ignore her the way Carys was.

"Hi, I'm Greta," she said. Shelly left her hand outstretched between them, and Greta squirmed at the awkwardness of not taking it. After a beat, she shook it quickly, then shoved her hands in her pockets, embarrassed that the tiniest bit of social pressure had gotten to her so quickly.

"Hello, Greta. Aren't you pretty. Carrie always did like the tomboys. You know, when she was about ten, she came to me and she said, 'Mama'—she used to call me Mama, not that she'd be caught dead in a ditch callin' me that now—she said, 'Mama, I—'"

"We're going to need to get going, Mom," Carys said. Then she took Greta's arm and walked away, back ramrod straight, shoulders unmoving.

"You're just going to walk away from me, Carysanne?" Shelly called.

"Just keep walking," Carys said, her voice tight. "Please."

"You think I'm gonna chase after you?"

Greta didn't look back, but Shelly's voice sounded like she was following them.

"Well, I'm not!" Then, in a very different voice, "My daughter, so silly, she loves this game, haha."

Carys kept walking. She was leading them away from the French Market, into the Quarter, and Greta kept pace. They didn't hear anything from Shelly again, so Greta relaxed, but Carys kept moving, squeezing her arm almost painfully tight. Then she turned onto a tiny side street, let go of Greta's arm, and leaned against the brick, eyes closed. It was only then that Greta realized Carys was shaking.

"Hey, come here," Greta said, reaching out to Carys.

Carys shook her head. "Sorry, not right now. I just need to be quiet for a minute."

Greta took a step back. She was a little hurt, and she tried not to take it personally. Clearly, this wasn't about her.

After a few minutes, Carys reached out a hand and squeezed Greta's arm. "Thanks," she said. "Wanna get some food?"

Greta nodded, and they settled in at a hightop table by the window of a Mexican restaurant nearby.

"So that's your mom," Greta said when they had their tacos and margaritas. She was shooting for casual so Carys could talk about it if she wanted, or not if she didn't.

"Yeah. I haven't seen her in two years. She almost never comes into town. She hates driving. Always talks someone into driving her anywhere she has to go."

"You sounded… When you were talking to her, you didn't sound like yourself."

"You can't have an actual conversation with my mom if you don't wanna get sucked in. I don't give her any information about me so she can't use it against me. I don't say anything about her because it all backfires. Even saying something that seems nice can get twisted. So you have to just be a rock—no info out, no energy in."

"Are you feeling okay now?"

"Better, thanks." Carys ate slowly. "It was just… I wasn't expecting to see her, so I wasn't prepared, and she…uh…she gets to me. Maybe she always will."

"Do you want to talk about it?"

"I don't know if I can explain it. It's like, intellectually, I'm completely resigned to her always being like this, because I know that narcissists don't change. But then there's a part of me that searches for a change every time. Or hopes for one maybe." Carys took a long sip of her margarita. "It's not logical, but it's like a tiny little part of my heart is hers, and no matter how long I go without seeing her, it wakes up when she's around." Carys made a face. "It's like dessert stomach. Narcissistic mom heart. There's always room."

After they finished their food and drinks, Carys seemed almost back to her usual self.

"I'm good," she said, almost like she was announcing it to herself. "Let's go party."

## GRETA

When Greta opened the door to Eleventh House two hours later, dressed for the party, it had been entirely transformed.

Three times the amount of paper chains now adorned the living room, the number (and colors) of stars suggested rifling through neighbors' recycling, and delicious smells spilled from the long table that had been pushed against the far side of the wall, where the stereo usually was.

Helen and Veronica lay sprawled on the couch, intertwined, snoring loudly.

Carys poked her head out of the kitchen, made a "quiet" motion, and waved Greta inside.

Carys wore a crepey silver-and-gold sleeveless dress that fell to the floor; a silver belt that looked like a snake wrapped around itself accentuated the beautiful curves of her breasts and her ass. Her hair was a cloud of curls, and she wore a 1920s-style silver sequined headband around her head. Her lips were bright red and her whiskey eyes were accentuated with a gold metallic shadow that made them mesmerizing.

"Holy shit, you look amazing," Greta said worshipfully.

"Thanks, baby. You look wonderful too. Damn!"

Greta hadn't packed any party-appropriate clothes, but she'd found a fitted tuxedo jacket at a thrift store the other day and wore that buttoned over black jeans and a bra. She'd smudged some black eyeliner around her blue eyes and tousled her hair into a bleach blond mess. She liked the look— half butch, half glam—but it was much more effort than she usually put into her appearance, and she blushed at Carys' clear appreciation.

"Um. Should we wake them?"

Carys snorted. "They were asleep when I got home. I bet they stayed up all night cooking and decorating. When they both get manic at the same time...hoo!" She shook her head. "They get a lot done, though."

"Yeah, it doesn't look like there's much to set up before people get here."

Carys nodded.

"Sooo, maybe I could just..." Greta ran a fingertip between Carys' breasts and raised an eyebrow.

Carys' smile was pure heat, and she turned and led Greta to her bedroom.

"Here's the thing, though," she said. "I just did my makeup and everything, so I'm afraid there's really only one place you can touch me..."

A throb of heat went through Greta, and she groaned and dropped to her knees. "Not a problem."

She pushed Carys gently back on the bed and buried her face between her legs. She was warm and sweet and so damn delicious that Greta never wanted to come up for air. She teased at first, then, when Carys was clutching at the duvet, she brought her to a quaking, hair-pulling orgasm. Her moan was low and throaty and made Greta feel like a god.

"Damn," Carys said, sitting up shakily. "That was art."

Greta wanted to ravage her. Wanted to ruin her perfect lipstick and muss her hair beyond repair. She also wanted to go out to the party still tasting Carys on her lips.

"Open your mouth," Greta said. "I promise I won't mess up your lipstick."

Carys did, and Greta gave her tongue a delicate swipe.

"I can taste myself."

"I love the way you taste," she murmured, and Carys groaned.

Satisfied, they made their way out of Carys' room to find Helen and Veronica smirking in the kitchen.

"Get it," Helen coughed, and Veronica just grinned. Greta automatically put a hand to her hair to try and smooth it, but Carys caught her wrist and tousled her hair even more. Then she gave a perfectly filthy leer and blew Greta a kiss. Greta felt like her spine had turned to liquid heat.

Then the doorbell rang, and the holiday party sprang to life.

Guests had sure gotten the memo about fancy dress and Greta appreciated the range of personal styles on display. She didn't know anyone except Carys, Veronica, and Helen, but people were friendly, and Carys introduced her to a friend who also loved plants so they had something to talk about.

When Muriel walked through the door, Greta thought she'd had too many lemonade Jell-O shots.

"You came!"

Muriel looked glorious. She wore one of her signature flowing outfits, but this one was a bright teal shot through with sparkling red threads that glinted in the light. Her thick hair was gathered in a braided crown on top of her head and studded with jeweled pins in the shapes of beetles, spiders, and one large green grasshopper.

"Of course I did," Muriel said breezily as she swept inside. "I wouldn't have missed it." She kissed Greta's cheeks without making contact, her bright pink lipstick perfect.

"Let me get you a drink." Greta took her elbow. "Er, I don't suppose you like Jell-O shots…"

Everyone stared at her as they made their way to the drinks table. Wide-eyed looks of admiration and compliments followed in their wake.

"You look amazing, ma'am," someone said.

"Thank you, darling," Muriel cooed. "As do you."

The guest in question, an androgynous black-clad butch with spiked blue hair and multiple facial piercings, blushed bright red and ducked their head with murmured thanks.

"So, um, a Jell-O shot is…" Greta paused, trying to figure out how disgusting a Jell-O shot might sound to someone as refined and, well, old as Muriel.

"I know what it is, dear," Muriel said. "Could I trouble you for something a tad more liquid?"

"Of course, sure, lemme just…"

Greta squeezed behind the drinks table and poured Muriel a glass of Veronica and Helen's lemonade that had not been gelatinized. "My friends make this. It's really good. Well, I like it…"

Muriel took a sip. "Delicious!" she proclaimed, and Greta felt a surge of pride. Her friends had made that. Her *friends*.

"Want to meet my…" She'd been about to say *girlfriend*. Could she say that about someone she'd only known for a few weeks? "Carys?"

Muriel nodded, a twinkle in her eye, and they crossed to

where Carys was arguing intently about math with two people who must've been fellow grad students.

"Omigosh, you must be Muriel," Carys said, interrupting herself midsentence. "I'm so glad to meet you. Greta's told me so much about you."

She held out a hand to shake, but Muriel leaned in and kissed her cheek.

"A pleasure, my dear. I hear you're a mathematician, so I wonder if you can explain something to me…"

Greta left them in deep conversation as someone grabbed her shoulder.

Ramona held out her arms.

"Hey, dude! I brought a friend. Hope you don't mind."

Ramona inclined her head to the man with her, who was dressed in purple from head to toe—suit, shirt, tie, and shoes—and mouthed, "Hot, right?"

Greta gave them both a thumbs-up and took them to get Jell-O shots.

After half an hour or so, Helen and Veronica emerged from the kitchen and struck dramatic poses in the doorway.

"The food's ready!" Helen yelled over the music. "Plates are by the door, garbage can is by the hallway. I know each and every one of you motherfuckers—well, okay, not you…or you," they said, indicating Ramona and her friend. "And, *damn*, why don't I know you?" they asked Muriel, who responded with a flirtatious wave. "Anyway, throw away your trash or you won't get invited back, you hear me?" they concluded.

A cheer and a flurry of thumbs-ups came from the crowd, and people made a beeline for the food.

Greta followed, stomach growling, excited to see what had kept Helen and Veronica up all night.

The large kitchen was lit by lava lamps, and platters of exquisite-looking morsels crowded every surface.

Lamb meatballs with mango-mint chutney; soppressata, pear, and brie muffulettas; red beans and rice arancini; fried green tomatoes with hot pepper jelly; baklava made with Veronica's honey; lavender lemon poundcake bites; cinnamon-sugar beignets with bacon glaze. Every platter was neatly labeled in Veronica's swooping handwriting.

And there, in pride of place on the stove, a huge platter heaped with latkes. HAPPY CHANUKAH! the label said. To the right of the platter were a dish of applesauce and one of sour cream. Behind each was a jar, and another sign said CAST YOUR VOTE: APPLESAUCE OR SOUR CREAM? Beads sat in a dish to be used as voting tokens.

Greta had waxed poetic to Carys, Helen, and Veronica about her mom's latkes the other day at breakfast. She'd told them about the applesauce versus sour cream debate that divided not only the Russakoff family but any group of latke eaters. Helen had instantly chimed in, voting for sour cream, Carys had scoffed and chosen applesauce, and Veronica had said, "I vote ketchup."

"A valid third-party vote," Greta had said.

There, next to the applesauce and sour cream, sat a bottle of ketchup.

Tears came to Greta's eyes when she saw that in addition to the latkes, Helen and Veronica had also made cookies in the shape of dreidels and kugel bites.

"Is it okay?" Helen said from behind her, voice just a touch uncertain.

Greta whirled around and grabbed them in a tight hug. "It's fucking perfect," she said.

Veronica approached, and Greta hugged her too.

"Thank you both," she said. "It's the best Chanukah I've ever had."

And it was.

"You haven't tried any of it yet," Veronica muttered.

"It doesn't matter."

But she piled her plate high with a bit of everything and was able to honestly tell them that their latkes were as good as her mom's.

The look of pride on Veronica's face was everything. She leaned in. "It was Carys' idea. She wanted you to feel like you weren't missing out on too much by not being at home."

Greta's heart melted, and she went to look for Carys. Greta found her in conversation with Muriel and slid her arms around her waist from behind.

"Thank you," she whispered, and even though she didn't explain, she could tell Carys knew what she was talking about.

Carys reached a hand back and squeezed her shoulder, imparting her tactile *You're welcome* without interrupting Muriel. Taking her cue, Greta pressed a kiss to her cheek, then left them to their conversation.

Greta stepped out onto the porch for a breath of fresh air. She didn't realize Ramona had followed her until she was deep in thought.

"Dude," Ramona said. "Just do it."

"Paid for by Nike," Greta chirped.

Ramona lit a clove cigarette, and instantly Greta was back in their shared freshman dorm room, trying a clove for the first time and nearly puking before she learned to love them (and not to inhale).

She took one from Ramona and accepted a light.

"What's stopping you?" Ramona asked, hooking a boot heel over the railing.

A flood of reasons and fears tidal-waved through Greta's mind.

"Um, hurting my parents, abandoning Ash, my sisters being mad at me, how expensive it is to move, not having a job here, things with Carys being so new, failing…"

"Failing at what?"

"Just…failing. Here. After leaving."

"How could you fail here?"

"I don't know, a million ways. I have to do better here than I would've at home, to…"

"To convince yourself it was worth it?"

Greta paused. "I guess?"

Ramona rolled her eyes. "I don't know what everyone's big thing about failing is. Failing rules. Failing is proof to yourself that you tried something. That you *did* something instead of just sitting on your ass letting life pass you by. How's that a bad thing?"

Greta hadn't thought of it like that.

"Plus who gets to decide what failure looks like for you? Oh, wait, lemme guess. Your family?"

Ramona didn't give her time to confirm that.

"Well, honestly, dude, fuuuuuck them. They wanna stay on Owl Island? Great! You're not trying to control their lives. You're just saying you wanna leave. You know, *Greta* is just *great* in a different order. You can't fail!" Ramona crowed.

A group of people walking past cheered at that, raising go cups high.

"See?" Ramona said. "The whole city agrees!"

A warm, sparkly feeling lit Greta up.

"Yeah!" she said. "Yeah, I can do whatever I want. Failure's, like, part of life. And I decide what it is."

"Exactly, dude! You just call your family and you say, *Hey, everyone, I'm outta here. Love ya, bye!*"

"Yes! I *do* love them, and I *do* wanna be out of there."

"There you go," Ramona said.

They clinked Jell-O shots, then downed them.

"I'm gonna call 'em right now!" Greta said.

"Yes!"

Greta fumbled out her phone and called her mom. It went to voicemail.

"Hey, Mom. I'm outta here. Love ya, bye!" Then she added, "This is Greta. Your daughter. And by here, I mean Owl Island. Love you, byyyee." She hung up the phone and turned to Ramona.

"I can't believe you did it," Ramona said, eyes wide.

"I did it!" Greta said.

They high-fived, and Greta's phone rang.

"Don't answer that," Ramona said.

"I'm not! Not answering, Mom!" she called.

Another group of passersby cheered.

"The whole city *does* agree," Greta said.

The door opened, and Carys came outside. She was the most beautiful person Greta had ever seen.

"The whole city agrees with me, baby," Greta told her, opening her arms.

Carys smiled and moved into them.

"Is that right?" she drawled. "About what?"

"That I decide what failure means and that I don't have to answer my mom."

Carys grinned. "Well, the whole city sounds right to me."

"Me too." Greta's voice was slightly slurred. She felt euphoric.

"I like you," Ramona said to Carys.

Carys replied, "I like you too."

"Sweet."

"Aww, you like each other. Yay," Greta said.

"If y'all wanna come back inside, we're gonna unwrap presents," Carys said.

"Oh, yes," Ramona said, jumping to her feet. "I brought the best thing. Can't wait to see it unwrapped."

Inside was glorious pandemonium. People were swapping gifts with ceremony and unwrapping each other's to reveal boxes of tissues, pairs of scissors, pillowcases, cans of beans, tubes of toothpaste, and various personal tchotchkes.

Greta exchanged her *Times-Picayune*-wrapped gift with Muriel, who handed her a box wrapped exquisitely in matte yellow paper embossed with shiny yellow pineapples and tied with a green bow.

She slid the paper off, careful not to rip it, revealing a fancy black box. She lifted the lid and peered inside. Nestled in glitter-specked black tissue paper was one of Muriel's signature pink sugar cubes.

Greta grinned. "Thank you ever so much!"

"My pleasure. Thank *you*," she replied, holding up one of Horse's dog toys.

Around them, people laughed and teased one another and exchanged the gifts back again.

"You know," Muriel said, leaning in conspiratorially, "I don't really need the sugar cube back."

Greta grinned and popped it in her mouth, letting the sweet sugar dissolve on her tongue. Then she paused. "Er, I do need mine back. It's Horse's favorite."

Muriel handed it back and leaned in again. "I like your Carys very much."

"Yeah?" Greta hadn't realized she'd been nervous about Muriel not liking Carys. "Me too."

She waited, hoping that perhaps Muriel might elaborate on all Carys' wonderful qualities. But instead, she just kissed Greta's cheek.

"Happy Chanukah, my dear. I'm going to take my leave. Thank you for inviting me, and please do pass my compliments on to your friends. Tell them that I'd be delighted to have them cater the next gardening get-together that I host."

"Oh my gosh, amazing. I'll tell them. Thank you!"

She walked Muriel to the door and confirmed that she had a ride. When her ride pulled up, Muriel cupped Greta's face in her hands.

"You can't know this yet. In fact, we rarely know it until it's too late to need to know it. But you are going to be just fine."

Then she was gone, waving a final time from the car window, and Greta stood at the curb, watching her drive away and trying to remember everything she'd just said. But it slipped from her tipsy mind one sentence at a time.

# 23
# TRUMAN

When Truman and Ash walked through the ornate wooden doors of Sunflower Seed, a small white woman with wild platinum curls was smoking out the tiny side window. She knelt on a stool and sucked hard on her cigarette.

"Hey, Ash," she said through a mouthful of smoke as they entered. Then she looked at her cigarette. "Hey! Ash." She pointed at the glowing tip.

"Rayanne," Ash said. "Got a sec?"

She waved them in, then waved them over, clearly unwilling to put out the cigarette.

"Day won't let me smoke in the kitchen anymore," she said with a roll of heavily kohl-lined blue eyes.

"Yeah, well. Food and all that," Ash said. "This is Truman. Rayanne owns the place."

"Guilty," Rayanne said. But whereas someone else might've said it as a quip, Rayanne seemed legitimately burdened.

Truman shook the hand not holding the cigarette and let go with the strong sense that his hand would smell of smoke anyway.

"She around?" Ash asked, looking toward the back of the restaurant.

It was cozy inside, with dark wood walls and flooring, a dark wood bar, gold chandeliers over the tables, and dark green tablecloths. Somber paintings of ships, gulls, lighthouses, and snowy farm scenes hung on the walls, and there were antler coat hangers near the front door. It looked nothing at all like the woman standing before them, who, Truman could see once she stabbed her cigarette out and uncrouched from her perch, wore a wildly printed jumpsuit so voluminous it swallowed her small frame and Doc Martens with a thick sole, even with which Truman still towered over her.

"Yeah," Rayanne said, then yelled, "Day!"

From the back of the restaurant strode a woman who looked straight out of Le Cordon Bleu. She wore a white chef's jacket, her hair was swept back into a tight bun, and she gave the impression she would be perfectly capable of spatchcocking anything you put in front of her. Truman took a tiny step back.

Ash, on the other hand, smiled wider than Truman had seen him smile at anyone else they'd encountered.

"Day, hi," he greeted her enthusiastically. "This is Truman. He's staying in Greta's place for a while. From New Orleans."

Day turned calm gray eyes on Truman and held out her hand.

"New Orleans. Excellent," she said and shook Truman's hand firmly.

"Thanks. I mean, I can't take credit. Obviously." Truman willed himself to shut up.

Day simply raised one perfectly arched eyebrow and stood, calm, silent, and intimidating. She seemed utterly at ease, which flustered Truman.

"So what's up?" Rayanne asked, lighting another cigarette.

Day reached over, slid it from her hand, and put it out between her fingers. Then she tucked it, filter side down, into the pocket of her chef's coat.

Ash outlined what they wanted to do, and Truman chimed in every now and then to add a detail. When they were done, Rayanne nodded. "Sounds great to me. As long as I don't have to make a bouquet."

"No flower arranging required," Ash assured her. "Day?"

Day hadn't given any response while they'd spoken, and now she simply nodded once and said, "I'll prepare a suitable menu."

Ash nodded back, and Truman had a vision of them hanging out, sitting in total silence except that each would say one sentence every couple of hours and the other would nod one time in acknowledgment.

He snorted a laugh.

Rayanne regarded him. "So you're the one Greta did the house swap with. What do you think so far?"

"Of Owl Island? I love it. It's really beautiful. I'm not used to the cold, but now that I've got the whole jacket thing down, it's great."

Rayanne narrowed her eyes, like she wasn't sure she could believe him.

"And what do you think of Ash?"

"Of…Ash?"

"Yeah."

"Rayanne," Ash said. "Don't mess with him."

"Fine," she grumbled.

Silence fell.

"Dolphins only close one eye when they sleep," Rayanne blurted.

"Oh," Truman said politely.

Day nodded.

"I'm doing this new thing where when I want to say something that's none of my business, I say a fact instead," Rayanne said. "I wanted to hear about how your relationship with Ash is going." She darted a look at Day. "But..."

"It rather mitigates the effect if you go on to report the thing you wanted to say, darling," Day said.

"Oh wow, are you guys a couple?"

Rayanne smirked and Day nodded that single nod.

"I was wondering if Ash and Greta were the only queers on the island."

"Well," Rayanne said conspiratorially and leaned in.

Day cleared her throat.

"Oh right, damn, that's a secret. Never mind. Uh, Greenland sharks can live up to five hundred years."

"Were you reading that book on oceanography that Don and Maisey keep trying to get rid of?" Ash asked.

"Yeah. They put it on the dictionary stand, so my facts will be ocean-related for the next while."

Truman's head was spinning.

"I'm sorry," he said. "Did you tell them we were...?" he asked Ash, surprised.

Ash shook his head. "Nope."

"Then how'd you—?"

Rayanne rolled her eyes again. "Oh, dear heart, it's all anyone's talking about!"

Day closed her eyes in what might have been apology or mortification.

Truman didn't have a response to that, so instead he said, "When's good for y'all to do the event?"

Rayanne and Day exchanged a speaking glance.

"We'll need some time to spread the word and put it all together. If we want anyone from the mainland to come, we'll wanna wait till after New Year's. No one comes out the week before Christmas, and all the local ads are sold months in advance," Rayanne said. While she spoke, she eased the purloined cigarette out of Day's pocket and flipped it to her lips. "We could do the first weekend after New Year's," she suggested. Then she knelt again, pushed open the window, and lit the cigarette, and Day did nothing to stop her.

"The first one could be a trial run for Valentine's Day," said Day.

"Oh, shit, of course," Ash said. "It's my biggest selling holiday," he told Truman.

"Makes sense. January, huh? Aw, I guess I'll miss it."

Because Truman was looking at Ash, he saw his words hit with tangible effect. Ash blinked his reaction away quickly, but Truman had seen it nonetheless.

It was the first time his impending departure had come up in conversation. Had he actively avoided mentioning it? Not consciously, but he could see now that he had. He hadn't wanted to do anything that would pop the perfect bubble that he and Ash were living in.

Ash cleared his throat, clearly searching for a response.

"We'll send you pictures," Rayanne said. She slung an arm around Ash's shoulder from her elevated perch. Her platinum curls got in his face, and he smiled and tugged one. Then he stole her cigarette, took a drag, and handed it back.

"Okay, well, glad you're on board," he said. He squeezed Day's shoulder and sketched a wave.

"Bye," Truman said, following him. "Nice to meet you."

"Yup," Rayanne said. Day simply nodded.

Flustered, Truman tripped out into the night after Ash.

"Wow. They're a strange couple," he said. "Have you known them long?"

"Yup. Rayanne was my student teacher one year."

Truman struggled to place Rayanne in the context of children. Or school. "Really?"

"Yeah. Well, not the whole year. She quit after a semester because she hated everything about it."

Truman laughed. "And Day. Man, she's super intimidating."

"I know. I've always had such a crush on her."

Truman raised an eyebrow. "Oh really? That's what does it for you: intimidation?"

Ash winked, but the silence between them as they walked back to Thorn felt heavy with uncertainty. Truman wasn't sure if acknowledging it would help or make it worse, but if he'd learned anything lately it was that it was better to say things than not say them.

"Listen," Truman said. "The thing I said about me not being here…"

Ash sighed and ran a gloved hand through his hair. "I know you're leaving," he said. It sounded almost neutral. If Truman hadn't seen Ash cry over his mother, whisper his desires, or play goofy games with Bruce, he might have believed he didn't care. But Truman had seen those things, so he knew. Ash cared. He cared a lot. And Truman cared too.

"Okay," he began.

But there was nothing, really, left to say.

# A MESSAGE FROM RAMONA

**RAMONA to TRUMAN CUTIE**

It's tempting to believe our own stories about ourselves more than the reality. Don't be so caught up in your own shit you can't smell the roses.

# 24
# TRUMAN

Truman was taking a bath the next night when someone rang the bell. He hadn't seen Ash all day, and he jumped out of the tub and swaddled himself in one of Greta's fuzzy towels to answer the door.

Ash stood, shivering, on the front porch.

"Come in, come in," Truman said, instantly regretting his choice of garb when the cold blasted through him.

"You were in the shower? Sorry," Ash mumbled.

"The bath. I was just reading and soaking. No problem. I'm glad to see you."

"Yeah?"

"Of course yeah."

Ash nodded, arms wrapped around himself, but stood just a step inside the door, making no move to come farther inside.

"I'm gonna just put some clothes on. Sit down, okay?"

Truman dashed into the bedroom and pulled on sweats and his heavy sweater, scrubbed the towel through his cold, wet hair, and went back into the living room to find Ash in the same spot he'd left him.

"Hey, what's wrong?" Truman led him to the couch by the arm.

Ash looked at him, eyes miserable. He seemed to start to speak several times, but each time, he said nothing.

"Is it your mom?" Truman tried. "Is she okay?"

"She's the same as usual," Ash said.

"Did she end up having those people over for coffee?"

"Yeah."

Truman was at a loss.

"Can I…do something?"

Ash seemed to deflate. He blew out a breath and sank deep into the couch.

"Do you think maybe I could hang out here for a little bit?" Ash finally said.

Truman's heart flooded with relief.

"Yes! Oh my god, of course. Please, hang out."

"You were reading," Ash said.

"That's okay."

"I mean…um…would you want to read it to me too?"

Ash couldn't know this, but reading to someone and being read to were two of Truman's favorite things. "Yeah, I'd love it. Do you wanna lie in bed? It's more comfortable."

Ash nodded and shambled to the bedroom, zombielike.

But clearly whatever was bothering him, he didn't want to discuss it right now, so Truman settled next to him on the bed instead and picked up his book. "I really think we should start at the beginning," he said, showing Ash the cover of book one.

"You can just read to me starting from wherever you were."

Truman waved him away. "I've read these a million times. I can start anywhere. And if you're giving me an opportunity to introduce you to the series, we are one hundred percent starting at the beginning. You need to understand the character arcs and emotional stakes!"

That got a small smile out of Ash, who acquiesced. Then he nestled into Truman's side and listened as Truman read the first sentence of the first book of the Dead of Zagørjič series.

An hour later, Truman's voice was threatening to give out, and he could sense Ash starting to drift off. He put the book aside and slid down beside Ash.

"Can I stay?" Ash murmured.

"Please."

And Truman was asleep within minutes, drifting off in the peace of Ash's strong arms and steady heartbeat.

↔

Truman awoke with the feeling of being watched. When he opened his eyes, he realized it was because Ash was gazing at him.

"Hey." Truman smiled and kissed Ash's full lower lip.

But Ash didn't kiss him back.

Something scared and desperate clawed awake in Truman's gut. "You okay?"

"No," Ash said miserably.

He sat up, and Truman, feeling too vulnerable lying down, sat up also. "What's wrong?"

"Truman, I…" Ash tugged on his hair with his fist. "I can't do this."

Truman blinked fast, trying to hold back tears.

*Oh my god, it's happening again. There's something wrong with me. No one wants me. Everyone stops liking me. I'll never find someone who actually wants to be with me long term. What's wrong with me?!*

"It's too hard," Ash choked out. "I thought about it all day yesterday. I came here to tell you last night, and I...I chickened out. I'm sorry. I couldn't stand not having one more night with you. But I just can't do this."

"Do what, exactly?"

His voice sounded thin and choked.

"I can't like you this much and watch you leave."

All Truman could do was blink.

"So you wanna stop...liking me."

Ash shook his head. "That's impossible. But I just...I'm sorry. It's just too much. Feeling like I have a par—" He swallowed hard. "I'm already starting to depend on having you here. But knowing you'll be gone in two weeks...it's too... I think it's better. Easier. If we stop now. Before I... Just before I can't take it anymore."

Truman was frozen, his heart shuddering to a halt with paralytic cold. "Can we...talk about it?"

"I can't," Ash said miserably.

Truman felt like something was happening that he should have some control over, but he didn't. So he defaulted to what he'd always said in the past when people broke up with him, and in saying it, he slid back into a version of himself that now felt like it didn't quite fit.

"Oh," he heard himself say, as if from a great distance. "I understand."

"You do?"

Now that Ash had dumped him, all Truman wanted was for him to leave before Truman fell apart.

"Sure. Yeah. I get it."

"Okay. I'm sorry."

"Don't worry about it," Truman said numbly.

Ash frowned, then nodded once, like this wasn't what he'd been expecting. Truman was excruciatingly aware of every gesture of Ash's leave-taking. The way he slid his keys in the pocket of his worn jeans. The plane of his shoulders beneath his sweater as he shrugged into his coat. How a lock of hair clung to his cheek as he stepped into his boots. At the door, he turned, began to say something, and seemed to think better of it. He waved and walked away.

Truman slunk slowly back into the bedroom, buried himself in Greta's bed, and pulled the covers over his head. They smelled like Ash. *Fuck.*

He must've fallen back asleep, because when he woke later, the sun was pouring in through the windows and he had to pee badly.

The latter discharged, he went about the morning plant chores, numbly ticking things off on Greta's spreadsheet.

Then he stood in the middle of the living room with no idea whatsoever of what to do.

He still hadn't cried. He felt stuck in the middle of the moment before crying, and he resented Ash for that too.

He replayed their conversation in his head. It had been habit that had made him capitulate quickly—after all, when someone told you it was over, it wasn't like you could *argue* with them, right? You couldn't convince someone to be with you if they didn't want you. But…Ash had given no indication that was coming. He'd just…

Anger rushed in to fill the empty space Ash had left in him.

"What the *hell* just happened?" he said. "What the *HELL*! Did he just…how can he…and did I really…? Again? What the *fuck*!" Truman rarely said fuck, but he said it now. Then he shouted it.

A rare fury clawed its way out of him like he was an eggshell.

How *dare* Ashleigh fucking Sundahl treat him like he was appreciated, admired, enjoyed, and then throw him away like garbage? How *dare* he make Truman get attached, start to picture the future with Ash in it, have some of the best sex of his life, and then tell him they should just *quit*?

And how the hell had he just *let* it happen?

Now Truman was supposed to, what? Stay in Owl Island for the next two weeks, avoiding Ash, avoiding Julia—hell, avoiding everyone, since apparently the whole *island* knew about them?

"How did this happen to me again?" Truman shouted at the pitcher plants. "How the fuck did Ash abandon me just when he was starting to make me fall in love with him? Asshole!"

Then his words caught up with him, and he collapsed on the couch.

"God damn it, Truman."

There was nothing for it now. He'd have to leave. He'd have to go back to New Orleans. Maybe he couldn't stay at his house because Greta was there, but surely he could stay with someone.

*At the holidays? People have plans, families, lives. Unlike you, who apparently just float around the globe, falling in love with assholes and then getting tossed away by them. Yeah, go spend Christmas in some shitty Airbnb in Metairie. Better yet, just go stay with Mom and Dad. They'll be thrilled to see you.*

Truman imagined the dreary trips to the mall to pick out Christmas gifts for his sisters, while his mother kept up a constant chatter about everyone he'd gone to school with as far back as elementary and their parents, siblings, and acquaintances.

Then Truman imagined driving a spike through his heart.

He couldn't go home. No. No way. No way was he letting this happen to him again. And wasn't *letting* the operative word? In every other breakup, he'd acted just the same. He'd never demanded that people explain themselves. Never asked Troy *why* it wasn't working, never insisted Jason tell him what would make him happy, and never fought for the relationships that were being wrenched out from underneath him.

But no more. He was *not* letting Ash leave him without a real conversation. And he was *certainly* not letting himself off the hook without fighting for Ash.

"Nope," he said aloud. "Nope, nope, nope. No sir."

Then Truman pulled on his outerwear, stomped into his boots, and stalked to Thorn.

"Absolutely not, Ash Sundahl!"

It would've been a strong opening gambit had it been Ash standing behind the counter of Thorn. But it was Rayanne.

"Oh," Truman said intelligently.

"Ash isn't feeling well today," Rayanne said. At least she said that with her voice. But with her face and her hands, she was very clearly saying (and pointing) that Ash was upstairs in his apartment and that he was sad.

But out loud, she only said, "Stubbs, a ginger cat, served as mayor in Talkeetna, Alaska, for twenty years," and pointed upstairs again. Then she made a heart shape with her fingers and broke it.

"No, he broke *my* heart!" Truman shouted.

Rayanne put her hand to her heart and shooed him away.

Truman slammed out of Thorn and knocked on the door to Ash's apartment. No one answered. Truman wasn't even sure if he could hear the outside door from up there.

"God dammit!"

He went back into Thorn, the cheery doorbell tinkling his presence yet again.

Rayanne just pointed behind the register, and Truman headed for the stairway to Ash's apartment.

This time, he didn't knock. He yelled.

"Ash, we need to talk!"

It took a minute, but Ash finally opened the door.

His eyelids were puffy, his skin blotchy, and his hair even more chaotic than usual.

Truman's anger deflated.

"Can I come in?"

Ash left the door open and drifted over to sit in the corner of the couch. When he settled, Bruce trotted into the room and jumped up to curl on Ash's feet.

Now that he was here, Truman didn't know what to say. He wished he could just yell at Ash the way he had at Rayanne.

He wished he could rant at Ash the way he'd ranted at Greta's plants.

But what came out was a pathetic near-whisper.

"I don't want to not see you anymore."

Ash cringed. "Please don't make this harder than it already is," he said. His voice was rough, and he didn't meet Truman's eyes. "I'm sorry, but I just can't."

Despair swept through Truman. "What is so wrong with me?" His voice was loud enough to startle Bruce. "Am I freaking cursed or something? Am I so unlovable that people can just throw me away?" His voice broke, and he sat down where he was, on Ash's gray-blue rug.

That was how Ash was in his mind too. Up until now, he'd focused on the blue—the calm, free, expansive blue that made him want to close his eyes and drift off under a serene sky or wade into welcoming waters. But now all he saw was the gray. A gray so heavy it could pin you forever to the earth or hold you beneath the waves until you were obliterated.

"God, Truman, no. The opposite. It's *too* easy to care about you. Too easy to fall—to feel like you're a real part of my life. But you're... You're *leaving*, man, and I honest to god can't take losing anything else right now."

"What if I didn't?"

The words came from somewhere deep in Truman, but he realized he meant them when he saw Ash's eyes light up for a moment. Then the light went out of them.

"You mean like with that guy you were dating at the end of college? No. I don't want to be one more person you do something for and then wake up in a year thinking how the hell did I end up on this island I don't even like."

"I do like it," Truman said softly.

"You know what I mean."

And Truman did. That if he stayed, he would be staying for Ash, just as he'd stayed in New Orleans for Tyler.

Only it didn't feel the same. It didn't feel the same at all. With Tyler, he'd stayed because he might as well have. He was happy to have the choice made for him. But this wasn't about having a decision taken off his hands. This was because he wanted to be with Ash.

*What do you mean you want to be with him?* the voice in his head hissed. *You've known him for three weeks. Normal people don't pick up their whole lives for someone after three weeks! He'll get sick of you soon enough, just like Manuel did. Or he'll cheat on you, like Brian. Maybe he already has a whole secret family, like Guy.*

Usually when the voice hissed at him, he listened. After all, it was his unconscious telling him things he didn't want to acknowledge but needed to hear, right?

Then he remembered something Charlotte had told him once. That witnesses lied on the stand all the time without knowing they were doing it. They lied because we quest for stories so we fill in narratives automatically, without evidence, without proof, supplied from our assumptions and the stories we've been told. When asked how they knew that something had happened a certain way, they said things like *It had to have happened that way because*…and then revealed that they saw step one and step three and filled in the blanks to make up a step two.

Assumptions break down under questioning because they're not made of substance but of assumptions.

Yeah, it was probably unusual for people to think of moving to be with someone after such a short time, but what did that matter? Why was he comparing himself with this idea of normal anyway? It didn't matter where he lived. He worked from home, and most of his friendships were long distance.

Cheat on him? Ash didn't really seem like a cheater. Get sick of him? Possible. But he could get sick of Ash too. Relationships didn't always last forever, but that was a feature, not a bug.

As for a secret family, well…even Truman had to admit that was likely a once-in-a-lifetime reason for a breakup.

"Okay, but seriously, Ash. What if I could stay?"

"Please, don't." Ash's voice was choked. "I know you can't. Or if you did, I'd feel like you messed up your whole life for me, and it's too much pressure."

"It wouldn't be messing it up. It'd be improving it, if I got to be with you."

Ash looked at Truman with the eyes of a ghost. He didn't look hopeful or excited at the prospect of Truman moving here. He looked haunted.

"You've done so much for me," Ash said. "Helped me so much. I'll never forget it, and I hope you know how much I appreciate it. But…it would never work. I barely have time to take care of myself, and…I'm no fun. With my mom, and the shop, and…"

His next words were so soft and choked that Truman wished he hadn't been able to hear them. But he could. And he couldn't unhear them.

"I don't have anything left to give."

And there it was. Ash didn't *want* him to move here. He didn't have the capacity for a relationship. He appreciated that Truman had helped the last few weeks, regretted catching feelings, and was now ameliorating the error.

Truman forced himself to stand up before he became rooted to the ground with misery.

"I understand," he choked out. "Sorry to have bothered you."

And then he darted for the door because in about two seconds an ocean of grief was going to drown him, and he couldn't let Ash see that.

# 25

# GRETA

"Kill me," Carys groaned into Greta's shoulder the next morning.

She was terribly hungover, and Greta felt awful for her.

"Want some water?"

Carys made a tiny sound in the affirmative, and Greta got her some water and two Tylenol, which she took gratefully.

"What can I do to help, baby? Want me to clean up? I could make breakfast?"

"No thanks," Carys croaked. "Honestly, I just need to sleep today. Can I call you tonight?"

"Okay," Greta said and dropped a kiss on Carys' cheek.

She went home and got Horse for his morning walk. As they approached the coffee shop, one of the regular baristas, outside on a smoke break, waved at them. Inside, another chatted with Greta about a play she was in and gave her a postcard with the information on it.

"I'll check it out," Greta promised as she left with her coffee.

She and Horse continued on what had become their regular route. Familiar faces waved to them and Greta waved back.

Other dog walkers smiled as they walked past. They stopped in a park, and Greta sat on her favorite bench to look at the flowers and people-watch.

*I have a life here*, she thought. *I have a regular coffee shop. I recognize people. I have a favorite bench. The people at the co-op recognize me. I exist here.*

Greta imagined herself as a piece of charcoal, deepening the mark she left every time she walked the same route, said hello, was recognized as part of the fabric of this place. When she'd arrived, she had felt anonymous. It hadn't felt bad or good, but she'd been aware that she was moving through the space without registering on it.

Now that she felt different, she was able to see that she'd felt that way for a lot of her life, even in the places she'd been far longer than New Orleans. Four years spent in Portland for college, and though she'd had friends, regular hangouts, people she recognized and who recognized her, it had all been tied up in a neat little package of impermanence. Whether because she knew her college years would come to an end or because they'd felt removed from the larger world, Greta didn't know.

More confusing was realizing that she'd felt that way about Owl Island too. She'd lived there her whole life, except those four years, and she knew nearly everyone. They all knew her. She had a favorite coffee shop there, which was easy since there was only one. She had favorite benches and hangouts and said hello to people and was waved to, just like here.

But because she'd never chosen to be there, because she'd always been part of a family unit, she still felt like she hadn't left a mark.

"I was invisible to myself," she said.

Horse turned his massive head and looked up at her questioningly.

*I want to do things. I want to leave an impression and be impressed upon. I want to choose. I want to be a singular person and not one limb of a family. I want to be myself,* Greta thought.

"Horse, I want to *do* things."

Horse nodded and bumped her knee with his head in clear support.

"Okay, let's go," she said, determined.

Two hours later, Greta had showered, changed, and let herself back into Eleventh House through the unlocked back door, patting Teacup on her way inside. There was no sign of any of its inhabitants having yet stirred, so Greta popped in her headphones, tuned into her new favorite podcast—*ShadowCast*, on Truman's recommendation—and began to clean up the living room and kitchen.

In spite of Helen's dire threats, there were still cups and plates on every surface. The garbage can was full, which likely explained it, so Greta gathered all the trash and took it outside. Then she started on the dishes. When those were done, it was nearing 2:00 p.m., and Carys still hadn't emerged from her room, so Greta decided to make her some food. It was what her mom always did when one of them was sick. She said food helped, whether you were hungry or not.

Greta found eggs in the refrigerator and some brioche buns that had been used in one of the dishes the night before in the bread box and made Carys an egg sandwich with cheese, ketchup, and hot sauce, the way she liked it.

Sandwich in hand, Greta knocked softly on Carys' door and was met with a bark.

"Hey," she said softly, easing the door open and perching

gently on the side of Carys' mattress. "I made you an egg sandwich and some coffee."

Carys made a disgusted sound and buried her face in the pillow.

"You've gotta eat, baby," Greta said. "You'll feel better."

Carys made another no sound, and Greta put the plate on her bedside table.

"Well, okay, I'll leave it here for you. Try and eat, okay?"

Carys didn't respond. Greta rubbed her back for a minute, then left her alone.

$\longleftrightarrow$

Greta went to a cheesy action movie on Canal Street, browsed her favorite bookstore, then walked down to the river and sat on a bench, staring out at its brown waters. On a whim, she started to look into the cost of movers and was instantly horrified. How did anyone ever move? She looked at renting a small moving truck instead, and that was much more reasonable.

The truth was, she didn't have very many possessions. She didn't have a car. Most of her furniture had come with the house, so it was just her clothes, books, and, most importantly, her plants. She walked home watching TikToks about hacks for moving with plants and felt pretty optimistic by the time she neared home.

Her phone rang, and she smiled when she saw it was Carys.

"Hey, how are you feeling?" she answered.

"Not great," Carys said.

"Do you want me to come over?"

"Yeah, if you're free. I'd like to talk."

Something lurched in Greta's stomach at her words. "Talk? About what?"

"I'll be around all evening, okay?"

"I can come now," Greta said. "I'm right by your place anyway."

Carys was installed on the couch, wrapped in a blanket when Greta arrived. She looked rough, and Greta was immediately in caretaking mode.

"God, babe, can I do anything for you?"

Carys shook her head and patted the couch. "Did you clean up in here?" she asked.

"Yeah. And the kitchen. It was no problem."

"And you made me food."

"Did you eat? Did it help?"

"Listen," Carys said. She sounded very serious, her expression stony. "I know that you meant well. You always do. But I really don't like that you didn't listen to me."

"Wait, sorry, what?"

"You offered to clean up and make me food, and I said I didn't want that. I told you I just needed to sleep."

"I know, I just thought..." Greta was confused. Was it *bad* that she'd cleaned up? "I didn't want you to have to deal with a trashed place when you woke up. You were all hungover and you were so generous to throw the party."

Carys shook her head. "We clean up together every year. It's a tradition, and part of the tradition is complaining about how horrible we feel. I know it sounds silly, but it's what we do."

The sick feeling in Greta's stomach intensified. She'd fucked up. Again.

"I'm sorry. I didn't know." Her voice sounded choked.

"I know you didn't *know*. That's why I explicitly told you."

Greta replayed their conversation in her head. Carys *had* told her explicitly not to. But that was what people always said.

"I guess I just thought you were being polite. But that anyone would want someone to clean up."

Greta thought of her mom. If you asked her if she wanted you to clear the table, she would say no, but if you just did it, she really appreciated it. Her father would never ask for assistance, so you just had to pick up a box and start helping.

Carys shook her head. "I wasn't being polite. I told you what I wanted, and you didn't respect it. This wasn't about what 'anyone' would've wanted. This was about what I wanted. I told you, and you did the opposite."

"I…" Greta didn't know what to say. "You're upset because I cleaned up and made you food."

She felt like her brain was glitching, because it came out sounding accusatory rather than clarifying.

Finally, Carys' voice rose, and Greta realized that she'd been keeping a tight rein on her temper. It reminded her of the detached way she'd spoken to her mother the day before, which horrified her.

"No. I'm *upset* because I was really clear about something and you didn't respect it. Listen, I understand that you were trying to do something sweet. Trying to take care of me. But it really bums me out that you didn't listen. I want you to pay attention to *me*, to what I *say* I want. Not to just act on your interpretation of what you think I want. I can't handle that shit. You know about my mom. This is a huge thing for me. I need to be able to say what I want and what I *don't* want and have it heard and respected. If I had wanted food, I would've told you. If I had wanted you to clean, I would've accepted your generous offer. But what I said was that I needed to sleep and be left alone, and you didn't respect it. You just did what you thought was best, and it wasn't."

Greta felt like her guts were turning inside out.

"Fuck. Carys, I'm so sorry. I didn't… I honestly was trying to take care of you. I didn't think about it that way at all. I'm really sorry."

"Thanks for saying that. This is, like, a thing you do. You know? You try to take care in the ways that you *assume* someone might want. But those gestures are about your assumptions and not about the person you want to take care of."

"I do?"

"Yeah. Like with the ice cream the other day—you did the same thing. So I'm telling you: when I say I want something, that's what I want. When I say I don't want something, I don't mean that you should go behind my back and do it anyway because secretly I do want it. Okay?"

Greta's stomach flipped. When Carys put it that way, what she'd done sounded absolutely horrible. Then another even more horrible thought dawned on her.

"Oh my god, I'm my mother. Fuck! This is exactly what she does! She thinks she knows what all of us *actually* need, and she just does it. I'm… Oh my god."

Greta shoved her hands in her hair and fisted it. Was this how it happened? Was it impossible to escape her family even seventeen hundred miles away? She hadn't even realized her own thought process, but she had done the exact opposite of what Carys had asked and hadn't even *noticed*. How? How was it possible?

She dropped to the couch like a stone. "Fuck, I'm so sorry," she said, horrified. "I'm *so* damn sorry."

Carys' expression had softened considerably. She laid a hand, palm up, on Greta's knee, and Greta took it, squeezing her fingers tightly.

"Thank you. I accept your apology, and we're all good. Just keep it in mind in the future, okay?"

Greta nodded avidly, thinking hard.

"God, now all I can think of is what other, like, grenades are buried in my brain just waiting to explode parent-ness all over you. I mean…um…all over…people. People I'm in relationships with," she amended awkwardly.

Carys smiled. "I'm sure they're in there. Lord knows we all have them."

Greta bit her lip. "That was a fight, right? We just had a fight. But we're…okay?"

"We had a talk about a thing that happened that I didn't like and won't accept," Carys said. "Is that a fight?"

"The word doesn't matter, I guess. Just…you were so calm."

Carys blew out a breath, curls lifting. "Yeah, well. Lots of therapy. Also, did I mention therapy?"

Greta smiled, settling into the couch more comfortably.

"My mom is totally activated by any emotion, so I guess I prefer conflict that's the opposite of the way it goes with her."

"And the other thing?" Greta prompted.

"Hmm?"

"Are we…okay?"

Carys looked her in the eyes and nodded. "We're okay. But I wanna be really clear. Apologies only mean something to me if behavior changes. So we're okay. But if this keeps happening after we've discussed it, I won't be."

Greta swallowed hard. It sounded so threatening.

Then she stopped herself. No, not threatening. Honest. Clear. Straightforward. Neutral. Greta was the one who was thinking about threats and ultimatums. Of course an apology didn't mean shit if you kept doing the thing you apologized for.

"Got it. I'm going to try really hard. But if it seems like maybe it's happening again, do you think—I mean, could you—or…" She stopped, trying to find a way to express herself without being like *Help me not hurt you.*

"Yes, if I see you unconsciously acting out patterns of socialization ingrained in you by your family of origin, I will point them out and suggest that you contemplate applying critical thinking to the situation." Carys grinned and stuck out her tongue. "How's that shit for therapy?"

Greta was too grateful even to laugh. "Very impressive. Thank you."

"And I know it's hard for you, but *you* can just say what you want too," Carys said. "I'll always respect it."

Greta was propelled to her feet. She began to pace the living room. Carys looked up at her.

"I can," Greta said. "I can."

"It takes some practice if you're not used to it. I really get that," Carys said sympathetically.

"It's so wild, because I *know* that I could just say what I wanted. But it feels so rude or selfish or something. But then I'm like, why on earth would it be selfish to ask for what you want? It's not like you're putting a gun to someone's head and making them do it if they don't want to. Right? Like, how fucked up is it that in my family, people don't ask for what they want, and they do the opposite of what people say because they *know* no one is asking for what they actually want? What the hell?"

Carys nodded the instantly recognizable nod of someone who has been through the same process of coming to understand. "It's so real. Families have these whole cultures of communication, and when you're in it, it's totally normal. Bonus points if it happens to work for everyone in that family. But it's often not transferable across family lines. Like, when I started college, I assumed that anyone who asked me about myself would use that information against me someday. So to avoid it, I would lie and tell them stuff that wasn't true, so when they inevitably tried to mess with me because of it, it wouldn't hurt me. Needless to say, I spent my first couple years of college without any friends, because I just didn't trust anyone or connect with them legitimately."

Greta nodded, listening closely.

"I had to teach myself, like, oh, okay, not everyone is the way your mother is, so you can't treat them like they are. And it was so damn hard, but over the next two years, I really made an effort to interrogate my thoughts every time I fell into that way of thinking. Anyway, you can do it. It just takes work."

"Can I tell you something true?" Greta asked.

"Always."

Greta's heart pounded in her chest, and she felt a trickle of sweat run down the base of her spine. "I want to move here."

She said it simply and clearly and without explanation.

A slow, delighted smile crept across Carys' lips. "I want you to too."

Well, that had gone well. Greta decided to try it again. "I'm scared because I don't want you to think that I'm only moving because of you and put some weird pressure on our relationship," Greta said.

"I can see why," Carys said. "I believe you."

"Fuck!" Greta exclaimed. "Holy fucking *fuck*, I really can say what I want."

Carys winced. "You totally can! Only, if you could just not yell it for, like, twenty-four hours, that would be amazing."

"Sorry, sorry," Greta said softly, dropping kisses on Carys' curls.

"Hey," Carys said, catching her face in her hands. "I'm really proud of you for wanting to change. And thanks for hearing me out and understanding."

"You're welcome. I'm sorry again about messing up today."

"Forgiven."

Greta kissed her softly and tucked her curls behind her ear. "I gotta do something," Greta said, standing up. "I can't leave messages on my mom's phone or text my sisters. That's what I would've done before."

*Before* flickered in her mind like a black-and-white high school yearbook photo, demarcated from *After*, where she stood in the present, in full, glorious, present color.

"I need to go home and tell them. I need to be honest."

"I really admire your emotional integrity," Carys said.

"What does that mean?" Greta was *very* much liking this whole say-what-you-mean thing.

"Um, people talk a lot about being honest, but honesty on its own is just kind of telling the truth about concrete things. But emotions are things you need to be honest about too, and some people can tell the technical truth about what happened or what they said without honoring their feelings. Without having emotional integrity."

"I think I've only had it once in my whole damn life."

"When was that?"

"Ugh. I was totally in love with my high school best friend, Tabitha."

Tabitha had been a constant in Greta's life from elementary through high school. They'd been best friends, confidantes, partners in crime. Tabitha, an only child, loved to sleep over with Greta's large, chaotic family. When her family made Greta want to scream, she sought out the calm and quiet of Tabitha's.

Somewhere along the way—she couldn't be sure exactly when, because it had grown as slowly and naturally as a plant in early spring—Greta realized that her feelings for Tabitha were *more*. Tabitha knew Greta was queer. Greta was pretty sure that Tabitha was not. So she said nothing. Besides, Tabitha was her *person*. She couldn't risk losing her.

But Greta wasn't secretive by nature, and it tormented her. Yes, she often kept things private from her family, but that was because their lives were all so intertwined that it felt like the only way Greta could have anything for herself was to keep it secret. But Tabitha was always the one she confided in. The one who made her feel more like herself for revealing it.

"Senior year, just before graduation, I couldn't stand it any longer. It just felt wrong spending all this time with her and being so close in all these ways but her not knowing this one huge secret about me. About *us*, really. And I was all amped up because of finishing school and knowing I was leaving. Anyway, I told her. I worked myself up to it all evening, while drinking three cups of Martin Wyland's trash can punch. Then, after I was lurchy but before I was woozy, I told her."

Carys cringed. "How'd that go?"

"Oh, very badly." Greta smiled. "I puked on her."

"I'm sorry, what?"

"Yeah. I was kinda tipsy, and when I told her, she made this face that was like—" Greta attempted an I'm-horrified-but-trying-to-be-cool-and-just-want-this-conversation-to-be-over expression. "She didn't even have to say anything. I knew she didn't feel the same. And then I threw up on her shoes."

Carys laughed and covered her mouth apologetically. "You're right. That is totally emotional integrity. Are you still friends?"

"Nah. It ruined everything."

She had apologized to Tabitha (for the puking) and taken it back (the declaration of love), and Tabitha had accepted both. When they went off to college, they'd tried to stay close, making plans for elaborate movie nights and metal detecting along the beach when they were back on Owl Island for the holidays.

But things had never been the same. They did all the same things they once had, but what had once been genuine was now pantomime, and no matter how she tried, Greta couldn't return to a moment before she'd spoken the words that had ruined everything. Semester by semester, they texted less and less until their entire relationship was birthday GIFs and dreading being home for the holidays together. Still, it was a small town—hell, it was an island—and they inevitably ran into each other from time to time.

"Anyway, we grew apart, but now... I don't know. For so long, I thought if I'd never told her, we could've stayed close. But now, I guess I'm not sorry I told her. It was the right thing to do, and who knows what I might've missed out on if I'd spent all that time channeling my energy into that relationship when I knew my feelings wouldn't be returned. Hell, maybe we'd've grown apart anyway."

This thought had never entered Greta's mind before, but

as soon as the words were out of her mouth, she knew they were true.

"And that's why it's integrity, right?" Carys said. "Because you honored the truth of your feelings above what the consequences were for speaking them. We're taught that what matters most is what *happens*. Did we get what we wanted, did we win, did we achieve the most. But what use is getting what you wanted if you get it at the cost of never being real about your own feelings?"

That hit Greta hard.

She'd spent so much time thinking what mattered most was the outcome. Did she succeed? Did her parents approve? Was she pulling her weight in the family? But all those things were done in *spite* of her feelings, not in line with them. She had always worried that telling her sisters she didn't want to do something would *result* in them being upset, but she never thought that doing the thing despite her own feelings was behaving as if her feelings didn't matter.

But they did. They mattered a lot.

"Fuck."

"Yeah. It'll mess you up when you fully realize how little you've honored your own feelings, which are, like, your whole self."

They were her self. What had she thought her self was? She didn't even know, but she'd been wrong.

"*Fuuuck.*"

Carys nodded in solidarity.

"And before, you were telling me your true feelings, and I was only thinking about the outcomes and my own habits of 'taking care of someone,' not about what you wanted at all. Damn. I get it. I really do."

Carys' smile was bright and fond. "Thanks, babe."

Greta was practically buzzing with determination. This was the piece she'd been missing. The thing she'd failed to understand. It was so crucial that she didn't think she could do anything else before she had a conversation with her family. It was scary and huge, but if she could express to them how she felt…how bad she'd been feeling…if they loved her, they'd want to help. Right? She had a free airline chit since her flight to New Orleans had been delayed and rerouted. She could go see them right now.

"I think I gotta go talk to my family. Can I…?"

She approached Carys, not sure if they'd repaired everything enough to warrant a kiss.

"Of course. Come here."

She sank down beside Carys, and they wrapped their arms around each other.

"I don't mean this in a patronizing way," Carys said, "but I'm really proud of you for confronting your family. It's so hard. You're really brave to do it."

Brave wasn't a word that Greta would ever have used to describe herself, but she liked it. She wanted it to suit her.

"Thanks. Is it okay if I call you and tell you about it?"

"You can call me any time, Greta. Any time." Carys looked down and fiddled with the blanket. "You're…you're coming back, right?"

Greta had spent weeks seeing Carys as mature and unflappable. She'd known, of course, that no one was confident all the time, but even seeing Carys' response to her mother hadn't shaken her vision. That one sentence, though, reminded her that Carys was scared and insecure like anyone. That she'd lost people and been hurt and had desires that she must fear not being fulfilled.

Greta was glad to see it. Glad to be able to offer something to Carys.

She cupped Carys' beautiful face in her hands and looked directly into her whiskey-brown eyes.

"You bet your sweet ass I'm coming back."

Carys closed her eyes and nodded, then kissed her so sweetly Greta almost couldn't pull away.

## 26

## GRETA

"Dude, you're saving my life right now."

"You know it, kid," Ramona yelled over the music.

Greta had found a flight leaving that afternoon and booked it after nearly an hour of being put on hold, told her free flight wasn't available yet, and being transferred ten times. When she'd texted Ramona to see if she could borrow her car, Ramona had offered to drive her herself.

Now they were cruising away from Ramona's house with Garden Gate's new album blasting.

They drove past the Lafayette No. 1 cemetery, and Greta felt herself flush at the memory of her encounter with Carys, and past Camilla's house, where she'd spent a lovely morning with the Garden Gang. At a stop sign, Greta thought she recognized a house.

"Wait, hold on, is that…" She checked her text thread with Truman, looking for the picture he'd sent weeks ago. "Ramona. That's Truman's shitty ex's house, right?"

"Yup. Bastard."

Greta thought of Truman—sweet Truman whose biggest regret about Guy had been that he hadn't exposed his cheating to Guy's partner. Truman, who had told her that he wished she'd go kick Guy's ass since he couldn't do it. She burned with an audacious desire for justice.

"Hang on. I gotta do something." Greta unbuckled her seat belt.

"What are you… Gasp! Greta Russakoff, you are *not*."

Greta raised an eyebrow. "Watch me."

"Omigod, *yesssss*!"

Greta stalked up the sidewalk to the house on the corner, primly decorated with white lights and a tasteful fir wreath on the front door. She felt like she was made of lightning, like at any moment she'd be blasted off the ground with the sheer energy of her conviction.

The doorbell chimed an echoey tune, and she heard footsteps.

"Oh shit, oh shit, ohshit," she muttered under her breath. It took every ounce of strength to plant her feet and not run back to Ramona's car.

A handsome man opened the door and smiled quizzically.

"Can I help you?"

"Um, are you Guy?"

"Nope, that's my husband. Want me to get him?"

"No. I need to tell you that your husband is a lying, cheating sleaze. I'm so sorry, because I know this is an awful thing to hear, but I wanted you to know."

The man's face went tight and his eyes narrowed. It was not the face of someone shocked at hearing unexpected news but of someone getting confirmation of something suspected or feared.

"Who's there, honey?" a voice called, and then Guy appeared.

"I'm a friend of Truman's, you scuzzbucket," Greta said.

The man's face was a mask of calm. "Who?"

It was chilling.

"Yeah, whatever. Anyway, I'm really sorry you're married to a dick, but I'm sure you can do better. Your feelings are important, and you don't have to put up with garbage!"

Greta's heart was pounding, and she knew she sounded ridiculous, but she didn't care.

"Happy Chanukah!" she yelled, and then she ran down the path and threw herself back in Ramona's car.

Ramona's eyes were wide and she was grinning hugely.

"Daaaaaaaamn, that was amazing!"

"Drive!"

Ramona peeled out of a stop and headed for the highway. With the windows down and Garden Gate blasting, Greta had never felt more alive.

"I can't believe you did that," Ramona said. "That was so deeply unlike you, and I fucking loved it!"

"He deserved to know his husband's a piece of shit, and that asshat doesn't deserve to get away with breaking everyone's heart! Truman told me his biggest regret was that he hadn't told Guy's husband. Now he knows."

Conviction, adrenaline, and shock at herself all mixed together, and Greta grinned at Ramona.

She leaned toward the open window and yelled, "Happy Chanukah, New Orleans!" out the window as they turned onto Washington Avenue.

"Okay, okay, not the place anymore," Ramona said, rolling up the windows as people turned, trying to figure out if they should be offended by whatever had been yelled at them. "Careful your enthusiasm for righting wrongs doesn't turn you into a total asshole."

Greta smiled. "I'll remember that," she said.

# A MESSAGE
# FROM RAMONA

**RAMONA to GREAT!A RUSSAKOFF**

You got this, dude. No matter what they say, you know you're doing the right thing! Text me from the airport and I'll pick you up.

# 27
# GRETA

Greta had kept her conviction through the flight, the ride from the airport, and the ferry. But when she stepped onto Owl Island, malaise dropped over her like a fog. This place trapped her, like a heroine in some gothic novel.

She hadn't told her family she was coming, preferring the element of surprise. Even though she'd only been gone for three weeks, it felt like everything had changed.

Now, when she walked through the slush on the uneven sidewalks of Owl Island, she compared them to the cracked sidewalks of New Orleans, with inset metal circles that had symbols carved into them.

Now, when she saw lights coming from the windows of houses she'd walked past a million times, she thought of the doors of restaurants in New Orleans, thrown open to the warmth of the day; of upper balconies spilling fragrant bougainvillea and jasmine and music into the night; of secret gardens and sagging porches and a purple sky over a brown-gray river that never stopped moving.

When she got to number 103 Mockingbird Lane, her heart was in her throat. Familiar silver-and-blue tinsel bedecked the trees outside her parents' house, and a blue foil star garland outlined the front door. On the windows were the peel-and-stick decals of dreidels, menorahs, and Stars of David that her father had brought home years ago so she and her sisters could decorate—and, more importantly, *re*decorate—as many times as they wanted.

That year, she and Adelaide had started a window decal war by sneaking out of their room late at night and collecting the decals from the whole house to plaster their bedroom windows. It had escalated when they woke two mornings later to find that all their light bulbs and mirrors had been removed—a power move when you were fourteen and had unpredictable hair.

It was only when Greta let herself inside and heard singing that she realized Chanukah had begun.

She walked into the dining room and gave an awkward wave. "Uh, hey."

Her mother jumped up. "You came home! Oh, honey, I knew you wouldn't miss Chanukah. Didn't I tell you?" she said over her shoulder to the table. Greta's shoulders tightened. "Oh, we've missed you so much." She hugged Greta and brushed her hair back. "You're tan!"

"Yeah, it's summer in New Orleans. Well, I mean, it's still winter, but their winter is warm like our summer. So it's sunny. You know."

"Oh my gosh, really? Turns out we've actually heard of seasons, even here in provincial Maine," Sadie simpered. Tillie shot Sadie a quelling look.

Greta began to explain that she'd misspoken and tried to correct herself, and why did Sadie always have to be such a rude asshole about everything? Then she paused. That was what the old Greta would have done.

The new Greta didn't need to explain because she hadn't done anything wrong. Sadie had interpreted her ungenerously, and that wasn't her problem.

So she moved on.

"Hey, I'm really happy to see you all. Sorry to show up in the middle of Chanukah without calling. But I needed to talk to you." She looked at Sadie. "And I'd really appreciate if you'd let me say what I need to say before you respond."

The flames from the menorah flickered. The third night. Greta had never spent Chanukah away from her family before. She waited for the sadness to come, but it didn't.

They all stared at her. Her dad had paused halfway through rising—presumably to come hug her—and sat back down half off his chair. Sadie was glaring expectantly. Tillie waited patiently. Maggie was leaning back, sitting cross-legged on her chair, smiling faintly like she couldn't wait to see what was about to happen. Adelaide watched with her head cocked as she always did when she was confused. Greta wanted to grab one of her braids and tug her head straight, only Adelaide hadn't worn her hair in two braids since they were eleven.

Although she'd spent the entire flight planning what she was going to say on cocktail napkins and the notes app in her phone, Greta's mind had become the blank blue sky above the bay on a summer afternoon. She searched for a beginning and found only edgelessness. The urge to squeeze her eyes shut or turn her back on her family so they couldn't see her was strong. There had been a time when anytime she needed to say anything important, she'd closed her eyes.

But now, instead, she summoned the person who had told Guy's husband the truth in his own doorway, the person who had told Carys she was coming back to her. The person who had gone someplace new and scary and fallen head over heels in love with it. She summoned the most powerful feeling she could conjure and opened her mouth.

"I'm in love with Carys" was what came out. Her eyes widened.

Sadie snorted.

Greta shook her head to clear it. "That's not what I meant to say."

*But it's true, isn't it?*

It was true. Greta put it in her pocket to take out and savor later.

"What I meant to say is that I love New Orleans. I've made new friends. I've met wonderful people. And yeah, one of them is someone I'm dating. And it's made me realize that…I've always felt so damn guilty when my desires didn't line up with what you all wanted for me. Like, I've tried to play along, but…it's okay if I want my own things that are different from what you want. Look, I love you all so much, but I *hate* it here. I don't want to live here. I don't want to work at Russakoff's. And I know that's what you guys want and I'm sorry, but…I'm gonna go back to New Orleans, and I'm…I'm gonna stay."

Greta felt like she was suspended between two weather fronts, held safe in limbo for the moment before she was sucked into the one looming on the horizon.

She expected—what? Tears, perhaps? Mostly from her mother, and maybe from Adelaide.

What broke the silence was a single laugh, like a cannonball.

Sadie's face was venomous, and when she spoke, her tone matched. "You're so selfish, Greta. Sorry Owl Island doesn't have enough drag bars for you or whatever. Just your family."

"Damn, Sadie, it's not about that! PS," Greta added, voice sharp, "your stereotypes could really use some work."

Maggie stifled a snort with her fist.

"Have you ever stopped to ask yourself why you care so much if I stay here?" Greta asked, squaring her shoulders. "You don't even like me."

"Oh, what, like you're a big fan of mine?" Sadie retorted.

Before Greta could reply, her mother chimed in. "Greta, you've had your adventure. Now it's time to come back home. Let me make you a plate."

Nell moved to the table where Greta now noticed a place setting for her was already laid.

"No thank you," Greta said. "I ate."

"Honey," Greta's father said. "Have you really felt like you had to do things you didn't want to go along with the family? We always wanted you to be who you are. All of you." He looked around at his daughters, and the guilt scratched at Greta's gut.

She looked at her sisters. Sadie looked scornful, but not as scornful as she usually did. Tillie looked sad. Adelaide's eyes were narrowed as if she too were confused. Maggie winked exaggeratedly and gave her a tiny thumbs-up. But her father looked shocked, drained. Her mother was working hard not to look at anyone.

"Am I, like, delusional right now?" Greta said. "Please someone tell me this isn't in my head, because I'm freaking out."

Maggie rolled her eyes at the silent room. "It's not in your head, dude! Come on, guys." She looked around the dining room table. "You know what she means. Sure, there was never, like, a you-do-this-or-else, but it was always just easier if we all agreed 'cause there're so many of us that we knew it could only ever be one thing. So if everyone wanted ice cream but you wanted cake, you knew it would be easier to just want ice cream rather than try and convince everyone else to want cake or to be disappointed that you didn't get what you wanted."

Her mom sniffed. "I'm sorry we didn't have the money to give each of you the snack food of your choice at all times," she said, sounding so much like Sadie that Greta almost laughed. Then realized that, no, Sadie sounded like their mom.

"It's not like that, Mom," Maggie said. "It's not a fault, just a fact."

"I know what you mean," Tillie said. "I just never care that much about the details, so I guess I was fine going with what everyone else wanted."

Greta had always looked up to Tillie. Sweet, selfless, agreeable Tillie was never the problem, always the peacemaker, and always seemed satisfied with whatever the outcome. Greta had felt like she could never measure up and had felt guilty for not being more like her.

Now, for the first time, Greta felt sad for her.

"You get what I'm talking about, right, Ads?" she asked her twin.

Adelaide nodded slowly but didn't say a word. Greta knew what that meant: she was processing something large, and she'd need to check back in later.

"Well, I don't," Sadie said. "Compromise is a good thing. Mom and Dad needed us to get along and share, so we did, because we're not spoiled monsters. The fact that you don't know the difference between compromise and martyrdom isn't their fault."

"I never said it was their fault, Sadie!"

Then the penny dropped, and Greta felt utterly foolish that it had taken her so long to understand.

"It must have been really hard on you to feel the strain to make us agree to take pressure off Mom and Dad, huh?"

Sadie started to snap at her out of habit but paused. "What?"

"You're the oldest. You must have seen how hard Mom and Dad worked to provide for us, to give us time. So of course you wanted to help, because you identified with them. So if we weren't compromising or sharing or whatever, you knew it meant more work for them. So you tried hard to help out."

Sadie narrowed her eyes.

"Probably you tried so hard to help out that there was stuff you wanted to do that you didn't get to, huh? You were so busy trying to be helpful that you didn't get to be yourself either."

Sadie sat back down. For a moment, she looked like she had absorbed what Greta'd said. Then she shook her head. "Whatever. I was the most mature, so sure, I helped keep you all in line. But I'm an adult now, and I can do whatever I want. I choose to stay here."

"Well, I'm really glad to hear that, Sadie. I want you to be happy."

And she really did. But it came out sounding sarcastic because she was talking to Sadie. So Sadie flipped her off.

"I'm going to the West Coast for the summer with Naveen, and I'm moving there after graduation," Maggie blurted.

All eyes turned to her.

"What?" their mother said, sounding horrified.

Maggie gave a nervous laugh. "Uh. Yeah. Seemed like an appropriately upheaval-y moment to bring it up."

"That's awesome," Greta said deliberately. "I can't wait to

come visit you there. And I can't wait for all of you to come visit me in New Orleans and let me show you around."

"Some of us have jobs and can't just pick up and fly across the country at a moment's notice," Sadie said.

Fury blazed through Greta, but before she could open her mouth, Maggie spoke.

"Would you stop being so shitty to Greta all the time, Sadie? I don't know what your deal is with her, but you never talk to the rest of us the way you talk to her."

Sadie blinked at Maggie. "She just swanned in here and accused us all of ruining her life and now is like, 'Oh, come visit my beautiful paradise that I've lived in for one second.'"

"That is not what I said, Sadie!" Greta exploded. "You're so determined to take anything I say in the worst possible way. But you know what, that's not my problem. I think you feel like since you've been the good, responsible oldest child your whole life, you're mad at anyone who hasn't. You're bitter and jealous because you think if you didn't get to do something, then no one else should get to do it either. But like you said, you're an adult now, and you can do whatever you want. So if what you want is to be a shady bitch to me all the time, then I guess that's your call. But once we aren't around each other all the time anymore, we won't have a relationship if you're like this."

"This is ridiculous," Sadie said and stood. "I'm going upstairs. Tell me when she leaves."

"Biiiitch," Maggie whispered to Greta.

"She doesn't mean any of that," Greta's mom said. "You're her sister and she loves you. We all do."

"What would you think if she does mean it?" Greta asked.

"No, no, she doesn't."

"Right, Mom, but I'm asking what your opinion of her would be if she really meant every word. Because it's a lot of work going around assuming someone doesn't mean 80 percent of what they say."

"I don't know what you're getting at, Greta Louise. She's your sister."

Greta's patience with her mother snapped. "I don't actually believe you're as oblivious to Sadie's shit as you make out to be. I think you know she'll stir things up so that you don't have to do it, and then you can sit back and act like you're the nice one while she does the dirty work. Like at the auction this year. You knew I'd hate it, because you know I'm queer and you know I think the auction is a horrific callback to selling enslaved people. But you *let* Sadie be the one I was mad at so your hands would be clean. You want us all to stay here, under your thumb, so you'll always know what we're doing and *you* don't have to do the work to figure out who you are or what you want for yourself besides being a mother."

Greta ran out of breath as her brain caught up with her mouth.

Her mother goggled at her, mouth open, but nothing came out.

"Greta, don't," Tillie murmured. Her sister looked scared. Even Adelaide wasn't meeting her eyes.

"No, I'm sorry, but I have to say this. I don't want this life. I have no scorn for it! It's just not what's right for me."

Greta could practically *see* her mother wipe her previous comment away and choose to focus on her most recent one.

"You don't need to work with us if you don't want to," Nell said stiffly. "You could do whatever you want and we can still be a family."

Greta wanted to scream. "We *are* still a family! Me living in New Orleans, or Maggie living on the West Coast, it doesn't make us any less of a family."

Their mother sniffed. "Is it so terrible that I want all my babies near me?" she said.

"No, of course it's not terrible," Greta said. "It's just not what's going to happen." She waited for Addie or her father to chime in, but they didn't. "I wish you could be happy for me," Greta said, taking them all in with her eyes. "Did you hear the part about how I'm in love with Carys and I adore New Orleans?" she added hopefully.

Tillie nodded absently. Adelaide chewed on her lip. Her father frowned at his uneaten plate of latkes and pot roast.

Her mother said, "You've only been there a few weeks, Greta. I'm glad you've had a fun trip, but we're talking about the rest of your life! How will you live?"

"I'll get a job."

Her mother was shaking her head. "I'll never get to see you," she said. She began clearing the dinner table aggressively, even though no one had finished their food. "We'll never be together the way we have been," she added when she reentered the dining room. "Nothing will be the same."

"Nope, it won't be. But that doesn't have to be bad."

Nell continued clearing the table, silent tears streaming down her face.

"I'm sorry, Mom. I'm sorry you're upset. I wish—"

Her mother waved her away and swept into the kitchen, closing the pantry door behind her. It was where she went to cry because she thought no one could hear her in there.

"Addie?"

Greta's twin was staring at her, the betrayal clear on her face.

"I'll miss you so much," she said. And before Greta could reply, she quietly went upstairs. Greta's heart broke a little bit more.

"Dad?"

She was hoping that he might give her his blessing. That he might understand. Her father just said, "You'll need to give her some time." Then he followed her mom to the pantry.

↔

The last time she'd left her parents' house three weeks before, she had been defeated and furious. Now, she was sad. Sad that her parents hadn't heard her the way she wanted. Sad that she hadn't left with their blessing. Sad that Adelaide wasn't on her side. But sad wasn't the same as defeated. For as heartbroken as she was, she *knew* she'd done what she had to do to be true to herself. And that? That felt really damn good.

Thinking hard about what had just happened, she arrived on her own front stoop before she knew it.

"I'm home, babies!" Greta announced to her plants as the door closed behind her. Then she saw unfamiliar boots and remembered that she didn't live here right now. "Oh, shit, shit!"

She debated backing out the door and closing it behind her. She could go to Ash's and crash on his couch. Hell, maybe Truman wasn't even in and hadn't heard her.

"Um, Greta?"

The first thing she noticed about Truman was that he was adorable. The second thing she noticed was that he looked awful—puffy eyes, a reddened nose, and lips bitten red.

"I am so sorry," Greta said. "Would you believe that I

somehow forgot that our entire house swap had happened in
the aftermath of a massive fight-slash-processing-session with
my family?"

"Yes."

"Oh. Well. Thanks. 'Cause that's what happened. Anyway,
I just need to crash for the night, and it's awesome to meet you,
but since I'm totally unannounced, I can go to Ash's. Sorry I
disturbed you."

Greta hadn't thought it was possible, but at the mention of
Ash, Truman's face became even sadder.

"No, no, that's okay," he said. "You should stay here. It's
your house."

He began bustling around, picking things up, and Greta
kicked off her boots.

"Hey, stop." She pushed him down on the couch. "What's
wrong?"

Truman closed his eyes and bit his lip, shaking his head
like he could banish the problem. "It's pathetic," he said.

"Oh, I assure you, no matter what's going on I will sympa-
thize. I just left my mother crying in a pantry."

The tiniest bit of interest peeked through his misery.

"So what's up with you? I know we don't *actually* know
each other, but I feel like we do, so do you want to skip the
small talk and just be friends? I could really use the distraction,
to be honest."

Truman looked up at her with brown eyes full of tears.

"I fell in love with Ash, and he doesn't want me to stay."

The tears spilled over, and Truman squeezed his eyes shut.

"Oh my god, that's amazing!"

Truman's eyes flew open.

"Sorry, no. That's horrible. No. I just meant Ash is so

great, and he deserves to have someone awesome fall in love with him."

Truman snorted. "Yeah, lucky him. And I offered to stay here with him. But what kind of total chump uproots their whole life to move thousands of miles away after knowing someone for three weeks? So obviously he told me to get lost."

Greta pursed her lips. "Erm. Well…"

And Greta told Truman about her own love affair with Carys and with New Orleans.

"And you haven't told her yet?"

"That I love her? No. But she knew I was coming back, so…"

"She probably knows," Truman concluded. "You're very… um…easy to read."

"Am I?"

Truman's smile was gentle. "Very. It's nice."

"Oh. Cool. Anyway, my point is that you're not a chump."

"Or maybe we both are," Truman offered.

"I choose to reject that interpretation," Greta said, and Truman almost laughed. But something was still niggling at her. "Okay, tell me what happened with Ash, because honestly, you seem like someone he'd totally adore."

Truman told her the sweetest story of kindness and help and love and care, and Greta's heart was full for her friend who had had such a tough life.

"Then he said he couldn't see me anymore because it'd hurt too much when I left. But when I offered to stay…" Truman's voice caught. "He said no."

"That's exactly what he said? He told you no?"

Truman threw himself back on the couch cushions.

"No, he's a sweetheart, so he was nice about it. He said he

didn't want me to do that just for him and that he didn't feel like he had anything to give me."

Greta rolled her eyes. That sounded like Ash. "And you let him get away with that?"

Truman looked up.

"You mean as opposed to looking the man I fell for in the face and being like, 'no, I demand that you give me things you don't have after I move somewhere you don't want me'? Um, yeah."

Greta shook her head. "No, as opposed to, like, asking him what he meant and talking about it."

"I tried to get him to talk about it, and he said he couldn't. Then he basically begged me to leave him alone, so I did."

"Listen, I'm not trying to do Ramona levels of witchy meddling here—P.S., has she been sending you strangely cryptic texts that, like, come true?"

"Yes!"

"Freak. Anyway, I've known Ash a long time. If he said he doesn't feel like he has anything to give you, it means he's scared that what he has to offer isn't *enough* for you, not that he *won't* give you anything. You need to talk to him."

She held up her phone.

"Um." Truman's expression was nervous, but he was nodding.

"I'll just tell him to come over, shall I?"

"Ugggghhhh," Truman groaned, burying his face in his hands. "Fine."

Greta dialed. "Ash Sundahl, I am at my house right now, and I demand your presence! That's right, I said demand, because I'm leaving first thing tomorrow morning, and I must hug you."

She hung up. Truman let out a breath of relief.

"He'll come over, and we'll talk about this," Greta said.

A buzz ran through her. She felt powerful.

"Did you know," she confided manically to Truman, "that you don't have to accept whatever happens to you?! That you have power over your life?!"

"Some people do," Truman mumbled. "I gotta take a shower before he gets here. I don't want him seeing me like this."

"I think some eye drops and an ice pack might serve you better." Greta grabbed the former from the bathroom and set Truman to making the latter by wrapping crushed ice in a towel that she applied to his eyes.

Twenty minutes later, she got a text from Ash that said Omw.

# 28
# TRUMAN

Before Greta burst through the door, Truman had been chatting with Germaine and Charlotte. He'd gotten as far as telling them what Ash said about not wanting him to uproot his whole life for him when Charlotte had dumped a wall of text. Often, when Charlotte wall-of-texted, it was simply because she'd switched to using voice-to-text, but sometimes—and this was one of those times—it was because she believed so fully in her opinion that she had to let you know right away. She was, it must be said, right approximately 93 percent of the time, by Truman's calculations. So he'd grudgingly read:

**Truman I love you immensely which is why I need to tell you that you MUST not tuck your tail between your legs and slink away!** (Too late. How had she known?) **You have always wanted a partner—like a full-on, share everything, we-are-a-team PARTNER. The dickwads you've dated haven't wanted that, so you've sanded off the corners of your desire until it's a damn circle. Sphere. Whatever. And NOW, Ash doesn't believe you want that because he can't imagine someone wanting that, but you DO WANT IT SO YOU HAVE TO TELL HIM! You rock so hard but sometimes you are your**

**own worst enemy and I want to SHAKE YOU because you're INFURIATING but I do love you. Goodbye.**

Okay, so she might also have been using voice-to-text.

Truman hadn't had a moment to think about it because of the aforementioned bursting in, but now, as he sat on Greta's couch with his head back and an ice pack over his eyes, as she walked around greeting her plants, he went over it again. He could see why Ash would think he would only be moving here because he did what other people wanted. He had, after all, done literally that. And he could see that Ash would suspect it in this instance, given the whole only knowing one another for three weeks thing.

But…but the part that he had to find a way to tell Ash was the other part. The wanting him part. The wanting to be with him all the time part. The wanting to be involved in all aspects of his life part. But in a partner-y way, not a stalker-y or savior-y way. The…the love part.

The doorbell rang, and Truman snatched the ice pack off his eyes, prayed it had done its job, and shoved it under the cushion. He heard Greta's jubilant exclamation as she launched herself into a hug and cringed, because he knew so well, so intimately, what it felt like to be wrapped up in Ash's arms.

Fuck.

"Where's Truman?" Ash asked. Then, "Oh, Truman."

Ash put a hand to his hair, changed his mind, and tugged on his sweater, changed his mind, and stuck his hands in his armpits, hugging himself. He looked exquisitely uncomfortable.

"Hi," he said.

Truman's *hi* stuck in his throat so only a gurgle came out. It was no more mortifying than anything else that had happened in the last twenty-four hours, so Truman just sat there, resigned to awfulness.

"I'm not gonna say this is an intervention," Greta said, "but I fear some deep miscommunication is going on, and I want to help."

She sat on the chair facing the couch and gestured Ash onto the couch beside Truman. Truman scrambled to the other side to make room. He could feel the air between them charge.

"It's so ridiculous," Greta said. "I feel like I'm just now learning how fucked up my approach to my whole damn life has been, and now I'm, like, a little bit high on the potential for freedom and self-determination, so forgive me if I sound like a total joke." She turned to Truman. "But I can't help but feel like you and I are on these parallel journeys, where we have inverse issues. I've spent all this time trying to live up to other people's expectations and resenting them because I wanted to do my own thing. And you seem like you've spent your time being perfectly happy living by other people's desires because you feel like you can't ever have what you want."

Truman cringed at the accuracy of the description.

"Too harsh?" she said.

"Nah. Just true," Truman said.

He refused to look at Ash even though he was desperate to see his face.

"And, Ash, we've known each other basically forever, so I feel at least partly justified in saying that your thing is that you think no one will ever want to share a life with you because you think your life sucks. But it seems like maybe Truman doesn't think your life sucks. Soooo... Discuss?"

"I don't think your life sucks! I love it here. It's so peaceful and genuine, and I love Thorn and—and—" Truman broke off before he blurted out *And I love you!* because, ya know, mortification.

When Truman managed to get up the courage to look at Ash, he was shaking his head.

"You don't get it," Ash said, voice thick. "My mom. It's like, every night, I'm there to make dinner, eat with her, get her settled, and by the time I get home, after that and working at the shop all day, I'm exhausted. And that's just how it is for…forever. I don't know. And I knew that when I came back here."

He sounded utterly resigned, the same way he had all those times they'd talked about the way the shop wasn't profitable. But Truman was a problem solver by trade and by inclination, and he refused to believe that Ash was consigned to things the way they were forever if he didn't want to be. Certainly there were problems that had no good solutions, but Truman didn't think this was one of them.

He didn't think it was really the time. After all, they were discussing why Ash *didn't* think he should move here. But also…if that was Ash's only reason, surely it was relevant? And what was the worst that could happen? Ash would want him to move here even less?

"What's the biggest reason you have that routine with your mom?" Truman asked. It was always the first question he asked to make sure he understood a situation.

"She gets confused in the evenings a lot. And having me there helps because I'm familiar. It's a routine. Plus she's not great about remembering to eat, so, dinner."

"Okay, so it helps her to have consistency and someone to share the evenings with. Someone familiar."

Ash nodded. He was twisting the bottom of his baby-blue sweater in his fingers, pulling the stitches to their breaking point.

"Could it be someone who wasn't you?"

"I can't afford to pay anyone. I looked into it before I moved back, but it's out of my price range."

"But hypothetically, it could be."

Ash frowned. "It could be if it was someone she knew. Someone consistent. Hypothetically"

"Okay, I have an idea. You know those people your mom invited to coffee?"

Ash nodded.

"She's friendly. She likes people. People like her."

Ash nodded again.

"What if she got housemates? Like, I know most of the older people are already set up. But Carla Muskee was talking about someone's son who's a painter, and I know those two kids who had coffee with your mom are young and probably have limited income. What if you found, like, two younger people who need super cheap accommodations, would be jazzed about having dinner together every night to share the cost and the company, and could be consistent people in your mom's life that would make her feel grounded and secure."

The silence was palpable. Ash looked utterly blank, and for a moment, Truman regretted saying anything. Then, he saw tears at the corners of Ash's eyes, and Ash tried to blink them away. Clearly overcome, Ash's tears came faster and faster.

Truman wanted to launch himself into Ash's arms and stroke his hair, his cheeks, his back. Hold him until he cried every tear he had in him and then could speak.

What actually happened, as he reached out a hand to

squeeze Ash's shoulder, was that something horribly wet and cold grabbed his ass, and Truman squeezed and jumped up.

"What the hell?" Greta said. "Are you okay?"

In the time it took Truman to get both feet on the floor, he realized what had happened.

"Yeah, uh, ice pack melt situation. Sorry. I'll…um…"

He wiped at the wet spot, but that just succeeded in more of the freezing wet spot coming in contact with his butt.

He looked over at Ash and saw that the tears were now streaming down his face.

"Oh, god, Ash, I'm so sorry. I didn't mean to…"

Then he realized that Ash was laughing so hard he couldn't speak.

"Hmph," Truman said and held his wet sweats away from him. "I'll be right back."

In the bedroom, he stripped out of his wet clothes and rummaged around for dry ones. As he was pulling on the new sweats, there was a knock on the door.

"Yeah?"

Ash slipped inside.

"Are you okay?" they both said at the same time.

Truman said, "Fine," and Ash nodded and said, "Yeah."

Ash sank onto Truman's bed and patted the spot beside him. "Do you really think there are people who I could trust who might wanna live with my mom?" he asked.

"Yeah. If that opportunity came up when I was in the situation of needing super cheap accommodations, I absolutely would've jumped on it. I watched this documentary about an experimental housing initiative that they tried in Sweden—or maybe the Netherlands? Shit, I don't remember. God, I'm such an American monster. Anyway."

Ash was smiling slightly and reached out a hand to tentatively stroke Truman's back. Truman smiled his encouragement.

"Anyway, it was about this idea called intergenerational living where students who needed cheap housing got housed in a retirement facility, and in exchange for the rent cut, they had to give five or ten hours a week being 'good neighbors,' which really just meant, like, hanging out and helping the older residents work their computers or paint their nails or serve food or whatever. But what they found out was that it was this amazing boon for everyone involved. The elderly residents who were often lonely and felt cut off from outside life suddenly felt like they were much more connected and felt younger. The younger residents felt like they learned amazing life lessons from the elderly and got to have friends with totally different life experiences. Before they knew it, everyone wanted to make the change permanent. And now it's sprung up all over the world because it's so mutually beneficial."

Truman felt himself getting choked up remembering the stories in the documentary.

"This one guy in his early twenties didn't have any family support because he wanted to be a dancer, and he made friends with this woman in her eighties who had been a dancer when she was young, and they became—" Truman broke off to avoid crying and laughed at himself. "They became best friends, and she was his biggest support system and he showed her contemporary dance videos on YouTube. Oh god, I can't believe I'm crying over dance videos." He laughed and wiped tears from his eyes. "*Anyway*, the point is that I bet there are a lot of people out there who would be super into the idea, and it would help them out just as much as it would help your mom."

Ash stared at him, and Truman found himself reaching out and stroking the tear tracks on his cheeks.

"Are you okay?"

Ash closed his eyes. His voice was rough when he spoke.

"Yeah. I never thought of that. Then when you said it, it was like the damn clouds parted and I thought I saw a ray of sun for the first time in so long. It's like…like I've been so deep in this whole thing for so long that I honest to god stopped trying to think of any solutions and just figured this was my life now. I feel pretty stupid, actually."

Truman caressed his cheek and his jaw and offered tentatively, "You know, that's why it's nice to have a partner sometimes. You can figure things out together. That's what I hear anyway," he hedged.

Ash grabbed his shoulders and looked deep into Truman's eyes. "You have to understand what you'd be getting into," he said fervently. "I couldn't stand for you to leave your whole life behind and then end up here and expect things from me that I can't give. I just…I'm no fun," he concluded.

"I hate fun!" Truman exclaimed. "The shit most people think is fun, I mean." Then Ash's words registered. "Wait. What I'd be getting into. You mean…you'd want me to stay?"

Ash's eyes burned with blue-gray fire. "I have never wanted anything as much in my entire life. I just didn't think it would be fair to—"

Truman knocked him onto his back on the bed and kissed him with everything he had.

"You're such an idiot!" Truman crowed. "I can't believe you said you didn't want me to come here when what you meant was *I don't want you to come here unless you really want to and with full understanding of the reality*. You get that's super confusing, right?"

"I...I just didn't want you to have to give up anything."

"Hey." Truman looked at his beautiful face and made sure he was listening. "I would be giving up things that matter very little to me and gaining things that matter very much."

Tears came to Ash's eyes again, but this time, a smile accompanied them. He pulled Truman down on top of him and wrapped those warm arms around him.

"I can't believe you would do this for me," Ash murmured.

"I'm doing this for us," Truman said. He didn't mention that it was precisely what Ash had done to be with his mother, because that seemed to kind of kill the romance, but he thought about it.

"Us," Ash murmured and kissed Truman. The kiss deepened, until Ash pulled away to exclaim, "Greta!"

"Um, what?"

"We left Greta out there."

Truman giggled. "Oh, right."

They trooped out of the bedroom to find Greta sitting among her carnivorous plants with her eyes closed.

"Hit me," she said without opening her eyes.

"Um. Any chance you might be interested in making this swap a little bit more...permanent?" Truman asked.

A slow smile spread across Greta's face.

"I was going to ask you the same thing."

They spent the rest of the evening talking, and by the time the wine ran out and Greta had to crash for a few hours before heading back to the airport, they had a viable plan.

# 29
## GRETA

Truman and Ash had trooped back to Ash's hand in hand when the wine ran out, and Greta had fallen asleep on the couch for a few hours, setting three alarms on her phone so she wouldn't oversleep and miss her flight.

She'd thought the first alarm was what jarred her from sleep, but it was a knock at the door and then the sound of a key in the lock. Assuming Truman forgot something, Greta grunted and pulled the blanket back over her head.

A moment later, she felt a weight on the cushion next to her, and a hand settled on her head. That didn't seem like something Truman would do. Greta sat up and pulled the blanket away.

"Mom. What are you doing here?"

Her mother looked awful, eyes puffy and nose red.

"I think I've always known you'd leave me," she said. But she sounded less accusatory and more mournful than before. She put a hand on Greta's cheek, and Greta leaned into it. "I'm sorry I didn't realize how unhappy you really were here," her mom said softly. "I...I never wanted that."

"You just wanted me to be nearby."

Her mother nodded. "I like having all my girls around me. I like knowing where you are and what you're doing."

"You know you can still know those things if I don't live near you."

"How?"

"Mom. You just ask."

Nell let out a bark of laughter that Greta recognized; she'd heard herself do it when she was nervous.

"And you'll tell me?"

Greta nodded soberly. "I will. I'll be excited to tell you because I'll be excited about my life. Don't you..." She screwed up her courage. "Don't you want that for me? A life I'm actively excited about, rather than one I just happened to be born into?"

Nell Russakoff tugged at the worn edge of the blanket covering her daughter. "Yes. Of course I do. I want that for you. I'm just sad for myself."

Greta sat up straighter. "Thanks for telling me. I'm really sorry that you have to be sad for me to have the life I want. And I hope you know how hard it's been for me to realize that I could leave. It hasn't been an easy decision. I love you. I love our family. I want us all to be close. But I can't give up my chance at the life I want so that you won't be sad."

"I know that," Nell said. "We know."

Greta twisted her fingers together. "Is Dad really mad?"

"No. Your father agrees with you. He's just protective of me."

"He does?" Greta's heart soared.

"You know what's funny," Nell mused, finally leaning back in the couch and taking her hand off Greta's.

"What?"

"This is what your father and I did. Left our parents

because the lives they lived weren't what we wanted. He didn't want to be in the restaurant business like his father, and I didn't want to live in the city like my parents."

Greta had heard about her grandparents in dribs and drabs over the years—her dad's father had owned a sandwich shop in Cleveland; her mom's parents had lived in downtown Columbus—but she'd never exactly put it together that her parents had *left* them rather than simply moving away as so many people did from their families of origin.

"Did they mind?"

"Oh yes. My mother told me I was selfish to leave. Who would take care of them when they were older? That's why you had children, to depend on in your twilight years."

Greta cringed. "Yikes, that's grim." They shared a conspiratorial eye raise.

"And your father...you know him. He likes everyone to get along. Likes people to be happy."

"Like Tillie."

"Yes. His father wanted him to take over the sandwich shop and be the next generation in the business, but your dad hated it."

"Yeah, I'm imagining him making sandwiches with about the same dexterity he brings to crafting."

"Yes, I'd say that's accurate. God save anyone who ordered a meatball sub."

They chuckled together and Nell reached for Greta's hand.

"I'm sorry," she said simply. "I'm sorry I overreacted earlier. I was upset. But if moving to New Orleans is really what you want, then...you have my blessing."

Greta threw her arms around her mother's neck, tears

threatening. She hadn't realized how much it would mean to her to have her mother's support—her mother, whom she'd thought of so often lately, and critically—and something occurred to her for the first time.

Maybe it wasn't that she didn't respect her mother. Maybe it was that she saw her mother's life as a failure because she didn't see that it was a result of her choices. For Greta, this life *was*, but for her mother? Nell had chosen this life, had built it into what she wanted, just as Greta would do.

"I think once I start doing things I like more, I'll want to tell you about them more," Greta said.

Her mother's face went soft. "I really hope you do. I miss our talks."

Once, she had cherished the moments she found herself alone with her mom, the only child in the room for a few moments, and the way they'd talked. It was only with dissatisfaction that true resentment had set in.

"I miss them too, Mom," she said, voice shaky.

Her first alarm went off then, and they both jumped.

"Hey, I don't suppose you wanna drive me to the airport and I'll tell you all about New Orleans?"

Her mother leaned in, conspiratorial. "Only if you'll also tell me about this Carys you're in love with."

Greta smiled, the word *Carys* enough to lift her heart like a balloon.

"I think I could probably handle that."

# 30
# GRETA

Three weeks ago, when Greta had stepped out of the car on Royal Street in the Marigny, she'd been running away. She'd thought she was running away from her family, and it had been the catalyst. But she had really been running away from the feeling that she felt powerless to decide the course of her life.

Now, she was running toward something.

Toward the place she wanted. The life she wanted. The person she wanted to share it with.

After a quick shower and a walk with Horse, Greta headed over to Carys' and found her in the backyard, feeding Teacup mini carrots and familiar pink sugar cubes.

The scene was magical and absurd and so beautiful that Greta felt her heart swell. "You're so lovely and amazing," she said to Carys.

At least that was what she began to say. She only got out "You're" before Carys shrieked and spun around, clutching her chest. Greta had not only startled Carys, she'd also startled Teacup, who let out what Greta had heard described in books as a whinny but sounded more like the baleful shriek of some creature Carys would describe on her haunted tours.

"Aw, baby, I'm so sorry," Greta said when Carys and Teacup were no longer in fear for their lives. "I missed you."

She wrapped Carys in her arms and felt instantly at home. Carys' body, her smell, her very being made everything in Greta feel at peace.

"I missed you too." Carys sounded almost surprised to hear herself say it.

Greta had talked with Carys at the airport about everything that had happened with her family, but she'd wanted to see her in person when she told her the rest.

"Can we go inside?"

They gave Teacup the last carrot and many caresses and scratches, then settled on Carys' bed beneath the painting of Carys riding Teacup. It looked so much like the scene she'd walked in on earlier that Greta grinned.

"Okay," Greta said. "I know that this is still really new, and I don't want you to feel like you owe me anything. I know you're a lot more experienced than me, and we haven't really talked about monogamy or…well, or a lot of things."

Carys was looking at her with such fondness that it emboldened her. She grabbed Carys' hand. This time, her rehearsing what she wanted to say during the flight paid off.

"I want to move here. Not for a month but permanently. I'm not saying this because of our relationship, I swear. Though I really love our relationship, and I hope it can continue. But I just need you to know that it's not *because* of you. You know?"

Carys smiled. "I understand. Thanks for thinking about how I might feel pressured, especially since it hasn't been very long."

Greta nodded diplomatically, congratulating herself on her clear and responsible communication.

"Do you *want* to have those conversations?"

Greta blinked. "Um, which?"

"The ones about monogamy and a lot of things." Carys smiled at her, but it was clear she wasn't making fun.

"Well…um…yeah. Do you?"

A fizz of excitement began to rise from her stomach to her throat, and Greta fought not to let it overwhelm her.

"Yup," Carys said.

"Oh, thank fuck," Greta breathed, and Carys laughed.

"Can we put a pin in them for the moment, though?" Carys said. "Because there's something very pressing I need to do."

"Oh, yeah, of course, sorry," Greta mumbled. "What do you need to do?"

Carys winked. "You, silly."

"Oh, right, well, yeah, I think that can be arranged," Greta said. Then she lost herself in the woman she loved.

# 31
## TRUMAN

*Six Months Later*

Truman hurried through the front door of Thorn with arms so full of wildflowers he could hardly see over them. Fortunately, Horse was tall enough that Truman stopped short at the last minute and didn't trample him.

The wildflowers were for what had quickly become Thorn's signature item, the Owl Island souvenir bouquet. They had small glass jelly jars with three different Owl Island stickers to choose from, and customers picked their own blooms from several different buckets of wildflowers. Then they chose from ten different string colors to wrap the bouquets so they were ready to hang dry as a souvenir when they began to droop.

It had been a long winter that most inhabitants of Owl Island were complaining about by February, but Truman had been reluctant for it to end. After all, he'd never been happier than when he was cuddled up with Ash under blankets, listening to music while they kissed passionately, told one another their deepest secrets, and fell asleep intertwined.

But when the first breath of warm spring weather touched the shores, it had been time to put all their winter plans into action. Those plans so carefully written up in bullet point lists and sublists in Truman's special Thorn planner were ready to become reality. While Ash had made contacts about the flowers and the jars, Truman had gotten to work designing multiple Owl Island stickers for Ash to choose from. In the end, Ash loved them all, and they decided on three different designs that might appeal to all kinds of tourists.

There was one where a stern and vaguely spooky owl perched on a branch with the shoreline of the island behind it. One had a brightly colored background of wildflowers and a wise-looking great horned owl in the foreground. The last had a vintage-inspired drawing of Maine with the state tree and flower, the white pine, featured behind a small flying owl and lettering that looked like it was made of logs.

Truman had believed deeply in the product when he suggested it, but when the first ferry of tourists had touched down, he was awash with nervous energy. What if Ash had trusted him with this and his idea was a flop? He'd practically bitten his fingernails to the quick waiting, but soon enough, the shop bell tinkled and a family with two teenage daughters walked in, interested in the signs they'd seen around downtown about creating a signature souvenir bouquet.

Truman had smiled calmly and shown them how to create their bouquets, upselling to the parents as well, while inside he was swooning on a fainting couch with relief.

It had gone on like that through all of May and June, Ash barely able to keep up with the demand for wildflowers and making plans to grow his own the next year to supplement supply. Now, as they rolled toward July, Thorn was functioning like a well-oiled machine. They'd sold enough bouquets to cover the shop costs through the winter when it was slow—although Truman had a lot of ideas to help—and were now using some of the profit to expand the small collection of cards they'd begun carrying along with flowers.

The night before, Ash had even told Truman that he'd be excited to expand into other flower-related merchandise, a holdout that had up to that point been based more in fear (in Truman's opinion) than lack of interest.

"Whoa, Tru, hang on."

Ash grabbed Truman around the waist to steady him and took the flowers from his arms, placing them into the waiting tubs of water. Then he wound his arms around Truman's waist from behind and nuzzled his chin in Truman's neck. "Damn, you smell good," he said.

Truman turned in his arms and squeezed him tight. "So do you."

Ash's smell was something that he now got to savor every morning and night.

After Truman and Greta had decided to make their swap permanent, he and Ash had gone back and forth staying at one of their houses one night and the other the next. Soon, though, it became merely a formality. They wanted to spend every night together. They had dogs. It only made sense to live together. And by Ash moving into Greta's house with Truman, he was not only able to save money splitting the rent, he was able to sublet the apartment above Thorn for some extra cash.

Between that and the new profits Thorn was turning, Ash could afford to hold on to Thorn for the foreseeable future, Mr. Crimm be damned.

A group of tourists approached the shop, so Truman

reluctantly let Ash go. It had been agreed upon that he would do front of house sales when he was there, since Ash couldn't bear to upsell and always wanted to give nice people deals on everything. Truman found this unutterably charming, but in the interest of their bottom line, he'd banished Ash to behind the counter where his hotness was an asset and his kindness didn't tank their profit margin.

"Good afternoon, y'all," Truman drawled as they came in. "How have you been enjoying the island?"

"Oh, it's lovely," a white woman in her forties said. "Such a beautiful view of the ocean. And the shops are all so charming."

"Did you know," Truman said conspiratorially as he led them toward the display of jars, "that it's actually the bay just out there? I didn't either when I came here…"

He winked at Ash and got down to business.

$\longleftrightarrow$

"Oh, Truman, good," Maisey said as he approached the Queen Bee.

She always acted like he was arriving at just the exact minute she needed him, even though she had his phone number and he'd encouraged her to text any time. This was, he'd learned over the last six months, common of the purveyors on Owl Island. They preferred to do everything in person, and it was always lucky or perfect timing when they ran into you.

"Have you had any luck yet in finding Agatha Tark? Don's going to want to make the posters soon, and we'd love to be able to add her appearance for a signing. It's going to be such a wonderful event for the community!"

Truman grinned.

In October, it would be the twentieth anniversary of the publication of book one in the Dead of Zagørjič series, and Truman had convinced Maisey and Don that the Queen Bee should have an event to celebrate, given that the series had been penned on Owl Island. They had ordered copies to sell and put on display, they were going to host a meetup discussion for any TDoZ fans who wanted to come, and they were designating the first in the series the community read for their book club. Granted, their book club only had six consistent members, but Truman had contacted libraries all over the mainland, and three of their book clubs were participating as well.

Honestly, Truman still couldn't believe that his lifelong obsession with the Dead of Zagørjič had culminated in him *living* in the house where Agatha Tark wrote the series. In fact, he couldn't help but think that it was a certain kind of cosmic meant-to-be that the books that had been his succor during times of loneliness would one day lead him to the place he'd call the home of his heart and the man he'd call the love of his life.

"I'm so close, Maisey, I swear. I found the last place she lived, and they have a forwarding address that she left, but I haven't had time to check it out yet."

This would be the icing on the cake: finding Agatha Tark and convincing her to come out of hiding and to the Queen Bee to sign books during the anniversary celebration.

"I'll tell Don," she said. "But you've got a week, and then we've got to get those posters done."

She stabbed a finger in his direction when she said *week*, and Truman nodded compliantly, even though he was fairly certain that she and Don never did anything until the very last minute.

"Noted." He put the box he was carrying on the counter.

"Okay, here are the planners. These are the weekly and the undated, like you said."

"Oh, wonderful." She began stacking them on the display beside the counter. "Nan Wilkins needs undated because she's developed her own method of keeping time, you see?"

"Oh?" Truman inquired.

"Yes, she's redistributed time so that there are more days in the months she likes best and fewer in the other months, and then more hours in the days she likes best of the months she most enjoys. It's very complicated, but those are the basics."

"Oh, well, great for Nan Wilkins, but these are still laid out in months, so I'm not sure they'll be to her, uh, specifications."

Maisey waved him off. "Doesn't matter, dear. She's loony as a toon, and besides, she prepaid."

Maisey winked at him and he winked back and waved goodbye.

Selling his planners at the Queen Bee was an experiment. In March, which had revealed itself to be an unendingly gray month on the island, Truman had put his head down and begun an Instagram for his bullet journal content. He'd also designed what he called a suite of "hybrid bullet journal printables" that he sold as digital downloads on Etsy.

These were pages that people could download and insert into digital bullet journals, print for their planners, or turn into stickers for their physical bullet journals. He showed how to use them on his Instagram account, which was growing every day.

He wasn't making a huge number of sales yet, but he was slowly adding more and more products to his shop. Building a business was a marathon, not a sprint, and Truman was still limbering up for that first mile haul.

When Maisey had overheard him telling his new planner friend Ginny about what he'd created over coffee at Bob's, she'd thought he meant physical planners and asked if she could sell them in the Queen Bee.

"My granddaughter says they're all the rage," Maisey explained. "She read about it in TikTok."

Truman and Ginny had nodded soberly and then cracked up.

"Does she think that's a book?" Ginny giggled.

"I have no idea."

Now, though, he was seeing that there was a market for independently designed and produced planners and journals. He thought with a little bit of time, he could create products that people would really enjoy.

And he enjoyed making them. There was a kind of user experience that you simply couldn't approximate if you weren't a bullet journal or planner devotee yourself. Truman knew what kind of bindings were best, what type of paper wouldn't let marker bleed through, how many pages were ideal, and what sizes worked best for different kinds of journalers.

Ash said he'd have an empire before he knew it. But Ash also said he was the loveliest, smartest, hottest person he'd ever met, so…

$$\longleftrightarrow$$

"Do you think it's weird to just show up there?" Truman asked Ash.

They were cooking dinner, Horse and Bruce lying on the kitchen floor in the hopes of gobbling some tender morsel as it fell to the ground.

"Well, yeah," Ash said. "It's undoubtedly weird."

Truman deflated.

"Yeah, okay. I know."

Ash eased the knife out of his hand and stepped close. His blue-gray eyes looked blue as the summer sky today. "But, well…" He stroked Truman's hair back. Truman hadn't cut it since he'd given his two weeks' notice in February, and now it curled freely around his face, always tickling his nose. He wondered how long he'd let it get. "Love, a lot of things you do are really weird. But it works for you."

He was trying very hard to make it clear that he didn't think weird equaled bad.

"So even if it's weird, if it's something you need to do, then you should do it."

"It's just…" Truman tried to pinpoint exactly why he needed to see Agatha Tark in the flesh. "She kinda saved me. As a kid and in my darkest moments, her world is what I escaped into. And I want to say thank you. But also, there are so many other people who I know feel the same."

When Truman had told Charlotte and Germaine that Julia remembered Agatha Tark living here, they had both been eager to get in their cars and make the trek.

Wow, thanks, assholes—you never offered to make a trek to see me, Truman had teased them.

*What?! I totally have!* Germaine protested, which was true.

At the same time, Charlotte wrote, **Yeah, duh, cuz you're not Agatha freaking Tark.**

Truman slid the chopped onions into the melted butter on the stove.

"And if I could get her to do the signing, people would get to tell her. I don't know. I guess if she's worked this hard to stay off the radar, then maybe she doesn't care about that. But *maybe* she doesn't want to deal with any of the publicity but she would be so happy to hear how much her work has helped people."

Ash kissed him. "You won't know until you try. I'll go with you if you want."

"Really? I'd love that."

←——→

And so, the next morning, they set off to the address Truman had gotten that might be Agatha Tark's. Ash was driving Truman's car because Truman was too nervous. On the ferry, they held hands and watched gulls soar and dive over the water, hoping a passenger might drop a tasty crumb overboard, though the captain always explicitly instructed them not to. Truman waited until there weren't many people around, then he pulled the last bite of his bagel from his pocket and dropped it over the side.

The gulls swarmed, and Ash turned to look back at him.

"You're such a softy," Ash said. Then he kissed Truman on the mouth, which took out any sting.

They were ten minutes away when Truman began to sweat and his stomach clenched.

"Oh god, was this a terrible idea? She's gonna think I'm a freak for tracking her down—I *am* a freak for tracking her down. Shit, shit, what am I doing?"

"Do you want to abandon mission? We can take a pretty drive or go into Portland for lunch," Ash offered, hand on Truman's thigh. "There's a place my friend works at that has the best blueberry pancakes you've ever had."

Truman loved blueberry pancakes, but at the moment, the idea of food made him feel ill.

"Maybe we should just go pick some wildflowers for the shop and forget this idea," Truman offered.

"If you want. Sure."

Ash leaned back in his seat and closed his eyes. He stroked Truman's thigh but didn't say anything more. It was one of the things Truman loved about him. He was patient and his patience never cost anything.

At the end of his first semester of college, Truman had returned to Metairie, relieved to be back in his own room. He loved Tulane and New Orleans, but he didn't feel like he fit in. Within a day of being home, though, he remembered that he didn't fit in there either. Remembered why he'd longed to distance himself from his family. That began one of the loneliest months of his life. During that time, he'd read the Dead of Zagørjič through twice. He'd finished the last chapter of book seven and gone right back to the first chapter of book one.

Maybe it hadn't saved his life, but it had held him all the times he needed to be held and didn't have any other way to be so. No matter what she thought of him, he had to look Agatha Tark in the face and tell her what her work had meant to him.

"Okay, let's go," he said finally. "I wanna do it. Don't let me change my mind, okay?"

"We'll go," Ash said, squeezing Truman's leg. "But you can always change your mind."

Truman closed his eyes. Appreciation for Ash brought tears to his eyes.

"Okay."

When they pulled up to the address Truman had been given, it looked so ordinary that his first thought was, *This can't be it.* But that was ridiculous. What had he been expecting—an ice palace?

"Ohgodohgodohgodohgod," Truman muttered as they walked up the steps. He wanted to hold Ash's hand, but his were sweating so much he didn't think he could. He pressed a shaking finger to the buzzer and stepped back. His heart fluttered like a jailed creature in his chest, and he felt light-headed. Then the door opened and he was looking at her.

At Agatha Tark.

He knew it was her somehow. In the opposite of how the house looked nothing like her, this person before him looked exactly how Agatha Tark *had* to look. She had broad shoulders, a severe short bob of thick, wavy gray hair, and eyes the color of the ice palace she should be living in.

"Yes?" she asked. Her voice was low and suspicious.

Truman's mouth simply would not function for a moment. Then he managed to croak out, "Agatha Tark?"

The woman's eyes narrowed, and she went to shut the door.

"No, please! I'm so sorry to bother you, but please wait just a minute."

She leaned on the door so only half of her body was visible, waiting. "How the hell did you find me?"

She was definitely angry, but Truman thought he detected the slightest hint of grudging awe in her voice, and he clung to it like a lifeline.

"Well, okay, here's what happened," Truman said. "My boyfriend was cheating on me—well, cheating with me, but I didn't know, so I had to get out of there, and I knew Maine was where you lived, so it was like fate, you know, when I switched houses with Greta, but then I got super drunk—wine, you know? And then when I fell off the bed, it was right *there*, the ship, in the floor. And I was like, no fucking way, this can*not* be happening, but then I woke up the next morning sober and it was still there, and I just knew it was connected because in book six, when Clarion finds the *Draggør* sailing ship, it's too specific. And I thought maybe it was just a Maine thing, but no one had heard of it, so I knew it had to have been what inspired you, and Ash's mom *knew* you—Julia! You remember Julia Sundahl? So then I just tracked all the leads because you have to know your books basically saved my life so many times, and I had to tell you."

Agatha Tark blinked those ice-blue eyes under thick brows, still dark brown, and said, "Good lord. I guess you better come in before you faint on my doorstep."

Truman opened his mouth to say he wasn't going to faint, but at just that moment, he realized he was breathing strangely and Ash was holding his elbow.

Then another part of him realized he was about to go into Agatha Tark's house, and he wondered if he really was going to faint.

"Just don't *Misery* me, okay?" she said. "I'd never hear the end of it."

Her house was completely brown. Not ugly wood paneling brown but the rich, subtle browns of the woods. Of tree trunks and soil and shallow water and dying leaves. The wood floors shone and the walls were painted a color between brown and gold. Bits of driftwood, twisted metal, macramé wall hangings, and towers of crystal decorated the walls and shelves. It was minimal and earthy and made Truman feel like he was inside the trunk of a tree.

They sat on a brown velvet couch, and Agatha Tark

lowered herself gracefully into the matching armchair across from them.

"I didn't comprehend a single word you said before," Tark said, "but I gather you are living in the house on Erskine Road?"

Truman nodded and geared up to try and explain about the house swap again.

"See, we have this mutual friend, Ramona, and she—"

"I don't care at all," Tark said. It was final and quelling, but it lacked any malice. She was simply stating a fact. "What I would like to know is how you know Julia Sundahl."

"You remember her?" Ash chimed in.

"Yes. She was a very good friend to me at a time when I needed one."

"She's my mom," Ash said.

Tark's eyes widened slightly, then she nodded.

"How is Julia doing?" she asked, and the first hint of warmth crept into her voice.

"She has dementia," he said. "Or early-onset Alzheimer's. They're not sure which. Some days, she's okay. Other days, she gets really confused. Thinks she's sixteen or thinks I'm my dad."

Ash swallowed hard. Truman knew those were the most difficult days for him—seeing the woman he'd once turned to for strength and support as helpless.

"I'm truly sorry to hear that," Tark said. And Truman thought that perhaps if she'd been a different person, she'd have reached out and squeezed Ash's hand.

"She remembered you, though."

Tark smiled, revealing sharp canines and crooked front teeth. It was a truly mischievous smile. "I should hope so."

She leaned back in her seat and fixed Truman with her lupine gaze. "So. You wanted to tell me about my books."

And so he did.

Haltingly at first and then with genuine pleasure at sharing with her the pieces of himself that he'd once shared only with her work.

He knew this was strange. Knew it was awkward. Too personal and too presumptuous, and probably she would laugh at him when he left or call a friend and roll her eyes. *You'll never guess what happened to me today!* And usually, such a thought would've stopped him in his tracks, his ideations of what others might think stronger than his own actual desires.

But here, now, with Ash by his side, whom he *knew* would not laugh at him, would not roll his eyes at him, would instead celebrate him for doing something hard and awkward and personal, his desire to place in Agatha Tark's hand his once-strangled heart won out.

When he fell silent, once-strangled heart galloping, she clasped her hands together and said, "Thank you."

And it was all she needed to say. Her gratitude and amusement and satisfaction were all apparent in those two words and in the quiet peace that had descended over them.

Truman felt like the moment might stretch in all directions for eternity—a beautiful, iridescent slide on the inside of a bubble.

Wanting to blow more bubbles, to give a moment like this one to every fan of the Dead of Zagørjič, he said, "In celebration of the twentieth anniversary of the series being published, I've arranged an event at the bookstore on Owl Island—the Queen Bee? And we'd love it so much if you wanted to come do a signing. Or a reading? Oh god, that would be magnificent!"

Agatha Tark said, "No."

"But, so, it's going to be great. We've made it the book of the island, really, and book clubs at libraries are going to—"

"No."

"Maybe you could, like, record yourself reading if you don't want to make the trip, and we could project—"

"No."

Ash squeezed his knee.

"Right. Okay. Of course. Sorry."

Truman studied his shoes. His first instinct was to feel like a failure. But lately he'd tried to ask better questions—less *I suck!* and more *What did I gain all those years from doing this thing, and why might I not need to anymore?* So instead of thinking *I'm a failure*, he asked her why. Why she'd always been so private.

"Because I have never wanted people showing up at my house trying to talk to me."

Truman flinched before he saw the hint of humor in her eyes.

Then her expression turned serious. "Creating something is very different from talking about it or interacting with people who consume it. Once it's out of my hands, it's no longer mine. I've never had any interest in seeing other people's interpretations of my work or answering their questions about what my characters eat for breakfast. The work is what's on the page, and anything else is in the imagination of the reader. It doesn't have anything to do with me." She cracked her knuckles. "Besides, I hate people. And they've never been terribly fond of me. Why do you think I created my own to play with?"

Then she smiled, a genuine, toothy smile, and stood up. It was clearly time to leave.

"Can I ask you one more thing?" Truman ventured.

"One more."

"Will you ever write anything else?"

"No."

And then there was nothing more to say. Truman had done what he'd come for, and he'd remember it forever.

Ash walked out first, and as Truman crossed the threshold, Tark grabbed his elbow.

"If you tell anyone where I am, I will have you murdered. Remember, I know where you live too."

Truman gave a nervous laugh, but Tark wasn't smiling.

"I won't. I swear."

She nodded once, and the menace was gone. "Please send my love to your mother, if you think it's appropriate," she said to Ash.

Then she closed the door and was gone.

# 32
# TRUMAN

July 2 was Ash's birthday, and Truman had strict instructions not to do anything that resembled a party or a gathering... or really anything that involved other people. It had become very clear to Truman over the last six months that while Ash enjoyed connecting with individual people, he hated being the center of attention.

Well, except when he and Truman were in bed. Then sometimes he let himself fall back into the sheets while Truman teased him slowly with kisses and caresses all over his body, until he was so sensitized he was writhing, desperate for more contact. Truman relished those precious moments of Ash's unselfconscious desire that were for him alone.

After waking Ash with just such single-minded devotion, they went to Julia's house for breakfast.

Tori opened the door with a cheery "Happy birthday," and they followed her into the kitchen where Julia and Bradley were cooking.

In January, Ash had brought up the idea of housemates to his mother, and Julia had been enthusiastic. Though she'd doubted young people would want to live with her, Bradley and Tori loved the idea. They were genuinely fond of Julia and jumped at the chance to help her and also live in a lovely house and split bills so that their costs were low enough for Bradley to pursue his art full time and Tori to take classes online.

They'd expected a transition period and some wrinkles they'd need to iron out, all of which happened. What they hadn't expected was the intense bond that Bradley, Tori, and Julia would come to share.

One morning in late March, when the temperatures had begun to creep up and optimistic Owl Islanders could be found enjoying the first bread crumb of spring, Ash had come home from picking up groceries crying.

"What's wrong, baby? Are you okay?"

Truman had begun patting him down, searching for a wound.

"I saw my mom," Ash got out.

Truman's heart sank. They'd just been getting into a rhythm where Ash didn't feel the need to check up on Julia every evening and didn't feel guilty when he wasn't with her.

Ash let the canvas totes slither off his arms and wrapped them around Truman.

"She was sitting outside Bob's with Tori and Bradley. They were talking. She was telling them a story. She looked so good," he said, then dissolved into sobs against Truman's shoulder.

Ash loved her so much. Though they'd talked a lot about the toll her care had taken on him and the devastation he'd felt watching her deteriorate in the years before he and Truman met, in that moment, Truman realized that he'd not fully understood the burden Ash had carried. It was only in his gutting relief at seeing his mom thriving that Truman could gauge the depths of his previous pain.

It had been a turning point. Julia had blossomed with her new housemates. She still got confused. She still had bad nights. Their presence was no magic bullet. But having people who were always there, who could redirect her and remind her of things, who she had a shared schedule with, had helped her quality of life immensely.

And Bradley and Tori had come to depend on Julia as well as on each other. They benefited from her experience, her perspective, her wisdom, and (as Tori mentioned whenever she was given the opportunity) her cooking.

"I make boxed mac and cheese and off-brand tater tots," Tori had said. "Bradley eats eggs for every meal except breakfast, and then he eats dry cereal. Julia's like a superhero."

Now, when they went to the house Ash had grown up in, it was a joyous affair, full of fun and warmth and family.

Truman had assumed the line between Ash's eyebrows was a wrinkle because it had always been there. But sometime in April, he'd looked over to find that it had disappeared. Now and then, it made an appearance when he was stressed about Thorn or his mom had a bad night. But most days, his brow was clear.

"Happy birthday, sweetie!" Julia said when she saw Ash and wrapped him in a hug. Bradley slid the spatula out of her hand before she got pancake batter in Ash's hair and gave Ash a nod.

Bradley didn't talk much, but he was incredibly kind and he adored Julia.

Over blueberry pancakes (Ash's favorite), bacon, and coffee, Julia told them stories of some of Ash's more memorable birthdays.

"There was the time I had to work on his seventh birthday so we decided we'd celebrate on Saturday, not realizing it was the Fourth of July. We turned onto Main Street, and Ash's eyes got huge. The whole street was decorated with balloons and streamers and those round ribbon things. He thought it was all for his birthday!"

Ash smiled and shook his head at his younger self.

"Everyone was wishing us happy Fourth of July, and Ash just kept saying thank you."

"I wondered why there was this uncle named Sam I'd never heard of who cared so much about me having a good birthday," Ash said, grinning.

"Oh man," Tori said, "that reminds me of the birthday when I thought my parents had gotten a clown for my party. I really hated clowns as a kid, so when I saw this lady coming toward us in the backyard at my party, I started backing away and saying to my parents, 'No clown, no clown!' Turns out it was one of the kids' grandma, she just had a really bad orange perm, and her lipstick was kind of smeared on."

Bradley snorted into his coffee. "I wanted a beetle cake for my birthday when I was ten," he said.

Before Truman could ask why on earth anyone would want to consume something that looked like a bug, he went on.

"My parents got me one in the shape of the Volkswagen instead."

Julia, Tori, Ash, and Truman waited for the story that would accompany this fact, but Bradley just tucked into his pancakes once more, and they all exchanged smiles around him.

After breakfast, Julia put a box down on the table in front of Ash. He'd been very clear that he didn't want this brunch to turn into a birthday party, and he narrowed his eyes.

"It's not a present!" she insisted. "Look, it's not even wrapped. It's just something I thought you might want to have."

Ash lifted the lid off the box to reveal a stack of papers. They were buckled, water stained, crumbled, and otherwise worn.

"Oh wow." Ash lifted the stack out. "These are all drawings I did when I was little," he explained.

The drawings were in crayon, marker, and pencil, and many had stickers and bits of decorative paper pasted on them. Ash flipped through quickly, pausing at one. "This is when I was obsessed with dogs," he said.

The drawing was one large dog in the center that looked vaguely like Scooby-Doo, and all around it were smaller dogs floating in space.

"That's adorable," Truman said.

"He used to stop to pet every dog we passed," Julia said. "Once we went into Portland, and it took us an hour to get down the street because he stopped for so many dogs."

"Awww." Truman's heart swelled. He loved imagining Ash as a sweet, serious little boy with so much love to give that he wanted to bestow it on every dog he passed.

While Julia told another story of Ash's childhood, Ash flipped through the drawings, then put the lid back on.

"Thanks, Mom. This is great."

"Happy birthday, sweetheart," she said. At the door, as they said their goodbyes, she whispered totally audibly to Truman, "His birthday present is behind the counter at the shop."

Truman gave her a thumbs-up, and Ash laughed and kissed her cheek.

Their hands found each other and they walked in joyful harmony for a few blocks.

"I think she's really happy," Ash said.

"I think so too."

"I think…I think I am too."

He said it so softly that at first, Truman thought he was joking and started to elbow him with a smile. Then he realized that although it was obvious to him that Ash was happy, they had never discussed it.

"I'm so glad," Truman said instead.

Ash simply nodded.

Truman had been planning for them to go home for a bit, perhaps take a postbrunch nap before heading out again. But this seemed like the right moment.

"Come with me?" he asked.

Ash raised an eyebrow in question, but when Truman didn't answer, he said, "Always."

They walked hand in hand to the shore. Warm sun, a cool breeze off the bay, and Ash's hand in his, Truman didn't think he'd ever been more at peace.

He led Ash to the mouth of the cave where Ash had first brought him all those months before. Inside, the cries of gulls echoed but all other sound was muffled.

From the bag he'd stashed there the day before, he took candles, a lighter, and a blanket and made them a cozy spot on the cave floor.

They sat facing each other, and Truman held Ash's hands.

"I wanted to come here for your birthday because meeting you, coming here, it's been like a rebirth for me. I know we talk a lot about all the plans we have for Thorn and for other projects we want to do. I think…I've always wanted a partner. Someone I would share my life with, and my ambitions. And I didn't really think it would ever happen. But then there you were."

Truman got choked up, and Ash's stormy eyes sparkled with unshed tears.

"I'm so damn glad you were born, Ash. And I feel so incredibly lucky that I found you. I know you didn't want a bunch of presents, but I just got you this little one."

He handed Ash the small packet. Ash tore off the paper and peered at what he held.

"It's seeds for your favorite wildflowers. I thought, since you mentioned you wanted to start growing them to sell in the shop next summer, maybe you could start with these. It's nothing really. I'm just so proud of you and all the risks you've—"

Ash knelt up and threw his arms around Truman. He didn't say anything, but Truman could feel everything he felt in his embrace.

Ash pulled a piece of paper from his back pocket and held it close to his chest when he sat down again.

"I drew this when I was, like, ten," he said, voice thick. "I'd forgotten about it until my mom gave me all those drawings today." He glanced at the drawing. "I told her it was me and a brother or something, but it wasn't."

Slowly, tentatively, he held the drawing out to Truman. His hand shook.

In colored pencil, Ash had rendered a house that looked very much like their house. In front of it stood a young Ash—Truman thought he would recognize him anywhere—holding the leash of a sweet-looking dog with its tongue out. But it was the person next to him that Truman peered at.

Ash was holding hands with another boy, who had light brown hair and a shy smile. He was holding a dog's leash as well. Around the house grew brightly colored tulips.

"I think I knew I wanted you before I was even old enough to know what that meant," Ash said. "I wanted this life. With you. The house and the dogs. When I left Owl Island, I left because I didn't think I'd ever find that here. When I came back to take care of Mom, I thought I was giving up my chance of ever having it."

Ash looked up at him, face shining with love.

"Truman, I love you so much. I never thought I could have this. And honestly, I'm scared of fucking up somehow and losing it. But I'm going to try so hard to be worthy of you. Of this."

He patted the drawing.

Tears streaked down Truman's face.

"You don't have to do anything," he said, stroking Ash's hair back. "You're what I want. This." He tapped the drawing too. "This is my dream too. I love you, and I love our life. I'm all in."

Ash rolled him onto his back and into Ash's arms, knocking over a candle.

"Please, please don't let our sweet moment end in a fiery conflagration," Truman said.

"I'll show you a fiery conflagration," Ash growled and kissed him. Their mouths met and Truman sank into the feeling of being touched by the man he loved, of hands and lips and tongues and smells that all said *home*.

Then he got a rock in his shoulder blade, and the tendrils of arousal that had begun to envelope him turned to pain.

"I love that kind of fiery conflagration, but also it's so uncomfortable here. Wanna go home and make out in our own bed?"

As Truman said it, his heart swelled. No word had ever sounded sweeter than *home*, when home was with Ashleigh Sundahl.

"Yeah. But can we stay like this for just a little bit longer?" Ash asked, face nuzzled in Truman's neck.

"As long as you want, love."

Truman and Ash held each other in their private universe until the tide began to rise. Then they walked in silence, hand in hand, back home.

It wasn't a drawing. It wasn't a fantasy. It was love and trust and choice. It was a life they were building, day by day, flower by flower, together.

# 33
## GRETA

Things grew like magic in New Orleans.

On Owl Island, Greta had required so much equipment to keep her plants alive, even inside. But in her community garden plot next to Veronica's, they thrived on neglect. Her tropical, carnivorous beauties were finally where they were meant to be. And when you were where you were meant to be, life required far less effort.

Of course, the process of relocating her plants had been a comedy of errors. She and Truman had set the week of their permanent swap, and when the time came, Truman had gotten Horse on the road with minimal effort, whereas she had to swaddle each one of her plants and place them in the moving truck individually.

It had been enough to make her think she'd never want to acquire another plant ever again.

Until she had them unloaded, some greening up Truman's house—now hers—some scattered around Carys, Helen, and Veronica's house, and some planted in the garden. It only took about two days before she was wandering through town and the garden, seeing all the amazing plants and deciding she couldn't wait to try her hand at them.

Now she was in the garden by herself, sun hat on against the summer heat, earbuds in so she could listen to *ShadowCast*. She'd begun growing lavender six months ago, and while it had been slow to start, once she'd figured out the perfect mix of soil for it, it grew in bushy swathes that scented the air sweetly and provided a feast for Veronica's nearby bees.

It had begun with lavender because Helen and Veronica needed an inexpensive source for it to use in their lemonade.

Now, Greta was growing mint, sage, tarragon, and other herbs for their infusions as well as the edible flowers they decorated them with. In Maine, she'd often saved seeds from her fruit to sprout in the hopes of growing fruit trees, but they'd never lasted more than a few months. Here, Greta had sprouted lemon seeds and pineapple tops that were on their way to becoming trees that would produce fruit they could eventually use.

And while Greta had volunteered to grow herbs for Veronica and Helen with no expectations, given that she hung around the house all the time, she'd contributed so many ideas for their burgeoning business that as of two months ago, they'd invited her to join them in making it a reality.

In just one week, they were launching Lagniappe Lemonade, a line of locally sourced, locally crafted beverages, bottled in New Orleans, for sale by subscription. Helen and Veronica had used the profit they made selling their Mardi Gras king cakes for the start-up costs.

Greta piled armfuls of lavender and mint into her harvesting basket to take to Eleventh House. She was in charge of making the bundles of fragrant herbs that were to be their business cards for the launch, and Carys had offered to help, so Greta wanted to make it a date night.

Carys had taught the first summer session because she needed the money, but she was on vacation as of the week before, so Greta was thrilled to be able to spend more time with her.

The first month of Greta's permanent relocation had been hard. Carys was busy and independent and had a large circle of friends. It was one of the things Greta admired so much about her. But it also took some getting used to on Greta's part. Even though her own family's hyperinvolvement with one another's every move had felt intrusive, it was what Greta was used to. And learning how to be mutually independent was something she was still working on.

Her involvement with Lagniappe Lemonade had helped a lot. Having a purpose made her feel like she belonged in New Orleans, and a collaborative business with two of your closest friends—which was what Helen and Veronica had quickly become—was a dream come true.

She had also begun a new internship, working with students on learning how to grow food. It had begun as a few workshops she taught at Tana's school with the monetary support of Muriel and the Garden Gang. When the students responded well and they got requests from other schools to run the workshops there, the Garden Gang set up a fund to provide regular workshops for ten local schools at no cost, and they'd reached out to three people to run them—two local farmers and Greta.

She'd demurred. She was a new transplant to the city and wasn't knowledgeable about its history, its politics, its inner workings. She was white while the students they'd be working with were majority Black. And her experience was more in house plants than in urban gardening. The opportunity should go to someone else.

The Garden Gang had respected her decision and hired someone else. But Muriel had suggested that she attend the workshops with the other three people they'd hired. That way, if they got the chance to expand the program, she would be in a better position to offer something to students at other schools.

Greta was thrilled she'd taken Muriel up on this idea. She'd already learned so much and was excited at the opportunity to someday pass that knowledge on.

And for the time being, she was working at the very coffee shop where she had first taken Horse all those months ago. A number of her coworkers were lovely, so she'd made new friends, and it still left her plenty of time to work on Lagniappe Lemonade.

By the time Carys got home from Jackson Square, Greta had turned the living room into a lavender-scented oasis. She'd bumped up the AC (nothing could have prepared her for the incessant heat of a New Orleans summer—although the daily tropical downpours were convenient, since they meant she rarely had to water her garden plot). She'd created an assembly line for putting together the bouquets. And most importantly, she'd made them an epic cheese plate for sustenance.

"Hey, baby," Carys said when she walked in. She threw her arms around Greta's neck and kissed her. "Wow, it looks awesome in here."

Carys had tied her curls up in a white bandanna and wore a mint-green linen jumpsuit in a pattern of broccoli florets and leeks that she'd found at a thrift store. She looked amazing, and Greta pressed another kiss to her lips and then her throat.

"How was the square?"

"Great take today," Carys said, pulling out her bag. "There's some kind of business conference at one of the hotels on Canal, and you *know* how business dudes are about wanting to prove that women don't know anything they claim to know. I raked it in." She grinned and dumped more cash than usual on the floor.

Greta high-fived her and helped order all the bills so they were facing the same way, the way Carys liked. *It just makes it easier for the bank teller*, Carys had explained the first time Greta asked why she did that.

They washed their hands, then settled down to make bouquets and eat cheese.

Carys thanked her for the cheese plate and made a blissful sound at the combination of a salty manchego and the sweetness of Veronica's lavender honey—a new offering, now that her bees had so much lavender to eat.

"How on earth do bees do it?" Carys mused worshipfully.

"I know, right? They make two of the best things on earth—honey and beeswax—and it's just like…their job. Good work, bees."

It didn't take too long before they'd gotten a rhythm down: tie the tiny bouquets, affix the card with sealing wax that Veronica had made out of her beeswax, and imprint it with the company seal. With breaks for cheese, weed, and making out, naturally.

"What's the latest on the family visit?" Carys asked.

For months, Greta had been hearing from her family that they were going to try and come visit her.

"I think it's finally materializing for November. At first they were going to try and come in August, but I think they'd legit perish, so I told them to hold off."

"Will Sadie come, do you think?"

"Psh, she might come just so she can't possibly be to blame if our relationship stays shitty."

Carys growled softly. She was not a fan of anyone who treated Greta badly, so when Greta had shown her some of their text exchanges, Carys had gotten mad. Which Greta found irresistibly hot.

"I will kick her ass if she's mean to you," Carys said.

"You could totally take her."

"Yeah, I could," Carys mumbled. She made a muscle jokingly. But Greta knew how fierce Carys' love was, and even though her sister had about six inches on Carys, she had no doubt who the victor would be.

Not that she actually wanted her girlfriend to beat up her sister. Much.

But while the reminder that she and Sadie didn't have the kind of relationship she had with her other sisters would've once made Greta's stomach cramp with anxiety, now she shrugged.

"Anyway, whether she does or she doesn't, I'll be excited to show everyone around."

Then, the final bouquet tied and wax seal applied, Greta tumbled Carys to the floor.

"Thanks for your help," she murmured into her neck as she placed kisses on all the exposed skin she encountered.

"Mmm," Carys said, which might've meant *You're welcome*, but Greta chose to interpret it as *Ravage me, you sexy beast*. So she did.

34
GRETA

The launch of Lagniappe Lemonade started in an hour. Greta, Carys, Helen, and Veronica had spent the morning setting up the dining room of the local barbecue joint that had volunteered to host.

The bar was stocked with the classic lemonade, the lavender lemonade, and two new varieties: a mint mojito lemonade and a spicy mango and cayenne lemonade, which was Greta's favorite. All were made with Veronica's honey.

There were cocktail suggestions to turn them into alcoholic drinks, and large posters of the label art hung on the walls. Postcards containing the branding on the front and the cocktail recipes on the back sat in neat stacks on every hightop table beside a plate of appetizers that Veronica had made. A table with the lavender bouquet business cards containing all their information sat beside the exit.

Everything was ready, and Helen and Veronica were staring at the space as if some cosmic horror was about to erupt from the floor and drag them all into the abyss.

"Are they okay?" Greta whispered to Carys, leaning close.

"Oh yeah. They always get like this before they do a thing

that really matters to them. They're both so stoic that neither wants to be the first to confess they're scared, so they just stare at each other until it passes."

"Okay. That sounds... Is there something we should be doing?"

Carys smiled at her. It was the *You're very sweet and I love you for it* smile that Greta could now recognize. "I got it." She walked to where Helen and Veronica stood and put a hand on each of their shoulders. "Darlings."

They both looked at her, wide-eyed. She pulled a joint from behind her ear and a lighter from her cleavage and handed Veronica both.

"Go smoke this and calm down. Greta and I will check to make sure everything's where it should be."

Veronica and Helen drifted out back as if in a trance. At the last minute, they both reached for each other's hands.

"They'll be fine," Carys assured Greta.

"Should they get stoned right before the launch?"

"Nah, it's like one part weed and three parts lesbian herbs," Carys said breezily.

Thirty minutes later, the bartenders had all arrived, and Veronica and Helen were back to their normal selves, emo panic having passed, and were talking a mile a minute about future, bigger launches.

"Okay, c'mere, y'all," Helen said, gathering Veronica, Carys, and Greta at the bar. They passed out cups of lemonade. "Toast time."

Veronica rolled her eyes but raised her glass indulgently.

"Carys, you're the raddest housemate ever. You've been so supportive and you almost never complain about there being honey everywhere."

Carys snorted.

"Greta, when you came on the scene…well, I'm not gonna lie. I thought y'all would break up in a week. You're so sweet, and I kinda didn't think you could hang."

Veronica snickered into her cup, and Carys elbowed Helen in the ribs.

"*But*—I was about to say but. But you're actually a total badass, and I'm so damn glad you're part of this honey, lemonade, wax crew. Whatever. I can't wait to see what you'll grow next that we can incorporate into recipes."

Greta tipped an imaginary hat and smiled at who she'd been the first time Helen had met her.

"Veronica. You're the sister I never had."

Veronica said, "You have a sister." But Greta saw her dab away a tear.

"You're the sister I *should* have had, and I'm so fucking excited that we're taking all this to the next level. You're the best. The total best."

"Damn it," Veronica hissed, tipping her head back so tears wouldn't run down her face. "Okay, since we're doing this. Helen, you're the brother I never had—yes, yes, I do have two brothers. They both suck. Never thought I'd meet someone as up for wild shit as me. I'm so damn glad we didn't work out, because otherwise I never would've gotten you as a best friend."

"Wait, you two used to date?" Greta's mouth dropped open.

"We went on a very ill-fated date five years ago. We were *not* compatible…uh…you know." Helen made vague gestures between them that Greta assumed meant *sexually*.

Veronica snorted and swatted Helen's hands away.

"*Anyways*, that's history. Here's to the future of Lagniappe motherfucking Lemonade!"

"Cheers!" they all chimed, clinking glasses—well, bumping, since the cups were cardboard.

"Knock knock," called a voice from the door. Greta recognized Ollie from Eleventh House parties.

The launch had begun.

They'd all reached deep in their social pockets to invite every contact they had. At first, Greta had thought she wouldn't have much to contribute since she hadn't been in New Orleans long. But when she began to invite everyone she knew, she realized how many points of connection she had already made in her new home.

The Garden Gang had been an invaluable resource, as they had forwarded her invite far and wide. The gardeners she was interning with had also been enthusiastic to come and to spread the word. Everyone Greta worked with at the coffee shop, the folks at the community garden, people at the co-op where Greta was a regular customer, Ramona and her friends...the list went on and on.

Greta had never considered herself very social. But here she was, only six months out, and she'd created an entire network that she could call on for support. It had made her proud of herself as well as eternally grateful to the people who had been so welcoming to her.

Muriel strode into the launch in a bright red jumpsuit and a yellow straw fascinator with a red feather. She lowered large white sunglasses to pick Greta out of the crowd, then glided over to her. Greta had the distinct feeling that if she hadn't peered over Muriel's garden wall all those months ago, her life might be very different.

"This is wonderful, darling," Muriel drawled. "How do you feel about it?"

Somehow, even in a loud crowd, Muriel had the ability to make you feel like it was just the two of you, sitting in her garden, and nothing else mattered.

"I can't even believe this is my life," Greta said. The lemonade toast (which had definitely had alcohol in it) had kicked in, and she was feeling deliciously honest. "I was such a loser when I moved here. I never would've believed I could be in business with my friends, have an amazing girlfriend… I can't believe it."

"You know, another way to say *loser* is *someone who hasn't bloomed yet*," Muriel said. "You'd never call a plant that had not yet put out its flower a loser."

Greta took a moment to be amused at the notion of wandering around the community garden lambasting all the plants that hadn't flowered yet for being losers. But she took Muriel's point.

"You're right, of course. And you were a huge piece in my flowering, if we're continuing this metaphor. Thank you so much, Muriel. Meeting you changed my life."

Greta couldn't be sure, but she thought Muriel might have dabbed at her eyes when she turned to survey the room.

"You changed mine too, Greta," she said, turning back.

"I did?" This had never occurred to Greta.

Muriel nodded somberly. "I wasn't feeling at all well the morning you poked your head over my garden wall. I was feeling rather sorry for myself, in fact."

"For what?" In all the time she'd spent with Muriel, Greta had never seen her anything but upbeat and future-oriented.

"Oh, well. For being old, for being alone, for being

ineffectual. The usual. But the point is that you were a surprise. You reminded me that there still *were* surprises that could happen to me. And that I still had something to offer. You can't know how essential that is—to feel as though one still has something to offer. And I hope it isn't too terribly patronizing to say that I'm very proud of you."

Greta bloomed. She threw her arms around Muriel.

"Thank you. Also, I've never said this because I thought it sounded weird, but you're the most glamorous person I've ever met."

Muriel's tinkling laughter glittered through the room as someone grabbed Greta's shoulder.

"Hey, bitch! Good work."

Ramona was wearing white linen overalls and a black bandeau, big red hoops, and platform boots, and she was smiling.

"Hey, thanks for coming!"

"Wouldn't miss it. This shit is *delicious*, by the way. I subscribed." She pointed to the lemonade.

"That's awesome, thank you."

"So how's your shiny new life going?" Ramona asked. She looked even more pleased with herself than she usually did.

"Very shiny indeed. How are you?"

"Two for two," she mused, smiling.

"Huh?"

"Oh, just both you and Truman. I'm amazing."

"You are? I mean, you are, but...why are you?"

"Duh, who do you think was Gossip Girl here?"

"I never watched it."

Ramona rolled her eyes. "You and Truman? Both of your lives sucked shit, but you were too scared and complacent and *nice*"—she said *nice* like she was saying *covered in pustules*—"to do anything about it. So you needed a little fairy godbitch to, uh, motivate you."

Greta laughed. "Well, thanks for your fairy godbitching. I hope you're proud of yourself."

"Oh, I am. I'm very proud of myself. You wouldn't even believe the altars I had set up for the two of you," Ramona muttered almost to herself. "You think it's easy to get two self-contained introverts to do *anything* that involves meeting or contacting other people?" She made a *phew* gesture of effort. "No, no, I don't need any thanks for my toil. I'm just glad you're both happy now."

"What do you mean, *altars*?"

Ramona waved that away. "Just don't worry about it, and enjoy your new life, Greta Russakoff, resident of New Orleans and lover of Carys."

Like *Carys* was a magic word, Greta broke into a grin. Whatever Ramona thought she'd done, Greta didn't really care. She had the woman of her dreams, friends she adored, and a life that felt like it was just beginning. She hugged Ramona hard, and when they let go, Ramona winked at her and slipped into the crowd.

The launch was a success by any measure. They got thirty-two subscription orders, myriad social media coverage, and two restaurants that were interested in contracts for their lemonades to feature in cocktails. By the time Veronica and Helen stood on the bar to thank everyone for coming, they were out of drinks and the moon was high.

Veronica and Helen were elated and, after they cleaned up, left with some friends for another party. After they waved goodbye, Greta took Carys' hand, and they strolled out into the night.

"I'm so proud of y'all," Carys said. And for the second time that night, Greta felt something inside her grow toward the sun. "How do you feel?"

The air was redolent with jasmine and cigarette smoke and the river. Greta pressed her free hand to her heart and felt its steady thump.

"I feel fucking alive. I feel...I'm proud of myself."

As she uttered the words, she realized it was the first time. She had been relieved to finish college, felt satisfaction at paying her own rent right out of school, but she had never known what it was to truly feel pride in herself until she moved here.

Greta stopped walking.

"Holy shit, this is where—"

Carys looked up at her and nodded. Her smile was radiant in the moonlight.

It was the spot over the river that they'd visited the day they met.

"You wanna?"

They both grinned and scrambled up the stairs, giddy with joy and sentiment.

"Oh my god, I can't believe there was a time when I'd never met you!" Greta announced to the Mississippi.

"You were so cute when you came up to me. So awkward. I'd seen you through the bar window, you know."

"What? No way. Tell me."

Carys smiled and sat at the edge of the pier. Greta sat beside her.

"I was chatting with a friend, and I saw you coming down the street. I thought you were hot. When I came outside, it might have been because I was gonna talk to you."

"What? And you just let me blather on like a doughnut?"

Carys grinned. "It was sweet," she insisted. "You were so nervous and so *not* slick. I liked it."

"And how 'bout now?" Greta asked.

"Now, you're still sweet, you're still occasionally nervous, and you're almost never slick. And I still like it. I love it. I adore you."

The lump in Greta's throat made it hard to force out words.

"Fuck, I adore you too."

"Listen," Carys said, twining their fingers together. "What would you think about moving into Eleventh House with me when your lease—Truman's lease—is up?"

"Really?"

"No, I'm playing a very mean and horrible prank. Of course really!"

A swarm of butterflies were fluttering in Greta's chest. She turned to face Carys, sitting cross-legged to try and stop herself from bouncing up and down. It didn't quite work.

"Yes! Yeah. Fuck yeah. Yes."

Carys let out a breath, and Greta realized she had been nervous to ask her. Self-possessed, confident Carys had worried she might not say yes.

"I love you so much," Greta told her, pushing her curls away from her neck and leaning in to kiss her throat, then her cheek, then the corner of her mouth.

Then something occurred to her.

"Wait, but are you sure, because I have a lot of plants. Like. A *lot*."

"Hello, yes, of course I know, and yes, I'm sure."

"I want to get a cat," Greta said. She hadn't even realized it was true until it was out of her mouth.

"Great. I love cats. Not a hairless one, though, okay? I think they're cute but Helen has a legit phobia."

"A full-of-hair cat, then."

Greta couldn't stop smiling.

"I take weirdly long showers for someone with almost no hair. And Adelaide says I snore, but I think she was just messing with me."

"Oh, I *know* you snore."

"I do?"

"Oh, honey, yes. You for sure snore."

"Wait, have I been snoring this whole time?"

Carys nodded.

"Why didn't you ever say anything?"

Carys shrugged. "I'm fairly sure it's not something you can control. I didn't want to make you self-conscious."

"Damn."

Greta didn't have it in her to be mortified about that revelation because Carys was looking at her with such fondness.

"I want to live with you. The idea of waking up with you every morning makes me so happy. I can't wait to make you coffee and bring it to you in bed because you're so snuffly and cuddly when you first wake up. I can't wait to eat dinner with you and plan our weekends together. I can't wait for Helen to yell at you for wasting water when you take really long showers."

Carys grinned but squeezed Greta's thighs tight.

"I...wow. I want all that stuff too. I just worried... You and Helen and Veronica have your whole thing going on, and I would never want to interrupt it."

"What? You're *part* of the whole thing we have going on. You're part of the business, not me. And V and Helen love you."

"I love them too."

"Listen, I only want this if you want it too," Carys said seriously, eyes anxious.

"No, no, I want it. I want it so much!" Greta grabbed her and pulled her close, heart zipping with joy. "I want it. Please don't doubt that for one second. I was just feeling a little insecure."

Carys stroked her hair. "Babe, you have nothing to be insecure about. You're so fucking lovely. I can't wait to plan all the things with you."

"Me too."

Greta had to work hard to keep herself from screaming her joy into the night.

But why? Why was she trying to hide her feelings from Carys? That was the whole point of joy, right? To feel it and share it?

Giddy and shaky with adrenaline, Greta stood.

"I'm gonna move in with the best girlfriend in the world!" she yelled at the dark, sludgy river. The Mississippi ate her words and skipped them out again, because someone shrouded in night called back "Congratulations!" (Someone else called back "Shut up," but it's all about mindset, so Greta ignored it.)

Carys snorted and stood up beside her, slinging an arm around her waist.

"I can't believe I used to live in *Maine*. On an *island*." Giddy had become slaphappy, and Carys squeezed her tight.

"I can't believe you came here as part of a *house swap*," Carys joined in.

"Omigod, I *know*!"

"So listen," Carys said, suddenly serious. "I want to run something by you."

"Hit me."

"I really, really want to kiss you," Carys said. "And I wonder what you think about that?"

Greta blinked at Carys asking, then she remembered. It was what Carys had said the first time they'd kissed, in this very spot.

"Shut the hell up and kiss me already," Greta replied, as she had all those months ago.

Carys' lips were lemon and honey, her mouth a luscious play of love and want. The kiss was sweet until it went dark and hungry, Carys' tongue sliding against her own and sending shivers through her legs and guts, directly to her crotch.

"Damn," Carys said as Greta breathed, "Wow."

Then by unspoken agreement, they reached for each other's hands and walked slowly, love-drenched, back to the home they would soon share, New Orleans providing the chorus.

**THE END**

# BONUS MATERIAL

Enjoy your very own holiday as Roan Parrish takes you on a tour of the world of *The Holiday Trap*, including:

1.  A sample from Truman's bullet journal, ready to be copied for your own use

2.  Questions for your next book club meeting

3.  Roan Parrish's latke recipe

4.  And even more holiday cheer!

# BOOKS

## GOALS

- ○ Read The Holiday Trap by Roan Parrish
- ○ Leave a review
- ○
- ○

## TITLE & AUTHOR

_____

_____

_____

_____

_____

_____

_____

_____

_____

## STARS

☆ ☆ ☆ ☆

☆ ☆ ☆ ☆

☆ ☆ ☆ ☆

☆ ☆ ☆ ☆

☆ ☆ ☆ ☆

☆ ☆ ☆ ☆

☆ ☆ ☆ ☆

☆ ☆ ☆ ☆

☆ ☆ ☆ ☆

☆ ☆ ☆ ☆

# READING GROUP GUIDE

1. At the beginning of the book, both Truman and Greta want to escape from emotionally difficult situations by going somewhere completely new. Have you ever imagined running away (even for a short time) and experiencing a completely fresh start? Where would you go and what would you do?

2. What it is about being in a new place that gives us perspective on our lives? Have you ever found changing your location changed your outlook?

3. Greta has a very involved family—sometimes a bit *too* involved for her liking. How might this have influenced Greta's personality? Is Greta's family anything like your own?

4. Ramona is Truman and Greta's mutual friend who "traps" them into confronting their dissatisfaction by coaxing them into leaving the comfort of their familiar lives. What do you think her role in the story is, beyond the

trap? Other than Truman and Greta, who else is trapped in *The Holiday Trap*?

5. By the end of *The Holiday Trap*, none of the characters work for anyone but themselves. The work force has shifted greatly over the last decade, with fewer and fewer people pursuing what we might call traditional career paths, and instead opting to work independently. What circumstances and shifts do you think are driving that impulse, and where do these characters demonstrate those shifts?

6. Ash's mother has Alzheimer's and dementia. Truman suggests that rather than Ash being her sole caregiver, she get housemates who can provide support, basing his suggestion on programs that have been tried internationally, pairing young people who can't afford rent with senior citizens who can't get out easily. The results were great community and joy among the participants. This works out great for Ash's mom! How do you think this might work on a larger scale? Would you want to participate if given the chance? Why or why not?

7. Carys' mother is a covert narcissist. As a result, Carys has learned highly adaptive survival and coping mechanisms for dealing with her. But these same mechanisms have influenced her emotional responses to the world. How has Carys adapted because of this dynamic? What moments in the text do you see evidence of what she's learned to do to work through conflict?

8.  Greta falls in with a group of gardening enthusiasts all in their sixties or older. What importance does intergenerationality play in *The Holiday Trap*? Are there lessons you've learned because you've had access to people much younger or older than yourself?

9.  Truman is obsessed (his word!) with The Dead of Zagørjič, a fantasy series by Agatha Tark. What role have these books played in Truman's life? Is there a book that was formative to you? In what ways did it shape you?

10. Greta grew up in the only Jewish family on Owl Island. Antisemitism is still very much alive in 2022. Even though she isn't religious, this cultural difference affected her. How do Greta's experiences differ from those of the gentiles around her? Have you experienced being in the minority because of any part of your identity or circumstance? How did it feel? Did it change how you view the world? Did it affect how you treated other people moving forward?

11. Helen and Victoria, Carys' housemates, become dear friends of Greta's as well. Helen is nonbinary and Victoria is trans. Both of them, and Carys, are queer. Most of their friends in the book are queer, trans, or gender nonconforming. Why is it crucial to the story that Greta joins a queer community? If you're part of the queer community, did a mainly queer friend/found family group feel familiar to you? Why is it so important for queer people?

12. By the end of the novel, Greta confronts her family about how she's been feeling and why she is going to make

her move permanent. They do not respond the way she was hoping. Why do you think some members of the Russakoff family have a hard time acknowledging Greta's experiences?

13. As of 2022, New Orleans is about 60 percent Black. In *The Holiday Trap*, though, there is only one Black character: Victoria. The author, Roan Parrish, is white. Conversations about who should write and publish stories across different experiences are always happening and evolving. Why do you think the author chose to make the four main characters white? Do you think it was the right decision? Why or why not?

14. One of Truman's regrets is that he didn't tell Guy's partner that Guy is a cheater. Greta ameliorates this and tells him in no uncertain terms. Do you think she did the right thing? How is her decision representative of the ways she's changed from the beginning to the end of the book? What would you have done in her situation? Would you want to know, if you were in the position of Guy's partner?

# ROAN PARRISH'S LATKES

*makes 8–10ish—scale up for more*

## INGREDIENTS

6 russet potatoes

2 onions

2 eggs (or, to make vegan, sub chia egg for each egg*)

salt

pepper

garlic powder

vegetable/corn/safflower oil

## EQUIPMENT

box grater or food processor

tea towel or T-shirt

cooling rack

## SERVE WITH

applesauce

sour cream

ketchup

*Chia egg = 1 tablespoon chia seeds mixed with 3 tablespoons water. Let it sit until it forms a gel consistency, and it'll bind just like egg.*

## INSTRUCTIONS

1. Shred your potatoes and onions.
2. Transfer shredded veg into a tea towel and squeeze into a bowl until all moisture is gone. This could take several minutes and if you tend to cry from onions you might want to see if you can con a housemate into squeezing it for you 😊. Whoever does the deed, you want as little moisture left as possible. The dryer your mixture, the crispier your latkes will be.

*NOTE: Do NOT dump out the water you squeeze. Let it sit in the bowl until you're ready to season your latke mix. Then slowly pour out the water, which will reveal a white substance at the bottom of the bowl. This is potato starch!*

3.  Scrape potato starch out of the bowl and add it to your latke mixture along with your eggs. Season with salt, pepper, and garlic powder to your taste. (I don't recommend using fresh garlic in your latkes because the temperature you'll be frying them at is hot enough that it'll burn the garlic on the outside.)

4.  Heat some oil in a pan on medium-high. You want enough oil to come halfway up a latke, but you'll be flipping them, so this isn't a deep-frying situation. It's the right temp when a little bit of potato starts to sizzle immediately when dropped in.

5.  Shape your latkes by taking a palmful of potato mixture and squeezing it into a patty. More liquid will probably come out, which is great—you want the latkes to go into the pan as dry as possible.

6.  Fry your latkes until browned and crispy, then flip and do the same on the other side. I go by color, but it's about 2–5 minutes on each side, depending on oil temp and size.

7.  Putting hot latkes on a plate will make condensation, which leaves latkes soggy. I recommend taking them from the pan and putting them directly on a cookie cooling rack, so air can circulate around them. Hit them with a good sprinkle of salt when they're still wet with oil, and you're ready to eat!

NOTE: If you're making a large batch, you can keep latkes warm out of the pan by putting them on a cookie sheet in a 200-degree oven.

**Now comes the most important question:**
**How do you like to eat your latkes best—with**
**applesauce, sour cream, or ketchup? Enjoy!**

# ACKNOWLEDGMENTS

Many thanks to my mom and sister, for letting me ramble endlessly about my ideas for this book. To my kickass agent, Courtney Miller-Callihan, for your excitement and encouragement about this project. To my brilliant editor, Mary Altman, for your belief in this book and for making it better in all the right ways. To the amazing team at Sourcebooks, for all your hard work and support in bringing the book to life and getting it into readers' hands. To Jasper Pyewackett and Dorian Gray, for being my constant furry companions (and sometimes sitting on my hands so I couldn't type—I'm sure you were right and we were supposed to just cuddle on those days). To artist Kristen Solecki, for the gorgeous cover. Most of all, to Timmi, for your endless support, your boundless excitement about my work, and for not laughing at me (at least not to my face) when I cribbed things from real life for this book. Having you in my life is better and more fun than even the swooniest romance comedy.

Finally, my deepest thanks to everyone reading *The Holiday Trap*—without you, none of this would be possible. <3

# ABOUT THE AUTHOR

Roan Parrish lives in Philadelphia, where she is gradually attempting to write love stories in every genre.

When not writing, she can usually be found cutting her friends' hair, meandering through whatever city she's in while listening to torch songs and melodic death metal, or cooking overly elaborate meals. She loves bonfires, winter beaches, minor chord harmonies, and self-tattooing. One time, she may or may not have baked a six-layer chocolate cake and then thrown it out the window in a fit of pique.